Christopher J Eddie graduated from Aberystwyth University in 2002, and after spending ten years working for the civil service, decided to train to be a primary school teacher — a career that he has followed since 2013. As well as writing, Christopher is also a musician and amateur herpetologist. The Covid-19 lockdowns saw schools close in the UK which afforded Christopher a little extra time to pursue a writing project. Taking inspiration from dystopian ideas and alternative history, Christopher completed his debut novel in 2021 and hopes to follow it up with further instalments in The Menorah series.

The Menorah
1979

Christopher J. Eddie

The Menorah 1979

Vanguard Press

VANGUARD PAPERBACK

© Copyright 2025

Christopher J. Eddie

The right of Christopher J. Eddie to be identified as author of
this work has been asserted by them in accordance with the
Copyright, Designs and Patents Act 1988.

All Rights Reserved

No reproduction, copy or transmission of this publication
may be made without written permission.
No paragraph of this publication may be reproduced,
copied or transmitted save with the written permission of the publisher, or in accordance
with the provisions
of the Copyright Act 1956 (as amended).

Any person who commits any unauthorised act in relation to
this publication may be liable to criminal
prosecution and civil claims for damages.

A CIP catalogue record for this title is
available from the British Library.

ISBN 978 1 83794 102 5

This is a work of fiction. Names, characters, businesses, places, events and incidents are either the product of the author's imagination or used in a fictitious manner. Any resemblance to actual persons, living or dead, or actual events is purely coincidental.

Vanguard Press is an imprint of
Pegasus Elliot Mackenzie Publishers Ltd.
www.pegasuspublishers.com

First Published in 2025

Vanguard Press
Sheraton House Castle Park
Cambridge England

Printed & Bound in Great Britain

PART 1

VON HINDENBURG'S BRITISH TERRITORIES

1

THIS IS WHERE WE ARE

The Second World War is initiated on the 1st September 1939 as Nazi Germany, led by Adolf Hitler, invades neighbouring Poland in order to regain lost territory and extend German rule to the east of Europe. In response to the invasion, the United Kingdom issues an ultimatum for Germany to cease hostilities but this is disregarded. As a result, the United Kingdom declares war on Germany on the 3rd September 1939. Into 1940, Adolf Hitler opens up a new front to the west by invading both Denmark and Norway in April of the same year followed by France on the 10th May 1940 — the same day that Winston Churchill is appointed as the Prime Minister of the United Kingdom.

The war in Europe rages through the remainder of 1940 but Allied Forces are quickly overwhelmed by the superior firepower and weapons technology possessed by the German Wehrmacht, who continue their sweep through Western Europe, forcing Allied Soldiers to retreat back across the English Channel to the safety of the United Kingdom. Hitler continues his advance across Western Europe securing a swift victory over most of the continent by the end of 1940. Towards the end of 1940, the Wehrmacht begin to assemble their forces on the coast of northern France in anticipation of an invasion of the United Kingdom.

On New Year's Day 1941, and in a devastating blow, Nazi Germany launches a successful invasion of the United Kingdom. A lightning strike involving hundreds of V-2 guided ballistic missiles quickly overwhelms the British coastal defence system (as well as targeting airfields and harbours), allowing thousands of German troops and thousands of tons of military hardware to land largely unimpeded on the southern shorelines of the

United Kingdom in multiple locations. Any resistance offered is quickly suppressed and British armed forces are forced to retreat further inland whilst being simultaneously pursued.

After securing the coastal regions of the United Kingdom, the Wehrmacht begin to move towards London on the 3rd January 1941 in a final attempt to secure a swift victory over the United Kingdom. Winston Churchill remains defiant in the face of invasion and pledges to defend the country with everything that is left, offering no surrender to Nazi Germany. London shores up its defences in anticipation of the arrival of the Wehrmacht. The Luftwaffe begin aerial bombardments on London with little discrimination as to who they target, the purpose being to break the spirit of the British people and force them into submission. So begins what becomes known as The Siege of London, a month long campaign by Nazi Germany to force Britain into a quick surrender and remove Winston Churchill from power.

Throughout January 1941, the German aerial bombing of London by the Luftwaffe continues with vigour. Vast swathes of the city are razed, thousands of innocent people are killed and numerous well-known London landmarks are deliberately targeted and destroyed in the attacks (including St Paul's Cathedral, the Tower of London and Tower Bridge) in further efforts to break the spirit of the British people. The advance of the ground forces of the Wehrmacht towards the capital continues, with any attempts to stall or halt it quickly overwhelmed. British military leaders remain shocked and taken aback at the effectiveness of the Wehrmacht and their superior arsenal which continues to decimate anything that stands in its path. Still, Churchill remains defiant and continues to refuse to surrender.

By the 20th January 1941 the aerial bombardment of London finally ceases. All air defences and anti-aircraft weaponry have been destroyed. The Wehrmacht reach the outskirts of London after quelling what little resistance has been encountered on their journey from the south coast and begin shelling the capital with heavy artillery. All supply lines to the capital are cut off. Fresh food and water are no longer accessible throughout London. Thousands of civilians attempt to flee the city but are stopped by the Wehrmacht who refuse to allow anyone to leave or to let any kind of aid into the city. On the 31st January 1941, Winston Churchill finally surrenders to Nazi Germany. The very same day, Nazi soldiers march into central

London completely unimpeded and the occupation of Britain begins. In the following months, the British royal family is subsequently abolished and members of the family are sent into exile with all their accumulated wealth being reallocated back to Nazi coffers.

Unbeknownst to the rest of the world, and in the years leading up to the invasion of Poland, Adolf Hitler had assembled a team of top nuclear scientists with the sole purpose of developing a nuclear weapon. The team of scientists, led by Professor Erich Bagge, worked tirelessly in a top-secret facility tucked away in the Bavarian Alps with the eventual goal of producing a functional atomic bomb. The top-secret project was known as Projektbefreiung (Project Liberation) with Hitler setting Bagge and his team of brilliant scientists a target to have completed their work by the end of 1940. Several months ahead of deadline, Projektbefreiung was completed with the production of the world's first atomic weapons, Der Befreier I & II (also known as The Liberators).

By April 1941, and following a swift victory in Europe, Nazi Germany begins looking further west to America who, up until this time, has not become involved in the European war but remains wary of both the ambitions of Germany to the east and Japan to west. Pre-empting the perceived American threat and how it would destabilise the Nazi grip across Europe, Germany unleashes its most powerful weapons — Der Befreier I & II. Within the blink of an eye, New York is destroyed by Der Befreier I on the 14th April 1941 and Washington DC the following day by Der Befreier II, killing hundreds of thousands of people instantaneously in the process. The resulting nuclear fallout across the East Coast of America kills thousands more in subsequent years and also leaves large areas of the country uninhabitable. Despite working tirelessly to create the atomic bomb first, American scientists remained years behind their counterparts in Germany. The blasts leave America in a state of panic with the president, Franklin D Roosevelt, declaring a state of emergency as well as immediate retaliation against Nazi Germany.

On the 20th April 1941, within days of the nuclear attacks on America's East Coast, the Empire of Japan capitalises on the ensuing chaos and launches its own attacks on the West Coast of America. Aerial and naval bombardments begin on military installations along the American West Coast as well as attacks on the American navy in Pearl Harbour, Hawaii. A weakened and disorientated America mounts a defence but is unable to divert enough military resources quickly enough to counteract the Japanese who, towards the end of the month, have mounted a successful invasion onto the American mainland. Upon seeing the East Coast of America destroyed by the atomic bomb and the West Coast fall to the Japanese Empire, President Franklin D Roosevelt formally surrenders to Germany and Japan on the 28th April 1941.

Learning of the arrival of the Japanese military onto mainland America, Hitler quickly diverts his own military as the two nations rush to claim as much territory for their own respective empires as they can. At the beginning of May 1941, Axis Forces (led by the German Wehrmacht) begin to air drop into key areas of America to commence occupation of the habitable remaining eastern states and central areas of the country. Simultaneously, any remaining American military are hunted down and destroyed to minimise the effects of any potential resistance or guerrilla insurgency. Similarly, the Empire of Japan continues its advance further east in an effort to lay claim to more territory. As supply lines widen across the huge country, the advances of both Germany and Japan are halted with Japan eventually laying claim to some of the far western states of America as well as the entire West Coast and Germany holding claim to the remainder of the country.

Having secured a swift victory over the United States, Hitler turns his attention back towards the east in the summer of 1941. Despite signing the Molotov-Ribbentrop Pact in 1939, the German Army commences Operation Barbarossa on the 22nd June 1941 with German divisions being launched against the Soviet Union from the Baltic to the Black Sea. In conjunction with a ground assault, the Luftwaffe begin attacks on Soviet airfields thus incapacitating much of the Soviet Air Force leaving the German offensive unstoppable. The Wehrmacht begin their advance towards Moscow; however, by the winter of the same year, the military offensive against the Soviet Union has stalled. As the harsh Russian winter begins, and as supply lines to the Wehrmacht become ever more distant, the advance towards Moscow is brought to a halt with the Wehrmacht taking up positions in Tver to the north and Kaluga to the south. Thousands of Wehrmacht die in the harsh conditions, being ill equipped to deal with such unexpected conditions. The better equipped Soviet army launches several counterattacks but while not being able to force the Nazis to retreat, manage to inflict severe casualties. This first major setback of the war for Germany begins to cause Hitler great concern.

Becoming known as the Christmas Day Apocalypse in later years, Hitler orders the dropping of the atomic bomb on Moscow on the 25th December 1941 to avoid the Wehrmacht getting bogged down in a potentially lengthy and costly conflict and to bring about a swift conclusion and victory on the Eastern Front. Known as Der Befreier III, hundreds of thousands are killed immediately in the blast, including premier of the Soviet Union, Josef Stalin. Thousands more die in subsequent years across the former Soviet Union from radioactive fallout. The following day, Hitler declares victory over the Soviet Union and over Europe as a whole. In the months following the end of the war, Germany begins an occupation of western Russia as far as the Sverdlovsk Oblast eventually annexing it from the remainder of the Soviet Union and renaming it Germanic Russia. The former Soviet Union (left without any form of leadership from Moscow) falls into a state of disarray leading to economic collapse, uncontrolled migration of the populous and years of civil strife and conflict as a result of the power vacuum created by the death of Josef Stalin.

By early 1942, the Japanese empire turns its attention towards Australasia and Eastern Asia. With the American, British and other Allies incapacitated during campaigns in the preceding years, the resistance met by Japan is minimal. Having already been at war with China since 1937, the Chinese remain stubborn and reluctant to submit. With its former ally, the Soviet Union, left in a state of chaos as a result of Der Befreier III and the death of Stalin, China finds itself particularly weakened and vulnerable in the face of the advancing Japanese who eventually declare a formal victory over China by mid-1942. Despite being asked to come to the aid of Japan with a nuclear weapon, Nazi Germany refuses such assistance for fear of Japan using reverse technology in order to advance its own fledgling nuclear weapons programme, thus creating a destabilising arms race.

In what would eventually turn out to be the final major campaign of the Second World War, Germany's ally Italy begins occupation and control over Northern Africa in August 1942. In the aftermath of the nuclear attacks in America and the merciless victories of Germany and Japan, very little resistance is offered for fear of reprisals and further nuclear attacks. The move prompts Arab countries, previously in support of the Allies, to declare their support to the Axis Powers, thus providing the German and Italian empires unlimited and unhindered access to a wealth of natural resources from the Middle East, in particular oil and gas, to fuel the fires of industry within both empires. The Second World War is officially declared as over in 1942.

The trial of Winston Churchill begins on the 2nd March 1943 in Berlin, Germany. He is charged with crimes against humanity and accused of using the people of London as human shields during The Siege of London, resulting in the indiscriminate deaths of thousands of innocent civilians. The trial is short and two weeks later, Churchill is found unanimously guilty by a panel of German judges and sentenced to death. A sentence that is carried out the following year.

On the 28th April 1948, exactly seven years after the surrender of America, an official partition agreement is signed by Germany and Japan effectively splitting America into an East and a West, with Germany controlling all eastern and most central states and Japan keeping control of the Pacific states and some of the central areas. Alaska to the north remains of little strategic significance to Japan and therefore becomes a neutral self-governing territory with an allegiance to Nazi Germany. Also to the north, Canada signs a non-aggression pact with Japan and Germany. Having remained neutral throughout the war, Canada also remains of little strategic importance to Germany or Japan. As part of the non-aggression pact, Canada agrees to not harbour any refugees from America or act as a platform for American guerrillas intent on destabilising the German governance to the east and the Japanese governance to the west. Any breach of the pact is to have serious ramifications for Canada, and the border between Canada and East and West America becomes one of the most monitored, secure and impenetrable in the world.

By 1953, and after several years without seeing any armed conflict and relative global peace, Hitler announces that the Jews have been eradicated from every Axis-occupied nation and officially shuts down former internment facilities used to house Jewish civilians both during the war and the subsequent years thereafter. In the same year, decorated German commander and war hero turned politician Klaus von Hindenburg is appointed as the governor-general of the British Territories; the previous names of Great Britain and the United Kingdom becoming defunct. As a senior member of the Nazi Party (NSDAP), von Hindenburg rules with an iron fist and freedom of speech and movement are both strictly controlled. Adolf and Eva Hitler welcome their first, and what would be their only, child to the world in the June of 1953. A son named Alois Hitler. The child is reportedly named after Alois Brunner, one of the key architects of the Final Solution and the annihilation of Jews in Europe, and a continued close friend to the Hitler family.

After spending several years living in South America, another architect of the Final Solution (Adolf Eichmann) comes out of retirement and is appointed by Adolf Hitler as the governor-general of East America in 1954. Like his counterpart in the British Territories, Eichmann also rules over East America with an iron fist, forbidding freedom of speech and ensuring minority races remain strictly segregated from the majority white population.

After thirteen years of civil conflict in the former Soviet Union, an agreement is signed in 1955 between warring factions within the former Union and Hitler's Reich to bring about the creation of five recognised independent nations, based to a degree on the boundaries of some of the former oblasts, krais and republics of the Soviet Union. These are: Yakutia, Krasnoyarsk Krai, Magadan, The Republic of Novosibirsk & Omsk and the Jewish Autonomous Oblast. The Jewish Autonomous Oblast remains a tiny nation state in the very far east of the former Soviet Union, closer to the Empire of Japan than the German Reich. Many Jews in hiding in Europe attempt to flee to the safety of the oblast in the years following the war but few are lucky enough to survive the journey from Europe due to: radioactive fallout from Der Befreier III, civil conflict during the reformation of the former Soviet Union, dire weather conditions or a combination of all three factors. Hitler remains vehemently opposed to the existence of the small Jewish enclave, but due to the sheer distance involved, proximity to Japan and the relatively small number of people, he is reluctant to invest manpower, weaponry and money to attempt a potentially costly eradication of the oblast that may also enflame an already fraught territorial relationship with Japan. The Jewish Autonomous Oblast is therefore left be but afforded no international recognition or rights by Hitler's Reich.

Towards the end of the 1950s, the world lives in relative peace and much of the planet is overseen by the three empires of Germany, Italy and Japan. While most of Central and South America remain set apart from any of the three empires, they are mostly propped up by strongmen fascist dictatorships with policies aligned to that of the German Reich. Northern African countries remain under the control of the Italian Empire with other African nations being exploited by both Italy and the German Reich for their wealth of natural resources. German advances in technology continue at pace and the Reich remains a leader in this field. Throughout the 1950s, the Reich is able to boast the construction of a giant road bridge linking the British Territories and France, setting up a network of satellites in low earth orbit as well as sending the first human being successfully into space.

In February 1960, a disparate group of surviving British soldiers and Jews in hiding since the end of the Second World War begin a campaign to overthrow the Reich in the British Territories. Led by a mysterious figure, who eventually comes to be known only as Hebron, the group begins by targeting official institutions occupied by the Reich including police stations, Reich ministries and the personal homes of senior Reich officials. Throughout the 1960s, the group detonates bombs and carries out assassinations of key figures associated with the Reich on British soil. As something of a calling card, the group always leaves a picture of a Jewish menorah at the scene of their campaigns (whether this be crudely and quickly sketched on a wall or drawn on a piece of paper and deposited at the scene) leading the group to become known as The Menorah and designated as a terrorist organisation. As time progresses, the group becomes more organised and advanced in terms of its capabilities. It is able to recruit men and women from every walk of life, even those working for a Reich ministry thus allowing them unfettered access to a range of sensitive information concerning the Reich and its workings. As well as carrying out a campaign of terror against the Reich, The Menorah also begin to intercept television signals in order to broadcast propaganda and raw footage of Nazi atrocities carried out during the war (and in subsequent years) in an effort to undermine the iron fist of the Reich and to incite violence and an uprising against it. Despite the best efforts of the Reich, the group remain ever elusive and the skilled tactician with a military mind,

Hebron, remains at large somewhere in the British Territories (but somewhat underground).

The ongoing campaign by The Menorah continues into the 1970s, becoming ever more troublesome for the Reich. The Menorah continue to recruit people to their ranks and continue to carry out targeted attacks both across London and in other parts of the British Territories. The rise of The Menorah gives inspiration to a similar group in East America who call themselves the Liberty Front, and in a similar vein to The Menorah, the sole aim of the Liberty Front is the eventual removal of Nazi presence and rule in America and a return to a system of democracy as seen before the war. Similarly, the Liberty Front remains an underground organisation keen to recruit operatives from every walk of life to help them work towards the final goal — the removal of Adolf Eichmann by whatever means possible.

On the 28th January 1979, the world begins to mourn the death of Adolf Hitler who passes away peacefully in his sleep.

2

THE DAY AFTER

APRIL 1980, ACTON, LONDON

As he flicked through the singed dossier, Peter Fewtrill felt a sense of rising urgency. The documents had been retrieved from the governor-general's attaché case, and since the events of the preceding days, had been largely ignored — until now. He had been taught German at school (as was the case with every child growing up in von Hindenburg's post-war British Territories) but he never excelled in languages. He knew enough though to remain deeply suspicious and concerned about what he was reading in the heavily burnt and damaged document. Peter scanned it again and again until his eyes began to ache. He held it close to his face to try and make out the vocabulary obscured on the burnt pages, desperately seeing what else he could piece together. It was almost like the most intricate jigsaw, an incomplete one at that. He had found himself a piece of paper and a pen, and as and when he was able to decipher anything, he wrote it all down. Some pages were simply undecipherable due to the fire damage; others were more revealing and after some time, two particular words stood out to Peter due to the frequency in which they appeared — Eiserne Festung (Iron Fortress when translated to English). Whatever this was, it was often sometimes accompanied by another phrase which Peter was unable to properly read each time but it looked like it was 'blau' or 'blauen' (roughly translated to blue) but he couldn't be sure. The damaged dossier also contained what looked like blueprints or designs of something but it was near impossible to tell what they were and such was Peter's knowledge of all things technical, he was unable to even guess at what they might represent. A lot of the dossier that he could decipher was information he didn't understand and it seemed quite technical but certain key phrases immediately jumped out of the pages causing him concern; more so those mentioning: maximum yield, casualties, devastation of the terrain and a few more spurious looking word choices.

Once he had thoroughly examined the dossier for what seemed like the hundredth time, he pocketed what he had recorded and left his flat in order to make a phone call. It was into the evening by this point and the sun was beginning to slowly set. There was a public telephone box on the junction of Saxon Drive and Noel Road (near where he lived) that he was sure was not covered by the multitude of security cameras. Over time, Peter had become quite adept at spotting the thousands of cameras dotted throughout London and he was sure that he was safe at his telephone box of choice. He dialled the number that he had memorised and waited for the person on the other end to answer. It was a secure line so, in theory, the authorities could not trace the call. The phone rang and rang and Peter thought it would never get picked up and it made him jump when the man on the other end answered.

"Hello?" the voice on the end of the line said with a gruff tone.

"Christian, is that you?"

"Who is this?" the man on the other end queried.

"It's Peter."

"Why are you calling this number?" the man on the other end replied curtly, sounding somewhat annoyed and irate that the number had been called.

"I need to speak to him, as a matter of urgency."

There was a slight pause before the other man responded, "That's not possible right now."

"Make it possible, Christian. I need to speak to him. Now!"

The other man could sense the urgency in Peter's voice. "What is it? Why do you need to speak to him?"

"I think I've found something."

15 MONTHS EARLIER

It is said that you always remember where you were, and indeed what you were doing, the day something of great significance happened — for instance, the day someone well known died. The same was true for Peter Fewtrill. Although the morning of the 29th January 1979 began in its stereotypically noneventful way, it was about to get a lot more interesting.

Peter lived alone in a small one bedroomed flat in a low-rise block in the Acton area of London. The block had been built at the end of the Second World War by the German Reich to replace those buildings that had been destroyed during the combined merciless bombings of London by the Luftwaffe and the equally merciless shelling by the Heer (the German Army) in the days leading up to Churchill announcing surrender — although Peter had only really heard about this and had not experienced it first-hand.

Born in 1949, he had grown up with tales of the war and how the dictator Winston Churchill had been defeated by the hero Adolf Hitler. Widely revered throughout the British Territories, images of Hitler (and other Reich heroes including Governor-General Klaus von Hindenburg) adorned what seemed like every street corner in the centre of the capital. Hitler was responsible for rebuilding the British Territories at the end of the war. Hitler gave the British people homes. Hitler gave the British people jobs and hope. Such was the cult of personality, who was Peter to even begin questioning the might of such an iconic leader? Woe betide those who ever did question the authenticity or greatness of this man. Criticism of Hitler and his Reich was met with a severe penalty — a statutory prison term of six months forthcoming for those foolish enough to dare speak ill. Likewise, criticism of Governor-General Klaus von Hindenburg was met with a similar sanction. The oppression of the former British Empire was well known and widely taught in schools. Hitler had freed the nation from the brutal reign of colonialism. Hitler was a hero!

His alarm clock rudely awoke him as usual at six thirty a.m. and he showered and shaved (as usual) and made himself his usual tea and toast whilst day-dreaming his way through the morning prior to leaving his flat. He was ready to leave for work by seven thirty a.m., so with a final comb of his cropped light brown hair and straightening of his tie on his slightly creased unironed blue shirt, he set off and headed for West Acton tube station. Peter didn't turn on the television in his flat that morning. He had little interest in what was being aired across the three channels at such an early hour, so up until that stage of his morning, he remained completely oblivious to the unfolding drama of the day.

Peter lived on Princess Gardens, a mere five-minute walk to West Acton Tube station. From here, he would get a train into Chancery Lane in the heart of London and do the short walk to a building on Grays Inn Road where he worked at the Ministry of Media, Propaganda and Information in the position of Information and Systems Data Analyst. He had held this position for nearly twelve years now. He neither liked nor hated the job. He was happy to be in meaningful employment and to be receiving a salary, but it was rather mundane.

Hitler's Reich was very careful indeed on how it presented itself to the public; therefore, information reaching any media or news outlet had to be very carefully and thoroughly vetted with any potentially defamatory information removed to ensure it was not reported. Any news reports to be published or broadcast were sent to the Ministry of Media, Propaganda and Information to be closely examined by a team of analysts who would redact, edit and improve any reports or scripts before sending them onwards. The ministry would also receive recorded footage, the intention for it to be broadcast alongside a news report. This too was closely watched by the analysts in the ministry and vetted for approval before broadcast. Any information relating to sporting events was also subject to an intense vetting procedure, being edited to present any sportsmen of the Reich in a more than favourable light, irrespective of whether they were the winning team or not. More often than not, information was edited by ensuring mention was given to Hitler and his enduring and positive influence over all these events.

One other major piece of information to frequently pass through the ministry was related to The Menorah. The organised terrorist group made up of the remnants of the Jews left over after the war, who were not confined to the borders of the Jewish Autonomous Oblast in the former Soviet Union. Bombings and shootings carried out by the group had become worryingly frequent in recent years. In the twelve years Peter had worked for the ministry, even he had noticed the frequency with which media reports relating to the group were coming through. It seemed as though they were attempting to ramp up their campaign to destabilise the Nazi-led government by assassinating political figures, targeting Reich authorities and killing innocent civilians. Under strict instructions, Peter and his fellow analysts had been ordered to tactically edit reports of Menorah attacks. If two had been killed, report it as ten. If one police building had been targeted, report as five civilian buildings. In von Hindenburg's British Territories, they knew better than to question the blatant bias, and so Peter remained in his steady job.

He had to undergo a rigorous vetting procedure that looked into every aspect of his life, his background and his family. Even his family holidays came under much scrutiny (something that would've been exacerbated had he actually travelled abroad at some stage, which he hadn't). Senior staff from the ministry even performed a home inspection which, rather disturbingly, entailed a thorough search of every cupboard, drawer, nook and cranny of his small Acton flat. He passed, but in recent years, the vetting process for every Reich job had become even more intense (thanks to moles from The Menorah) so he dreaded to think what lengths they would go to now to assess the suitability of a candidate.

The Propaganda Department of the ministry was on a different level in the building. Again, vetting was strict to get a job there. It wasn't even possible to access the floor itself without the necessary security pass. The folk who were lucky enough to be offered a position in Propaganda were often ridiculed by the folk in Media for being 'just a little odd' not only in the way they behaved if passed awkwardly in a corridor but also for how they looked. Even though he never openly expressed it, Peter had always wanted to work in Propaganda but could never seem to find the motivation to ever look at how to get there. His manager, the war veteran Heinrich Stein, was a ball breaker so he figured that whoever headed Propaganda would be just as bad, if not worse. Stein was bad enough. He was happy to leave you well alone if you got on with your work but more than happy to let you know if you messed up. Thankfully, Peter hadn't fallen foul of the grizzled war veteran too often but he knew about it when he did.

The first thing that struck Peter as rather peculiar that morning was just how quiet it was. It was a Monday and the usual daily bustle of people and vehicular traffic in the vicinity was lacking which was odd. People and cars were usually busy milling about (even in this relatively quiet area of London) all on their way to work but not this morning. It seemed eerily quiet. Even the dull and distant rumble of cars from the main arterial routes around Acton seemed absent. Whilst he found it odd, it wasn't that strange or unbelievable that it particularly bothered him, so he proceeded on his journey towards West Acton Tube station.

As he approached the station (which also sat on Princess Gardens), there was a tobacconist at the junction with Queen's Drive. Peter knew it well as he often popped in there to buy cigarettes. Outside the shop was a woman who could only be described as in an inconsolable state. She was doubled over, in floods of tears and periodically howling almost as if suffering an injury. This made Peter slightly uncomfortable but also worried and concerned for the stranger. So much so that he felt as though he had to at least step in and see what the problem was, what was troubling her so and if he could help.

"Excuse me, are you all right?" questioned Peter as he approached the woman with caution. She did not respond but continued to wail with tears running down her face. Peter got a little closer and placed a soft hand reassuringly onto the woman's shoulder. "Are you all right? You seem—"

"Get off me!" the woman yelled in response as she knocked his hand away with considerable force.

The look on her face conveyed a mixture of different emotions: anger, confusion, grief and even an element of sheer insanity. The tears continued to stream down her cheeks and without saying anything else, she promptly stomped off (continuing to wail as she went) leaving Peter feeling a little bemused as to what had just happened.

In his shocked state, he watched as the woman disappeared up Princess Gardens and around the corner into Noel Road before he decided to continue towards the station. At the front door of the tobacconist, the proprietor — Stan Myers — was stood behind the counter with his back towards the door. He was transfixed by the black and white television mounted behind the counter and whatever it was that was being broadcast on it. He was a potbellied individual who stood with a half-smoked cigarette hanging from his lips.

"Morning, Stan," Peter called in.

Stan didn't respond verbally but simply raised his hand in acknowledgment of Peter's presence in the doorway. Keen to know what was wrong with the woman he had just encountered on the street, he continued talking to him.

"What was her problem? You been upsetting the locals again?"

It was said in some amusement. Peter had lived in the area for long enough to establish a nice friendly relationship with the tobacconist. Stan did not respond.

Peter muttered under his breath, "What the hell is wrong with everyone today?" Before addressing Stan again but this time with more volume and urgency. "Stan? Stan?"

Stan half turned around and finally spoke. "What? Oh morning… erm… Pete."

"Stan, that woman, what was her problem?"

Stan looked confused and stared quizzically at Peter. "What?"

"The woman. The upset one. What's up with her?"

Stan still stared quizzically at Peter before eventually responding as if having something of a lightbulb moment. "Oh, her? Yeah, the news. She saw it… on the… up here… news…"

Stan trailed off and returned his attention to the television. All the while, the cigarette never left Stan's lips.

Peter gave up and decided to move on. "Helpful. Thanks, Stan," he said sarcastically as he continued on his daily journey towards the tube station.

Peter was beginning to think that the whole world had gone a bit mad! In reality, he wasn't too far off the truth.

His journey on the train to his final destination was similarly odd. Firstly, the train was eerily quiet (like the streets) which was strange. Most who got onto the train were vacant with a look of confusion, some with sadness others with shock. Some with a combination of all three. It was only when he disembarked in the heart of London at Chancery Lane station that all the bizarreness of his morning was finally explained, in only two very simple words. At top of the stairs as he exited the station was a newspaper billboard stand with a man selling copies of the daily newspaper stood behind it. The words on it, in large black bold print, were simple enough to understand and straight to the point. He needed no further explanation to the strangeness of his morning.

HITLER DEAD!

He didn't know how long he had been stood there. It was only when someone knocked into Peter (no doubt whilst in a similar state of shock) that he snapped out of his trance. Adolf Hitler was dead. This was the man he felt as though he had personally grown up with. The man every child learnt about in school and his heroic conquests in the Second World War. His pursuit and destruction of all things evil in an effort to create a purer world. The defeat of the cruel British Empire, the defeat of the cruel communists of the Soviet Union, the defeat of the cruel American dictators, and finally, the defeat of the Jews — surely the biggest enemy — who were intent on world domination. Everyone in the British Territories could thank Hitler for at least one thing in their lives. The man was an idol, loved and revered by all. But this day had to come. Hitler was, after all, only human but it did leave the burning question on Peter's mind — as it no doubt did on everybody's mind. What now?

The grief was all too palpable as Peter walked into the ministry to begin his day at work. He swiped himself in through the main door with his security badge and walked through the metal detector in the foyer. The two security guards solemnly waved him through and nodded in acknowledgement as he passed by them. The ministry building was a large place. An old Victorian building with several floors. Propaganda sat at the very top of the building but all data analysts were located on the third floor. He waited for the lift and got into it with several other people. One woman was silently weeping, the tears running down her cheeks like raindrops. The other people stood silent with a stunned look on their face. When he reached the open plan office he worked in, he went straight to his desk. He did walk past Heinrich Stein's office, but rather uncharacteristically, the door was shut. Sat opposite him was his colleague, and closest friend, Danny Want. Slightly older than Peter, Danny was sat back in his chair, his black tie slightly loosened with his fingers clasped together behind his head. He was silent as Peter took his seat, and at first, didn't acknowledge him.

"Bloody hell," said Peter.

Danny rocked gently back and forth in his laid-back position and nodded gently to acknowledge his friend. "I know, right?"

"I have literally only just found out. People were acting all weird and I just didn't click. How bloody stupid am I?" Peter paused for thought before continuing. "When did it happen?"

"Some time yesterday apparently," responded Danny. "There was an announcement at about two o'clock this morning. Hindenburg said he'd passed away in Berlin. National televised address."

"How?"

"Natural causes apparently. The old man went in his sleep."

It was a sombre day. Perhaps the most sombre day Peter had ever experienced at work. He quietly got on with his job (although it remained unusually quiet with not a lot landing on his desk or in his tray to edit, improve or redact and then repeat). Likewise, Danny also quietly got on with his job — which was the same as Peter's. To edit, improve, redact and then repeat. The office all seemed to just quietly continue. Stein remained well out of sight for the remainder of the day. He had served in the Wehrmacht during the war as an officer. Peter never really knew the rank and had never wanted to ask but the man idolised Hitler and everything he stood for. He even had a picture of himself shaking hands with the Führer proudly framed and displayed on his desk. He was likely in a period of some grief whilst trying to process the dreadful news of the day.

By the end of the day, Peter and Danny had made the decision to go and drown their own sorrows at the pub after work. Peter never really knew for sure what Danny's own personal feelings towards Hitler were. He always had such a lackadaisical demeanour about him that he was sometimes a difficult person to read. He also never really gave much away about himself. In fact, when he thought about it, Peter really didn't know much about his best friend at all. He was aware Danny's father had fought (for the British) in the war but that he had perished during the Siege of London. Danny himself, along with his mother, had — to the best of Peter's knowledge — remained in London in the years following the war. Peter therefore made the assumption that growing up in a Nazi world was all Danny truly knew.

Danny had never once overtly expressed his allegiance to any party or faction, political or otherwise. He would quietly watch the news reports of attacks by The Menorah, expressionless, whilst quietly shaking his head in disgust; at the same time never truly condemning their actions. Similarly, he never condemned or approved the policies of Hitler, the NSDAP or the Reich. Then again, who would dare to condemn them anyway for fear of reprisals? Criticism of Hitler or any government aligned to the Reich would lead to a hefty penalty so only those foolish enough would dare express a view on the matter in the first instance.

That being said, Peter always remained surprised that Danny wasn't more forthcoming to him; particularly as the two were so close. Either Danny still had a subconscious mistrust of his friend or was living with the quiet acceptance that the Reich existed, and well, that was that.

Danny wasn't a bad looking chap by any means. Indeed, it seemed as though he took care of himself outside of work and ate well, exercised and remained a non-smoker. But he remained ominously single. Sure, he could easily attract the attention of the ladies if he wished but more often than not he would shy away in such a situation or make a polite excuse to be somewhere else. Peter was almost certain his friend was not attracted to those of the same sex. Maybe it was just that Danny preferred the single life? Either way, he remained a dark horse shrouded in perhaps more mystery than Peter would sometimes like, but nevertheless, he trusted his friend. Danny was reliable if nothing else. When he said he would be somewhere, he would be there. If he said something would be done, he'd get it done. If you asked him for help, he'd help you out, no questions asked. When you invited him to the pub, he'd join you at the pub. What more could you ask of a friend?

And so it came to be that the two men found themselves later that evening walking down Kings Cross Road towards their favourite pub, the Highwayman, on Cleveland Street in the Fitzrovia area of London. It was a trek from the ministry and somewhere they had stumbled upon some time ago whilst indulging in perhaps one too many drinks after work one Friday night. They liked the place though and it was worth the walk.

The grief surrounding the death of Adolf Hitler was evident on every street corner and in every shop front. People were distraught and it was clear that this would remain a newsworthy story for some time. On their journey, they walked past an electronics store where the numerous televisions in the window were all playing the same news report on the same channel. Alois Hitler, the Führer's only child, was pictured leaving the Reich Chancellery building in Berlin. He was a handsome young man with dark hair, parted and gelled to the left, with a thin frame and prominent cheek bones. He was always clean shaven and of average height. He was wearing a dark suit and sunglasses and was filmed entering a chauffeur driven, black (no doubt armoured and bulletproof) Mercedes before being driven away at speed. Alois Hitler had been named after Adolf Hitler's close friend and one of his right-hand men, Alois Brunner — a former Schutzstaffel (SS) officer and former right-hand man of the now governor-general of East America, Adolf Eichmann.

Brunner had been instrumental during the war in the rounding up and detaining of thousands of Jewish civilians and, along with Eichmann, had become a close confidant of the Führer in the years following the war. Upon the appointment of Eichmann as governor-general of East America, Brunner also took up a high-ranking position in East America taking the lead in the Ministry of Aeronautics and Weaponry, developing projects alongside other top Nazi scientists whose knowledge and skill had been so instrumental in securing a swift Nazi victory during the war. While there remained a tentative peace between the Nazi East America and the Japanese West America, it was rumoured that — towards the end of his reign — Adolf Hitler expressed ever more vocal ambitions to extend the Reich further west. Therefore, having a figure such as Brunner heading up weapons projects on that side of the Atlantic was seen as somewhat of a strategic (as well as a political) move and a consistent reminder to Japan as to who, and what, was sat on their very doorstep and the capabilities of the Reich should it ever chose to use them.

While no official announcement had been made, it was widely assumed that the twenty-six-year-old Alois Hitler would be stepping into his father's shoes to become the new Führer. Alois Hitler had remained largely out of the public eye throughout all his life and he was rumoured to be a shy man. Unlike his father, Hitler Jr was not known for his passionate speeches and fiery rhetoric. From a young age, he had taken to his father's side and appeared in public with both his parents with a nervous smile on his face and never seeming to know what to do with his hands — whether to pocket them or leave them dangling awkwardly by his side. Even into adolescence, the younger Hitler seemed uncomfortable in the limelight leading many people to question his suitability to lead the NSDAP and an empire. Particularly his ability to step into the shoes of his father, the most revered leader in history. Rumours abounded that the mantle would pass to Hitler's wife, Eva Hitler, but these remained wild and unfounded yet not entirely implausible. Eva Hitler was a matriarchal figure who, unlike her son, oozed charm and charisma. She remained active in public life across Europe appearing at many sporting events, parades, openings of new hospitals and all similar such activities where she would act as the face of the Reich. Like her husband, the cult of personality followed her wherever she went, and also like her husband, she was always greeted with rapturous applause and praise wherever she appeared. Yet, Alois Hitler remained lacking in the charisma and personality espoused by his mother and father leaving many (even within the highest echelons of the Reich) to ask serious questions amongst themselves as to how effective the younger Hitler would be.

Peter and Danny walked up Kings Cross Road and cut through into Fitzrovia. As they walked through Fitzroy Square they continued towards Cleveland Street, where the Highwayman was located. As they turned right onto Cleveland Street, they could see the Highwayman tucked away approximately two hundred metres on the left-hand side. To the right (a little closer to them) was a small police building adorned with the Swastika on a pole hanging at a forty-five-degree angle in front of the building, swinging gently in the frosty winter evening breeze. A small outpost. One of many dotted around London. Sparsely manned but a constant reminder to all residents that the Reich was very much there and keeping a close eye on the populous at all times.

The explosion that ripped through the outpost as the two men rounded the corner was both shocking and unexpected. They were immediately thrown backwards and knocked to the floor. The momentary and sudden blast of heat washed over them, and this (combined with the noise) left their faces scorched and their ears numb, yet ringing. While not knocked completely unconscious, it took both men a moment or two to gather their senses and begin to comprehend what had happened. As they pulled themselves up from the ground, they surveyed the ensuing carnage all around them. The explosion had happened at, or around, what looked like the police post and had created a cloud of dust and debris that was hanging in the air and slowly descending onto the street below. Both men were covered in a thick layer of dust and dirt, their ears yet to adjust to the sounds all around them at that point. They could make out an enormous hole in the buildings to the right-hand side roughly where the police post had been. The flag of the Swastika was by this point in flames but most disturbing of all were the numerous body parts that were strewn across Cleveland Street.

After what seemed like some time, the two floored men began to regain their auditory senses and were immediately greeted by a wall of screaming and sobbing as people caught up in the blast scattered in every direction from the scene. They hadn't realised how busy the street had been until this point. Most people were running away from the explosion. A few individuals were searching through the debris looking for survivors. Injured people were staggering away from the scene, clutching their wounds, covered in dust and detritus. It was impossible to ascertain exactly who the body parts belonged to, whether they were of any police inside the post at the time or of innocent bystanders. It was nothing short of carnage. The sort of scene Peter could only imagine in a warzone. The dust kicked up into the air by the explosion had obscured the street lights and it seemed almost as though they had been instantaneously transported into the middle of some kind of dark abyss.

Before the light dimmed to a point where visibility was near zero, Peter noticed something. Something he had seen before. The first time when he had been a child but it was something that had become increasingly more common in recent years. Graphitised on the wall of the building approximately two doors from the police post was a symbol that had become synonymous with terror and also a cruel indication of who the perpetrators of such carnage could be.

3

RAID

At roughly the same time the bomb ripped through Cleveland Street, the police were conducting an operation of their own in the Wembley area of London. They had been watching the comings and goings relating to a house in Norton Road for weeks now. In fact, unbeknownst to the residents, the authorities had set up covert cameras in the house opposite and they had been recording and photographing those visiting and thought to be living at the address. The police had been acting on intelligence from their undercover operatives, one of whom had successfully managed to penetrate a suspected Menorah cell.

Members of the group were notoriously difficult to locate as, more often than not, they were nothing more than ordinary citizens carrying out ordinary jobs and living an ordinary life. Many worked directly for the Reich and in recent years, more and more Menorah terrorists had infiltrated various Reich departments or ministries in an effort to further the cause of their group. Vetting procedures for any Reich position were now more stringent and thorough, making infiltrations more of a rarity but such incursions were still not entirely unheard of.

Infiltration of terrorist cells was an activity also carried out by the Ministerium für Infiltration und Intelligenz (Ministry of Infiltration and Intelligence — or IUI), a specialist Reich ministry populated by highly trained former military personnel. Set up by Hermann Göring, with a headquarters in East America, the IUI despatched its operatives wherever their services were required; usually acting on initial intelligence gathered by the police. However, on this occasion, the Intelligence Branch of the Reich Police of the British Territories were taking charge of the Wembley operation which was on verge of being brought to what was deemed to be a logical conclusion.

Detective Sergeant (DS) Jonas Weber had been within earshot of a conversation in a café some months prior to the night of the 29th January 1979 that had sparked suspicion. It was a purely coincidental occurrence, involving someone called Paul Fuller and another member of The Menorah, yet one that began an intense and undercover operation to expose other members of The Menorah and put an immediate halt to their activities. After some careful intelligence gathering, and surveillance over a considerable period of time, DS Weber made contact with the man in the café — Paul Fuller — and gradually gained his trust, eventually becoming a trusted member of The Menorah (or so they thought) under the alias of Jonathan Webster.

Like the Reich, The Menorah had their own vetting procedure. They too had access to the same fingerprint scanning technology used by the police and were able to identify anybody as and when they chose to do so. This required DS Weber to have a completely new tailor-made identity created so he was able to penetrate deep into the ranks of The Menorah and help weed them out. His initiation was brutal. Days of interrogation in a dark room. Sensory deprivation. Sleep deprivation. No access to food and water, but he passed and was able to withstand what The Menorah was able to throw at him. He had them convinced and so he was able to begin gathering intelligence and report back (covertly) to his colleagues in the police.

The double life was not easy by any means but the fruits of his labour eventually bore the necessary results. The house on Norton Road was eventually identified as a property of some interest. DS Weber was never allowed access himself, leaving the police to assume it housed someone (or something) of great importance hence why covert surveillance was set up to monitor the property more closely. Those higher up in The Menorah were reluctant to give too much away about the house, but further gathering of intelligence over a period of time eventually led the police to believe the property was being used to plan further attacks against the Reich and that it was possibly also being used to intercept and jam television signals and make broadcasts with false propaganda and fabricated historical footage. It had to be shut down and, while senior officers wanted a swift resolution, they had to act with caution and some trepidation. The time to strike had to be correct and the evening of the 29th January 1979 was that time.

The intelligence DS Weber had gathered as part of the operation was accurate. At least as accurate as it could be and The Menorah was indeed in the process of once again preparing to jam the television signal across the capital in order to broadcast their own message. Their technology was crude, it didn't always work but their knowledge was such that they were able to, on occasion, scramble the signal — albeit only briefly. It was risky attempting to do it too often and for too long. The technology of the Reich was better and a lot more reliable. Still, they were able to outsmart it enough to get their messages across on a semi-regular basis. The broadcasts were designed to show people the truth about Nazi Germany and what it did during the war and the subsequent years. There was plenty of footage out there showing what really happened on the day London was finally liberated. The triumphant lines of panzers and goose-stepping ranks of soldiers being cheered on by the grateful British citizens of London in 1941 was (in reality) actually nothing short of a massacre. Indiscriminate bombings, summary executions, brutality of the highest order. While Germany had sought to destroy all such evidence of their atrocities (both in Britain and elsewhere in the world), there was still plenty of footage and other evidence to indicate what the real story was. It had been hidden away by some of the same people who would go on to form The Menorah. More was out there if you looked hard enough for it. In fact, The Menorah was always keen to try and convince and recruit members who worked for the Reich. They would have access to a wealth of intelligence on the Reich and their activities but vetting processes for potential employees were becoming so stringent, this was becoming increasingly difficult. Not impossible — but increasingly difficult.

Paul Fuller was one of the members of The Menorah lucky enough to be granted access to the Norton Road address for he had been a trusted member of The Menorah for many years. His father had been a soldier in the British army and had witnessed first-hand the New Year's Day invasion of 1941. Along with thousands of other soldiers, he was forced to flee in the face of the Nazi invasion and was hunted down mercilessly by the Heer as they advanced through England from the south coast. His father was one of the few who managed to evade capture and make it back to his family in the Midlands where he kept his head down and maintained a low profile. In the subsequent years, Paul Fuller's father worked a series of menial jobs, keeping his military past a well-guarded secret but he remained traumatised by what he had seen and experienced.

To cope, he often turned to alcohol and would switch between terrible anger and sheer grief within a heartbeat. Such was his unpredictability, he was eventually placed in a secure hospital environment where he succumbed a few years later with his mind well and truly broken. For this, the now forty-four-year-old Paul blamed Nazi Germany. In the space of a few years, he had seen his father transformed from a loving family man into nothing more than a rambling lunatic. Even though he had not witnessed what his father had, the stories of the invasion horrified him and as a result, he grew up with a deep-seated hatred for anything associated with Hitler and his Reich. When presented with an opportunity to join The Menorah in the 1960s, it was a decision he didn't have to ponder over for too long.

Paul stood outside in the back garden of the Norton Road house having a cigarette whilst the broadcast was underway. It had taken some time to get set up, but as it approached midnight, the transmission was in full flow. He believed this one was more of the raw (and genuine) footage detailing the events following the Siege of London, primarily the execution of civilians by the Heer in the streets. The air was cold and he shivered as he puffed away and blew the smoke into the night sky. It was quiet that evening, almost eerily so. Paul stood alone in the unkempt garden thinking to himself how oddly quiet it was. The enormous crash made him jump nearly out of his skin. It took a few seconds for Paul to process in his head what was going on. He froze and listened carefully.

He could hear shouting and while most of it was indecipherable, he could make out what he thought was something like, "Police! Don't move!"

They were being raided. He had no time to think. He had to get out of there. Without thinking the situation through any further, he dropped his cigarette, ran to the back of the garden and vaulted the fence into the garden of the house at the rear. He crouched down on the lawn and remained deadly still and silent. Listening. He could hear the shouts as the police had forced their way into the property. There was screaming and shouting and more crashing as if something was being smashed to pieces. No doubt the transmitter being used to broadcast the footage. Paul looked around him.

The noise didn't appear to have alerted the occupants of the house, whose garden he was in, and it remained in darkness. He could see a gate to the left of the house that would take him onto the street so, as light-footed as he could be, he made his way to it in order to escape.

The gate was unlocked and he opened it quietly and peered through. All was silent in the street ahead of him. There was a street light in front of him that cast a dim yellow glow down the side of the house and onto the driveway. He looked up and down the street. All silent. He knew he had to get out of the area and quickly. He had to alert others within the group as to what was happening and they themselves may need to relocate depending not only on what the police knew but what they would find out from the occupants of the house under what would no doubt be an interrogation of the most extreme order.

Rommel Way, Themse Marschland in East London was where he would need to head to. The locations of the safe houses set up by The Menorah were dynamic but this one, despite being miles away from Wembley, he knew in all certainty was still very much active and in use. There was no way he would make it that far tonight. Not on foot and during the curfew hours. He would have to find somewhere safe to hunker down for the night.

When he thought the moment was right, he moved onto the quiet street and began walking swiftly but not quickly enough that he might arouse any unwanted attention. As he walked, he heard a car coming up behind him. To his horror, as it passed by, he noticed it was a police vehicle. Further to this, he was out well after curfew hours. The car braked and came to a halt. He knew he was about to get questioned. Perhaps he could get away with it? An officer exited the passenger side of the vehicle and stood in Paul's path forcing him to slow his pace.

"Evening. Any reason you're out after curfew?"

"I'm really sorry, I've just been to see a friend and completely lost track of time."

The officer raised his hand. "Stop there for me, please."

Paul stopped dead in his tracks at the request of the officer, not wishing to enflame an already tricky situation.

"And where's home?"

Now he had a problem. His real address was miles away. Would he get away with trying to lie his way out of this situation?

"Just round the corner," he responded vaguely.

The officer paused and looked at him quizzically. "Whereabouts 'just round the corner'?"

"Look, I'm sorry I'm out. Like I said, I just lost track of time, I'll go straight home. There'll be no more problems."

"Let me decide that," the officer replied before reaching to his utility belt upon which was a loaded sidearm and a fingerprint scanner.

The scanners were small enough to strap to a belt and light enough to be carried by all officers and were an invaluable resource allowing the police to identify anyone, anywhere at any time.

"Step forward please, present your right hand so we can see where 'just round the corner' actually is."

He wouldn't get away with it. Not a chance. Not if they intended to scan him and refusal to be scanned was not really much of a viable option. This would only anger the officer who would either force a scan, arrest him or beat him. If he were really lucky, he would be treated to all of this. Without further thought into the situation, Paul turned and sprinted as fast as he could. As quickly as he had about turned, the officer had drawn his sidearm and fired off two shots towards Paul. They cracked and echoed into the still night air, setting off the barking of some nearby dogs. The bullets missed Paul and he continued his desperate sprint away from the patrol car which itself was beginning to perform a turn in the road in an effort to pursue him. As the car accelerated towards Paul, the officer who had attempted to scan — and then shoot — him was immediately on his radio.

"All units, all units, we've got one of them heading east on Maple Avenue, immediate assistance required. I repeat, immediate assistance required."

4

UNWANTED VISITOR

Peter and Danny never made it to the Highwayman. Any suggestions that they might even get close were quashed following the explosion at the police post. Within minutes, the area was flooded with police officers who immediately cordoned the area off, shut the street in its entirety and ushered everyone away from the scene. By the time the dust had settled, a helicopter hovered overhead and the devastation was truly evident. Not only had the explosion completely destroyed the police post, but it had also ripped apart the adjacent buildings, exposing their interiors. Ambulances were also quick to rush to the scene to attend to those lying injured on the street. After being abruptly ordered away from the scene, the two men made their way back to Kings Cross Road and headed to the Puffing Billy that sat roughly opposite Kings Cross train station.

Aside from being covered head to toe in dust and detritus (much to the amusement of some of the other patrons in the pub), they remained uninjured. Shocked, yet uninjured. The first pint of beer they drank was done so largely in silence while they mentally processed what they had just witnessed. More ambulances and police vehicles with their sirens blaring raced past the window in the direction of the explosion while the judder of the helicopter could be heard as it continued to circle the scene. It was yet to make the news. The television above the bar in the pub was still broadcasting news of Hitler's death alongside archive footage of him being paraded through the streets of a newly liberated London. The story would make it there in due course though. Terrorism by the group calling itself The Menorah always did eventually, it was only a matter of time. So the men drank into the evening before deciding to part company thus allowing one another time to get home before curfew hours.

After leaving the pub, a slightly foggy headed Peter Fewtrill made his way back to his flat in Acton. He had consumed maybe more alcohol than he should've done for a weeknight but the mass outpouring of grief over Hitler's death coupled with his near-death experience on Cleveland Street had left him feeling pretty depressed. His journey back on the tube and short walk from West Acton station to his flat (accompanied by a belly full of booze) had given him some time to reflect on the events of the day, and indeed, his own feelings towards the death of the Führer.

He was born after the war, into a world already occupied by Hitler's Reich so he knew little else. Much the same as his friend Danny. What he did remember was the huge effort made by the Reich to rebuild a London left shattered by war. A war fuelled by Churchill's belligerence. A war where Churchill had refused outright to submit to the Reich and how he had used thousands upon thousands of innocent people as human shields. A war where Churchill had sent thousands of ill-equipped British soldiers into battle whilst remaining in the comfort of his secure bunkers feasting on the finest food and drinking the finest wine, all the while having little to no concern over the plight of his people.

He was not too young to remember the Swastika flags, proudly flying atop any building considered to be of importance or significance. The German soldiers standing on every street corner in the early years of the occupation. The great Wehrmacht, as his school taught him. Watching over the populous, keeping everyone safe and quickly suppressing any who remained in support of Churchill's ideology. Churchill was tried, convicted and executed before he was born and he was too young to remember a great deal about the appointment of Governor-General Klaus von Hindenburg, the steely scar faced war hero who gallantly led the Wehrmacht as they landed on the British beaches years before.

Peter had never really ventured far; for doing so was often met with difficulties and much bureaucracy. He had family to the north, who he visited with his parents on a semi-regular basis, and he remembered that even in the north, the stories were the same. Von Hindenburg was considered a hero and a key factor in securing a swift victory in the United Kingdom. He was a brilliant military strategist who stared death square on in the face and defeated it. It would be fair to say that much of the population had, over time, become almost indoctrinated to the Reich way of thinking and their take on history.

There remained, however, a nagging doubt in the back of Peter's mind. He vaguely remembered first seeing a picture of a menorah when he was a lot younger. Some time back in his earlier childhood. It had been crudely painted on a wall somewhere and while he couldn't remember exactly where, he remembered asking his parents what the 'funny looking candle thing' was. His parents remained dismissive and told him to ignore it but the symbol began to appear more frequently as the years went on. As quickly as they would appear, they would be removed by the authorities. Only through rumour and word of mouth did he discover the real name for the 'funny looking candle thing' and that it was actually called a menorah, a seven-lamp (six branched) ancient Hebrew lampstand, a symbol of Judaism. An outlawed religion, its people the primary instigators of the Second World War. A greedy and selfish race of people who caused a massive wealth divide throughout Europe at the behest of the ordinary working-class citizen. A race that was determined to one day dominate the globe until Adolf Hitler decided to rise up against and confront such an existential threat. At least that's what the Reich would have you believe.

Into his teenage years, and becoming more self-aware, Peter began to hear another side of the story and that the Jewish people were in fact not the cockroaches Hitler had made them out to be, but an ordinary race of people simply discriminated against because of their religion. Either way, Peter remembered being taught in school about how they had been largely erased from the face of the planet with the exception of some place in the far east of the former Soviet Union called the 'Automatic Jewish Blast' or something equally tongue-twisty. Possessing the ability of independent thought, Peter often thought to himself that this was incalculably cruel, yet he daren't express this other than in his own thoughts. The penalties for saying such things were harsh. Rumour had it people disappeared for saying such things. The same rumours would say that some people disappeared only to return weeks later having received a lobotomy! His current stance was mixed. Part of him hated the Jew, because that's all he knew. Hatred towards an entire race he had never even met. But then, that's what seemed to him to be, at times, utterly incomprehensible. How can you hate someone or something that you know nothing about?

The first time he ever heard of a terrorist attack was in 1965. He had just turned sixteen-years-old and graffiti of a menorah had appeared on a tube train. Shortly thereafter, there was a bomb explosion on the very same train. Luckily, it had been late at night so there were no casualties and it seemed as though it had been done to make a point. Make a point it did. Weeks later, another device was detonated, this time outside the headquarters of the Reich Metropolitan Police of the British Territories. A painting of a menorah was found nearby. In subsequent years, attacks against Reich targets (accompanied or preceded by a picture of a menorah) became increasingly commonplace. Sometimes there were Reich casualties, sometimes there were none. Sometimes, innocent people were injured or killed, prompting outcry from the Reich and widespread panic amongst the general population.

In 1967, The Menorah was officially declared a terrorist organisation. No one knew or could say for sure exactly who they were or where they came from. Much of it was only assumptions but intelligence gathered on the group was able to deduce that the leader of the new terrorist group went by a singular name — Hebron. The Reich take on The Menorah was that they were a small band of Jewish 'leftovers'. Those who managed to escape the clutches of the Reich during the final months of the war or who were unable to flee into the former Soviet Union to the safety of the Jewish Autonomous Oblast. Now they were hiding out, occasionally launching attacks if only to make a point. Again, rumours, hearsay and word of mouth would offer an alternative take on the origins and purpose of this group but God forbid you ever discuss this outside the boundaries of your own conscious thought.

When Peter arrived at home, he settled down in front of the television but the viewing was hardly stimulating. All three channels were dedicated to the same thing: the death of Hitler, the death of Hitler and the death of Hitler. Occasionally there was some old grainy footage of Winston Churchill's trial and of panzers patrolling through central London on the back of a British surrender, but apart from this, it was pretty boring viewing. So much so that Peter eventually drifted off into a drink induced deep sleep whilst sat up on his sofa.

As Peter slept on the sofa, the newscast on the television continued. He never knew (because he was sleeping) but there was a grainy, crackling sound of interference and static on the television before the newscast suddenly cut off. The screen went blank for a few seconds before grainy black and white silent images were broadcast in place of the newscast. The images showed rows of people (men, women and children) kneeling on the street. It was impossible to tell exactly whereabouts this was. As they knelt, five German soldiers stood in front of them watching over them talking amongst themselves. One of the soldiers then stepped forward and removed a sidearm from its holster and began indiscriminately shooting the kneeling people one by one in the head leaving them to slump forward dead in a pool of their own blood. As this unfolded, a voice began to narrate on top of the footage. The voice had clearly been disguised and sounded almost metallic in nature and as if it were being spoken into a bucket. The words, however, were clear and spoken slowly and deliberately.

"You have been lied to. This is what the Reich did to British citizens during the war. Tens of thousands of innocent people have been murdered in atrocities across Europe. The Menorah know the truth. We will expose the Reich. Rise up and fight back against—"

Almost as quickly as the broadcast had begun, it was cut off and the screen returned to noisy, psychedelic looking static interference before eventually returning to the news — as if nothing had even happened. Little did Peter know, or would have known were he awake, that the broadcast was coming from a house some miles away in Wembley and that it had been brought to an abrupt end as the police raided the house smashing the transmitting equipment to pieces in the process. Little did Peter know that this was around the same time Paul Fuller had vaulted a fence and evaded the police and through nothing more than sheer coincidence, he was about to have an encounter with the very same man.

The crash awoke Peter with an almighty jolt. His heart nearly burst from his chest cavity such was the ferocity of the bang. He had no time to gather his thoughts or his faculties or even properly determine what was going on. The first thing he did see was that someone had forcibly entered his flat and they were stood in front of him. The man was a tall skinny thing. He was wearing dirty jeans and a raggedy dirty white shirt that was untucked and ripped in several places. His auburn hair was matted with dirt and beads of sweat were prominent on his forehead. His face was also streaked with dirt and grime. It looked as though he had been dragged through a hedge and in reality, this wasn't too far from the truth. He had actually traversed more gardens than he could count in his attempts to escape his pursuers.

Instinctively, Peter leapt from his slumber and pushed at the man, aiming to get him towards the front door and out of his flat. But the man was strong, almost inhumanly so and his eyes were filled with a rising sense of panic. He lurched forward grabbing Peter by his lapels and pushed back against him, almost (but not quite) knocking him off balance altogether. So the shouting began.

"Get out my flat!" Peter yelled with blind panic. But the man would not give and continued to push back. "Get out!"

"Help me, please! Help me, you have to help me, please!"

"I said get out!"

"Help, help me please, help me!"

The look of panic in the man's face was rising. From behind him, out in the corridor of the block, there was the noise of more voices and shouting and stomping as if more bodies were making their way up the stairs. This only served to increase the man's sense of panic.

"Help me, please! They're coming. You need to go... You need to go to—"

The man loosened his grip on Peter and began to ferret around in the back pockets of his jeans leaving Peter stood there thoroughly confused. Was this some kind of drunken dream? As the man was searching for something, so the footsteps and racket from outside the flat were becoming louder and louder. The man then pulled from his back pocket a scrap of paper and handed it to Peter.

"Take this." Peter said nothing and looked at the man, still confused. "Take it! Please!"

Peter extended his hand and took the scrap of paper from the mystery man. Before he had a chance to look at it in any detail the man began talking again.

"Go to the address on that bit of paper and tell them that they have Paul Fuller, tell them that they have Paul—"

"Don't move! Get on the floor! Get on the floor! Now!" was the next thing both men heard, as the police finally barged through the door and rushed into the room where they were.

There were several of them and they were all armed with firearms aimed forward and it was obvious they meant business. It all happened so quickly, Peter had no chance to remonstrate with the police or even begin to explain what had happened. Something struck him in the belly. He wasn't sure exactly what, but it was likely the butt of a police weapon, and he dropped to the floor winded before having a hood slung quickly over his head and tightened with a cord around his neck. He was unable to see the intruder who had barged his way into his home but he heard the beating he was receiving and the cries of pain after each punch or kick.

It was clear almost immediately that the armed men were the police. While they didn't take the time to identify themselves, it was quite clear. Black body armour, black helmets, wielding automatic weapons; they were more than the standard beat officers but likely an operational unit engaged in an operation that had unwittingly spilled over into Peter's block — specifically his flat. Peter was hooded, cuffed and then manhandled from his flat and down several flights of stairs and into the back of a vehicle of some description. The cacophony of voices, shouting and sirens was deafening and it was impossible to make out an individual voice. With the exception of Mrs Banks, the old lady next door. She didn't like Peter, a feeling that was reciprocated. He never really knew why but she never cracked a smile or even acknowledged Peter with a "good morning" if they ever passed one another on the stairs. Sometimes, she would open her door a fraction and watch him leave his flat, almost having some kind of extra sensory perception by knowing exactly when he was planning to leave. Peter suspected she was just being cantankerous and nosey and in recent weeks had begun to greet his little spy with a polite little wave and a cheery "hello".

The reception on this night was less than cheery though as Peter could make out her voice screeching angrily at the officers. "Do you know what time it is?"

The hood was finally removed when Peter's journey to the police station was completed. He didn't know which station he had been taken to. There were hundreds dotted across London, some small outposts (like the now defunct Cleveland Street) and some more grandiose, serving multiple functions. By this point, he had been strapped to a chair in a small interrogation room. His eyes took a minute or so to adjust to the light in the room and he squinted to see who was in front of him and indeed, where he had actually ended up. His journey had not been particularly comfortable and the police officers involved in his apprehension had been quite heavy handed in removing him from the block, throwing him into the rear of what he assumed was a police van and then keeping him stationary on the floor with what felt like their feet on his back and arms. The fate of the man he could only remember as being called Paul was unclear. As Peter was being dragged from his home, Paul was still taking a considerable beating, his cries of pain becoming ever weaker between each strike leading Peter to assume he hadn't fared at all well in the confrontation.

When his eyes had adjusted to his new surroundings, Peter was finally able to cast them on who was sat in front of him. It was a man and a woman, both with almost identical humourless expressions on their faces. The woman was surprisingly attractive (at least that's what Peter thought) and was slim and had auburn hair that hung straight, roughly down to her ears. Her cheekbones were well defined, giving her an almost sleek cat like appearance. The man on the other hand Peter naturally considered the less attractive of the two. He was clearly a well exercised individual as indicated by his broad shoulders. He had short dark brown cropped hair and a few days of dark stubble growth. Handsome to some? Maybe, but not to Peter.

The woman started talking first. "I'm Detective Inspector Jo-Anna Harding and this is Detective Sergeant Dean Fellows. Do you know why you're here, Mr Fewtrill?"

Rather taken aback and equally amused, Peter responded with a scoff, "Well, funnily enough, Detective Jo-Anna, no. However, if I were a gambling man I would bet it's got something to do with that other guy."

"You know him then do you?" Detective Sergeant (DS) Fellows interjected.

"What?"

"The 'other guy'. You know who he is?"

"No! Not a clue."

"So why was he in your flat then?" continued Detective Inspector (DI) Harding.

"He forced his way in. He barged in, while I was sleeping, I had no choice."

"Why did he come to *your* flat?" Back to DS Fellows.

"I don't know, ask him!"

"Why did he choose to break down *your* door?"

"Man alive, I haven't got a clue. Ask him!"

The questioning ceased momentarily and the two police officers maintained their fixed humourless glance towards Peter, who was still utterly clueless as to why he had ended up in this position. It didn't take long for the interrogation to continue.

"What do you know about a group called The Menorah?" DS Fellows continued.

Peter paused and considered his response. He was in a volatile situation with a couple of potentially rather volatile individuals. He knew that he was innocent of whatever it was they thought he was guilty of in the first instance. However, he sensed they were maybe looking to incriminate him. To lure him into a trap, so he had to play along to save his own skin if nothing else. The trouble was, which direction should he play it?

"I know that they're a terrorist organisation. Intent on… terror," Peter responded clumsily.

The interrogators remained stoic and silent on the back of the response. So too, Peter remained silent as the two officers continued to eye him quizzically.

After what seemed like an eternity, Peter continued, "I don't know what else you want me to say. I have nothing to do with The Menorah if that's what you're getting at. Was he something to do with them?"

"Who?" DS Fellows enquired.

"Him… what was his name… Paul."

"Ah, so you do know him then," stated DI Harding. "And now we seem to be getting somewhere."

Despairingly, it seemed as though Peter had walked into a small hole but he was determined to not dig it any deeper than was necessary.

"Oh for crying out loud, I don't know him. He told me his name when he came into my flat and—"

"When you invited him in you mean?"

"No, I didn't say that. He was rambling and he… he… just told me his name. Look what do—"

"Well acquainted by the sounds of it, DI Harding, wouldn't you say?"

"I absolutely agree, DS Fellows."

"No!" snapped Peter. He was becoming more panicky now. "I don't know him. And I am not a member of any terrorist organisation! You've got the wrong person. Check my record for God's sake. Look at who I am and who I work for. I'm one of you!"

"Oh we've looked at your record Mr Fewtrill," DS Fellows interjected.

A brilliant advancement of Reich technology was fingerprinting of every citizen. A mandatory requirement making it quick and easy for police officers to scan anybody and everybody in situ and retrieve an immediate photograph and record of the person in question. A record containing every feasible personal detail down to blood type and parentage. Another way for the Reich to keep a close eye on everybody under its control. DS Fellows continued.

"You are one of us all right. Ministry of Media, Propaganda and Information. Very privileged. You must have access to a lot of really sensitive information. Am I correct?"

Peter paused to consider the question. He wasn't wrong in all fairness. "I guess so, yeah."

"Information that, in the wrong hands, could be potentially damaging to the Reich. Am I correct Mr Fewtrill?"

"What are you implying?"

"What do *you* think I'm implying?"

"Well, it sounds like you're accusing me of passing information to a terrorist organisation."

"I didn't say that did I, DI Harding?"

"No you did not, DS Fellows. But it's interesting that that's the connection you made, Mr Fewtrill. So have you been passing sensitive information to a terrorist organisation? Maybe that's why you had arranged to meet 'Paul'? To pass on information that you shouldn't have been passing on."

Peter began to laugh almost maniacally. "No! This is ridiculous. I haven't passed anything onto anyone. You've got it wrong. I want to see a lawyer."

Whilst freedoms for all were severely restricted, anyone arrested was still entitled to legal representation and still within their rights to request it. Although the quality of such representation was at times questionable (and more often than not downright bias), Peter felt it was the only card left to play at this stage. The request for a lawyer, however, was met with a hood once again being placed over his head from behind — by someone Peter was unaware was even there — and his world once again plunged into darkness.

So the interrogation continued on and off for what Peter could only guess was hours, well into the night with no sign of letting up and even less sign of any legal aid. His mouth was dry, his lips felt cracked, yet they did not give him a drink. When hooded, he could feel himself drifting into sleep only for the hood to be ripped away and the same questioning continuing over and over again: what's your relationship with Paul Fuller? What information have you passed to The Menorah? Where are the headquarters of The Menorah? Why was Paul Fuller at your flat? How long have you known Paul Fuller? It was relentless.

The final time Peter was hooded, he heard the people he was sharing the room with utter something to one another about taking a break before leaving the room. What he didn't hear was someone else enter and sit next to him. He thought he had been left alone, bound to his chair, until the person who had walked in lifted the hood from his head and placed it on the table in front of him. Having thought he was alone, this came as a surprise, and as his eyes once again adjusted to the light in the room, he was met by the sight of a fair headed young lady who was dressed in a smart suit. She was bespectacled and Peter estimated her as being late twenties maybe even early thirties. She looked tired and had placed an attaché case on the table that was open. She had in front of her a file and she seemed to be furiously reading the notes within the file, as if trying to familiarise herself with the contents before the officers returned.

"Hello," said Peter but the fair headed lady didn't respond. "Are you my—"

Peter continued but he was cut short as the lady raised a finger into the air — without looking up from the file — thus stopping Peter in his tracks. The finger remained where it was as Peter could see her eyes frantically moving side to side as she read the notes in front of her. When she reached the end, the finger lowered, she removed her glasses, placed them next to the attaché case and met Peter's gaze.

"I'm Susan Scott, duty solicitor."

"Hi. I'm—"

"I know who you are," Susan replied while pointing to the file she had been reading and smiling rather sarcastically.

"Oh right, yeah. Of course. Are you going to get me out of this?"

Susan's response was as curt as it was abrupt. "Just sit there, shut up and let me do the talking. Right?"

Rather taken aback and not entirely sure how to respond, Peter reluctantly agreed. "OK."

DI Harding and DS Fellows re-entered the room after a few minutes, both wielding what smelt like cups of bad coffee in paper cups. The third person (the phantom hood man — or woman) did not come back. The officers retook their seats opposite Peter and Susan. Peter wasn't sure who was going to begin this time but Susan was the first person to address the others in the room — specifically DI Harding and DS Fellows.

"Let him go. You have nothing to hold this person on."

"Excuse me?" questioned DS Fellows, a hint of some frustration in his voice.

"He's clean and you can't possibly expect to build a case against him. Reich employee for nearly twelve years, no criminal record, no intelligence against him, no known associates, no family history. His only run-ins with the law are two breaches of curfew which were both dealt with by a fine. Both of which were paid well on time. He isn't associated with your prime suspect in any shape or form. From what I can see, they have never even been in the same place at the same time other than this evening which, from what I can make out, was nothing more than an unfortunate coincidence. At least for my client. I hate to say it officers, you have nothing to make anything stick. At least not at this stage. If you want my advice, invest your time on someone else because this man has no worth to you."

The two officers looked at one another and seemed to be lost deep in thought. DI Harding reached up and stroked her face with her left hand and looked to the ceiling in thought before finally shrugging and saying, "OK. You're free to leave, Mr Fewtrill. Thank you for your time."

And with that, DI Harding rose from her seat, uncuffed Peter and both she and DS Fellows left the interrogation room leaving Peter and Susan sat at the table. Peter was in a state of some shock. For hours, he had been mercilessly questioned over and over again. He was beginning to think the questioning would never end, but as abruptly as this situation had begun, it finished.

"Thank you," Peter said to Susan who was now hurriedly packing her belonging back into her attaché case.

Susan smiled and nodded without making eye contact.

"Bloody hell, I'm thirsty," he said, noticing just how dry and uncomfortable his mouth was.

"Here, drink this," said Susan passing him an unopened bottle of water that had been sat in her case.

"Thanks," Peter responded whilst wasting no time whatsoever drinking the small bottle of water in one huge gulp.

Some of it had clumsily dribbled down his chin but he didn't really care. He wasn't attempting to impress anyone. His only intention was to quench his unbearable thirst. The water was cool, refreshing and he could feel it flowing into his stomach making it cramp upon contact. His wrists were red and sore where he had been tightly cuffed for the past few hours. Susan finished packing away her things before rising from her seat.

"Come on, I'll show you out. If you're lucky you might catch a night bus. Avoid another curfew breach."

Although everyone was required to be off the streets by eleven p.m. each night, exceptions were in place for a minority of those pursuing night work who thus needed to move around the city during curfew hours. Such people were granted a curfew pass to show to any police officers inclined to perform a stop check. A very limited public service transport (in the form of some night buses) was also operational to facilitate the movement of any night workers. The problem remained that Peter didn't actually know whereabouts in the city he was. A night bus would be wonderful but would it get him back to where he needed to be? This was yet to be determined.

"Thanks. How long have I been here for? I've lost all concept of time."

"Long enough, Mr Fewtrill."

Susan didn't seem to be in the mood for small talk but Peter was happy that she had helped him and continued to try to engage with her.

"You got any more work on this evening?"

"No, I'm done."

There was an awkward silence for a moment or so with Peter not really knowing what to do, what to say or how to act (or even dare to act). He didn't know where he was and was somewhat reliant on following her from the room so he could finally be shown the door to this dreadful place and somehow navigate his way back to the safety of his own home.

"Well, thanks again," continued Peter, breaking the awkward silence. He was met with no response from the lawyer who was still organising her belongings.

"He's a character isn't he," Peter mused.

This had piqued the young lawyer's interest who looked up at him quizzically. "Who?"

"That DS guy. You put him in his place. Who does he think he is anyway? Hitler?" The tone in his voice oozed sarcasm and it made the lawyer crack a smile.

"Oh, he's not so bad," Susan responded lightly. At last! It seemed as though Peter had found a chink in the armour of the young attractive hard-nosed lawyer.

"Oh yeah, how do you know that?" queried Peter.

The face of the lawyer dropped almost instantaneously from one of joviality to stone-faced seriousness and she fixed him with a steely gaze before responding. "He's my husband."

5

THE SECRETARY

At about the same time as the raid on Peter Fewtrill's flat and his lengthy interrogation, Superintendent (Supt) Rolf Becker had paid a visit to the Security and Surveillance Control Branch of the police force. This was a huge imposing concrete structure built in the aftermath of the Siege of London. Located in the White City area, it stood four stories tall, was cuboidal in shape, grey in colour and intimidating to look at. This was not helped by the presence of a tall (and electrified) razor wire fence around the perimeter and a number of security cameras operating round the clock to protect the building, its residents, and above all, the goings on inside. Originally built as a Reich ministry office, it quickly became taken over for police usage and now acted as the nerve centre and the brain for the entire capital city's security camera network (which was extensive to say the very least).

London was dotted with two types of camera on nearly every street corner and every public space. The first type of cameras were the regular security cameras, operating twenty-four seven and being monitored from the White City building twenty-four seven by a task force made up of hundreds of employees. All paid to monitor the activity of the citizens of the city and call through any misdemeanours to response officers as and when spotted. This is, in part, what made the police so efficient and so quick to respond and quash any disturbances. Crime rates in the city remained low, and in many parts virtually non-existent. The network of eyes in the sky, on every street corner, in every shop and every other public building made committing and getting away with even the slightest of crime a near impossibility on every level.

The second type of cameras were the curfew cameras. London remained on a strict night time curfew beginning at eleven p.m. and ending at six a.m. the following morning. During this time, no one was allowed to be on the streets with the exception of essential night workers; those carrying out paid work that could only be conducted during curfew hours. The curfew cameras would switch on at exactly eleven p.m. every night and would target vehicles on the road after this hour. Every vehicle passing within sight of a curfew camera would have its registration scanned. Every vehicle registered to a night worker would not create an alert. However, any vehicle not registered to a night worker would generate a very swift alert to operational officers who would duly mount a pursuit to ascertain exactly why the vehicle and its occupant(s) were out during designated curfew hours.

Supt Becker was interested in footage from one of the regular cameras, particularly the one in Cleveland Street that covered the location of the now destroyed police post and the surrounding area. It didn't take him long to find it. Each section of the building covered different areas of the capital so locating the relevant section and section operator was easy enough for Supt Becker to achieve. He specifically requested the raw footage of the explosion itself and the preceding twenty-four hours' worth of footage, which was duly granted and provided. He needed no authorisation to request this, his rank was sufficient to see it so. The section operator copied the relevant footage to a data disc for Supt Becker, after which he was requested to delete the original footage of the explosion and the preceding twenty-four hours. Again, this was done without question by the section operator who had no need or authority to question such orders from a high-ranking officer.

Once Supt Becker had obtained the footage of the explosion and the hours leading up to it, he left the White City compound and headed back to his designated station in Ladbroke Grove, coincidentally the same station Peter Fewtrill was being held at and questioned. Upon arrival, Supt Becker headed straight to his office where he had his own personal computer. The Reich had been quick to computerise all police records, something that had begun in the late 1950s. By 1979, all police forces under the control of the Reich shared the same systems allowing easy sharing and transfer of data both nationally and internationally thus speeding up investigations into crime and the hunt for any criminals. Specifically, Supt Becker wanted to check the footage from the day of the Cleveland Street blast. He couldn't do it at White City, it wasn't private enough and he was under strict instructions from a higher power to conduct his investigation with the utmost secrecy. He was therefore left with little choice but to copy the footage for viewing in a location he knew he would not be disturbed or interrupted.

So he inserted the data disc into his computer and it duly loaded and he sat and watched intently. The footage was good. It covered the police post in all its glory (and in colour too) as well as the buildings either side. It remained static. Whoever the operator had been at that time had had no reason to adjust the angle as nothing had alerted them to do so. He continued to watch. Sometimes he would stop to rub his tired eyes, to use the toilet or to refill his coffee. Then he saw what he was looking for.

Approximately three hours before the blast, he saw them. Two figures dressed in black had approached the police post. He could clearly see they were both male and neither was making any attempt to hide their identity. One of them had a small rucksack on his back. They were stood outside the police post and one of them had lit a cigarette. Outside the automatic doors of the police post was a litter bin. They were talking and looking cautiously around as if looking for — or waiting for — an opportune moment. That moment came a few minutes later when the footfall on Cleveland Street seemed to go quiet. The smoking man dropped his cigarette and stubbed it out underneath his shoe. *Would've made a great piece of evidence*, Becker thought to himself but was likely vaporised by now such was the ferocity of the explosion. The other man reached into the backpack and pulled out what looked like a shoe box. It was difficult to see an immense amount of detail and it was only momentarily in sight as it was then placed inside the litter bin located outside the automatic door of the police post. Once placed, the two men took one final look around before walking from the scene towards Euston Road, never to be seen again on the camera. Becker continued to watch and sure enough, three hours later the explosion occurred. He had to rewind the disc several times and slow down the footage at the exact time of the explosion but it was clear where it had emanated from. The bin.

He had seen enough. There was no need for him to sit there watching the emergency services rush in to pick up the pieces. He had seen who had planted the bomb and where they had planted it. He also knew exactly who the two men were. However, this was not the job he had been assigned. His orders were implicitly clear. Obtain the footage, ensure it was footage of the bomb being planted and the subsequent explosion, destroy any originals and any copies of the footage. He had ensured the operator at White City had removed the original recording and, now he had double checked that he had the correct footage of the correct time period, his copy too would now need to be destroyed.

By this point it was well into the following day. Becker had been up all night reviewing the footage. His secretary had arrived by that point and was going about her daily duties.

"Morning, Sally," Supt Becker cheerily said to his secretary as he exited his office.

"Morning, Rolf. How are you today?"

"Tired, my dear. But other than that, I'm good. I have a little job for you to do before I head off if it's OK with you?"

"Of course, what is it?"

Becker had placed the data disc into a preprinted and premarked envelope clearly stating 'For Destruction' on the front of it in large red letters. This wasn't the sort of thing you threw into a bin on the off chance it should end up in the wrong hands. This was a top-secret item that needed to be disposed of securely. This usually meant by way of incineration (along with any other confidential or secret documentation) so it would need to be directed accordingly. There were set procedures in place that had to be followed. Becker had worked with his secretary for years. They had embarked on a brief yet torrid affair in 1975. Although short-lived, the two remained close friends and Becker trusted her implicitly.

"I need you to make sure this goes to disposal. Soon as you can please if that's OK."

"Not a problem, let me take it."

Becker handed the disc and the envelope over. "Oh, it will need sealing first if you don't mind."

"Certainly."

And with that, the disc had been handed over ready to be disposed of. Becker returned to his office, made a brief phone call to his superior to say that what was on the disc was what was expected and it had been dealt with, packed up his belonging, bid his secretary a good day and went home.

At twelve p.m. that day, Sally the secretary was beginning to get hungry and decided that she would take a slightly earlier lunch break. No one would mind, they were quite a flexible bunch on this floor of the building. Before she took her break, she realised that the envelope left by Supt Becker had to be dealt with first. As she picked it up from her tray, the disc slipped out and fell onto the carpet under her desk. She cursed under her breath at her clumsiness and immediately got down on all fours to retrieve the disc — which was easily located — and placed it back on the desk. At the same moment, her telephone rang. It made her jump and she banged her head on the underside of her desk. She again cursed under her breath. She crawled out and took the call. It was one of the other officers after something or other. She politely informed him she was taking a short break but would deal with his request upon her return. Once the call had ended, she placed the disc back into the envelope, sealed it (tightly) and then dropped it into the secure waste disposal bin at the other side of the office. She then went off to have her lunch.

Little did she realise that in the mild confusion of dropping the disc, hitting her head and being caught out by a phone call, she had then gone on to place the wrong disc back into the disposal envelope. There had been another disc on her desk which was intended to be sent to the Data Analysis section of the Ministry of Media, Propaganda and Information. In her hurry to get to lunch, this disc had been placed in the secure disposal envelope in error instead of the Cleveland Street footage. When Sally returned from lunch, the Cleveland Street footage was placed into a different envelope, marked for the attention of the Ministry of Media, Propaganda and Information and posted accordingly.

Sally never knew what she did or the wide-reaching ramifications of her actions in the weeks and months that followed.

6

THEMSE MARSCHLAND

"Shit!" muttered Peter Fewtrill. "Shit, shit, shit!"

He was late for work. Very late! After making a complete fool of himself in front of a rather attractive lawyer and then navigating his way home from what turned out to be a police station in Ladbroke Grove, it was four fifteen a.m. He figured he could squeeze in a couple of hours of shut eye before having to get up and go to work. Unsurprisingly though, he overslept and by the time he woke up, work had already started. So began his rush to get into the office before he got into real trouble.

His head was throbbing in pain and his ears were still ringing from the explosion at Cleveland Street. That was certainly going to be a story to tell when he got into work (if Danny hadn't already told everyone). His headache was only exacerbated by a combination of dehydration, fatigue and the two police officers from the night before who had been like a dog with a bone. His front door had been bashed open in the melee of the previous night. He was unlikely to get a refund from the police for that one although the Yale lock was just about functional. At least functional enough to hold the door shut. Mrs Banks next door would no doubt keep an eye on the place while he was at work.

He rapidly got his suit and tie on in a bid to make himself look vaguely presentable for work. He brushed his teeth quickly and took several long swigs of water from the tap. When he looked in the mirror he could see that the left side of his face was mildly singed with a hint of blistering. He hadn't noticed it until now, and now he had noticed it, he felt it and it was pretty sore. Mild burns as a result of being in close proximity to the blast on Cleveland Street. Anyhow, no time to worry about that, he had to get to work quickly.

Before he exited his flat, he couldn't help but see the stained carpet by his front door. It was bloodstained where the mysterious man had clearly received what looked like one heck of a beating the previous evening. Poor man. Peter did wonder what became of him. He had been a member of The Menorah, the feared terrorist organisation intent on bringing the Reich to its knees by whatever means possible. Peter figured his fate was probably none too pretty. Either way, he doubted any recompense for his carpet would be forthcoming — something else for him to deal with later. He grabbed his keys from the small coffee table in the living area and a few other bits from the floor (what he assumed were his work ID and underground pass) and left the flat. Mrs Banks was peeking through a gap in her door. She had likely been there all night.

"Good morning, Mrs Banks," said Peter cheerfully (yet sarcastically) with a quick wave of his hand. "Show's over now!" She didn't seem to appreciate the sarcasm and quickly shut the door.

He dashed to the underground station and boarded the very first train that came along. *Thank God for German efficiency* he thought to himself as the train rumbled its way towards Chancery Lane. From there, Grays Inn Road was a short sprint. If he were lucky, he would only be an hour or so late for work. He could make the time up by missing a couple of lunch breaks; maybe work late. He knew the boss wouldn't be happy. Heinrich Stein was a ballbreaker at the best of times. Typical hardened war veteran. A participant in the Siege of London, he had enjoyed it so much he had decided to stay after the war and rose through the ranks of the Reich ministries now heading up the Ministry of Media, Propaganda and Information. As with all things German, he prided himself on efficiency, led largely by example and expected all those beneath him to fall into line. Sick days (while permitted) were frowned upon and in some cases could work against you. You took time off when it suited Stein, not when it suited you and God forbid should you arrive late without any kind of decent excuse.

The burning question was — should he divulge to Stein what had happened to him the previous evening?

That question was pretty much answered as soon as he arrived at work. No sooner had he signed himself in and cleared the mandatory and daily security checks that Herr Stein called him into his office for a little 'conversation'.

"You understand why I'm concerned, Herr Fewtrill?" asked Stein.

"Of course I do, Herr Stein, but you have no reason to be. It was… well, it was wrong place, wrong time I guess."

The police had notified the ministry. Unbeknown to Peter at the time, this was standard procedure. Every Reich ministry and associated agency shared information concerning employees. It was only a matter of time before information relating to his arrest was disseminated to old man Stein — although he remained shocked at how quickly it had happened.

"Wrong place, wrong time? You were arrested for terrorism!"

"No, Herr Stein. I wasn't arrested. I was… questioned. Not arrested."

"Were you taken to a police station?"

"Well, yes."

"Then you were arrested were you not?"

Clearly, Peter and Stein's ideas about the definition of arrest differed somewhat but Peter felt this was an argument he clearly wouldn't win.

"I guess so."

"Right, thank you, Herr Fewtrill."

He seemed almost happy that Peter had yielded and accepted that he had been arrested. Stein took some deep breaths before continuing. "But I am informed you were released without charge and that they have no interest in you."

"That's correct, Herr Stein."

"I know it's correct, you don't have to tell me that!" snapped Stein in frustration. "Take this as a warning, Herr Fewtrill. If you are dealt with by the police again for anything, and I mean anything, and if you are late one more time, I will see that you lose your job. Are we clear?"

"Yes."

"Yes what?"

"Yes, Herr Stein."

"Fine! Now get out of my office. You can miss your lunch break all this week to make up the time."

This was clearly too much but Peter knew better than to argue with the cantankerous old bureaucrat. He had to take the punishment on the chin and get on with his day in the hope he would not receive another unwanted house guest anytime soon. He was annoyed with Stein. He didn't like Stein and he figured Stein cared little for him but he was thankful he still at least had a job (as much as he also held an element of disdain towards that as well).

Elizabeth Reuben walked past his desk with a chirpy, "Morning, Pete." It was accompanied by a cheeky smile — one that knew he had just received a dressing down. He didn't know her that well but appreciated the little sly jibe. If it hadn't been her, it would've been Danny who was not currently sat at his own desk.

When Peter did finally get himself seated, he took a few minutes to compose himself and began addressing the workload that had already accumulated in his tray. In comparison to the previous day, there was a sense of more normality in the office. People were still grieving the loss of the Führer but it seemed marginally less sombre and people spoke to one another, telephones rang and everyone seemed to be just getting on with it. It looked as though his tray was full: mainly of new scripts and unedited newspaper reports that all needed editing before being passed onwards. Nothing that would greatly enhance his day but then again, when did his job ever do that anyway?

As he shuffled in his chair, Peter realised he had something in his back pocket that was proving to be marginally uncomfortable to sit on so he reached behind him to retrieve (and dispose of) whatever it was that was making him feel this way. What he retrieved was a tatty scrap of paper with, at first glance, what looked like some indecipherable scribblings upon it. Peter thought nothing of it for a second and was about to dispose of it in the bin, when he suddenly remembered the events of the previous night and the man who had burst into his flat. The man (Paul Fuller) had given him a scrap of paper and told Peter to go to an address and sure enough, upon the piece of paper, there was an address that looked as though it had been rather hastily and clumsily scribbled.

Flat 304
Block 87
Rommel Way
Themse Marschland
SE478-99

Peter stared at the address. What exactly was he looking at? He knew it was an address in the Themse Marschland area of London but whose address? He sat pondering until his thought process was interrupted by an ever-cheery Danny.

"Hey buddy. What's up?" Danny had taken Peter by surprise and made him jump. He quickly scrunched up the piece of paper and put it back into the back pocket of his trousers.

"Hey… nothing. Just, you know, getting on with it."

Danny nodded. He had no reason to question what Peter had just been looking at.

"Where were you this morning?" Danny questioned, as he moved in closer speaking in a quieter more cautious tone. "Did Stein have your arse?"

"Jesus. Yeah. I guess everyone noticed didn't they?"

Danny laughed. "Yep. Don't miss a trick mate."

"Great. I had a… well, let's just say I had a bad night."

Danny could sympathise. After all, he had been there on Cleveland Street and witnessed first-hand the devastation that had occurred. It had been mentioned in the office but talk of The Menorah was generally not accepted by Stein — irrespective of how derogatory it may be.

He didn't know, of course, that his friend was in fact referring to what Stein had earlier referred to as his 'arrest' and the encounter with the mysterious Paul Fuller.

"Oh right. Wanna talk about it over a beer later? Go down the Billy again if you're up for it?"

That was the good thing about Danny. Loyalty. He always seemed to care for Peter and would be the first person to offer a shoulder in the event of any perceived crisis. There was no doubt about meeting for a beer after work. Peter needed no encouragement to do that.

The question was, should he tell Danny about the drama of the previous evening and his interrogation? The stigma of being apprehended could linger. It could damage his friendship with Danny who may think less of him or become increasingly suspicious of him. However, at the same time, Danny was a friend. Surely, he wouldn't think less of him? Particularly as he was released with no further charge or even any action being taken against him. Was he now more permanently under the radar of the police as a result of the previous night? And what about the address that was given to him? Should he tell Danny? No, but it should be handed in to the police as a key piece of evidence. Peter knew this. Yet he decided that he would not divulge this piece of information to anyone. Not yet at least.

"Beer yes! Let's do that. You know, it's just personal stuff. I don't want to bore you with it."

"Pete, that's what I'm here for, mate. To be bored senseless by your so-called problems!"

"Yeah thanks for that." Peter laughed in response. "I'll take that under consideration. I better get on. Stein has his eye on me today I think."

"All right, catch you later. I got to fly to a meeting."

With that Danny slinked off in his charismatic way back to wherever his meeting was taking him, leaving Peter to continue tackling the workload in his tray and ponder further over the address.

They never stayed out for long that evening. Peter was shattered. He needed sleep. One quick beer at the Puffing Billy was enough for him, and the two men parted company fairly early in the evening. Peter returned home to Acton (struggling to hold his eyes open on the tube) and settled into his flat in front of the television. Every channel was still broadcasting the same thing. The death of Adolf Hitler. The world was in mourning for the great Führer and would be for some time to come. More images of his son, and heir apparent, Alois were broadcast. The strangely nervous looking young man was still seemingly reluctant to appear a great deal in front of a television camera or indeed provide any interviews to any media outlet. Any glimpses of the next Führer were brief and usually involved him moving in or out of the Reich Chancellery in Berlin, sometimes accompanied by his mother, sometimes alone.

One more event was also making the news and that was the explosion at Cleveland Street. The Menorah had been blamed and police were working flat out to capture the culprits who had clearly decided to capitalise on the death of Hitler to continue their reign of terror. It was anticipated that more attacks would be forthcoming and everyone was urged to be vigilant in the coming weeks and months as the transition to a new Reich leadership continued.

Peter awoke the following morning feeling rather more refreshed and rested than he had done the previous morning. The daily ongoing news bulletins once again remained focused on the worldwide mourning still ongoing for Adolf Hitler. Peter took a long shower during which he continued to reflect on the Themse Marschland address he had been passed by the member of The Menorah who had barged his way in a couple of days earlier. He was continually questioning himself: why had he kept it? Why had he not handed it into the police? Why had he not destroyed it? What was he going to do with it? The questions circulated almost continually in his head seemingly leaving him with somewhat of a moral choice as to what to do.

In the eyes of the law, the best thing to do would be to deliver the address to the nearest police station and be done with it. Then again, his nagging doubts and deep-seated feelings towards the Reich were telling him to hang onto it and do one of two things. Option one was to keep hold of it, sit on it, do nothing with it. Option two was to go to the address in question and tell them that Paul (if that was his real name) had been arrested. But what benefit(s) would option two have? How would that impact on Peter? Was it a trap? Was it a test? Was it genuine? His moral compass was circling uncontrollably and his conscience was far from clear.

It troubled him for all that day and even throughout the following day. He daren't be even a second late for work. He knew Stein was watching him like a hawk, ready to strike at the slightest excuse. He did struggle to concentrate and, on the Thursday, he received an unusual package into his tray. It wasn't often that he received data discs but they did sometimes find their way onto his desk, sometimes erroneously. More often than not, they contained footage of some so-called newsworthy story that had to be checked to make sure no one involved was deemed to be saying or doing anything that may paint the Reich in a bad light. He was sure someone else in the department usually dealt with them but he would pass it to them if it turned out to be beyond his remit.

He inserted the disc into his computer and waited for the content to load, which it did after a few seconds. It didn't register with him immediately exactly what he was watching. It was clearly security camera footage — but of what? So much had been distracting him recently that he didn't realise he was viewing the security camera footage of Cleveland Street and the hours leading up to the explosion. The very same footage that just days before, Sally (the secretary to Supt Rolf Becker) had erroneously placed in the wrong envelope and forwarded to the wrong department.

"What the...?" muttered Peter.

"What's up?" Danny's entrance made Peter jump which Danny noticed. "Sorry, I should've given you a bit more notice." Danny looked quizzically at Peter's computer screen. "What's this?"

"I have no idea, mate." The two sat in silence viewing the footage for another few seconds before Peter ejected the disc and placed it back into his tray. "Looks like it ended up with the wrong person."

"Yeah. Anyway, we at the Billy later?"

Ordinarily Peter would've jumped at the opportunity but he didn't feel in the mood for it today. The Themse Marschland address was playing on his mind. He was too conflicted to be in the mood for drinking. Even with his best friend.

"You know what, not tonight, Dan. Still got stuff on my mind, I'd be crap company."

"You're bloody useless," Danny mused with his friend. "You're always crap company anyway. I've come to expect it of you. Is it anything you wanna talk about?"

"Nah. It's just... stuff."

The following day was Friday and Peter was glad it was the weekend. A chance to have a break from the boredom of his job. As soon as five p.m. came, Peter turned everything off and left his work station. He hadn't seen Danny today (which was unusual as he was usually pestering Peter for a

Friday night session in the pub). Maybe he had got the message that Peter wasn't much in the mood for socialising.

At Chancery Lane station, Peter headed for a different platform. He didn't want to go west back to Acton. Instead, he boarded a train taking him east. As part of Nazi Germany's numerous reconstruction projects in the years after the war, an enormous amount of money was ploughed into infrastructure, much of which had been destroyed during the Siege of London. As thousands of new houses were constructed in the suburbs to replace the ruined inner-city slums, a new network of train lines were created to adequately serve them. As part of this project, the von Hindenburg (or VH) underground line was constructed. Named after the governor-general, the line intersected London from west to east — beginning in the Buckinghamshire countryside, cutting through the middle of London and ending in the southeast of the city, the last stop being Themse Marschland. Along its route, the VH Line shared several stations with other existing stops, including at Chancery Lane on the Central Line.

Evening had well and truly set in when Peter arrived at Themse Marschland. He exited the tube station and began to navigate his way to Rommel Way. Following the siege of London, a sizeable portion of the city lay in complete ruins. While thousands had tried to flee, Churchill had not allowed them to do so and had instead used his own people as human shields in the face of an advancing Nazi army. At least this was what the Reich had everyone believe. As a result, tens of thousands of people were left either dead or homeless and living a life of utter squalor amongst the inner-city slums. As the German Army advanced into London and began its occupation, Hitler pledged a swift rebuilding of the city of London, and as promised, the reconstruction began in earnest in the late 1940s onwards in an effort to rehome the thousands left without a home due to the recklessness of Churchill and his wartime policies.

Earmarking East London as an ideal place for redevelopment, the Reich quickly set about draining and converting marshland on the southeast banks of the River Thames. With its easy river links, the transportation of building materials from the European mainland and up the Thames estuary made land along the banks of the Thames ideal locations for new and upcoming developments.

So up sprung the Themse Marschland estate. A series of rapidly constructed concrete monolithic blocks designed to house thousands upon thousands of people, whether they be the homeless native Londoners or immigrants of Germanic descent, keen to resettle in a new outpost of the German Reich. With its straight roads and grid like road system, navigating the Themse Marschland estate was an easy enough endeavour but above all, made monitoring and watching the residents a lot easier. The estate had not escaped the hundreds of security cameras and round the clock monitoring from the White City compound.

With its concrete walkways intersecting the streets and inter-linking each rising concrete tower block, it was far from the utopian paradise it was promised to be by the Reich upon its completion. But no one dared say otherwise. People lived on top of people in cheap (and now often rapidly decaying) housing provided by the Reich. Transport links to the centre of London were adequate with the VH Line and main arterial roads (covered by curfew cameras) in and out of the estate. Keen to solidify their mark on the city of London, the streets were all named after various German figures. Fearless soldiers or leaders of the Wehrmacht who were instrumental contributors to the Nazi war effort. And so, street names such as: Rommel Way, Schorner Avenue and Von Kleist Road (to name but a few) sprung up across the new estate.

Peter wasn't entirely sure where he was going or indeed which direction to head in so he asked one of the station attendants for some guidance on how to get to Rommel Way and he was duly directed accordingly. As he exited the station, he couldn't help but feel an air of stagnation and borderline depression. The tower blocks were immediately visible and their colourless, concrete and weathered look was imposing. A representation of everything the Reich stood for. As with other areas of London, cameras were on every street corner; some static, some moving as the invisible operator zoomed in and out and followed people around the streets.

The people Peter could see milling about in the area appeared as equally humourless and as stagnant as the surrounding buildings. Almost as if the very place had sapped their souls away from them. Hardly the utopia it was intended to be. Nevertheless, Peter knew he had to move with caution. He didn't know the area. He had never ventured to this area of the city (and he was glad he had never had a need to). The cameras were evident everywhere, he knew he would have to be savvy in order to avoid them.

Lifting the collar of his jacket up towards his face, he hunkered down and crossed the main road outside the station to avoid the first camera in his path. He headed straight on, as directed, towards the address he was looking for on Rommel Way. His stomach turned over and over and his palms sweated. His breathing was erratic, and as he continued on his journey, he continuously questioned why he was doing this and what the outcome would be. Yet he had been brought, almost lured, here by something in his own head. A continuing nagging doubt. He knew he could abort this journey at any time but there was a stronger part of his subconscious that wanted to continue and so he did.

As directed, he found Rommel Way. Locating Block 87 was an easy enough endeavour as each block along the street was clearly numbered in sequential order. Even numbered blocks to one side of the road and odd numbered blocks to the other side. As Peter stepped onto Rommel Way, he stopped and surveyed his surroundings. The cameras were in place on either side of the street providing full coverage for what looked like the entire street in both directions. Looking at the camera on his side of the road, it was facing away from him so this would be the best side to remain on. It would only capture the back of his head, not his face. That wasn't to say another camera further along wouldn't be pointing in the opposite direction and thus capture his front profile. He didn't know this but that was a part of this risk he had chosen to take and he knew it. Rather fortuitously, the odd numbered blocks were also on the side of the road he was currently on, negating any need to cross over the road and be spotted face on by another camera.

Block 87 was different from the other blocks along Rommel Way. All the other blocks up until that point — on both sides of the street — had been high rise concrete monoliths. Peter figured at least twenty stories tall. From Block 87 however, the number of storeys reduced dramatically with there being only three from 87 onwards (for however long the blocks went on for). Flat 304 was the one he was looking for. As he stood outside Block 87, there was a map of the layout of the block on the wall at the entrance to the main stairwell and Peter took a moment to survey this. He wanted to enter the block with confidence. With the look of someone who knew where he was going and had a clear purpose. Not with the look of someone who didn't know what he was doing or why he was there in the first instance. The slightest bit of suspicion could attract unwanted attention from particular authorities and he had already received enough of this in recent days. Flat 304 was on the third (and final) floor so he ascended the stairwell cautiously, yet confidently, in order to reach his final destination.

Flat 304 was located at the end of a short corridor. Flats 300—303 were along the same corridor. It was a dimly lit affair and in fact, not all the lights appeared to be working. They were not damaged in any way, just not functional. Neglected. Much like the rest of the area. This block was no exception either. The corridor had a damp musty smell about it. There was a hint of urine too, maybe a sign at the lack of pride the residents took in the block. The corridor had been painted with what looked like cheap, thick orange paint that was peeling in a lot of places revealing the dank concrete beneath it. Patches of damp were evident in various places along the corridor. Each door to each flat was a dark green with the flat number embossed in gold at the top. The door to 301 had what looked like a plank nailed over the bottom of it, almost as though it had been kicked in at some point in the past and hastily repaired.

Peter's heart was beating in his chest so hard that it hurt. He tried to control his breathing, which seemed to be hurtling ahead of him. His palms were sweaty. This was his last chance to turn away and go home. To forget about this address and whoever — or whatever — might lie behind the door at 304. But he couldn't walk away surely? He had come this far. Risked everything. The time was now. It was now or never. Peter gently knocked the door three times. There was silence. He waited. Nothing. He was about to knock the door again when all of a sudden there was the sound of someone putting a key into the lock and turning it. Then the handle of the door turned…

7

LOOK BEYOND WHAT YOU CAN ALREADY SEE

The door was on a chain; therefore, the occupant only opened it as far as the chain would allow. It was a man and he peered out through the small gap. He had chin length greasy dark brown hair. He was thin, almost emaciated and unkempt. There was a waft of cigarette smoke from the flat and although Peter couldn't see inside, other odours (along with the sight of this man) indicated that the property was perhaps not the tidiest or indeed the cleanest. He didn't look happy to see Peter and his tone of voice only served to confirm this.

"Yeah?" he barked.

He had a twang to his voice and Peter was struggling to place it. It was northern but he couldn't quite figure out the exact origins of the dialect. Maybe Mancunian, maybe Yorkshire, he wasn't sure. Peter hesitated. So much so that the man barked at him once again.

"What do you want, mate?"

"Hi. Is this flat 304?"

The man didn't verbally respond but tilted his head upwards to where the gold embossed numbers were located as if to indicate to Peter that he had just asked a rather silly question, which he had but in his state of nervousness and apprehension, he had approached the situation with some clumsiness.

"Right, yes of course. Sorry. Look, I know this will sound a bit odd and I am sorry to disturb you but I'm here about Paul. Paul Fuller."

"Who?" the man barked again.

"Paul Fuller."

"Never heard of him," responded the angry man and he went to close the door; however, he stopped on Peter's insistence.

"Wait!" Peter snapped. He didn't mean to come across in an aggressive manner but he hadn't finished telling the man what he had come to tell him in the first place, "I'm sorry. I didn't mean to snap at you. It's just… well, he's been arrested."

"Who has?"

"Paul Fuller. And he told me to come here and tell you. I don't know why. Are you family? A friend maybe? I'm just trying to—"

"Never heard of him!" The man eyeballed Peter intently without blinking.

He clearly wasn't happy about the disturbance or by having some other man stood on his doorstep telling him about somebody called Paul.

"They gave him a beating," Peter continued.

"Who did?"

"The police. When he was arrested, I don't know what state he's in but it—"

"Are you fucking deaf?" The man was clearly getting more and more angry as the conversation continued.

"What?"

"I told you already, mate. I don't know who you're talking about. I don't know any Paul Fuller and I don't know you. So jog on! Before I really lose my temper."

With that, the man slammed the door with surprising ferocity considering it was only open by a few centimetres in the first instance. Peter stood where he was momentarily before turning around and making his way back to the stairwell. He had clearly wasted his time coming all the way to the estate. In a way he was relieved that he had visited the address as the anxiety throughout the week had been somewhat overbearing at times. He didn't know who that man was but his work was done now and he intended to return to Acton and forget all about Paul Fuller, the Themse Marschland estate and everything else even remotely negative that had happened to him at various intervals during the week.

It was a case of wishful thinking though. As he reached the bottom of the first flight of stairs, an unknown assailant rushed up behind him, hastily flinging a hood over his head. Peter began to instinctively struggle in order to get away, but within seconds, something large and heavy had struck him on top of the head and he slumped to the ground in an unconscious heap.

When he awoke, it was black. Jet black. Peter found himself gasping for air but all he inhaled was fabric of some kind. He shuffled but could feel that his hands were bound behind him and he was sat on what felt like a wooden chair. The disorientating nature of his new situation was making him panic and he started to struggle and gasp even more for precious oxygen. All of a sudden, the hood was whipped from atop his head and he gasped heavily as the cool and fresher air hit his face and was drawn into his mouth and into his lungs. In front of him was a lamp directed straight into his face making him squint as his eyes struggled to adjust to the bombardment of light. It took him a while but eventually, Peter slowly adjusted to his new surroundings. Unfortunately, it looked all too familiar.

Under a week ago, he was cuffed to a chair in an interrogation room. And now, he was cuffed to a chair in what looked like an interrogation room. He couldn't tell if it was the same one he was in at Ladbroke Grove as he didn't take the time to examine it in great detail. Either way, it was similar. Similarly, to Ladbroke Grove, there was a table in front of him (on which the lamp sat) but just one person sat on the other side of the table. A steely face looking man. He was bald and heavy jawed. His arms were folded and Peter could see he was clearly a very well exercised and heavily built man. Clearly not the same police officer who had questioned him a few days previously. Almost immediately, Peter knew he had made a terrible mistake by going to Themse Marschland. How could he have been so stupid? Clearly after his encounter with Paul Fuller, he had come under the radar of the police. They must have been watching him ever since. They must have followed him to the estate. They must have been waiting for him.

"I want to see a lawyer," Peter began, his head throbbing.

His neck felt moist but he couldn't tell whether it was sweat or blood from being struck so forcibly over the head. The man opposite didn't move or react in any way. He sat and stared at Peter with his arms folded.

"I want to see a lawyer please. I'm entitled to that much."

"All in good time," the man responded in a monotonous (and hushed) tone.

The two men were silent and looked at each other across the table. Who was going to be first to break the deadlock of silence? The man on the other side of the table was the first to crack.

"Why were you in the Marschland?"

Peter shrugged and huffed, "You know, I don't know. I really don't. I made a stupid mistake and I'm sorry."

"How do you know Paul Fuller, Mr Fewtrill?"

This was almost a repeat of the Ladbroke Grove interrogation. "I don't know him. I told you this a few days ago. I don't know him. He just burst into my flat, you arrested him, that's it. Beyond that, I don't know him. Ask the lawyer I had. She'll tell you."

"Who was your lawyer?"

Peter wasn't great with names but he remembered the name of the lawyer for two reasons. Firstly, because she was incredibly attractive. Secondly, he put his foot in it with her whilst trying to lighten the mood and made an inappropriate remark about her husband.

"Susan. Susan Scott. Married to that DS... what was his name... Fellows. Yes, Dean Fellows," Peter eventually responded. "I want to see her please."

The bald man nodded. "All in good time, Mr Fewtrill. All in good time. First of all, I'd like you to tell me why you went to Themse Marschland."

"I've told you already. I made a terrible mistake and I'm sorry. I don't know why I—"

"How long have you known Paul Fuller?"

"I don't know him. I've told you this before, I don't know him."

"Who lives at the flat in block 87 on Rommel Way?"

"I don't know."

"Why did you go there then?"

"I don't know!"

The man unfolded his arms and leant forward onto the table whilst taking a large intake of breath. "You don't know a lot do you, Mr Fewtrill?"

Peter responded by shaking his head solemnly.

"And that presents me with a lot of questions. Unanswered questions. Peter Fewtrill, Reich civil servant. Someone in a very privileged situation with access to a wealth of sensitive information, associating with a known terrorist — Paul Fuller. Someone who claims he has no links to this person whatsoever yet, decides to go and visit a suspected terrorist safe house. Do you see why I have a problem with that?"

"Look, I know how it looks. I get that but I swear, before last week, I had nothing to do with Paul Fuller and that's the truth."

"And I would've believed that had you not have turned up on the doorstep of a terrorist safe house."

To be fair, the bald man had a point. Peter really had dug himself a great big hole. "I know how it looks."

"I know, you've said that already and it looks pretty bad from where I'm sitting."

"He gave me the address!"

"Who did?"

"Paul Fuller. When he came into my flat, before you arrested him, he gave me a scrap of paper with an address on it and I was stupid enough to bloody well go there. Stupid, stupid, stupid!"

The bald man leant back in his chair and looked up and beyond Peter as if acknowledging someone stood behind him. Peter had begun to cry, out of frustration in his own stupidity. The tears were rolling down his cheeks and the bald man sat and watched him sternly.

"What are your views on The Menorah?"

"I don't know anything about the bloody Menorah."

"I didn't ask you what you knew. I asked you what your views are on them."

The question had Peter puzzled and he pondered over the answer although, however he responded it would likely be wrong.

"I... I don't have views on them. They're a terrorist group that go around bombing things and killing you lot."

"Our lot?"

"The police. Everything else to do with the Reich."

"Including you."

"What?"

"Including you. I mean, you're an employee of the Reich. So they would kill 'you lot' as well wouldn't they? In a heartbeat."

"Maybe. I don't know."

"So, what are your views on The Menorah?"

"What do you want me to say? Shall I tell you what you want to hear? Is that it?"

"It isn't a trick question, Mr Fewtrill. What are your views on The Menorah?"

"If I tell you I hate them, that I despise every one of the bastards for what they do and what they are, you'll accuse me of being a barefaced liar. If I tell you I support everything they do and their little campaigns, you'll shoot me dead where I sit. Or beat me to death. Just like you did with Paul Fuller."

"Why would we go so far as to kill you, Mr Fewtrill?"

"Because that's what you do! That's what the police do!"

Peter was at his wits end. They should just be done with it and do what they had to do. Put a bullet in his head. He had lost everything anyway by being stupid enough to visit Block 87, so what was the point? Before he was aggressively hooded again, the bald man responded with something that left Peter pondering even further. A response that was both surprising as it was intriguing.

"Who says we're the police?"

While he was hooded once more, Peter could hear the comings and goings in the room. No one spoke but he could hear footsteps entering the room and shuffling around before leaving again. He remained on edge and was feeling ever more bewildered. Initially, he was certain that his captors had been the police but that comment from the bald man had left him with even more questions. Who were these people? Was he being played? He was thoroughly confused and wished he had been given an opportunity to turn the tables. To ask him who he was and what his intentions were. To try and find out more about his motives.

As he sat bound in the chair, his head continued to throb with pain as a result of receiving a hefty blow. Peter eventually drifted off into a light, uncomfortable and slightly restless sleep but was awoken when he was roughly removed from the chair and frog-marched from the room by what felt like two people — each gripping an arm tightly. He was guided out of the room and outside. He could tell he had left the building as the air felt fresh and cold on his body and smelt clean, devoid of the grime and dirt associated with the city. The ground underfoot felt soft and slightly muddy and it was quiet. No sounds of the city either, making him wonder where he had been taken. He could hear birds chirping as if singing their morning song and he figured he had been taken far away from the city altogether.

He was manhandled into what felt like the back of a car and forced to lie in the rear footwell. As per his apprehension by the police days before, he was held firmly in position by what felt like a set of heavy boots. The drive was performed in silence and no one spoke. Peter drifted in and out of light and uncomfortable sleep. He didn't know how long the drive took, it felt like many hours. It may have been more; it may have been less such was his disorientation. Eventually, the journey came to an end.

Peter was pulled from the car and immediately he was struck by a smell. It was the smell of the sea. He could also hear the gentle rumbling of the water as it lapped the shore. His location was confirmed when the hood was removed for the final time and as his eyes adjusted, he could see he was indeed at the shoreline. The bald man was stood next to him and pulled a knife from his pocket. He grabbed hold of Peter's wrists and with one swift motion, cut the cable tie that was binding them together. He felt the blood rush almost instantaneously back into his numb hands, giving him pins and needles in the tips of his fingers.

As his eyes adjusted once more to his new surroundings, it became almost immediately obvious where he was. He was stood on the beach in Dover. The great England to France road bridge was to his left-hand side. Completed in the years after the war, it was another incredible feat of German ingenuity and engineering. A four-lane super highway linking the British Territories to the European continent. Another way to unify the great Reich and make the British Territories as much a part of the empire as the rest of Europe. On a clear day, it was possible to see the great bridge as far as the French mainland. Today (on what Peter assumed was an early morning), the busy bridge disappeared into the mist that hung lazily above the English Channel, as if being consumed by some unearthly and ethereal entity.

The bald man ushered Peter onto the beach and then pointed. Peter looked in the direction the man was pointing and could see he was pointing towards another man stood at the shoreline facing out towards the English Channel. He was a tall man with short grey hair and he wore a long dark mackintosh. Peter turned to ask the bald man exactly what he was meant to do but the bald man had already turned and started to walk back to the car leaving Peter to assume he was to go and speak with the man stood by the shoreline.

He approached slowly and with caution but the man knew he was coming. Not only had he been told but he could hear the footsteps on the stony beach as Peter walked towards him. Peter stopped at the man's side and looked at him. His gaze remained fixed across the sea and he had a thoughtful look on his face. Peter figured him to be in his sixties or thereabouts (give or take a year or so).

As he gazed, he spoke, "Thirty-seven years ago I stood on this beach and watched them arrive. The Nazi liberators. I saw their weapons and their bombs and their rockets. The way they wiped us all out and hunted us down. I lost a lot of friends that day." He paused and then turned to face Peter. "I'm truly sorry for how you've been treated. We have to act with an element of… caution these days. We never know who's watching."

Peter stood, perplexed. "I'm sorry, I've been dreadfully rude," the man continued politely. "Allow me to introduce myself. I'm Hebron."

He extended his hand towards Peter wishing for it to be shook. Peter was stunned and remained motionless. Was he really standing face to face with the most feared terrorist leader in the world? The mighty Hebron? The man claiming to be Hebron began to laugh gently.

"You may shake my hand. It won't poison you. Despite what they say." Peter extended his right hand and the two shook hands. "There we go, that wasn't so bad was it now. You don't need to introduce yourself, Mr Fewtrill. I know who you are already."

This made sense. After all, he had no doubt had his fingerprints scanned and had undergone a thorough enough interrogation.

"I expect you have a lot of questions you'd like answered. Am I correct?" Peter nodded. "Then walk with me. I don't have a lot of time."

Hebron (or at least the man claiming to be Hebron) ushered Peter away and the two walked slowly along the beach leaving the great road bridge behind them. Peter began the conversation.

"I don't understand. What's just happened to me?"

"Well, that's an interesting question, Peter. Do you mind if I call you Peter?"

"No, not at all."

"Well, Peter, the question I have for you is why did you go to the Themse Marschland? What compelled you, a servant of the Reich, a believer if you please, to go to an address given to you by a known terrorist?"

"I told your friend the answer already. I don't know. I really don't. It was a moment of stupidity."

"And curiosity?" Hebron interjected.

"Well, maybe yes. I was curious. Maybe even duty bound."

"How so?"

"I didn't know who Paul Fuller was and I guess I figured that the address might have been that of… I don't know… his wife maybe? Perhaps even children. Perhaps some other family. They would have wanted to know."

Hebron thought for a moment. "Well, we appreciate you coming along and letting us know of Paul's fate. He was involved in another one of our operations. One that was recently shut down. We were unsure as to his whereabouts but you have confirmed our deepest fears." He paused before continuing. "Could it be you have doubts I wonder?"

"Doubts about what?"

"About who you are. About whom you believe. About the Reich. About everything you've grown up with and everything they've taught you to believe. You see, in my mind, anyone else would've given that address to the police straight away. If only to exonerate themselves and their own involvement in any terrorist activity. But you walked straight into the lion's den. And I want to know why you did that. What compelled you to put everything you have on the line for the sake of an address on a piece of paper?"

They continued walking and Peter remained silent, still unsure how to respond. Hebron continued, "You see, I believe that you doubt what the Reich tell you. I believe that you question it, more often than you think as well. I believe that's why you went to the address given to you by Paul Fuller. Not through any sense of duty you may have had towards the man."

He wasn't entirely wrong. Peter had doubted the authenticity of the Reich's claims on a number of occasions. The very nature of his work had caused him to call it into question: why tell someone to report five deaths when there were none? Why say three buildings were blown to pieces by

The Menorah, taking many innocent lives in the process, when it was a single assassination of a high-ranking police officer? It was all he knew but he daren't speak his mind for fear of the dire reprisals. It was also becoming clearer to Peter what the intentions of Hebron (if that's who it really was) were and the very reason why he was stood on the beach with him.

"Are you trying to convince me of something?"

"Such as...?"

"Are you trying to convince me to join you?"

Hebron let out a laugh. "I'm not trying to convince you to do anything. You have to make a decision such as that for yourself. Any other person, we probably would've ignored. But you're different."

"How?"

"By virtue of who you work for. The information you have at your fingertips. This could prove valuable to us."

"But how? I see nothing in my work that has any worth to you. Or your cause."

In reality, he could probably tell Hebron about the hundreds, if not thousands, of times he had edited, redrafted and redacted various news scripts to suit the Reich mantra, but he couldn't see how this would prove particularly beneficial in terms of significant influence — or worth — for Hebron or The Menorah.

Hebron stopped and turned to Peter. "That's because you haven't looked hard enough. If you did, I almost guarantee you'd find something that would truly shock and horrify you. Something to make you cast doubt over everything the Reich has taught you to believe."

"And something that you could use on your little pirate broadcasts?"

Hebron smiled broadly. "Exactly. Something we could use for our 'little pirate broadcasts'. The Reich is deceiving us, Peter. They have been ever since they marched onto these shores back in 1941. And any bit of information, no matter how small, to convince everyone out there that this is the case, the better in my book."

As they stood there, a car had pulled up on the road running parallel to the shoreline. It was the bald man.

"And now," Hebron continued, "it's time for us to part ways. My friend will take you back to London. It's Sunday morning by the way so you have time to rest before you go back to work tomorrow."

"And that's it?"

"For now."

"So what's stopping me from going to the police?"

Hebron stood for a moment pondering his answer. "Now that is a very good question. You could well do that. And others have. But just be aware that we know who you are, where you live, who you work for, who your family are. Shall I continue, or do you get the picture?"

"What about the Themse Marschland address? I could send the police there."

"Why? What did you find there of any interest?"

Hebron had a point. There was nothing there other than an incredibly grumpy and rude man. Peter suspected the man had indeed played some part in his most recent abduction and interrogation but this was probably an operation that had been slickly organised and no doubt all tracks would be covered and Hebron was probably right in that nothing of interest would be found at the Themse Marschland address.

"You must go now," continued Hebron. He ushered Peter towards the car.

"What if I want to contact you?"

"We'll contact you in due course. At the right time and in the right place. Any more questions before we part company?"

Peter did have one question, something that many people across the British Territories had wondered. "Why do they call you Hebron?"

The other man laughed and was clearly rather amused by the question. "I have no idea! Do you know what makes it funnier? I'm not even Jewish."

There was clearly a story behind how the man had acquired a moniker but that would be a different story altogether for a different time.

"Maybe one day I'll get a chance to tell you how it came about."

Peter nodded. As they both reached the car, Peter opened the rear passenger side door and sat down. He was not asked to wear a hood this time. Before Hebron bid them both farewell and shut the car door he said one final thing to Peter.

"Just remember, you haven't been looking hard enough. Look beyond what you can already see."

And with that, he closed the door and the car drove off back towards London.

Peter sat silently in the back of the car. The two men didn't speak a word all the way back to London. The bald man drove cautiously and obeyed all the road rules to avoid being pulled over by the police. He didn't ask for any directions and seemed to know exactly where he was going and by early afternoon, Peter had been dropped back at his flat in Acton and the bald man drove away without saying another word.

Look beyond what you can already see. The words resonated with Peter and he kept saying them back to himself over and over again. He drifted off on the sofa (again) when he got into his flat. He was truly exhausted and had hardly slept since Thursday night.

When he woke up it was late into the evening and it had gone dark. He decided to shower and as he did, the water turned a light red as the blood caked into his hair (from being knocked unconscious) was washed out. He felt around the wound. It was sore but didn't feel too deep and he had no intention of seeking further medical treatment. As he stood under the warm jets of water, he felt his body becoming clean and purified. Then it struck him. Look beyond what you can already see. On Friday, he had briefly viewed some camera footage at work and then stopped it; believing it was nothing important and likely intended for someone else. It had come to him all of a sudden. He knew where that was now. It was footage of the police post at Cleveland Street.

Later into the very same evening, the bald man pulled up at the farmhouse and exited the car. It had been a long drive from London and by now, darkness had descended on the surrounding countryside. It was going to be another cold night; he could feel it. He went into the house and could smell the burning wood and hear the crackling of the wood burner in the living area. It was comforting and a welcome change from the forbidding cold evening air. He went into the kitchen where Hebron was sat at a table having just poured himself a strong cup of coffee.

"Ah, Christian. You're back. Everything go OK?"

"Absolutely fine, yes."

"Good. Pour yourself a coffee."

The bald man — Christian Bonner — poured himself a fresh cup of coffee and joined Hebron at the table. The two men savoured the flavour of their warm drinks.

"So, what do you think about Fewtrill?" asked Christian. "Do you think he'll be of any use?"

"I think he could be, yes. I think he could be very useful indeed."

Christian nodded approvingly before continuing, "Do you think he could prove useful with the other operation we spoke of?"

"The von Hindenburg mission you mean?"

"Yes."

Hebron paused for thought before continuing. "Now that, I'm not sure of my friend. I'm just not sure."

8

MAN OF THE HOUR

When he arrived in work the following day, Peter rummaged around in his tray for the data disc that he had started to watch at the end of the previous week. Danny was absent for some reason. He wasn't sure why but figured that this was probably a good thing, under the circumstances, as he wanted time to watch the footage without being disturbed or questioned as to what he was looking at. Peter wasn't sure exactly why the data disc had ended up on his desk and he would never know that it was all down to an administration error by a remiss secretary.

He placed the disc into the drive on his computer and began to watch the footage. Just as he had suspected when it finally came to him in the shower, it was Cleveland Street and the footage was covering the police post and the buildings either side. Looking at the time stamp, it was displaying 16.45 28/01/1979. This was the day before the explosion that he had been caught up in alongside Danny. He watched intently for some time but could not see anything noteworthy. He decided to fast forward the footage to the evening of the explosion and he recommenced watching from about roughly five minutes before the blast.

There it was, in all its glory. An enormous explosion that ripped open the police post killing and injuring dozens in the process. He stopped it and took it back and watched again. It took a few more very close examinations for Peter to finally deduce (correctly at that) that the explosion had emanated from the litter bin placed just outside of the automatic doors.

The questions began to flow through his head. Who had planted the bomb in the bin? Would the footage show who planted it there? Carefully and methodically he began to rewind the footage from the point of detonation. Stopping every few seconds to see if he could see anyone approaching the bin and placing anything inside it. It was a laborious task but he was determined to see if he could spot the culprit.

He missed it at first and it wasn't until later in the day, in between completing other tasks, that he finally spotted what Supt Rolf Becker had spotted. The time stamp on the footage was now showing 15.12 29/01/1979. This was approximately three hours before the explosion. Just like Rolf Becker, Peter saw the two men approach the bin and loiter outside the doorway before placing a shoebox size package into the bin. Peter didn't recognise both of the men but to his horror, he recognised one of them. It was DS Dean Fellows, the man who had interrogated him at the Ladbroke Grove station. He was under no illusions of this whatsoever. Peter swallowed hard and stopped the footage. What had he just seen? Had a serving Reich police officer really planted an explosive device outside one of his own police stations and killed several of his colleagues in the process? Why had he carried out such a terrible act? Was he working for The Menorah?

He had so many unanswered questions and it drove him to distraction for pretty much the remainder of the day and he struggled to be tremendously productive. Danny reappeared shortly after he had taken his lunch break. He had to attend a doctor appointment which explained his absence. Danny could tell Peter was distracted but did not pressure him into giving anything away. Peter had considered on several occasions telling Danny all about what he had experienced over the past week or so but as he began getting deeper and deeper into the shady world of The Menorah, the more he thought that this would be a severely unwise idea.

It was towards the end of the working day that the police arrived at the ministry. There were four of them in total, two uniforms and two plain clothes officers (most likely detectives). As soon as Peter saw them enter the office, he began to panic. Had they found out about his meeting with Hebron? Did they know about his visit to Themse Marschland? Were they here about the disc? Getting up and trying to make an excuse to be elsewhere would be too obvious and perhaps even suspicious, so he made the decision to remain put and act as innocently as he could. The disc was still sat in the drive of his computer. He left it be. To try and remove it and swiftly hide it would also look suspicious. The four men (led by the plain clothes officers) walked straight past Danny and Peter and knocked on the door of Stein's office who beckoned them in. There were hushed tones from within the office.

"Check this out. They come for the old man?" Danny asked quizzically.

"No idea," Peter replied believing they had gone to Stein to ask him who Peter Fewtrill was and where he could be found.

After a few seconds, Stein emerged from his office and looked in the direction of Danny and Peter — at least that's what Peter thought but it could've been his paranoia playing tricks with his mind. His mouth went dry and he felt sick to the stomach. Stein then signalled towards someone at the other end of the office and the four men marched off in that direction. They seemed to stop by another analyst and surround her. Peter knew her, albeit vaguely. It was Elizabeth Reuben, the young lady who had made a guarded jibe towards him the day he was late for work. He had also said hello to her on occasion but other than this, contact between them had been minimal. Danny and Peter looked on curiously as the officers pulled her from her chair, cuffed her and then led her out of the building. Stein returned to his office without saying another word, the officers were gone and everyone got on with their work. Peter breathed a huge sigh of relief.

Everyone in the department was too nervous to ask what had just happened and no one was brave enough to go and approach Stein to ask him so it remained unclear what she had been arrested for although, it wasn't long before rumours of her being a Menorah spy began to circulate — but these were only rumours. Life in the office remained consistently mundane through the remainder of the week. Peter chose to not watch the surveillance footage again but at the same time, he kept hold of the disc and concealed it in one of the drawers in his desk under a pile of junk that had been accumulating during his time at the ministry. It got to Thursday and Peter enquired as to whether Danny fancied joining him for a quick pint after work. Uncharacteristically, Danny refused claiming that he would rather head straight home but would be happy to go another night. Nevertheless, Peter fancied a drink so he headed to the Puffing Billy in Kings Cross by himself.

It was quiet in the pub and he positioned himself at the bar and ordered his drink. As he sat quietly, he noticed a young lady sat in the corner on her own. She appeared to be writing something and was deep in concentration.

He recognised her from somewhere and before too long, he realised it was the lawyer who had come to his assistance at Ladbroke Grove — Susan Scott. The last time they had met, he had made a complete fool of himself by saying what he had said about her husband. In a strange way, he felt a little guilty. Then again, after seeing what he had done on the camera footage of Cleveland Street, should he feel guilty? He wondered if she was involved with the bombing. Having experienced everything that he had over the past couple of weeks, and becoming drawn ever deeper into the world of The Menorah, he wanted to know more.

Again, Hebron's words resonated in his head — look beyond what you can already see. As he sat nursing his drink, he weighed up all of the options in his head and these were: leave her well alone (easily the most prudent option on the table), make an approach to see if she can offer any further information about how her husband is linked to the bombing (easily the riskiest option) or make an approach and buy her a drink because she's a nice looking young lady (easily the stupidest option and he immediately wondered to himself why he would even think such a thing in the first instance). She looked as though she was getting ready to leave and seemed to be gathering together her things in a nice tidy pile. He had to act quick. Option number two (the riskiest one) it was.

"Hi. It's Susan isn't it?"

Susan looked up at Peter blankly. She didn't recognise him which was not the best start. "Yes. I'm sorry, do I know you?"

"Erm, yeah. Peter Fewtrill. You helped me out at Ladbroke Grove station."

Susan still stared at Peter blankly before it finally dawned on her who he was. "Yes, sorry. I remember. How are you?"

"I'm very well thank you." There was an uncomfortable silence between the two and Susan now had a look on her face that looked to be asking what exactly he wanted. "Look, I don't mean to disturb you but I was just wondering if I could get you a drink?"

Susan scoffed. "Excuse me?"

"Could I get you a drink? I mean, to say thank you for the other week. And for saying what I did about your husband. I feel bad."

"Really?"

"Absolutely. I was rude. I'd like to make it up to you."

Susan pondered momentarily before responding. "I don't think so, Mr Fewtrill. I'm not in the business of accepting drinks, gifts, handouts or anything else for that matter from any of my clients, irrespective of how briefly I may have dealt with them. But I appreciate the apology for what you said about my husband. Oh wait… you didn't apologise did you."

Susan looked at Peter awaiting a response to the passive aggressive sarcasm.

"Erm… no. I… sorry. Sorry I was rude about your husband."

"Apology accepted, Mr Fewtrill." Peter stood where he was not too sure how to react. "You may leave now."

"Right, yes. Sorry."

With that, Peter awkwardly backed away feeling embarrassed. His intelligence gathering skills needed work — a lot of work. His first unofficial assignment had got off to a less than brilliant start. In retrospect, option number one would've been the far better choice to make and she was best left alone. So he sat and finished his drink and ordered another one.

He was about to pay when a voice from behind him chimed in, "I'll pay for it. And I'll have the same as well please."

Peter turned around. It was Susan. She had come to join him at the bar.

"Thanks," Peter said, taken aback by the sudden change in tone. "Should it not be me buying you the drink?"

The young lawyer had watched Peter back away from her, clearly terribly embarrassed by his actions and attempts to make what seemed like an apology — albeit a clumsy one (although she remained blissfully unaware of his true intentions for making an approach in the first instance). She hadn't remembered him at first. Such was the nature of her work, she dealt with a high number of individuals, some proving more memorable than others. She did remember Peter though (eventually), more so as he had been dealt with by her husband, DS Dean Fellows. He had seemed quite upset with her when she had seemingly admonished him in the interrogation room that night by telling him that Peter was of no evidential value — which he wasn't. He had just been unlucky getting caught up in the whole Paul Fuller incident. It hadn't gone down well at home later that day but that was something she was beginning to get used to as work and personal life often locked horns with one another. She found herself feeling bad for

Peter. She had treated him unfairly and for this, she felt more than just a modicum of guilt.

Susan smiled. "Well, maybe this is my way of saying sorry to you. It was me who was rude. Intentionally rude at least. There was no need for me to behave like that. So, I'm sorry."

Peter was hesitant at first and slightly suspicious of the young lawyer and her sudden change in tone. Susan could see this in his face and could see he needed a little reassurance.

"Look, do you want me to buy you a drink or not? Most men would jump at the chance. I was unnecessarily rude to you, and I'm sorry. So, will you join me in drinking to that or should I make you pay for our drinks?"

Peter hesitated a moment longer but could see that the lawyer's face had lightened considerably and that it had even cracked something resembling a smile.

He laughed lightly and nodded. "Well, I'll drink to that. I'd be a fool to turn down a free drink, right?" The two clinked their glasses together and took a sip of their drinks.

What had started off as a slightly awkward encounter that night eventually turned into a surprisingly pleasant evening, for both of them. Susan was not half as steely as she had been that night in the police station and presented a much different persona. A lot less regimented and serious and a lot easier going and amenable. While they didn't have an enormous amount in common with each other, they still seemed to get on and the conversation flowed. It flowed so well that Peter almost completely forgot that his reasons for approaching Susan were to try and find out more about her husband. Such was the surprisingly pleasant nature between them, it almost seemed irrelevant.

What he did find out was that the two met at Ladbroke Grove seven years earlier. She was a young duty solicitor and he was a young and upcoming constable. They had married quickly (within a year of meeting) but did not have any children as both were focused on their respective careers. Her husband's career had flourished and he was still hoping to proceed ever further up the ladder to an even higher position. He took his job incredibly seriously and, from what Peter could gather, was a staunch and unwavering supporter of Adolf Hitler — making it increasingly harder for Peter to fathom out his reasons for wanting to plant a bomb outside a police station.

Susan's career had not moved as quickly as her husband's and she spent most of her time acting as a duty solicitor and dealing with people who had committed very minor infractions such as: curfew breaches, daring to speak freely and other similar such events. She was at the Puffing Billy that night to meet a client charged with such an offence to discuss the case but they had not turned up. From an early stage, Susan had decided to not use her married name.

When questioned on her political alliances, Susan simply smiled and replied with, "Well, it isn't really relevant. We do as we're told."

Peter didn't push it any further than this as political discussions were risky at the best of times, irrespective of who it was with, but the rather non-committal nature of her response suggested to Peter that they may share at least some of the same reservations about the Reich. It was difficult to be certain though.

As she had shared details about herself with Peter, so he also shared his own (omitting the events of the past two weeks, his suspicions about her husband and his motives for coming over to talk to her in the first instance). She listened with interest and was curious about the nature of his job but he was dismissive and reassured her that it was nowhere near as interesting as it sounded but he was grateful to have a job that offered a regular salary — if minimal future prospects.

Time passed by quickly that evening and it soon became time to part company before breaching curfew. They finished their drinks and prepared to leave the Puffing Billy.

"Well, it's been nice, Mrs Scott. Or do I call you Mrs Fellows?"

"Susan is fine. Call me Susan, and by the way, I accept your apology."

Peter laughed. "Thanks. Likewise, I accept yours and again, I really am sorry. Incidentally, won't your husband be wondering where you are?"

"No, he's too tied up with work. Plus, he knew I was meeting a client tonight and that I might be late."

There was a slightly uncomfortable pause. "Well, I guess we should, erm, go?"

Peter extended his hand out to shake Susan's and she reciprocated.

"We should do this again." He immediately regretted what he had just said.

Doing this again was simply not an option and he had overstepped the mark. Susan looked at him wide eyed but he wasn't sure if it was shock or amusement. He immediately backtracked.

"I didn't mean… erm, I… sorry. Look, it's been really nice but I didn't mean that."

"It's fine. Really," Susan responded.

Peter smiled and gave an awkward wave by half raising his right hand and turned to walk off.

"Do you know where the Tavistock Metropolis is?"

The question took Peter by surprise. He knew exactly where the Tavistock Metropolis was. It was a mid-range hotel located on Tavistock Square, not far from Kings Cross. It was part of the Metropolis chain and many were dotted across Europe.

"I know it yeah."

"Well, I've got a meeting there with a client next Thursday which should be finished at six or thereabouts."

"Right?" he wasn't entirely sure where this conversation was heading.

"Just thought I should mention it. You know, in case you got thirsty on your way home."

He knew what she was getting at now. He was no expert by any means but could tell that this was a discreet invitation to meet again. He knew that deep down it would not be a good idea. In fact, it would be a downright dangerous idea. Her husband was not only a police officer but also responsible for committing an act of mass murder. To complicate matters even further, he had no idea which side her husband was fighting for or indeed whether Susan herself was involved in any shape or form. All these concerns had been forgotten during the course of the evening as the two had clearly shared a mutual attraction to one another. Everything else had all of a sudden become irrelevant. Peter had to make a prudent choice though, even more so considering his recent involvement with The Menorah. To meet again would surely be near suicidal. He had no idea what or who he was dealing with.

"Well, I'll bear that in mind."

"I hope so."

With that, the two parted company and Peter proceeded back to his flat. He was getting used to the sleepless nights by this point. So much had happened in recent weeks and his head felt as though it was spinning. With still so many unanswered questions, he wondered when (or even if) The Menorah would get in touch again. Of course, there was nothing stopping him going to visit Themse Marschland again but he figured that such a move would not be the best of ideas and could have an unfavourable outcome.

He could continue to try and find out more about DS Dean Fellows from his wife but he would only ever really know the truth about him and his involvement in the Cleveland Street bomb by asking The Menorah. The only logical explanation was that he was indeed an undercover agent of The Menorah. He had to be — surely? If he wasn't though, what had he witnessed on the camera footage that day? Then there was Susan. What was he to do about that? Once again weighing up options, the most sensible one was to walk away but he was genuinely attracted to her, something he was certain was reciprocated. He eventually drifted off into somewhat of another restless sleep little knowing that at least some of his questions would become answered within the space of a week.

On the same night that Peter and Susan met at the Puffing Billy, DS Fellows and DI Harding had arrived together on the Greenwich Peninsula. Once an industrial hub, the factories and gas works were long gone and had been razed to make way for numerous high-rise slab block housing. Organised in its typical grid fashion and interconnected by numerous underpasses and walkways, the area had the same look and feel of Themse Marschland. In fact, to the untrained eye there would be very little to really distinguish the two areas from one another. Like Themse Marschland, it was designed to be somewhat of a Reich utopia but had decayed over the years and now stood grey, neglected and depressed. It was also where the person they had come to see lived. While they had to exercise an element of caution so as to not be seen, their contact knew more than enough about the area to direct them to somewhere that would assure them the maximum amount of discretion. Away from the prying eyes of the security cameras dotted around the estate.

The two officers parked up and walked to their final destination which was underneath one of the many walkways traversing the streets which, like

Themse Marschland, were all named after German figures — military heroes or otherwise. Shortly after they arrived, the person they had arranged to meet also arrived on foot. DS Fellows and DI Harding saw him approach and knew exactly who it was. It was the man who had, over a period of time, been monitoring the activities of Elizabeth Reuben at the Ministry of Media, Propaganda & Information. The same man who had gained her trust and discovered that she was harvesting sensitive information from the ministry and passing it to The Menorah. The same man who was working at the ministry as an undercover police officer.

"Here he is. Man of the hour!" DS Fellows said happily and triumphantly. "Good work, my friend."

"Thank you very much," the other man said, extending his hand towards DS Fellows who took it and shook it heavily. "Evening ma'am," the man said towards DI Harding, who nodded in acknowledgement.

"I think DC Daniel Want is going places," Fellows said. "We've got Elizabeth Rueben bang to rights, Danny. Confessed everything. No issues with Stein and you being away this morning for the briefing?"

"No, he was fine."

"That's good," DI Harding replied. "The longer we can keep him out the loop, the better. We need your cover to be watertight."

"Anyway," Fellows interjected, "Reuben was small fry really. Been passing information to The Menorah for months. Unedited news reports. Not enough to cause the Reich a massive headache but if we didn't have you on the inside, we never would've got her and who knows what else she might have got her hands on?"

"That's good," Danny replied. "To be honest, she made it easy for me. I said that to the guys this morning when I briefed them. I've had a lot tougher assignments. Has she given anything away about the chain of command?"

"Not yet," Harding continued. "We don't know how much she knows about that but it's given us plenty of lines of investigation to follow which is good. So thank you, couldn't have done it without you."

"My pleasure, ma'am."

"One more thing, Danny, what about Fewtrill?" Fellows enquired.

"Pete? What about him?"

"Well, you know we pulled him in the other week, right?"

Danny remembered. He was informed about it and remembered Peter being late for work and getting a mouthful off old man Stein in the process.

"Yeah I remember."

"Is he involved?" Harding asked.

Danny thought this over for a moment. He had known Peter for some time now and the two were undoubtedly very close (if not best) friends. Although he wasn't sure if Peter would feel the same should he find out that he was actually an undercover police officer. Nevertheless, he had never suspected Peter. He was fully aware of his arrest and the Paul Fuller incident (having read the file) but had concluded that it was nothing more than a case of wrong place, wrong time. Peter had given him no other reason to be suspicious.

"No, ma'am. I don't think you need to worry about him."

9

TAVISTOCK METROPOLIS

After Peter and Susan had initially met at the Puffing Billy, they met once again at the Tavistock Metropolis in Tavistock Square near Kings Cross station on the same night that Susan had indicated the last time they had met. Peter was still approaching the young lawyer with considerable caution. Even when he made it to the hotel doors, he found himself turning around and walking away, only to turn back round again and finally find the courage to go in.

True to her word, she was there. Sat alone at a table in the bar, looking considerably more relaxed than the time he had approached her at the Puffing Billy. She also looked beautiful and he was pleased he had gone along — if not apprehensive. It was a natural encounter and the two chatted like they were old friends. She wasn't sure if he was going to turn up and he confessed that he nearly didn't. Peter complimented her on how pretty she looked and she blushed in response. Before too long, they found themselves in one of the hotel rooms becoming more intimate with one another than either imagined they ever would. The bruises on her arms could not be hidden though. It was as if someone had grabbed her roughly around the upper arms, and as they prepared to part company for the evening, he couldn't help but ask.

"How did you get these?"

She was reluctant to speak though and pulled her blouse over her head and adjusted the sleeves to place the bruising well out of sight.

"Oh, it's nothing."

She continued to get dressed in silence looking uncomfortable when it came to discussing the injuries. Maybe foolishly, Peter continued, "Was it him?"

"Who?"

"Your husband."

Again, she seemed uncomfortable at the question but also keen to come to his defence. "He's a good man."

"Doesn't really answer the question, Susan."

"Look, he… it was nothing. It was… we argued. That's it."

"And he hurt you? He beat you?"

"I said that's it. Please! Just… it's best left alone. Please."

"I'm sorry."

He could see that he had upset Susan which was not his intention. He felt almost hypocritical raising the injuries with her, especially considering his recent involvement with a group responsible for killing hundreds of people over the years. There also remained the unanswered question over DS Dean Fellows and whether he was involved with this group or not.

"Will I see you again?" Peter asked before they once more parted ways.

Susan looked over at him and smiled. "Do you want to see me again?"

Peter leaned over as she sat on the bed and tenderly kissed her on the lips. "What do you think?"

"I guess that's a yes then."

As they checked out, the hotel clerk (an elderly gentleman) gave them a disapproving look. They had only checked in two hours earlier. He wasn't stupid and had seen this happen at the Tavistock Metropolis more times than he cared to recall. Each time he hardly approved but they had paid their bill so who was he to be overtly verbal over it? They would visit the hotel a few more times over the coming months but never tried to use the same location on more than two consecutive occasions, to avoid raising unnecessary suspicion.

Peter went home that night feeling almost like a teenager in love for the very first time and positively bounced back to his flat in Acton. He reached the front of his block and still had a big smile on his face but the voice from behind him made him jump almost out of his skin.

"Evening."

He swivelled round and was faced with the bald man — Christian Bonner — from The Menorah who had interrogated him.

"You made me jump! Shouldn't sneak up on people like that."

Christian looked at him and remained unwavered. "Get in."

"You what?"

"I said, get in." He signalled towards a car that was parked on the street behind him. "Now!"

"As long as you promise not to stick that hood on me again."

Christian didn't respond verbally but pulled Peter towards him before then pushing him towards the car. He clearly meant business and wasn't prepared to engage in any form of conversation with Peter. When they got to the car, Christian pulled open the rear passenger side door and pushed Peter towards it. He climbed in and the door shut behind him. Hebron was also sat in the back of the car and looked at Peter feeling rather amused at his ungraceful entry into the vehicle.

"Sorry about that," he said. "Christian can be a little, how can we put it, heavy handed."

"Heavy handed? Say that again."

Christian got into the driver's seat of the car and started the engine. The car then left Princess Gardens.

"We don't have long. For reasons I'm sure you probably understand, I don't come to London too often and I'd like to be out of London before the curfew cameras decide to turn themselves on."

Peter nodded. "Understandable."

"So, Peter. How have you been? Have you had time to reflect on our last meeting?"

He had done nothing but reflect on their last meeting. "I've thought about it a lot. About looking for what I can't see."

"And what did you find?"

Peter considered his next choice of words carefully. The one burning unanswered question was Dean Fellows and the bomb.

"I found out about the bomb you planted at Cleveland Street and that you have a serving Reich officer working for you."

Hebron didn't say anything. He just stared at Peter blankly giving absolutely nothing away. Inside, he was shocked that such an accusation had been levelled in front of him with little in the way of hesitation. Clearly, Peter had found something of considerable interest.

Peter continued, "I've seen it with my own eyes. I have the camera footage. DS Dean Fellows and someone else. I don't know who the other person was. They put the bomb in the bin outside the station and then a few hours later... well, you know full well what happened next. In fact, was it you that organised for that footage to even end up in my tray in the first place?"

Hebron was still looking at Peter with no expression on his face. "You think we carried out the bomb attack on Cleveland Street?"

"Yes. You even left your little calling card. The symbol on the wall. Not only was I there but I've seen the camera footage. With my own eyes."

Hebron nodded. "And you think we have a serving Reich police officer, this Dean Fellows, working for us?"

"Yes. Like I said, saw it with my own eyes and the camera doesn't lie."

Hebron remained with his gaze fixed on Peter before taking a deep breath and continuing.

"You're right, the camera doesn't lie and I dare say what you did see was a loyal and faithful servant of the Reich indeed planting a bomb outside a police station, killing their own in the process. But as much as I would love to sit here and claim responsibility for the coordination of it all, we are not responsible for that. As much as I would also like to say we have been accomplished enough in our methods to recruit a serving Reich police officer, we are also not responsible for that. In fact, we make a point to generally avoid trying to recruit police. They aren't tremendously trustworthy from my experience. And I am most certainly not responsible for putting whatever it is you've seen into your tray at work. So, I'm very sorry to disappoint you."

Peter was taken aback not really knowing how to respond. "You're lying. If it wasn't you, then who?"

"Who did you see plant the bomb?" Peter looked confused. "It isn't a trick question. What did you see and who planted the bomb? It's a very easy question."

"I told you, I saw a police officer plant it. Dean Fellows."

"Then, it was the police who did it. Simple as that."

"What? Are you telling me th—"

"It was the police who did it."

Such was the intense tone behind what Hebron had said — coupled with his gaze which seemed to be burning holes in Peter — he thought better than to continue to question him. The two men sat in silence as Christian continued to drive the car. Peter had well and truly lost track of where they were in London at this point.

"When we last met, I said to you to look beyond what you can already see. Now, I totally understand why you would think that it was us who planted the bomb at Cleveland Street but it wasn't. The bomb that destroyed a police station and killed lots of police officers and innocent people was engineered by the police themselves. They engineered it, they planted it, they killed their own. They painted a symbol of a menorah on the wall. It was all them."

Peter was bewildered. "But... why?"

"Because we're at war, Peter. Only the sort of war that they want to wage is desperate and doesn't discriminate. Even against their own. It's been happening for years. Well, as long as they started to view us as a threat at least."

"I'm sorry... I don't understand."

Hebron breathed deeply before continuing. "I don't really know how else to explain it other than it's nothing more than an act. A set-up. An elaborate fabrication of the truth. All engineered by the mighty Reich. If I had the time, I would tell you in detail about all the attacks that we supposedly carried out. I would tell you about all the people we have supposedly killed and all the atrocities we've supposedly committed. And that's the key word — supposedly."

It was all beginning to fall into place. "So you're telling me that all those attacks and assassinations carried out by The Menorah, they weren't done by you but they were all carried out by the police? And then blamed on you?"

"Largely."

"Largely?"

"Peter, I won't lie. We are responsible for some of the attacks that have made the news in recent years. I won't ever deny this, but everything we do, and I mean everything, is clearly thought out and we avoid civilian casualties as and when we can. At all costs. Our only interest is in members of the Reich. Anybody else who has been killed as a result of our actions has been purely accidental, and believe me when I say, that eats me up every single day, hour, minute and second that I draw breath.

"But what you have seen? Cleveland Street? We will never lay claim to that one and the man you mention is not one of us. I don't pretend that our methods are entirely peaceful because we're at war after all but we are methodical. Our aim is to free the British Territories and start the revolution. A ripple effect that will spread across the world. There's more like us in America attempting the same thing. We want to show the world what this regime is and the magnitude of the atrocities it has carried out, not only against the Jews but against the everyday man and woman."

"So what are they trying to do by blowing themselves up?"

"It's an attempt to discredit us as well as being the biggest conspiracy in a generation. It isn't the first time it has happened and it won't be the last.

"Cleveland Street? Not us. Marble Arch underground explosion, twenty-three innocent people killed June 1978? Not us. Drive by gun attack on the Mill Hill police post April 1978? Not us. Detonation of a bomb outside White City Stadium after a football match killing seventy-four December 1977? Not us. Shall I continue?"

Peter shook his head. It made sense now. Sure, The Menorah had been behind some attacks but those yielding a high death toll of largely innocent people had been carried out by someone else, no doubt on the back of orders from a very high place. Attacks carried out to discredit The Menorah and to paint them as a threat to the very existence of the Reich. In much the same way as the Jews were made out to be a threat to world existence in the years leading up to the Second World War.

Like Hebron had said though, this was a war they were waging; a less than conventional conflict with less than conventional means. Peter could now see more clearly why he had been of such interest to Hebron for, at his very fingertips, he had access to information that would discredit the Reich. How would the people of the British Territories feel knowing that their own were being murdered by the ones there to protect them? The very ones who had triumphantly paraded through the streets of London promising a brave new world under the Führer. How would they feel seeing the Cleveland Street footage in all its glory with a serving police officer being identified as the culprit? What he possessed in the top drawer of his desk back at the ministry was an invaluable piece of information — and he could get hold of more of it if he really wanted to. He had finally begun to look beyond what he could already see. He didn't like it.

"I can give the footage to you. You can broadcast it and I can get more. As much as you like—"

Hebron raised his hand to stop Peter. "You don't have to give us anything you don't want to. I will never force you into a situation that may lead you into danger. However, do I make the assumption that you want to continue to help us?"

"If what you've said is the truth, then yes."

"It's the truth, Peter, I can assure you of that. And you've seen it with your own eyes. I can't explain why or how you ended up with that footage but it seems rather fortuitous that you did. You must, however, proceed with caution. One of our operatives in the very same ministry as the one you work for was captured only recently."

Peter remembered now. It was the lady sat on the opposite side of the office.

"Elizabeth Reuben?"

"Yes indeed. Regrettably, she will likely spend many years imprisoned. Her only crime being to simply tell the truth. Are you prepared to take that risk, Peter? To be imprisoned, maybe for the rest of your natural life?"

"I am," Peter responded, without hesitation.

"Well, it's easy to say that now in the heat of the situation. But I would suggest you maybe sleep on it. The footage of Cleveland Street would be ammunition for our cause, without a doubt but I think you need a little more time to think through whether potentially spending the rest of your natural life incarcerated courtesy of the Reich is a realistic sacrifice you really want to make. And if you decide it is, only then will I happily accept that footage from you alongside anything else you may wish to share. Until you reach that decision, I don't want it. Unlike the Reich, I prefer the idea that we're all free to make our own choices."

There was one thing that was still worrying him. "But how did they find Elizabeth Reuben?"

"The eyes of the Reich are everywhere. I dare say that Elizabeth Reuben was rooted out by a mole within the ministry. I cannot say for certain and we will never know for certain but you must never discuss what you do for us with anyone else. No matter how much you trust them. Discussing your activities could prove to be an existential threat to us. Do you understand? You must never disclose the nature of your work with us. The consequence of doing so would not be good for you." Hebron's tone was one of the utmost seriousness.

"I understand."

"Christian, let's take Mr Fewtrill back home. It's getting late."

A few minutes later, they had arrived back in Acton outside of Peter's block. He had not mentioned that he had, earlier that evening, had a romantic encounter with Susan Scott, the wife of the Cleveland Street bomber. While he now desperately wanted to tell her that her husband was nothing more than a terrorist, he knew he would not be able to do so. To do so would, as Hebron eloquently put it, be an existential threat that would have dire consequences for Peter and no doubt others within The Menorah. The car came to a stop in Princess Gardens.

"So what now?" Peter questioned. "How do I get in touch with you?"

"It's early days, my friend. We'll contact you as and when it's safe to do so. For now, the only advice I can offer you is to be normal. Act normal. Continue as normal. But continue searching for more of the same material that you have already found. Elizabeth Reuben found it, so can you. Elizabeth was careless. I can't say for certain how she was discovered. It could be that she put her trust in someone she shouldn't have done. Don't make the mistakes she made. If you are captured, there will be very little I can do to help you."

Hebron extended his right hand towards Peter who took it and shook it. They parted company once more and Peter returned to his flat.

The next day, and as advised, Peter prepared himself for work as normal and went about his daily journey, as normal. He arrived at the ministry as normal and went about his job, as normal. Danny arrived on time and also began to carry out his job, as normal — the two friends remaining completely oblivious to the fact that they were both playing for opposing teams. Peter sworn to secrecy; Danny sworn to secrecy. Peter was keeping a very close eye on old man Stein's office waiting for the door to open for he had an idea that he wanted to discuss with him. When the door was closed, it was usually a signal that he didn't want to be disturbed. When he did finally open it again, Peter took his chance. He had been thinking about how he could aid The Menorah, and sure, he could get his hands on a wealth of information from where he was in the ministry, but he knew where he could get more valuable information but he needed Stein's advice and maybe even his help so he had to sweeten the old man up.

As he lightly rapped on the door, an impatient Stein responded from within. "Yes?"

"Sorry to disturb you, Herr Stein," Peter replied quietly and nervously. "May I take a moment of your time, please?"

"Yes, yes, come in. I only have a minute though so make it quick, Fewtrill."

"Thank you, Herr Stein."

Peter paused, not really sure how to continue the conversation which seemed to make Stein even more impatient.

"Well? What is it?"

"Herr Stein, I was wondering if I may apply for a position in the Propaganda Department?"

10

THE VON HINDENBURG MISSION

As the summer of 1979 approached, it seemed as though the world was finally beginning to settle following the death of the Führer. At least it seemed that way. There had been no more (Reich engineered) attacks by The Menorah on British soil since the Cleveland Street incident. There was a globally reported coup d'état in Berlin a week after Hitler's funeral which had provided a momentary period of drama; however, by the time summer approached, Klaus von Hindenburg, and other Reich appointed governors-general, were declaring that everyone should heap endless praise onto the new Führer who would continue with the policies of his predecessor — the great Adolf Hitler.

For Peter Fewtrill, he had continued to take the advice of Hebron and was carrying on with his life whilst maintaining as much normality as he possibly could. Old man Stein had seemed rather amused and perplexed at his enquiry to apply for a position within the Propaganda Department, particularly as he had been arrested weeks prior to his expression of interest — if not then fully exonerated of any wrong doing.

Nevertheless, Stein was still a professional and took his enquiry seriously, and to Peter's surprise, went away and enquired as to whether there was indeed a position vacant in the secretive department upstairs amongst the slightly odd and uncomfortable looking crowd. To Peter's delight, there was and he was advised to contact the head of the department, Almut Muller, which he promptly did. He had never even seen or met Frau Muller during his years working at the ministry but she seemed affable enough when they did meet for the first time. She was a middle-aged German with a broad German accent yet had an excellent command of the

English language. She was happy to show Peter around the department which was laid out in much the same way as his own. An open plan office layout with people sat behind their desks quietly working away.

Frau Muller was keen to find out more about the prospective candidate and took time to question Peter on his motives for wanting to work in Propaganda as well as his past experience. Peter was eloquent in his explanations and tried to sell himself in terms of his years of experience and his impressive track record in the department within the floor below. Frau Muller seemed impressed.

There were other candidates looking to fill the vacant position, all of whom had to submit a formal application and then undergo an interview if shortlisted — which Peter was. To his surprise and delight, he was finally offered the position of propaganda analyst subject to background checks. As expected, these were rigorous and thorough. References were checked and a search of his property in Acton was also carried out with every drawer and cupboard thoroughly searched with not a single stone left unturned. He understood that his colleagues were interviewed at great length, Danny included. He knew he could rely on his best friend (and undercover police officer) to paint a glowing portrait. His family history was also checked as were his travel records, both of which revealed nothing untoward as he had never travelled abroad. He was interviewed heavily in regard to his arrest in the January of that year. Once again, the conclusion was that it was nothing more than a 'wrong place, wrong time' scenario and there was no need for it to cause any concern whatsoever.

All searches and checks revealed nothing and Peter was eventually cleared to start his new position. Packing up all his belongings from his desk (including the camera footage of the Cleveland Street explosion), Peter bid his best friend Danny farewell and made his way upstairs into the secretive Propaganda Department at the beginning of April 1979 to begin his new job — and to also begin harvesting a wealth of sensitive and confidential information serving to expose a range of atrocities committed by the Reich.

Peter's clandestine meetings with Hebron continued periodically but he still had no idea how to contact him if he wanted to. Any contact would always be initiated by Hebron and always involved Christian Bonner who seemed to act almost like a second in command to Hebron.

In reality, the depth of their relationship stretched back almost forty years and Christian owed Hebron an enormous debt of gratitude as a result of what Hebron did for him in the years following the war. Even though Hebron had no children of his own, he viewed Christian as the son he never had. Likewise, Christian viewed Hebron as the father he had lost at the hands of Nazi Germany.

Hebron had remained reluctant to accept the Cleveland Street footage from Peter, along with anything else he was offering from his new role within Propaganda. To be captured by the authorities would be nothing short of life changing for Peter, and if he didn't stand up to what would no doubt be an uncomfortable, prolonged and painful interrogation, potentially devastating for The Menorah. As a result, Hebron wanted to be beyond certain that his newly acquired asset would be willing to sacrifice everything without question (and also keep his mouth shut if captured) for the sake of the cause before committing him to smuggling harvested information out of the ministry. That time wasn't now, but it would come soon enough.

At the same time, Peter's affair with Susan Scott gathered pace and their liaisons had become more frequent but continued to be restricted to hotel rooms for a brief period only. Peter had remained true to his word and not discussed the nature of his involvement with The Menorah with anybody, not even Susan. As much as it pained him, he had also been unable to reveal the activities of her husband, DS Dean Fellows, with Susan and his responsibility for a deadly bomb attack on members of his own. One of many carefully staged terrorist attacks engineered by a higher power within the Reich, the sole purpose of which to further discredit the activities of The Menorah. As much as he wanted to reveal the truth, he couldn't.

What pained him even more were the injuries Susan seemed to be picking up with increasing frequency. Fellows was brutally clever and only seemed to leave bruises where they wouldn't be immediately visible. If it wasn't the arms, it was the legs. If it wasn't the arms or the legs, it was the ribs. She would often try to hide the marks from Peter as they were making love but sometimes it was impossible. She would occasionally defend him, claiming he was a good man really but just struggled with his temper due to the nature of his work and the awful things he would sometimes see and that he was getting help and things were improving. They never seemed to improve though.

He wished so much he could tell her the truth or that one day she might choose to leave him altogether. For now, they continued to enjoy one another's company on an intimate level but Peter could feel himself falling deeply in love with the young lawyer, and although she hadn't said it, he suspected that his feelings were reciprocated.

As his secret relationship with Susan continued alongside his covert activities for The Menorah, so did his friendship with Danny who became known within the Propaganda Department as 'Downstairs Danny'. The two still met regularly after work for drinks at the Puffing Billy. As spring approached and the evenings began to draw out, they even ventured back to the Highwayman on Cleveland Street and sat on the small outside terrace enjoying their drinks, although the view was not much to look at. There was still a gaping hole in the buildings where the police post had once stood. Some of the surrounding area had also been demolished. Oddly enough, the graffiti of the menorah was still visible and Peter figured it had been left there as a reminder to everyone as to who was responsible for the carnage (even though he now knew full well that it wasn't The Menorah who were responsible for the attack).

Danny remained oblivious to his friend's involvement both with the lawyer or The Menorah but still continued to covertly monitor the activities of others within the ministry building, hoping to once again catch someone out and expose them as a mole, just like he had done with Elizabeth Reuben. He continued to remain blissfully unaware that the man sat opposite him on the outside terrace was also one of the people he was trying to find.

As with his relationship with Susan, Peter was desperate to share his secrets with his best friend but again, he remained true to his word and kept quiet. Too many people knowing too many things would be dangerous.

All the while, Hebron and Christian continued with their planning of the von Hindenburg mission. A plot to kidnap Governor-General Klaus von Hindenburg. Hebron did not often talk of his experiences in the Second World War but they were memories that would never leave him. He had stood on the shores of Dover and witnessed for himself the almost God-like power of the Nazi military as it wiped out the British sea defences from the air with pinpoint accuracy, leaving the way open for tens of thousands of German soldiers to land unimpeded onto British soil.

The guided missiles were like nothing ever seen either before or since the New Year's Day invasion. He remembered fleeing from the military advance and the ruthlessness of his pursuers who mercilessly shot and killed any remaining soldiers and indeed anyone else who decided to try and stand in their way. All under the orders of one man. One of the architects and leaders of the invasion and subsequent occupation — Klaus von Hindenburg.

It went beyond being a personal grudge though. Von Hindenburg would be a valuable prisoner and their aim was to have him confess to a range of atrocities committed under his command and broadcast the event live on the television across the British Territories by once again jamming the signal. To show the people that their great governor-general was really nothing more than a cold-blooded killer and a war criminal. Another slice of ammunition to further the revolution. If they could get him to also confess that the many bomb attacks in peacetime were also engineered by the Reich and not The Menorah, this would be a bonus revelation that would only serve to further tarnish the reputation of the Reich.

It wasn't going to be easy though and to pull off the kidnapping, they would have to plan meticulously over a long period of time. Upon taking office as governor-general, von Hindenburg took up residence in the building formerly known as Buckingham Palace. After the war, the king, along with other members of the royal family, had been forced into exile and the palace stripped of all its material wealth to be distributed back to the Reich. Much of this wealth had taken pride of place in Hitler's Chancellery building. This left the palace largely empty so it was assigned as a headquarters for the NSDAP during the occupying years. By the time von Hindenburg was appointed to governor-general, the building was reassigned as his personal residence and promptly renamed as the Palace of the Governor-General. Much like the Reich Chancellery building in Berlin, the palace was not only the personal residence of von Hindenburg and his family, but also a place for his cabinet to meet. It remained a highly fortified building, covered from every angle by security cameras, armed guards or both.

Christian Bonner had been carrying out surveillance on the palace for many months to try and get an accurate picture of von Hindenburg's daily activities and movements. Frustratingly, he never seemed to venture very far but then again, he had little need to do so for the palace acted as both his home and place of business and the grounds were plenty large enough for the aging governor-general to get a daily dose of fresh air and exercise.

A full-on frontal assault of the palace was simply not an option for The Menorah. Such were the fortifications, it would be a suicide mission and they were not equipped adequately enough to raid such a large building, and resources (in terms of manpower and weaponry) were precious. Even more frustrating was Hindenburg's lack of regularity on the occasions that he did venture outside of the palace. Not only were they infrequent, but when they did happen, it was a large cavalcade of no doubt armoured vehicles that would never adhere to the same route more than once. Von Hindenburg was a top military mastermind and clearly this was something that had not left him in his older age and he remained insistent on his drivers pursuing a different route around London whenever the need arose for him to leave the palace. This would make setting up an ambush nigh on impossible. His theory was indeed correct as The Menorah could not identify anywhere in London where an ambush could realistically be set up such were the seemingly random routes and lengthy diversions the von Hindenburg convoys would take.

Von Hindenburg also remained deeply paranoid when venturing away from the palace and would sometimes send out a decoy convoy, before then leaving the palace in a separate convoy sometime later. The former war hero had been shot in the face during the war years during an ambush, losing an eye in the process and leaving him with his trademark facial scarring. The experience had nearly killed him and had the bullet entered his face at a marginally different degree, it no doubt would have done just this — but he had survived. In the process of surviving, the governor-general had developed a sense of paranoia when away from his comfort zone or in the company of others he was unfamiliar with. The erratic drives around London and frequent decoys were all put in place to suppress his fears and keep any potential ambushers off his scent.

The strategy was working as Christian had also noted the numerous decoy convoys leaving the palace and cursed in frustration at seeing them.

Similarly, he had cursed when following a genuine convoy around London whilst disguised as a motorcycle courier as it snaked its way in yet another seemingly totally random direction on some wild detour. To snatch the governor-general outside of the palace walls was the only realistic option but it was going to be difficult. Very difficult.

As Christian and Hebron walked the grounds of the farmhouse on a warm spring evening, they discussed the options that they had in front of them.

"There's no way we can stop the convoy in the city. It's too difficult and dangerous. Firstly, I can't say for certain which route he'll take but also, in terms of getting him out? That'll be tricky if we stop the convoy in a built-up area."

Hebron nodded and pondered for a moment. "Getting into the palace is clearly out of the question, unless we can acquire some kind of air support. Stopping the convoy in the city is possibly off the table. So, can we stop it as it leaves the palace? This seems to be our only option wouldn't you say?"

Christian sighed heavily. "Out of all the options we have, yes. But it still won't be easy. Hindenburg sends out decoys. Sometimes, they go out before him. Sometimes, they go out after. Again, it's the regularity of it all."

"How do you mean?"

"I mean, there is no regularity. If we knew he left at, say, seven o'clock every morning without fail then we could be ready and waiting. As it is, I haven't been able to ascertain when he leaves, when he plans to leave, what time he's likely to leave and if it'll be him out the gate first or a decoy. We can't exactly stand outside waiting for him in the hope that we don't accidentally ambush one of the decoys. In terms of getting away, an ambush outside the palace is definitely the best option."

"I see. It's a shame we haven't got someone on the inside who can tell us his schedule."

"Could we get someone do you think?"

Hebron shook his head. "In a circle as tight as the one around von Hindenburg? I doubt it. Even if we could, the time it would take to build up the trust and confidence is not time that we have or that I wish to invest."

The two men continued on their evening stroll around the farmhouse. Christian did have another thought.

"We could scare him out."

Hebron looked at his friend thoughtfully. "Go on."

"So we don't know when he's scheduled to leave. But we could force an evacuation of the palace."

The idea had Hebron's full attention. "And how would we do that?"

"I'd need to think it through in a little more detail. We've got enough in the way of weapons to send some grenades over the wall towards the palace. If we can convince him the palace is under attack, he might make a dash for it and try to get out. When he does, we can be waiting outside to pick him up."

"Sounds risky."

"Whatever we do, it'll be risky. It would have to be quick. The authorities would pounce so we'd need to look at blocking routes in and out of the palace. There would have to be diversion tactics so we could get away with him. But it's a viable option, one that I think we should look into in more depth."

"All right, let's look into it."

On that very same spring evening, the man who lived in Flat 304, Block 87 in Themse Marschland was hurrying back to Rommel Way. He had been out to the shops to get some cigarettes and decided to drop by the local watering hole, Brandenburger Tor, for a swift beer — or three. He was alerted to the presence of two people who he was absolutely certain he recognised from somewhere but he couldn't initially place them. As he watched the man and woman closely he desperately tried to think where he had seen them both before. They were acting suspiciously and asking questions of the barman. Very discreet, yet specific, questions relating to The Menorah, and the man had a strong German accent. Where had he seen them before?

It was only when he was halfway back to his flat that he remembered and he immediately picked up the pace. When he finally made it back, he headed straight to the phone and made the call and eventually Christian Bonner picked up.

"Chris, it's Lewis. You need to listen. I've just seen something you might be interested in."

Christian could hear the urgency in Lewis' voice. The man that Peter Fewtrill had encountered some months before had been based in Themse

Marschland for many years, manning one of the many satellite safe houses dotted around London for The Menorah.

"What is it, Lewis?"

"There's a couple of folk wandering round the estate asking things, certain things. About us."

Christian didn't see that this was anything unusual. The authorities (amongst others) were always enquiring about The Menorah.

"So? Is this a problem?"

"Not exactly no. It's who it is that's interesting."

Christian was intrigued. "Why? Who is it?"

"Well, unless I'm mistaken, it looks like Richard Frick and that Ukrainian woman."

Christian was shocked. "Are you sure?"

"Sure as I can be. It didn't come to me at first but I'm almost certain it's them."

Christian sat at the other end of the phone in a state of shocked silence. He knew immediately who Lewis was referring to for his name had been all over the news for many months now. Richard Frick was a member of the NSDAP (or at least a former member) — specifically the minister for Food and Agriculture. While he didn't know for certain, it was a strong possibility the woman he was with was Bohdana Melnik, a Ukrainian Nazi sympathiser. Why was this so significant? They had been on the run since February (something to do with the coup d'état in Berlin that made the news some months earlier) and were currently two of the most highly sought-after fugitives in Europe which begged the question — why had the two Nazis turned up in Themse Marschland asking suspicious questions concerning The Menorah?

"All right, Lewis, leave it with me. I'll talk to him about it."

It was in the June of 1979 that Klaus von Hindenburg returned from his meeting with the new Führer and Adolf Eichmann at the Berghof in the Bavarian Alps. He had returned to the British Territories with a highly decorated member of the IUI — an Italian by the name of Zappa who had found favour with the new Führer and had been given a fresh assignment to pursue within the Territories. Alois Brunner had also been present at the Berghof and the meeting in the picturesque location had been held to discuss the ongoing security concerns in relation to The Menorah and the Liberty Front — two active terrorist organisations who had not gone away.

As part of the meeting, the Führer had presented each man with an eyes-only top-secret dossier and they had discussed the contents. It was a plan conceived by Adolf Hitler in the years after the Second World War but one that had never quite come into fruition. The plan had lay dormant for many years but since coming to power, the new Führer had wanted to reactivate it and so the men read through the pages of the dossier one by one.

Most of it was not the concern so much of Governor-General von Hindenburg. At least not in the short term but the longer-term implications of the plan would no doubt have their ramifications for the British Territories and indeed the wider world at large. As he sat in his personal study in the palace, von Hindenburg once again leafed his way through the top-secret document and read with interest about the work of Alois Brunner and his team of elite scientists at the Ministry of Aeronautics and Weaponry in East America. He looked at the blueprints and designs of the Iron Fortress. He didn't much understand it but it looked impressive, whatever it was. He read about Brunner's Project Bluebird, as well as the mobilisation of the Wehrmacht in Wyoming. Again, he didn't much understand the technical language behind Project Bluebird, but Brunner's work definitely looked interesting. He finished reading the dossier and placed it into his safe. It seemed as though the future was looking bright for the Reich as it cast its gaze west.

PART 2

HITLER'S GERMANY

11

CANARY

JUNE 1962 — THE BERGHOF, BAVARIAN ALPS, GERMANY

A nine-year-old Alois Hitler had enthusiastically gathered up his collection of toy soldiers and taken them out onto the terrace of the Berghof, one of his father's holiday residences in the Bavarian Alps. The Berghof also served as one of his father's many headquarters during the war but these days, it had become one of his favourite holiday locations. The view across the mountains was glorious and the property sat above the market town of Berchtesgaden. Over the years, the property had been renovated and extended and looked very different to how it had done during the war years. Nevertheless, it remained lavishly decorated and full of valuable and rare antiquities from across the world. Adolf Hitler retained his own private study where he would often sit for hours by himself: writing, reading or painting. His mother also had her own private quarters to use at will. Security was tight and the property was fenced and patrolled by a team of security specialists thoroughly checking the identity and intentions of any visitors. Local people knew the property well and knew to stay away. The Berghof was often lent to close friends of Adolf Hitler including Alois Hitler's namesake, Alois Brunner, who would often fly over from East America to take in the mountain air, the beautiful scenery and everything else associated with his home country. Similarly, Governor-General Eichmann would also visit the Berghof. On occasion, the three men would meet there simultaneously and sit on the terrace: drinking, smoking and reminiscing about days gone by and their respective successes in the war.

On this sunny June day though, it was Alois Hitler who was currently occupying the terraced area of the Berghof that overlooked the Alps. He had assembled his plastic toy soldiers in a particular way. On one side was Germany led by General Alois Hitler himself. On the other side, the rest of the world! The mighty General Hitler ordered his infantry into battle. The famous Wehrmacht, each one a trained killer, an expert in their art. The forces of the rest of world would stand no chance. They were nothing more than men press-ganged off the street and given a gun. Sure enough, the brave general's forces immediately took out the front line of enemy troops with minimal casualties. Those Germans who did fall in battle screamed at their brothers in arms to continue without them. Let them die a brave and honourable death on the field of battle. And so the German forces marched on, cutting down the enemy indiscriminately. But wait, surely not. The enemy is fleeing back to the safety of their trenches. But General Alois Hitler is having none of this. The Führer has ordered total annihilation of the enemy. The general is not prepared to disappoint. He wants to return to Germany a decorated hero. A revered general who would go down in history. He was about to order his troops to pursue the enemy when his concentration was broken by someone coming to join him on the balcony.

"Are you winning, my boy?" It was his father.

The seventy-three-year-old Adolf Hitler was taking a break with his family. Away from the pressures of Berlin and all that came with it. He had aged since the end of the war. His hair had greyed and his posture had become stooped as his bones had aged. He was now relying on the aid of a walking stick to move around due to arthritis in his hips. He retained the characteristic moustache but this too had also greyed over the years. He had become a father late in his life and had, at times, struggled to keep up with his son. Adolf Hitler always had his own plan for his child. He wanted him to follow in his footsteps. To be the leader that he had become. To inspire the world over with his inspirational speeches, to continue to lead the world in technological advancement, to extend the boundaries of the Reich (if he had not completed such a feat by the time he died). He loved his son but he was also infuriated by him at times. He was painfully shy and appeared to lack many social skills. He was uncomfortable around others, and to his frustration, had developed a stammer in his early years.

In reality, Alois Hitler was terrified of his father. His earliest memory of his father was of being dragged up the stairs by one leg whilst being in floods of tears. He never knew what he had done that was so dreadful that it warranted being treated in such a disgusting fashion. Alois had asked his mother as he got older why it had happened but she had remained dismissive. He suspected she knew what had happened but she was always keen to defend her husband (his father) at every opportunity. Adolf Hitler had dressed his son the way Adolf Hitler wanted to dress him and this always made the young Hitler uncomfortable. He hated the clothes he was forced to wear. They were always mismatched and he felt as though everyone was laughing at him when he went somewhere with his parents. Alois also had his hair styled by his father. Again, he hated it. The ridiculous amounts of gel were almost like lacquer and he hated the left parting. He just wasn't comfortable with any of it. Alois Hitler was also sent to the very best school in Berlin. A prestigious and elitist school, Alois always felt out of place at the Berlin Academy for Exceptional Boys for the simple reason, he didn't consider himself exceptional in any way. He was never top of the class, he was useless at sport and not musical in any shape or form. He was escorted everywhere in the school by two burly looking former special forces soldiers and chauffeured in and out of the school in a bulletproof Mercedes each day. As a result of this, and his noticeable stammer, he was ridiculed frequently by his peers.

Yet every time he tried to speak up or didn't perform as he should at school, his father would simply explode in an enormous fit of rage. His beatings were frequent. His father's verbal abuse towards him was inappropriate and harsh and by the time the boy had reached the age of nine, he was a frightened shell of a child with little confidence in his own abilities. His mother would make minimal effort to defend her son, more often than not sitting idly by while his father would berate him once again. The childhood abuse had brought to the surface a darker side to Alois Hitler.

He had always had an interest in nature and animals from across the world and when he was eight years old, his parents had managed to acquire a pair of yellow canaries for him. He adored them and would spend hours watching them happily hop between the perches in their cage, pecking away at the millet and chirping happily.

One day, his father returned home in a rage over something. He quite often didn't need an excuse to be angry but he did use his anger as an excuse to abuse young Alois who received a clout across the scalp sending him running to his bedroom and the company of his canaries. Alois was hurt, physically and mentally and his self-esteem was at an all-time low. In his own fit of rage, Alois removed the canaries from their cage and placed them into a cardboard box. He then proceeded to shake the box roughly. He could hear the canaries becoming more and more distressed but he continued until their panicked tweets and frantic flapping finally ceased. When it did, he opened the cardboard box and peered inside. They were dead. He felt nothing. No remorse. No sadness. No regret. Nothing.

Even though his father was now elderly, he still feared him and nothing had changed that day on the terrace of the Berghof. He didn't respond to his father's question but his father continued anyway.

"I asked you a question. Who's winning? And who's that?" He pointed towards the lead figure of his make-believe German Army.

"Th-th-that's General Alois H-H-H-Hitler. He's leading the German advance."

"I see. And are the German's winning?" his father enquired. He seemed to have a genuine interest in what his son was doing and had a smile on his face.

"Yes, Father. They're winning."

"Good, that's good to hear. Well, General Alois Hitler. Who are you fighting against?"

"The rest of th-th-the w-w-world."

Hitler remained quiet and nodded approvingly. "I hope that includes Japan?"

Alois was confused. He was only nine years old but his understanding of the war was that Germany and Japan had stood side by side fighting a common cause. "I thought Japan were on our si-si-side, Father?"

Although he was an old man, he was still quick and never failed to surprise his son with his volatile and violent outbursts and this was no exception whatsoever. As fast as lightning, Adolf Hitler struck his son across the face with his open palm with such ferocity that it sent him sprawling across the balcony.

"No! You're weak!" he yelled. "A weak and silly boy. And this?" He pointed at the general leading the charge. "This will never be you!" With that, he stamped hard on the toy soldiers and they shattered in every direction. Alois raised his hand to his face instinctively to protect himself from the flying debris. His father continued on his furious rant at his son, who was by this stage cowering in fear on the floor in floods of tears.

"One day, I have to pass all I have onto you. As my only son, it is down to you to lead what I have created. It's my legacy. But you are weak. And you are foolish and I only wish I had another son who was strong enough to lead an empire. Because you are not fit to lead a group of toy soldiers let alone an empire! You're nothing but a stuttering idiot!"

TUESDAY, 6th FEBRUARY 1979 — BUDENHEIM, RHINELAND-PALATINATE

Götz Koch was worried. Deeply worried. He had known the Führer had been unwell for some time and he was also aware of the deep reservations he held over the capabilities of his only son and heir apparent — Alois. He vividly remembered the last time he saw the Führer alive. It was four days before his death and he had been shocked at the appearance of the once charismatic leader. The skeletal, bedridden elderly man had been nothing more than a shadow of his former self and the ferocity of his deterioration was shocking to see. The night Götz Koch arrived at the Reich Chancellery in Berlin to visit the Führer, he took over from Alois Hitler who had been keeping a vigil at his father's bedside for some hours. He had sat with the Führer who was barely able to speak and only able to ingest small amounts of fluid periodically. It seemed as though it had taken the Führer all his remaining strength to beckon Koch forward in an effort to try and say something to him and the two words he was able to eventually utter to Koch were a weak and raspy, "Not him." These were the final words the Deputy-Führer was to hear Adolf Hitler speak before he passed away a few days later.

The words had stuck with Götz Koch who had been appointed as the second highest ranking member of the NSDAP upon the death of Martin Bormann in 1970. Like his predecessor, the new Deputy-Führer (and head of the Nazi Party Chancellery) was the only member of the NSDAP allowed unfettered access to Adolf Hitler. The only person controlling the flow of information and access to the Führer. A former tank commander, Götz Koch had served throughout Europe and had proved himself to be a formidable opponent on the battlefield. With a strategic mind and natural leadership qualities, he rose up the ranks of the Wehrmacht quickly finding favour with Adolf Hitler for his numerous victories in Europe. After the war, Koch took a sidestep into politics where, in a similar way to his rise in the Wehrmacht, he rapidly rose up the ranks of the NSDAP eventually being selected by the Führer himself as the successor to Martin Bormann in 1970. The now fifty-three-year-old Koch had served the Führer loyally in his last years, but like many others, had become increasingly wary of the Führer's son, particularly in the final few months of his life.

He found it unusual to be so wary of someone he had barely even spoken to but as the Führer had aged, it was only natural that talk of his successor would become more prominent — and more prominent it had most definitely become. It was becoming increasingly evident within the NSDAP that many were concerned about the leadership qualities and abilities of Alois Hitler, for he had never once stood out in the same way as his father. He came across as painfully shy, socially awkward, frustratingly quiet and lacking all the charismatic qualities possessed by his father. Most in the NSDAP had been reluctant to discuss the issue (for fear of reprisals) but as the Führer entered his twilight years, Koch could not help but notice an underlying unrest and deep-seated concern with the future of the Reich under the leadership of Alois Hitler. The eventual demise of the Führer would leave the Reich vulnerable to not only internal threats but also from more far-reaching elements. It was no secret within the NSDAP that there had been much sabre rattling on the East/West American border and that the Führer had been working closely with Adolf Eichmann to come up with a solution. Would Japan seize the instability of a new ineffective leader to further their own cause? Would Alois Hitler be able to continue the legacy of his father? Or would he prove to be nothing more than an existential threat to the Reich? In addition, pressure had to be maintained on the dissident groups intent on continuing their underground guerrilla campaigns against the Reich. The Menorah and the Liberty Front had gained momentum in recent years with the former of the two groups now attempting to spread their influence across Europe. The Reich leadership had to remain resolute in the face of the continued threat, and committed to suppressing the terrorists.

Although she had never overtly expressed it, Koch often suspected that Eva Hitler too was concerned for her only child. Concerned that he would not be able to carry the mantle of his father. While she had not openly said so, he deduced that she may have reservations of her own based on the few conversations he had had with her over the years. Now the Führer was dead, the Reich was in a precarious position. While Germany — like many other places in the world — was in an early state of mourning, the dust would eventually settle and when it did, Koch remained deeply concerned of what would be left over. Even more so upon hearing the final words spoken to him by the Führer.

The other two men arrived at Koch's house early on Tuesday morning and were driven to the location from Berlin in the same chauffeur driven vehicle. It was Konrad Lange (the chief of the Reich Chancellery) and Lothar Krausse (the chief of the Chancellery of the Führer) — two of the highest-ranking members of the NSDAP behind Koch. Both men had expressed concern over the 'Alois Hitler issue' and Koch had decided that it was time to begin discussions on a way forward to ensure a smooth transition of power — whether that involved Alois Hitler or otherwise.

Koch's house was sat on the banks of the River Rhine in Budenheim, Rhineland-Palatinate. It was a cold and frosty winter morning when the two men arrived at the house and the mist hung above the gently flowing and calm river. Koch's house was rather grandiose with three floors and a garden set on a hill that descended all the way down to the banks of the river. In the summer, Koch would sit by the river and fish or tend to the wealth of flowers in the garden itself. Today, the three Nazis sat in Koch's private study area where his housemaid brought them all tea.

"I think we all know why we're here, gentlemen," Koch began on that cold frosty morning. The other two men nodded in agreement. "The day has finally come and the Führer has gone, but like myself I'm sure, many of us are left wondering what happens now."

"People are talking, Götz," Lange cut in. "Across all ministries. We should have had this conversation a lot earlier."

"I know but it's a sensitive situation and I was hoping that the boy would have stepped up in recent weeks and proved us all wrong. Or that his mother may have had some kind of influence and made him step up. It saddens and worries me somewhat that neither has happened."

"Are you surprised?" Krausse questioned.

Koch shook his head solemnly. "No, Lothar. I can't really say that I am. We're left on somewhat of a precipice though and the next steps need to be considered carefully. Japan will be watching, as will the rest of the world. If the transition isn't smooth, if there's the first hint of any kind of unrest, our enemies will work to capitalise on it. The situation could very easily, and very quickly, begin to work against us."

The three men sat in quiet contemplation. If any action were to be taken, it had to be carried out on the highest level — and they were the highest level.

"What about the boy's mother?" Lange asked. "Even if she can't convince the boy to become what he should be, can we convince her to take the boy's place? She's done more for the Reich than he ever has after all. There's no denying gentlemen, she's a wonderful ambassador. Always has been. She was the closest person to the Führer. Can she be convinced?"

"To take the reins from the boy and lead the Reich?"

"Yes."

Koch had, on occasion, thought the same and had certainly got the feeling that Eva Hitler had her own reservations about her son. Would she be prepared to usurp her own child? This, he was not sure of. He had a family of his own and despite occasional divisions (as with any family), they were loyal to one another and would stand by one another no matter what. The Hitler family would no doubt be the same.

"I don't know, Konrad, I really don't. I absolutely agree with you. She's an excellent poster girl and ambassador for the Reich. But a politician? I just don't know. I suspect that Eva has her own doubts but I don't think her loyalty is frail enough to incite her to go against one of her own." Koch diverted the issue as he had a specific question for Lange. "What about the Wehrmacht? Can we rely on their support?"

"I've spoken to the High Command," continued Lange. "Obviously I haven't appraised them of the exact situation that we speak of today but they are ready to mobilise on your orders if necessary. They're on alert as it is, the situation being what it is. They're only a call away."

"Good."

In legal terms, the commander-in-chief of the Wehrmacht was the Führer himself in his position as Germany's head of state. Under any other normal circumstances, any orders to mobilise the Heer, Luftwaffe or Kriegsmarine would be from the Führer, but these were not considered to be normal or conventional times. Götz Koch was prepared to circumvent and bypass current procedures by ordering the Wehrmacht into action if necessary. Likewise, the High Command were prepared to act on any order issued to them from the Deputy-Führer. There was, however, another obstacle standing in their way.

"What about Brunner?" Lange asked.

It was a subject that they had all thought about at one stage or another and it was only a matter of time before his name would be mentioned — Alois Brunner. Young Hitler's namesake. Although disliked greatly in the higher echelons of the Reich, Alois Brunner remained a highly influential figure and firm favourite of the Führer. Alongside Adolf Eichmann, Brunner had been one of the key architects of the Final Solution during the Second World War and was known for his ruthlessness and cruelty. In the years following the war, he had followed Adolf Eichmann to East America and was currently heading an elite weapons programme within the Ministry of Aeronautics and Weaponry — somewhat of a political and strategic move aimed at keeping the Japanese at bay and away from the border. Even though he was thousands of miles away, his influence stretched far and wide and he was one of the very few people considered to be close to Alois Hitler and this was a worrying problem. A potentially very dangerous thorn in the side of any plans to unseat the new Führer and his continued influence on Governor-General Eichmann.

"Brunner is a worry," Koch continued. "But in a matter of days, he will be in Berlin for the funeral. We can apprehend him at the earliest opportunity if needs be. Let's face it, gentlemen, few will be too sad."

"Eichmann will," Krause interjected. He had a point too. It was no secret that the governor-general of East America and Alois Brunner were close — both professionally and on a more personal level. This created a potential difficulty in apprehending Brunner. How would Eichmann then react? Would he have to be apprehended at the same time?

"Apprehension of both of them is an option," Koch continued after contemplating the potential Eichmann issue. "An option I would rather avoid though. Brunner? No problem. But to apprehend Eichmann as well could be folly. The American border is delicate as it is. To remove the governor-general paves the way for Japan to potentially act as they please. That gentlemen, is an unacceptable risk. The western borders need to remain secure. If they fall, so will the East."

The other men knew exactly what Koch was talking about. Removing the leadership of East America could incite Japan to further its own ambitions to the west which, if successful, could then begin a campaign on a western front. The strategy had to be carefully thought out to ensure a smooth transfer of power and indeed, one that — to appear to the rest of the world at least — had been mutually agreed by all parties. A strategy that would see an end to the Hitler dynastic leadership without a single shot being fired or a single life lost in the process. Only then would Japan be kept at bay, seeing that the Reich remained strong in the face of change. To see Eichmann lose his grip on East America could prove devastating; his support in the plan was paramount.

"I think we all agree, gentlemen," Koch went on, "that there is little love lost between ourselves and Brunner. I am on good terms with Eichmann though. I know he supports the boy but he does not favour him as much as Brunner. I would like to think that I could convince him to lend us his support. He wouldn't want to lose his position as governor-general anyway, irrespective of how he feels about the boy's capabilities. So one would hope we will be able to convince him to make the right choice."

As the men talked into the early afternoon, they had decided upon a strategy. It was too early to act at the present moment anyway, they needed time to prepare. The funeral of the Führer was approaching, and out of respect if nothing else, this was not to be disrupted under any circumstances. The world was grieving, Germany was mourning and the people needed time to process this. To attempt to launch a coup d'état at this moment would be foolish. As their discussions continued, it was agreed between the three high-ranking officials that any removal of Alois Hitler and his mother was to be done as peacefully as possible. While this would involve the Wehrmacht in some capacity, exactly what their role would be would need to be determined. The three men pledged that no shots were to be fired and the loss of life was to be avoided at all costs. The transition of power was to be achieved as peacefully as possible with Alois Hitler and his mother unseated from power without them coming to any harm in the process. This was likely to happen when they were both at the Chancellery building in Berlin where they could be contained by the Wehrmacht with the minimal amount of attention being drawn to the situation. It was agreed that Alois Hitler and his mother were to be detained — as was Alois Brunner — and that Deputy-Führer Götz Koch would assume power as the de facto commander-in-chief, head of state and Führer of the German Reich. As for Eichmann? Koch was hoping to be able to reach out to the governor-general and gain his support to secure the future of the Reich, if nothing else.

It was hoped that any resistance to the plan would be minimal. Any instability in the Reich or power vacuum would be capitalised upon by others. Not only the terrorist groups of The Menorah and the Liberty Front (who would no doubt be keen to take the opportunity of uncertainty to try and further their own campaignshigh of terror) but also the Empire of Japan sitting to both the far east and west that had, to a degree, fallen out of favour with Adolf Hitler due to its own ambitions and influence on the world stage. Little did the three men know that in a leafy Berlin suburb, another group — led by a father and son — were planning a more violent and bloody coup d'état of their own.

12

MARBLE MAUSOLEUM

FRIDAY 9th FEBRUARY 1979 — REICH CHANCELLERY, BERLIN, GERMANY

Alois Hitler had retired to the private living quarters of the Reich Chancellery following the funeral of his father. The body of Adolf Hitler had lain in state in the week leading up to his funeral. He had died an incredibly weak and emaciated man who had wasted away gradually over a period of time, but a team of highly experienced morticians had worked round the clock to restore the body to something resembling its former glory. Even though the Führer had lost all of his hair and his trademark moustache, this was restored with expert precision (albeit in a greyer form) giving the appearance that neither had ever fallen out in the first instance. He was dressed in a beautifully manicured black suit, white shirt and black tie; all discreetly packed out to give the dead Führer a little more bodily consistency (and to disguise the fact the corpse was little more than a skeleton). In a rare step by the Reich, the Chancellery building was opened so mourners from across the world could come and pay their respects to the body as it lay in an open casket in the Mosaic Chamber.

Condolences had come from far and wide, from leaders across the globe and Adolf Hitler was afforded a lavish state funeral — also at the Reich Chancellery — before the body was driven to St. Barbara Friedhof Cemetery in Linz, Austria, the Führer's birthplace and childhood home. Alois Hitler and his mother did not accompany the body on its near four-hundred-mile journey into Austria. The enormous cortege snaked its way out of Berlin in the late afternoon, past the crowds of weeping mourners, and headed towards the small Austrian town. Prior to his death, the Führer had ordered the construction of a grandiose marble family mausoleum at the Austrian cemetery. Somewhere to lay not only his body to rest but the bodies of his family — his entire dynasty laid to rest in the same place. Built from white creamy marble, the structure had a similar appearance to that of the Parthenon in Athens (albeit smaller in size). Its numerous pillars surrounded the main structure of the mausoleum and supported a pitched roof, at the front of which was a giant golden Nazi eagle with the swastika in its claws. The huge mausoleum would become a shrine to those unable to visit Berlin in person to pay their respects to the dead Führer. Such was the significance of the building, it was afforded an armed patrol around the clock and would become somewhat of an attraction to anyone who would visit the Austrian town.

Although the Führer's body had been on display for the public, the funeral itself was a marginally quieter affair. The service was held in the Mosaic Chamber of the Chancellery building — the same room where the body had lain in state. The Reichsbischof of the German Evangelical Church performed the service itself before the attendees watched as the casket was loaded into a hearse and driven away from the Chancellery building towards its final resting place in Austria. Alongside immediate family members, leading figures within the NSDAP and a number of world leaders were also in attendance; amongst them the governors-general of the British Territories and East America (Klaus von Hindenburg and Adolf Eichmann). The Duce of Italy (Aberto Bianchi) was not in attendance due to illness but a representative in the form of Pietro Casati (the Italian Minister of Agriculture) had been sent in his place. There was no personal representation from the Empire of Japan but the condolences of Emperor Hirohito were conveyed to the grieving son and widow of the late great Führer. All high-ranking members of the NSDAP were in attendance including the three men who, a few days earlier, were discussing their concerns over the very future of the Reich: Götz Koch, Konrad Lange and Lothar Krause. As expected, yet equally to their dismay, the highly influential Alois Brunner was also in attendance. Brunner was not a well-liked man within the NSDAP. His contribution to the cause during the Second World War had no doubt proved to be invaluable but as a person, he was an arrogant and rude man with a sometimes-over-inflated opinion of both himself and his abilities. He had revelled in the fact he had been assigned to East America to lead a weapons programme and many believed that this had only served to inflate an already over-inflated ego. He was to be approached with caution and remained one of only a very few people who seemingly had some form of personal attachment and relationship with Alois Hitler.

The three high-ranking members of the NSDAP greeted one another as they would do any other day but did not discuss in any way the meeting that they had held a few days before but Koch had made some progress. He had spoken to the leaders of the High Command and insisted that they remain on full alert in the coming days and be prepared to be called into action at a moment's notice. Worryingly, he had heard rumours of other members within the NSDAP planning their own actions against Alois Hitler. As much as he tried to find out who or what this involved, he proved unsuccessful in securing any further information. He would find out who they were in time though — as would the rest of the world, for it was about to be broadcast across the globe. For the moment, Koch remained oblivious and attributed the talk and hearsay to nothing more than idle rumours; probably to be expected given the gravity and shock of recent events.

Once the cortege had left Berlin, Alois Hitler and his mother returned to the Chancellery, the main headquarters of the Reich and the permanent home of the Hitler family. Hitler had instructed the architect Albert Speer to construct a new Chancellery building, considering Otto von Bismarck's old Chancellery unfit for purpose. Hitler deemed any costs associated with building a new Reich headquarters to be immaterial and four thousand workers toiled round the clock in an effort to complete the building within the given time frame of less than a year, something that was miraculously achieved. So impressed was Hitler, Speer was branded a genius and earned himself a promotion to Armaments Minister and a director of forced labour during the war years. As well as housing some of the Reich ministries and separate living quarters for the Hitler family, the Chancellery also had a large and equally lavish garden area and the Führerbunker, an underground compound intended for Hitler, his family and other senior members of the NSDAP to take shelter in during the war years should enemy forces decide to drop their bombs on Berlin. German victory was so swift and decisive that this was never the case and the Führerbunker had remained largely unused and somewhat redundant for many years.

So Alois Hitler and his mother Eva stood in the great study, a particular favourite room of the late great Adolf Hitler. It was a room used during the war years for military conferences and had been used to host various other meetings in the years following the war. The walls of the room were adorned with some of Adolf Hitler's most prized artwork and paintings and there was a large marble-topped table sitting at one end of the room. As the mother and son entered the great study, they had remained silent. Alois stood in front of one of the many of his father's paintings that he had acquired over the years. Many of these he claimed had been saved during the war years, some had been acquired from elsewhere in the world. He didn't know a lot about art and he cared little for it; unlike his father who had a love of fine art and was a talented artist in his own right. Alois observed the painting quietly whilst contemplating the events of the day. His father had finally been laid to rest after what had been a period of ill health and he was finally at peace. He had watched his mother weep; he had witnessed the thousands of mourners weep yet he had not shed a single tear. He was unsure how he felt. He was somewhat conflicted. Part of him was sad, after all it was his father who had been buried. Yet a larger part of him felt very little. Much like the canaries in the box. What weighed on his shoulders was the responsibility now levelled at his feet. He was now taking over the reins from his father and was by default the new Führer of the great German Reich. He had known since childhood that it was coming. He never wanted it though. He knew he had been a let-down to his father and this had been made very clear to him on more than one occasion. He knew his father lacked the faith in him to carry on his legacy. So how was he meant to lead an empire in the same way his father had done for so many years? More worryingly, he strongly suspected others in the Reich lacked faith in his abilities — a suspicion that was all too true. This was going to be a pivotal moment and the young Hitler and his mother both knew this.

Eva Hitler was just shy of her sixty-seventh birthday when her husband had passed away on the 28th January 1979. She had been by his side in the hours leading up to his death and he passed in his sleep, in no pain or discomfort. Her birthday on the 6th February (three days before the funeral of her husband) was nothing to celebrate. She was dressed in black funeral attire but had since removed the accompanying hat, veil and gloves. She approached her son, who was still gazing at the artwork on the wall, and touched his arm gently in order to get his attention.

"What are you thinking, Alois?"

Alois shrugged and shook his head. "Nothing. Just looking at all of this. I never understood it mother. His love for this art. It's so... materialistic."

Over the years, Alois had largely lost his stammer although it did come back to him on occasion, mainly if he was feeling particularly nervous or on edge. He didn't understand the arts. Never did. It was beautiful to his father. To Alois, it was nothing. Just pictures. Nothing more.

"We need to talk, Alois," his mother continued. Alois turned to face his mother.

"About what?" he responded rather nonchalantly.

"About what happens now. Your father has passed the Reich over to you to lead. And lead you must. Alois, there are some out there who don't believe in you. Not like they did your father and you must show them that you are strong and capable. It's your time."

"Would they like to see me dead?" the young leader questioned sounding sarcastic and almost unsurprised at what he had just asked his mother. After all, it wasn't an entirely inaccurate question to have asked.

Likewise, he was unsurprised by his mother's response. "I dare say they would, Alois. There are some out there who see your father's death as an opportunity. There are usurpers. There are those who doubt you. Who doubt us."

It was statements such as this that made Alois question his mother's intentions. What did she mean by this? What was her motivation? His father would not have tolerated this. He led the Reich, no one else. So why should that change all of a sudden? Eva Hitler was the face of the Reich, an ambassador, but she was not part of the leadership. At least not to Alois' knowledge so when she referenced 'us', this left Alois confused as to who really was in charge in this particular situation and indeed, who really wanted to take charge.

"What would you have me do, Mother? Tell me. Should I order the deaths of all those who have no faith in me? Surely if I do, there'd be nothing left of the Reich. Especially if so many people think so little of me.

Who are they anyway? Maybe they could come to me in person and tell me to my face of their so-called lack of faith. Would they do that, Mother?"

Eva grabbed her son by both arms tightly and looked him in the eyes intently. She was angered by his sarcasm and what she perceived to be a lack of clarity over the urgency of the situation. "Be the leader you were born to be, Alois. As soon as the time is right, assemble your cabinet and lead them. Show them that you will not tolerate the usurpers. Show them that you intend to continue your father's legacy. You need them firmly on your side so those in the west know that they cannot take advantage of you."

"Those in the west? Who do you mean by that? The Japanese?"

"Yes. That's exactly who I mean. They're waiting for an opportunity to make gains of their own in the world and they are watching your next move very carefully, Alois. Believe me they are watching you."

Alois knew exactly what his mother meant by this. Yes, the Germans and Japanese had stood side by side in the war years and had agreed to a partition of America into Germanic East and Japanese West but for Adolf Hitler, this wasn't enough. He wanted to expand the Reich to take control of the entire globe and in order to achieve this, Japan would have to be defeated first. It controlled swathes of the Asian continent, all of Australasia and the western states of America. If he were to make progress in his eventual plans of complete world domination, they would need to be dealt with first. This is why he stamped on the toy soldiers in a fit of rage in 1962 and this is why, seventeen years later, his mother was encouraging him to look to the west. To carry on with his father's legacy. To finish what his father had never quite managed to start.

His mother was desperate and he could see this in her eyes but Alois remained silent. He gently removed his mother's hands from his arms. Her fingernails were digging into his flesh (even through the fabric of his suit) and he despised physical contact with his mother. In the same way he had despised physical contact with his father on the rare occasions he had extended any form of affection towards his son.

Once released, Alois quietly told his mother that he was tired, then left the great study and ascended the stairs to the private living quarters of the Reich Chancellery, leaving his mother standing alone.

13

THE SYNDICATE

After the funeral cortege had departed the Chancellery building, the many guests in attendance and thousands of mourners gathered outside on the street all began to disperse either back home or to their hotels (if visiting from abroad). The Italian minister of Agriculture, Pietro Casati, returned briefly to the Berlin Metropolis where he was temporarily residing. He rested for a few hours and waited for the crowds in the streets to disperse. He also took the time to examine the Berlin street map. He wasn't familiar with the German capital but he knew he had to make his way to a house in the Hermsdorf area of the city. This he had to do without attracting the attention of others. In reality, he was unlikely to be recognised but he had to take all the necessary precautions anyway such was the nature of the meeting he was due to attend later that evening. It was a long walk but that was fine. He considered himself fit enough to carry it out and it would also allow him plenty of time to be sure he wasn't followed and to abort at the first sign of a tail. It was roughly ten miles (as the crow flies) to get to Hermsdorf from the Berlin Metropolis and he set off in the late afternoon with an anticipated arrival of later that evening when darkness had finally descended over the capital city.

After taking several planned detours and some strategic stops along the way, he finally arrived in the leafy and quiet Berlin suburb of Hermsdorf. He had memorised the relevant section of the map back at the hotel and without too much difficulty located the street he was looking for — Gartenstrasse. Before making his way onto the street, he stopped once more and took a minute to look all around him to make one final check and make sure he had not been followed. It was a crisp and still evening. The rumblings of the traffic through the city could be heard in the distance, but all was quiet apart from this so he made his way onto Gartenstrasse to locate his final destination.

As described by his contact, he found the house with no difficulty. The unkempt front garden was the clue. The house itself was set back from the road, and other than the garden, there was nothing to distinguish it from any other house in the area. It looked like a timber framed one-storey house and there were no visible lights on in the property and no cars were parked outside. As Pietro approached the house, the front door automatically opened and he walked into the building without saying a word. The door closed silently behind him and the mysterious occupant who had let him into the building spoke in a hushed tone. He spoke in German which Pietro was fluent in. Such was the nature of his work with the Italian government and its close alliance to that of the German Reich, the ability to speak fluent German was pretty much a prerequisite for getting a job within the government in the first instance.

"You're late. Were you followed?"

"Not to my knowledge."

The man behind the door gave Pietro a look as if to say his response wasn't entirely satisfactory. Pietro therefore felt as though he maybe had to elaborate to placate the man and put his mind at ease.

"I took all the precautions I had to. It's for that very reason I'm late. I haven't been followed. At least not to my knowledge."

"You're certain?"

"Absolutely."

The mysterious occupant hesitated and looked Pietro up and down. He had changed from the suit that he had worn for the funeral service and was now wearing something more casual in the form of jeans, comfortable walking shoes and a padded black jacket to keep the February chill off his body as he traversed Berlin. He stood just shy of six feet tall and had a heavy build. Not fat by any means but more of a stocky muscular individual with jet black hair, a Mediterranean complexion and light stubble. The occupant would've placed Pietro at around forty-five-years-old (give or take a year or two) and he wasn't far from the truth as Pietro was forty-three-years-old at that moment in time.

"Go through. They're in the back room waiting for you." The man gesticulated with his head the direction that he should go, to which Pietro complied and made his way to the rear of the house.

This involved walking through the kitchen. As he entered the kitchen (which, much like the rest of the house, remained shrouded in darkness) he could hear low voices in a room beyond this and there was a dull light emanating from underneath a door at the far end. He slowly opened the door so as to not cause any undue alarm — he knew the people on the other side of the door would likely be a little on edge given what was no doubt being discussed inside. On the other side of the door in the back room there was a table and there were six people sat around it talking. An elderly man was sat at the head of the table. He looked frail, his cheekbones protruded from his thin face and his thin white hair was combed backwards. His clothes seemed to hang from his frame and beside him there was a walking stick to assist him when he moved around. Sat to the right of the old man was his son, a German that Pietro knew to be called Wolf. As he entered the room, the old man smiled and slowly, yet clearly uncomfortably, rose from his seat to greet the Italian.

"Pietro, you made it. We've been waiting for you." He extended his right hand towards Pietro. The two men shook hands. The old man's grip was weak and felt as frail as he physically looked. Pietro took a seat at the table and the old man also sat back down before continuing.

"We were just discussing the final arrangements of our plan, Pietro. You all know I've waited years for this day. I thought it would never arrive but it has and we are all here for the same reason. We all possess contempt and disgust for one man. But that man has gone. He is dead. And that, my friends, is a good thing. Let there be no doubt about that. What are we left with?" The man's tone when he posed the question was one of disgust and disdain and Pietro knew exactly who he was referring to. No one answered and the old man repeated the question, "What are we left with my friends?"

"His son," responded a woman who was sat around the same table. "Who will be no better than his father." Pietro knew her as Bohdana Melnik, a police officer from the Ukrainian district of Germanic Russia who, like the others around the table, had been drawn in and recruited into the planned armed coup to overthrow the Führer that was now being discussed around the table.

The old man slapped his hands together before exclaiming, "Yes! Exactly, my friend. But do you know what else we are left with?" There was silence. His tone changed from one of excitement to something a lot quieter, almost a whisper. "Opportunity. That's what we are left with. Opportunity. Alois Hitler is a weak man. Be under no illusions whatsoever, my friends. He may be from the Hitler bloodline but he doesn't have the heart or the courage of his father. He is weak and lacks the heart to lead the Reich. He will never live up to the reputation his father made for himself. Why is this good for us you may ask? Because it makes it a perfect time for us to act. Alois Hitler is vulnerable. His only ally is his bitch mother." The old man awkwardly rose from his seat, supported by his walking stick with his son watching on ready to catch him if he fell. He eyed everyone sat around the table and pointed to them one by one as he continued.

"Round this table we have representatives from within the very heart of the Reich, from the Ukraine, the British Territories and the Italian Empire. It has taken us years to get to this point but now my friends, we are ready to strike at the very heart of the Reich when it is at its most exposed. The sooner, the better. We will strike and we will assassinate Alois Hitler and so a new Reich will begin under my command."

It had been nearly a year earlier that Pietro Casati first became aware of discontent within the Reich. The Führer was advancing in years but his grip on power was still firm. The rumours of his weak son seemed to be rife within Reich circles and it was something that Pietro picked up on when visiting his counterpart within the Reich — Minister for Food and Agriculture Richard Frick. Frick had opened up to the Italian minister, probably more than he would have done with a fellow member of the Reich, and been overtly verbal in his criticism of Hitler and his leadership. Even more so at the prospect of what he described as 'his strange little son' taking over when the Führer did eventually die, believing it to be a certain death sentence for the Reich. After becoming initially acquainted, the two men had formed a close and lasting friendship largely based around a mutual interest — their dislike of Hitler and the worrying prospects of 'his strange little son' seizing power.

It had turned out that Frick was somewhat of a hardliner, determined to see that change was brought about forcibly but he was being led from outside of the NSDAP, by someone else. As Pietro became closer to Frick so it was revealed that the old man and his son, Wolf, were in control and pulling many strings from the safety of other locations as part of a much larger group Pietro came to know as The Syndicate. On the instructions of the old man, Wolf had spent years travelling across Europe, painstakingly gathering intelligence and recruiting more hardliners prepared to answer the call to arms and to seize control of the Reich. This explained the multi-national coalition assembled round the table that night. Each representative at the table had, under their own command, more people from all walks of life willing to join their cause and bring about a forcible change of leadership within Europe. Pietro had taken advantage of his position within the Italian government, taking every opportunity to meet with Frick and to eventually become a fully trusted member of The Syndicate. He had served in the Italian military, and although he had not been involved in any combat action, he was handy with a weapon and prepared to offer whatever advice and assistance he could to his fellow militia.

All members of The Syndicate saw the old man as the next Führer, and his son the heir apparent. The old man had worked alongside Adolf Hitler for many years and had an in-depth knowledge of the NSDAP (having served in the party himself before falling out of favour). The old man had been disgusted and terrified at the use of Der Befreier I, II & III. While he was a staunch Nazi and a loyal supporter of the Nazi ideology, he had found the use of nuclear weapons over-zealous, unnecessary and a threat to the very existence of the world. As a result, he had fallen out with Adolf Hitler. This was the person who would lead the Reich in a different direction, one that would serve a wider world peace with no fear of nuclear destruction, not one committed to constant tensions with the Japanese. He may have been old but everyone round the table had no doubt in their minds that this man would succeed in the plan he had been forging since as early as 1941. It had taken him years to find allies and accompanying manpower from around Europe to help him but at last, with the aid of his loyal son, he had a team and they were in the final stages of piecing together their plan.

Each member of The Syndicate had mobilised their members of the militia and hundreds of militants were now surreptitiously positioned in and around Berlin ready to strike on command. Some posing as mourners from abroad and staying in the many hotels in and around the capital; some staying at campsites and hostels; some being accommodated in houses within Berlin itself. In the mass outpourings of grief, The Syndicate had taken the opportunity to begin to meticulously piece together their final plan to dethrone the new Führer and replace him with the old man. To the best of their knowledge, the authorities remained blissfully unaware of the existence of The Syndicate, and anyway, their attention would likely be directed towards the known terror groups (such as The Menorah or the Liberty Front) who were probably going to cease upon an opportunity to continue their own campaigns. Which they indeed had, and the Cleveland Street explosion in London had been broadcast on German television as well as on the British television channels.

The Syndicate was heavily armed. In the aftermath of Der Befreier III, hundreds of Soviet military outposts were abandoned, leaving huge caches of weapons (both light and heavy) largely up for grabs. Whilst much of this was seized by the Wehrmacht, an enormous amount was ceased by others and transported east, into the feuding former Soviet Union not annexed into Germanic Russia, to fuel years of civil unrest with many different factions vying for power. So Wolf travelled east in the years leading up to that night in the Hermsdorf house, bargaining and negotiating with various warlords and regional leaders to acquire a wealth of leftover Soviet weaponry. His father, along with other high-ranking Nazis, had plundered a vast array of valuables during the war years (including a sizeable amount of secretly stored gold bullion) and this was used to finance the acquisition of all that was required to build a small army — and build a small army they had done. In the process, Wolf had also been able to recruit a number of members from the remains of the now partitioned former Soviet Union. Men and women bitter at seeing the Union destroyed by Der Befreier III; men and women who had lost their homes to Nazi Germany; men and women bitter by the years of civil turmoil caused as a result of the loss of Josef Stalin; men and women desperate for revenge. They were now a force to be reckoned with. A small multi-national army of fascists, Nazis, Nazi sympathisers and disgruntled members of the former Soviet Union all possessing one common interest. A hatred of Adolf Hitler and his Reich along with a desire to enact change for the benefit of all.

The team had laid out maps of the Reich Chancellery as well as maps of the surrounding area to discuss their approach. In a timed lightning strike, The Syndicate planned to storm the Reich Chancellery. They would be led by Wolf and the very front of the building would be blown open by heavy explosives (planted in a huge car bomb — which would unfortunately involve a member of The Syndicate sacrificing themselves in order to detonate it) before being entered. It was hoped that the shock and awe of the explosion would disorientate the security within and around the Chancellery enough to allow Wolf's team entry and to immediately seal off the ground floor, thus preventing anyone from being able to access the garden area and more importantly to isolate the Führerbunker and to stop Alois Hitler from taking refuge inside it. Each floor of the Chancellery was to then be 'cleared out' and Hitler and his mother assassinated at the first opportunity, without hesitation.

The minds around the table that night were such that they knew full well seizing control of the Chancellery would not be enough in itself to gain complete control in Berlin. The explosion of the car bomb would immediately trigger a huge security response that would have to be quelled. Two further teams would provide cover in the immediate area surrounding the Chancellery, sealing all access routes both in and out and securing the perimeter around the Chancellery itself. This would leave the remaining teams of The Syndicate to suppress any responses called in from elsewhere in Berlin and they would be ready to swoop on the major security outposts within the city and stop them attending the Chancellery to assist. The threat of air support was prevalent and realistic and it was likely that assault helicopters would be called in upon the raid commencing but Wolf had managed to secure enough surface-to-air missiles to counter the threat from above and there were enough military minds within The Syndicate with the knowledge to operate the equipment. Within a very short timeframe, the plan was to have Berlin secured and all immediate security responses to the crisis quelled. Finally, upon completion of the mission and the assassination of Alois Hitler and his mother, the old man would be transported across Berlin and installed as the new Führer in the liberated Reich Chancellery where he would make a live televised address declaring himself the new leader and the beginning of a new era for the Reich.

In the short term there would inevitably be those who would oppose him but all within the NSDAP knew who he was and while many would need convincing to accept him as the new Führer, he was confident that more would not need convincing for he knew the doubts that existed about the young Hitler and he knew the level of unrest there was within the NSDAP. It was all intelligence he had gathered from his Syndicate moles who worked within the NSDAP — such as Richard Frick. He didn't think it would be easy by any means but in his heart, he knew that what he was offering the Reich was a more viable alternative to the current young Führer, and he remained resolute in his determination to bring about reform and restructure and an overall different approach in Reich policy across the world.

As the leaders within The Syndicate planned well into the night, their hundreds of members waited in locations across Berlin in anticipation. Their weapons had been moved into the city and were currently being stored in vehicles hidden out of sight in underground parking lots or private garages. The gathering of men and women from across Europe all waited with bated breath for the instruction to mobilise to come through. The leadership team of The Syndicate drank whiskey in celebration as their plan became largely finalised into the early hours of the following morning. Their job from here was to brief and prepare their respective teams for the all-out assault on the Reich Chancellery and the installation of a new Führer. More importantly, all being well, the date of the armed coup d'état was decided upon — Friday 16th February 1979.

14

BEST LAID PLANS

FRIDAY 16th FEBRUARY 1979 — REICH CHANCELLERY, BERLIN, GERMANY

A week after The Syndicate had met in the Hermsdorf house, they set about carrying out their armed operation to overthrow the new Führer and install their own leader in the form of the old man. The plan failed. Little did they know that it had been doomed for failure before it had even commenced. The SS commando sniper on the roof of the Chancellery was the first to fire a shot, and with deadly precision, the single high velocity bullet struck the driver of the car carrying a quantity of high explosives square on between the eyes. This caused him to slump over the wheel, sending the car into a hard-left turn before making it roll, with it eventually grinding to an awkward halt on Vossstrasse approximately two hundred metres from the entrance to the Chancellery. The explosives inside the car then detonated but aside from smashing some surrounding windows and spewing debris across Vossstrasse, little damage was done to the Chancellery building itself.

As the vehicle exploded, so the SS commandos who were poised waiting inside the Chancellery sprang into action and stormed out and so began a fierce and bloody, yet brief, gun battle. Finding themselves pinned down by sniper fire, as well as heavy fire from the SS commandos, the teams of The Syndicate who had taken up position to either raid the Chancellery or secure the surrounding area were forced into a retreat but not before either being captured by the commandos or killed in the gun battle. The few who managed to escape the unfolding scene of utter carnage dropped their weapons to seek sanctuary within the alleyways and side streets of Berlin; however, few were able to make a successful getaway.

Similarly, the teams of The Syndicate assigned to quell the response anticipated by security forces away from the Chancellery were met with a similar level of success. To their horror, the snipers and SS commandos had been lying in wait for their arrival, and as soon as the teams made their approach at the agreed time, they were immediately peppered with bullets from every conceivable angle leaving most of them dead, some captured and a few managing to flee the scene back into the depths of Berlin.

The ensuing carnage would go on to claim the lives of most of the members of The Syndicate who had chosen to partake in the attempted coup d'état that night and within the space of an hour, Berlin (including the Reich Chancellery building) had been secured by the crack team of SS commandos. The Syndicate's plan, a plan just shy of forty years in the making, had been brought to an abrupt and rather unceremonious end on the streets of Berlin in under an hour.

As the members of The Syndicate around the Chancellery (who had not either been killed or fled into the surrounding area) surrendered, they were quickly flanked and surrounded by a number of masked commandos, ordered to throw down their weapons and lie face down on the ground, which they duly did. They had seen the devastating impact of the sniper fire and knew that a bullet to the head would no doubt be forthcoming if they resisted. The commandos moved in, kicked away their weapons and searched each member of the group one by one before dragging them away and making them all kneel with their hands atop their heads at the foot of the steps of the Reich Chancellery in Vossstrasse. The leader of the group, Wolf, had survived the failed attempt to storm the Chancellery and in total, twelve others had also been captured. From one end of Vossstrasse, a black armoured Mercedes-600 came to a halt by the captives and their captors. From the rear of the vehicle, a man was roughly pulled out and forced to kneel next to the other captives. It was the old man from the house in Hermsdorf. He had received a beating and his face was bruised and bloodied. He looked solemnly at his son Wolf at the other end of the line of captives, who looked back at his elderly father equally solemnly.

A few minutes later, a small cavalcade of vehicles began to drive towards the steps of the Chancellery from the other end of Vossstrasse, past the burning wreckage of the car bomb. In total, it was five black Mercedes-600s and they all came to a slow halt by the steps and the captives. The headlights of the lead Mercedes blinded the group of men and women as they knelt on the ground with nervous anticipation. The doors of the first Mercedes swung open and two men stepped out of the rear of the vehicle and approached the group. The old man at the end of the line was the first to speak as he saw who they were. "You!" he spat in anger, as it became apparent who it was who was approaching him. "Traitor! I trusted you."

Pietro Casati stopped short of the group. He was dressed in the military fatigues he had worn earlier in the evening when the group had met for the final time to wish each other good luck in the execution of their operation. He wielded a machine gun and also had a sidearm holstered on his thigh. He looked on with a sense of satisfaction. His mission was complete. It had been a tough mission at that. Pietro Casati was not a member of the Italian government at all and he never had been. In fact, Pietro Casati was his assumed identity and one that he had used for the duration of his mission with the Ministry of Infiltration and Intelligence (Ministerium für Infiltration und Intelligenz) or the IUI — a clandestine and specialist Reich ministry and successor to the Gestapo. His real name was Giovanni Zappa and he had managed to fool all within The Syndicate such were his skills in deception and the high level of military experience and training he already possessed.

His mission had started when Adolf Hitler was still the Führer (albeit in his twilight months). Upon receiving disturbing rumours that many within the NSDAP were beginning to express concerns about the viability of his own son, he had initiated an investigation to determine the legitimacy of such claims. Not wishing to jeopardise such a sensitive investigation, Hitler had instead decided to use a foreign agent. Someone with no previous ties to the Reich and someone who would be less likely to arouse any suspicion and force any traitors or usurpers even further underground where their threat would exponentially grow. So it was that Giovanni Zappa was assigned the mission to assess the rumoured threat and to infiltrate any potential dissident groups, and to report back to Hitler himself.

Zappa had worked for the IUI for years and was chameleon like in his abilities. A skilled former special forces operative for the Italian military, he quickly moved up the ranks, eventually capturing the attention of the head of the IUI — Hermann Göring — who vigorously attempted to recruit him into the new discreet ministry purposely set up to deal with growing militant threats on both sides of the Atlantic. The multi-lingual Zappa had a skill to be able to blend into any situation and penetrate even the tightest of circles. So he had posed as an Italian politician for many months and followed up on every lead provided to him. This way he was able to gain the trust of NSDAP minister Richard Frick, who eventually allowed him access to the old man and The Syndicate. The same old man who now knelt on the floor looking up at Zappa in utter horror.

The sensitivity of his operation had meant that Zappa was required to report to Adolf Hitler directly thus bypassing the Deputy-Führer Götz Koch who, all the while, had remained blissfully unaware that a plot to forcibly seize power was underway — although he had heard rumours which he had deemed to be without foundation. Upon Adolf Hitler's death, Zappa's mission continued in earnest and he reported to the new Führer who, to the old man's horror, was the other man who had exited the Mercedes and was now stood alongside Zappa. Dressed in his best suit and tie and wearing a long black leather overcoat, the young Führer looked over the group with particular disdain before walking down the line looking closely at each and every one of them in turn. Most of them averted their gaze away from the Führer and maintained fixed eye contact on the street upon which they were knelt. Some of them were bloodied and wounded from the brief firefight. Some appeared uninjured. All were fearful of what the Führer would now do and how he would act. One man who had remained defiant throughout and kept his gaze upon the young leader was the old man at the end of the line. The Führer stopped at the end of the line and the two men's eyes met and they stared at one another intensely.

"So, you are the great Rudolf Hess I assume?" Hitler asked the old man, who said nothing in return but fixed Hitler with his furious gaze. "You know Herr Hess, my father told me all about you. He used to speak of you often. I have to say, I found his tales of your… cowardice, rather amusing."

Until 1940, Rudolf Hess had served as Hitler's Deputy-Führer, a position he had held since 1933. He was one of Hitler's most trusted servants. A man with equally anti-Semitic and extreme views and they rarely differed in discussions on how to deal with the Jewish 'problem'. As

Hitler began to plan the invasion of the United Kingdom in late 1940, so the collapse of the relationship between the two men began.

While Adolf Hitler ambitiously planned to mount an invasion onto British soil, so Hess began to secretly plan a peaceful solution without the knowledge of Hitler. The two men remained largely at loggerheads in relation to German war strategy, with Hess preferring to focus on defeating the Soviets to the east and investing German resources on this front. Hitler, however, remained determined to focus on the British problem. Despite being a staunch ally and confidant of Hitler, Hess was becoming increasingly concerned about the threat of nuclear strikes and Projektbefreiung and wished to avoid mass destruction happening at any cost, seeing nuclear strikes as a threat to the very existence of humanity itself. If Britain would submit peacefully without the necessity of armed conflict, this would allow Hitler to plough the Wehrmacht into the Eastern front, thus necessitating swift conquest of Moscow, thus avoiding using the atomic bomb. As Hess prepared to take off for England in his Messerschmitt BF-110 from the Augsburg-Haunstetten airfield in an attempt to broker a peaceful solution with British politicians in November 1940, he was captured by the SS. To that very day, Hess never knew how the SS had found out about his plan but it had been foiled. Subsequently, the United Kingdom was invaded and Moscow was razed with Der Befreier III. Hess had failed.

In the aftermath of Hess' attempts to negotiate with the United Kingdom, a furious Hitler removed him from his position of Deputy-Führer, replacing him with Martin Bormann. Initially, Hitler imprisoned Hess, wishing to have him executed for treason. Eventually, after recognising his former friend's contribution to the NSDAP, he exiled Hess to Austria allowing him to live a quiet and modest life on a reduced military pension on the agreement that he was to never show his face or make his presence known in Germany ever again. In subsequent years, Hess became a fierce opponent and critic of Hitler, beginning to see his willing use of weapons of mass destruction as the greatest threat to the very existence of humanity. Hess retained his anti-Jewish doctrine and beliefs but had slowly come to the realisation that Hitler's ambitions went far beyond his extermination of the Jews and were becoming something far more dangerous to the world at large. For years Hess sat, waiting in the shadows, seeking allies from both within the Reich and also from around the world. People with similar views to his own, with fears of Adolf Hitler's true ambitions for complete world domination and people with concerns about his son and eventual successor — Alois. Over the years, and with the aid of his son Wolf, Hess had gathered together a large group of dissenters from all walks of life and formed The Syndicate. Importantly, he had been granted an insight into the current inner workings of the NSDAP in the form of Richard Frick — who had managed to escape into the Berlin night after the firefight with the commandos. While this had proved an invaluable source of intelligence over the years, it had also inadvertently brought the Italian master spy Giovanni Zappa into the mix. Something that Hess had now realised was a fatal mistake. Zappa had fooled everyone in Hess' circle of trust and they were now paying the price.

"I knew I never should've trusted an Italian," Hess said furiously as he addressed Zappa. "I trusted you, I brought you into my circle. Italian bastard!"

Zappa said nothing but the young Führer responded for him. "Well, hindsight is a wonderful thing isn't it, Herr Hess? I'm sure my father thought the same thing when you betrayed him all those years ago."

"Your father was insane! All I was trying to do was stop him destroying millions of innocent people with the atomic bomb."

"Right, and how did that work out for you, Hess?" the Führer responded, with the sense of some amusement in his voice.

As the two men conversed, three other figures had exited the other Mercedes-600s from the convoy. One person from each vehicle. They had all been summoned from their home addresses at exactly the same time, and with precision timing, had all arrived in convoy at the steps of the Reich Chancellery. The three men who exited each respective vehicle were the very same high-ranking figures who had, but days earlier, discussed their own marginally less bloody and destructive plans to overthrow the Führer — Götz Koch, Konrad Lange and Lothar Krause. All three men stopped and stood by Giovanni Zappa and looked on at the situation with a sense of horror, surprise and confusion. Seeing them all arrive and take up their positions, the Führer turned from Hess and approached them all with a friendly smile upon his face.

"Gentlemen, welcome. Thank you so much for turning up on this fine evening."

The men stood to attention as their new Führer approached and cheerily greeted them although there was something rather sinister about what was unfolding here.

Götz Koch was the first to speak on behalf of the other senior members present. "With respect, Mein Führer, may I ask why we are here and who these people are?"

"That is a very good question, Herr Koch. A very good question indeed. Let me introduce to you someone who you probably already know, Rudolf Hess." The Führer immediately swung round and extended his arm triumphantly to a kneeling eighty-four-year-old Hess at the end of the line of prisoners.

"My God!" exclaimed Koch in utter horror at the sight of the bloodied former Deputy-Führer. He knew exactly who Hess was although he never recalled meeting him in person.

"Hardly," laughed Hitler. "He is anything but a god, Herr Koch. In fact, he is nothing but a pathetic old man. An enemy of the Reich who was intent on bringing me, no, bringing us down and installing his own government with its own ideologies. A traitor, Herr Koch. Nothing more than a traitor."

"I don't understand. How did you... how did you find out about this?"

Hitler placed his hand firmly onto the shoulder of the Italian spy who remained staring over the prisoners. Once again with an air of smugness in his voice, the Führer replied, "I have people everywhere, Herr Koch. I have done for months. People watching and listening. People letting me know who I can trust and who not to trust." He paused. "Can I trust you, Herr Koch?"

"Excuse me?"

"I said, can I trust you, Herr Koch? Because the eyes and ears I have within the party would suggest that you are maybe not as trustworthy as you may make out. And you address me as Mein Führer or have you forgotten this?"

"My apologies, Mein Führer. Of course you can trust me. I'm shocked at the suggestion that you may not be able to." He wasn't shocked in reality, as it was the truth. He couldn't be trusted and somehow, word of this had got back to the Führer.

The young Hitler, as well, knew this was not entirely truthful. As Zappa had penetrated the ranks of the NSDAP, not only had he uncovered Hess' armed insurrection, but he had also uncovered intelligence to suggest that several senior members of the NSDAP were disturbed at the prospect of Alois Hitler taking over from his father. While such figures were not part of Hess' separate operation, rumours of their dissatisfaction were becoming increasingly commonplace and worried Adolf Hitler and his son alike. The new Führer had to put talk of doubts in his ability to bed once and for all. He knew that his father doubted him, he knew high-ranking members of the NSDAP doubted him and he knew his father's former deputy was planning to kill him. The time had come to step up and deliver.

"I hope I can trust you, Herr Koch. I sincerely hope I can. The same for you gentlemen." Hitler now turned his attention to Lange and Krause who, like Koch, had remained stationary and in shock at the situation that was now unfolding before their very eyes. "I hope I have your trust too." The two men were about to respond but Hitler had turned his attention back to Zappa. "Herr Zappa, your weapon, if you please."

"Yes, Mein Führer," Zappa responded as he retrieved his automatic pistol from his thigh holster and removed the safety catch.

With that, the new Führer walked up to Wolf Hess, pointed the gun at his forehead and fired one shot, sending him reeling awkwardly backwards onto the steps of the Chancellery and killing him instantly. His father at the other end of the line let out a bloodcurdling scream of agony as he watched his son's life be extinguished immediately by a single bullet. It was almost as if it happened in slow motion and every moment he had ever had with his son, from his birth up until that moment, flashed before his very eyes. The senior members of the NSDAP looked on in utter horror. Lange swallowed hard, resisting the urge to vomit. Their ears rang as a result of the gunshot.

The Führer handed the weapon back to Zappa and walked over once again to Rudolf Hess who was crying uncontrollably. By this time, his defiant gaze had vanished and he wept with his head down, his tears falling onto Vossstrasse.

He then addressed the soldiers surrounding the group. "You know what to do with these people. Make sure it is done. Except for this one." He pointed at Hess before addressing him directly. "Death is too good for you Hess. You will spend the rest of your life wallowing in your grief. I will make sure that you are reminded on a daily basis of this night and your failure. I will see that you are held accountable for the death of your son and you will spend the rest of your days being eaten away by your own incompetence in a very small cell." He turned away and went back to Koch, Lange and Krause. "Do you have a problem with what you have seen tonight?" he asked of his leadership team.

Each man responded in turn. "No, Mein Führer."

"From now on, things will be different. I am not my father. Everything you do, and I mean everything, will be passed through me. I want to know where you are and what you do at every minute of the day. You make no decisions without my authority. Any independence or autonomy afforded you by my father ends. Right here and right now. If you ever doubt my authority, you will meet the same fate as these people here tonight. Do we understand one another, gentlemen?" He was greeted with a less than enthusiastic response which sent him into an immediate blind rage. "I said, do we understand one another?"

The three men jumped nearly out of their skin. This was the first time they had ever seen or heard the shy Alois Hitler act like this. It shocked them deeply and they all responded with more gusto and enthusiasm so as to not upset the Führer.

"That's better. Now show me the respect I deserve." The three men looked at each other not entirely sure what he meant or how to respond. "Salute me, damn it!"

The three men jumped once again but the second brief outburst had made it quite clear what he wanted from all of them so they threw their right hands into the air, whilst saying in unison, "Heil Hitler!"

The Führer cast one last disapproving glance over the prisoners before getting back into the rear of the black Mercedes, where his mother smiled approvingly at him. Despite all her reservations, he had come of age. He had not only thwarted an armed insurrection by her husband's former deputy and ultimate traitor Rudolf Hess, but he had also put to bed any doubts the current Reich leadership may have had about her son's position. As the Mercedes drove away from the Reich Chancellery building, they heard the clatter of machine gun fire as the commandos who had been lying in wait cut down the prisoners in the street outside the Chancellery. With the exception of Rudolf Hess, who would suffer the remainder of his life in a prison cell. As this happened, the three senior members of the NSDAP —

Koch, Krause and Lange — looked on in horrified silence and departed the scene in no doubt whatsoever as to who was now in charge. As the Führer had stated — and as they would find out — things would change over the coming weeks and months. The boy they had known as the slightly strange, shy person who looked scared of his own shadow had come into his own.

"I'm proud of you, Alois," his mother said to him in the back of the car with tears of pride in her eyes. "Your father would be proud of you as well."

The Führer said nothing. He was deep in thought about his intentions for his beloved mother. He needed her for now. She was a fantastic ambassador for the Reich and had promoted his father across the world. He needed her to now do the same for him. This, she was very good at doing and she would no doubt continue to flourish in such a role. But she wouldn't be required forever. In fact, she was expendable and he knew that. As soon as her job was done, she would no longer be required. She was very much on borrowed time.

SATURDAY 27th JANUARY 1979 — REICH CHANCELLERY, BERLIN, GERMANY

Nearly three weeks prior to The Syndicate's failed coup, Adolf Hitler lay in his bed in his private bedroom on the top floor of the Reich Chancellery. He had been drifting in and out of consciousness for nearly a week now and he could feel his body weakening with every passing hour. He had been taken aback at how quickly his condition had deteriorated. He had struggled with mobility for some years as his arthritis had become gradually more debilitating but the sickness, the malaise and the fatigue were something else. No matter how much rest he took, he never felt fully refreshed. He knew he was dying and no matter how hard he fought, he knew he couldn't hold on forever.

At regular intervals, in the days leading up to his eventual demise, his wife, son and physician, Dr Meyer, would all take turns in holding a bedside vigil with the deteriorating Führer. He was too weak to eat and he would find himself choking on even the smallest piece of food. He could, however, still drink fluids in small amounts and through a straw. On the evening of the 27th January 1979, Alois Hitler took over the bedside vigil from Dr

Meyer, who gave him a brief update of his father's condition before leaving. His father was sleeping. He looked weak and thin. Over time, most of his hair had fallen out, including his trademark moustache. His muscles had wasted considerably, leaving him with a skeletal and fragile looking frame. He was wearing a loose fitting set of white cotton pyjamas and he breathed gently through his mouth as he lay on his back in the large bed, his back propped up by three large white pillows. It was dark outside and the room was dimly lit to create an ambient atmosphere. It was quiet too. The comings and goings in the Chancellery building could not be heard on this level of the building; neither could the hustle and bustle of Berlin whose residents (with the exception of those within the Führer's most inner circle) were unaware of what was happening to their leader.

Alois had been sat by his father for about an hour when he noticed him shuffle a little and slowly open his eyes. He could no longer speak, such was his weakened condition, but he turned his head to look at his son. Alois looked back at his father and the two men made eye contact. His father's breathing quickened and his eyes darted back and forth as if indicating something. He was signalling to the jug of water on the bedside table.

"What is it, Father? Are you thirsty?"

His father managed a gentle yet laboured nod indicating that this was so. Alois poured some water into a glass and placed a metal straw in it. His father could no longer hold on to anything so Alois guided the straw into his father's mouth and he sucked up the fluid which immediately quenched his thirst.

"There. This will make it better, not long now," said Alois with a smile on his face as his father swallowed the cold water.

Adolf Hitler would never know that his son had been poisoning him for many weeks now. The amounts of arsenic he had been putting into his father's drinks were negligible and such that the colourless and odourless substance had been impossible to detect. He knew though that in his elderly and fragile state, it would not take long for it to have the desired effect. And have the desired effect it did. Soon his father was bedridden and becoming weaker and weaker with each day that passed. Alois had been so surreptitious in his activity that even the physician had not suspected. He was no longer a young man and all who surrounded him in his inner circle believed it to be down to nothing more than deterioration through age. No one knew, or would ever know, any different. As he finished giving his father what would turn out to be his final dose of poison, he watched as the old man slipped back into unconsciousness. He hung on for a few more hours but would go on to eventually pass the following day. As he sat and watched his father's demise, he cared little and the last two words he ever spoke to him as he sat and watched were a rather sarcastic, "Heil Hitler."

15

TWO FUGITIVES

The failed coup made the news worldwide, and without any further delay, Berlin was placed into lockdown in an effort to apprehend any outstanding members of The Syndicate. On the instructions of the Führer, the Wehrmacht simultaneously flooded the streets to not only provide reassurance to the people of Berlin but also as a show of strength. Much to the shock and disbelief of many (his mother included), Alois Hitler had outsmarted those plotting against him from both inside the NSDAP and outside the party. In the aftermath of the attempted coup, there were few now left in any doubt as to who was leading the Reich as the new Führer brutally and ruthlessly consolidated his power.

In the chaos and confusion of the firefight outside the Chancellery, Richard Frick had been lucky enough to escape into the network of surrounding side streets. Similarly, Bohdana Melnik (the Ukrainian police officer and Nazi sympathiser) had also managed to evade capture when the team she was leading failed to take control of a nearby police post. Through nothing more than sheer luck, the two had managed to meet up with one another as they ran for their very lives just as the streets began to fill with military personnel and hardware. Frick had hidden his car in a nearby underground parking lot as the trunk had been packed full of light weapons, all of which had been removed by members of The Syndicate who were now lying dead on the streets of Berlin. He figured that no one would know he had left it there so, with Melnik in tow, they made their way to the vehicle with the aim of getting out of Berlin before the streets were locked down completely. Both Frick and Melnik remained blissfully unaware that the undercover IUI operative Giovanni Zappa had proved instrumental in the failure of the coup. Rather fortuitously, Zappa remained blissfully unaware of the location of Frick's car full of weapons in the parking lot.

An immediate arrest warrant had been issued for Frick and Melnik (along with the other members of The Syndicate whose identities were known) and it would only be a matter of time before their pictures were broadcast across all news channels and details of Frick's vehicle circulated to ensure an immediate stop if picked up by one of the thousands of cameras throughout Germany. The two were somewhat panicked by the time they reached the car but it was dark and no one knew they were there, but they wouldn't be safe for long. As they sat in the underground carpark, they could hear the military hardware rumbling through the streets alongside the shouts of the Heer who had been mobilised to stand guard on every street corner. Getting out was going to prove difficult but they still had darkness on their side.

"We won't make it, Richard," Melnik said with a sense of much urgency in her voice. Frick didn't respond but he sat thinking hard about their next course of action. "Richard, what are we going to do?"

"I don't know!" Frick snapped back. "I don't know, Bohdana. Let me think."

As the cacophony on the street level continued, Frick continued to think about the next course of action. To leave the parking lot in the car would be dangerous. The Heer would be stopping all vehicles and severely restricting all vehicular movements around the city. It would be unlikely that their pictures would have been circulated too widely at such an early stage and moving on foot seemed like a more feasible option. He knew Berlin well enough to be able to dip into any side streets (something not possible in a car) so as to avoid the patrols plus they would be moving under the cover of darkness which would be advantageous. If they were going to escape though, they needed one more thing. Money. Frick knew where there would be lots of it, but firstly, they had to get to where it was, and secondly, there was a real risk that someone else may have already found it.

"We can't stay here and I'm not taking the car."

"Are you crazy? Why not?"

"They'll be stopping all the cars and checking them. There's no way we'll get out. We should go on foot."

Melnik was dumbfounded and couldn't seem to understand the logic behind Frick's suggestion. "And go where exactly?"

"Hermsdorf."

"What?"

"Hermsdorf. To Hess' house."

Mclnik was even more awestruck at the suggestion. "You're insane. Why would we go there? It'll be crawling by now."

"I know, Bohdana, I know. It seems crazy but there's something there that we need."

"What could possibly be there that's so important?"

"Money, and lots of it."

"What?"

"Look, do you want to get out of this alive? Yes or no?"

"Of course I do."

"Right, then you either trust me and come to Hermsdorf or you leave. Now. Because I'm going back to that house whether you like it or not. It's up to you Bohdana…"

Melnik thought it through carefully and thought to herself that she must be crazy as she reluctantly agreed to go with Frick back to Hermsdorf. Darkness was definitely on their side that night as they snaked their way through the quiet side streets of Berlin that ran roughly parallel to all the main routes leading to Hermsdorf. Where they could, they either jogged or ran. Whenever it looked as though there were other people in the area, they walked so as to appear as inconspicuous as they could. Whenever there was sight of the Heer, they would duck into a doorway or quiet alleyway and wait for them to pass. The further away from the centre of Berlin they got, the less military activity there seemed to be.

The journey was roughly ten miles and they managed to cover it within a couple of hours but were exhausted and thirsty as a result. When they reached Gartenstrausse, they paused and took the opportunity to seek cover in the garden of one of the neighbouring properties. They were within sight of Hess' house and from the outside, it looked quiet.

"Looks as though they've already been and gone," Frick said hopefully.

"What is it you think we'll find anyway?"

"Like I said, money. Hess has a safe hidden under the floorboards in the living room. I was one of the few people he trusted the code to and one of the few people who even knows it's there. Well, hopefully still there."

"Do you think it would've been found already?"

"I don't know. Let's go and find out."

The door to the property had been kicked down and the whole house completely ransacked. Frick was correct. The Heer had been and gone and performed a cursory search of the house, looking mainly for other members of The Syndicate rather than any specific property. He dared to think that a more forensic search would be carried out in due course but it seemed as though the main intention was to get in, get Hess and get out again. He did find it bizarre that there was no one standing guard over the property. They had certainly not spotted anyone and they had to act quickly.

Melnik remained in the front reception room, keeping an eye out over the unkempt front lawn, ready to alert Frick to anyone approaching the house. While she did this, Frick made his way into the living room at the rear of the house. It was dark and the floor was covered with overturned furniture. He moved it aside and pulled up the carpet from the corner. It was looking positive and it did not look as though anyone had tampered with the floorboards. Running to the kitchen and retrieving a table knife from one of the drawers, he slotted it in between the floorboards and lifted them enough to get his hands underneath and pull them up. His stomach bounced with joy and he breathed an enormous sigh of relief as he saw the safe, seemingly untouched, in front of him. So far, things were going to plan.

Thankfully, he had remembered the correct combination for the safe under the floor and it clicked open. To his relief, what he had expected to be in there was indeed still there. It was some of the funds left over from Wolf's efforts to acquire all the weapons needed to carry out the failed coup. Bundles of Reichsmarks (he didn't have time to ascertain how much) and four gleaming bars of brilliant gold bullion. This would be enough to hopefully secure them a safe passage out of Berlin and indeed out of Germany altogether.

As he quickly gathered all the items together out of the safe, he called out to Melnik, "Bohdana, I've got it. Is everything OK?" When there was no response, he called again, "Melnik? Is everything all right?" Still no response.

He placed the money and the gold into a satchel he had found emptied of its contents on the floor, closed the safe, placed the floorboards back and made his way into the reception area to see where Melnik was.

As he rounded the corner into the reception area, he froze. Melnik was stood with her hands in the air with two soldiers stood behind her pointing their rifles at her back. They had not seen anyone outside as the soldiers had already been inside the house, having being ordered to lie in wait for anyone who may decide to pay the address a visit. Such was the urgency of Frick and Melnik's journey out of Berlin, they had failed to perform a thorough reconnaissance of the property prior to entry.

"Drop the bag, get your hands in the air. Now!" one of the soldiers barked.

Frick placed the bag slowly onto the ground and raised his hands. "You don't have to do this, guys. We can talk."

"Don't think so," said the soldier who had spoken. He seemed to be the chatty one. The other soldier kept his rifle closely pointed at Melnik's back. "Get on your knees, keep the hands where I can see them. Or I'll put a bullet in your face."

Frick slowly complied and dropped to his knees. "We can make a deal."

The soldier laughed. "I doubt it."

"In that bag there." Frick gestured with his head to the satchel on the floor. "There's a lot of money. More than you'd ever earn on a soldier's wage. Get us out of here and it's all yours."

"Yeah right," the soldier said clearly rather amused by such an absurd suggestion.

"Check for yourself." Frick started to move his hands away from above his head when the soldier tensed up.

"Get the hands up! Now!"

"OK, I'm sorry. Look, check it for yourself."

The two soldiers looked at one another suspiciously and hesitated before the one who had done all the talking stepped forward. The room was largely in darkness but the dim light coming in from the street lights outside was enough to illuminate the soldier's way. All the while, he kept his weapon raised and pointed towards Frick.

When he got a little closer, he said, "Push the bag towards me."

"OK, I'm lowering my hands slowly. OK?" Frick cautiously lowered his hands and pushed the satchel across the carpet towards the soldier.

In the process, it tipped and spewed its contents on the carpet right in front of the soldier who looked at it in awe, all the while keeping his weapon raised and pointed at Frick.

"Shit," uttered the soldier. "Look at this Hans. You ever seen anything like it?"

The other soldier leant his head forwards so he could see what his partner was seeing and was equally stunned, so much so that he was only able to utter the same as his colleague, "Shit!"

"Where did you get this from?"

"Does it matter? Look, help us get away from here and it's yours. Keep it. Just help get us out of Berlin. We won't say anything, I promise."

The soldier looked at Frick and seemed to be mentally weighing up the options for himself and his partner. They had been told to wait in the darkness of the house as they suspected someone might return there. When they did, whoever turned up was to be immediately apprehended. To be presented with an untold amount of money and gold was not at all what either of them were expecting but it was presenting options. Some rather appealing options at that.

"So, let me get this straight. You want me and my friend here to get you and your lady friend out of Berlin. Right?"

"Right."

"And in return, we get all of this?"

"Right."

The soldier nodded thoughtfully before continuing, "I've got a suggestion."

"Go on."

"How about, we take all the money — and the gold — and turn you pair over. How does that sound?" It was said with an air of menace and the soldier had a cruel smile on his face.

"Come on, be reasonable. I'm offering you both enough to retire on. I can tell you where you can get that bullion melted down and cashed in so its untraceable. The least you can do is return the favour."

"More than our job's worth. Letting you pair go. I still fancy getting all the glory for catching you pair of idiots. All that money and gold is a bonus. Double the glory. What do you think, Hans?"

"Yeah, sounds pretty good to me."

Frick dropped his head in despair. They wouldn't buy the deal and it was only a matter of time before one of the soldiers had the common sense to get on his radio and report that they had captured two people in the Hermsdorf house — although the bag of money and gold would clearly not receive a mention.

"Right, it's agreed then. We take all this and call it in. You spend the rest of your lives in jail. On your feet." The solider gestured with his weapon for Frick to rise from his kneeling position on the carpet.

As he rose, he looked Melnik dead on in the eyes and hoped to God she was able to read in his face what he was about to do. It seemed as though she could, because as he made a lunge towards the one soldier, she immediately about turned and lunged for the other one and a fight ensued. The talkative soldier managed to let off a shot from his rifle into the darkness of the room before the two men fell to the floor struggling over control of the weapon. As they struggled with Frick on top of the solider, another three shots were let off into the darkness. In the melee, Frick hadn't realised that one of the shots had struck the other solider in the belly making him release his weapon and drop to the floor in agony. Seizing upon the opportunity of no longer having to grapple with the man, Melnik instinctively reached to the floor and grabbed one of the bars of bullion that had spilled out onto the carpet and proceeded to smash it against the head of the soldier Frick was still wrestling with until he went limp and he too let go of the weapon. It was over quickly, although they were worried the shots fired would alert the attention of the wrong people.

Frick immediately rose and stepped over the bloodied solider (who he assumed was dead from the trauma of being bludgeoned with a gold bar). He went straight to the front window and looked out across the unkempt front lawn. All seemed silent and it didn't appear that the brawl had drawn any unwanted attention.

Melnik was standing over the wounded soldier who was bleeding heavily from his wound. "H-h-h-help me," he pleaded as he lay there.

"I'm sorry," Frick responded. "There's nothing we can do for you. I'm sorry." He wasn't lying either. Such was the nature of his injury, he would soon lose consciousness and die of blood loss, there was little either of them could do. As for the other solider? They were pretty sure he was dead.

While Melnik kept watch, Frick undressed and then dressed himself in the soldier's uniform. Melnik was unable to do the same due to the sheer amount of blood covering the other soldier's clothing. By the time Frick was changed, the wounded man had lost consciousness. Frick and Melnik searched both men for anything of use, recovering what looked like a set of car keys from one of the dead men. Gathering together all their belongings, the weapons of the dead men and the money bag, they left the Hermsdorf house for the very last time. The set of what looked like car keys led them to an army G-Wagen, set back off Gartenstrausse, out of sight. They loaded it up, got inside, and with Frick taking the wheel, they drove off away from Berlin as the light of a new day was beginning to break through the darkness of the night.

It was another four hours before the alarm was raised that there was a problem in Hermsdorf. The two soldiers were found bloodied and dead, one with his uniform missing, their G-Wagen also absent and an empty safe discovered under the floor boards. Immediately the alarm was raised and all security services were put on alert and ordered to look out for person or persons unknown posing as members of the Heer, driving a G-Wagen. Frick and Melnik made the most of the four-hour limbo period and were well away from Berlin by the time the alarm was raised. They had in fact made it to the safety of the small Brandenburg town of Kyritz by which time it was early morning. Their journey out of Berlin had been unimpeded and the Heer had no need to stop and search one of their own for they were not suspects at that particular point in time. They had aimed for Kyritz for a very good reason, as it was the home of another member of The Syndicate. A non-combatant by the name of Maksim Turgenev. Originally from Moscow, Turgenev had fled his home country in the aftermath of Der Befreier III. Having seen first-hand the devastation the Nazi weapon of mass destruction had had, as well as the subsequent annexation of swathes of Russia, Turgenev had developed a deep-seated hatred towards Hitler and the Reich. Migrating west into Germany, Turgenev had set himself up as a seemingly innocent antiques dealer. In reality, he was a master forger and worked tirelessly for The Syndicate producing false documentation for the likes of Wolf Hess, allowing him to transition effortlessly between Germany and the former Soviet territories to the east without question — allowing him to smuggle weapons to The Syndicate.

The Russian lived in a small and discreet house on the edge of the town and welcomed Frick and Melnik into his home without hesitation. He had met the NSDAP minister once before and Melnik once or twice over the previous years. They had abandoned the G-Wagen some half a mile from Turgenev's house in some bushes and walked the rest of the way. It would be found eventually but there were no clues as to where they had gone. Turgenev made them both a hot drink and some food while listening intently to the details of the failed coup d'état the night before. At that point, they were unaware of the fate of Wolf and Rudolf Hess but they suspected that both were dead by now — which was partly true. Frick and Melnik remained at Turgenev's house for three more days, lying low and keeping out of sight.

The Heer did indeed find the G-Wagen and came to Kyritz but they found nothing of interest and didn't stay long. Turgenev was kind enough to acquire some new clothes for Frick and Melnik as well as produce a new set of identity documents that would allow them to traverse the European borders hopefully without question. This was on the provision their fingerprints were not scanned. Turgenev was clever but not clever enough to be able to outsmart some of the best technology possessed by the Reich. He liked to do things the 'old-fashioned way' and if they were lucky, Frick and Melnik would make it out of Germany but where they were to go after that remained a topic of discussion.

"We should head east," Melnik suggested. "I have friends in the Ukraine who can protect us."

In theory, Frick thought this was a good idea — in theory. To stay in Germany was not an option as they were now two of the most wanted fugitives in the country. However, he remained sceptical for one very good reason. "I don't disagree with you, Bohdana, and I'm sure you're right and that we could be protected."

Melnik sensed a 'but' coming on. "But?"

"It's too far, Bohdana. Whichever route we choose to take, there's hundreds of miles to travel before we even reach the border with the

Ukraine. We don't have many friends left between here and there and there's thousands of soldiers standing in our way. We can't travel by air which means we'll have to go overland. Using the roads is risky, we don't have a car and there's several international borders to navigate on the way. Do you understand why I have concerns?"

"Of course but I don't know what else to suggest. It's the only place I know we can be protected."

"I don't like it, Bohdana, I'm sorry. I don't like it."

Melnik was frustrated. In light of recent events in Berlin, she was now desperate to return home and knew with much certainty that she would be offered the protection from the Reich that she needed, that they both needed. The distance was an obstacle though. An obstacle that seemed almost insurmountable

"What do you suggest, Richard? If not the Ukraine, then what? Where do we go?"

Frick had thought it through over the past few days. It was all he had thought about. Personally, there was nothing or no one keeping him in Germany. He wasn't married and what few friends he did have would no longer wish to be associated with him. The family he had in Germany would not be able to offer him any protection and the money they had would not last forever. There would be only so many people they could bribe and pay to keep them hidden well out of sight. Even some of them would undoubtedly be less than reliable and probably beyond bribery, much like the two soldiers in Hermsdorf.

"I think we should head to the British Territories."

Melnik recoiled in shock. "What? Why? Are you crazy?"

It was pretty much the reaction he expected. After all, without any further explanation, it did indeed seem like a crazy suggestion but there was a method in his madness and he hoped he could convince Bohdana of it. "Look, I know it seems mad—"

"Because it is!"

"Hear me out, please. Just hear me out."

Melnik settled down and reluctantly sighed. "OK, go on. I'm listening."

"Firstly, we don't have the distance issue. It's nowhere near as far as the Ukraine which means bribing, or paying, our way there won't cost as much and we hopefully won't run out of money. Now, exactly how we get there depends on the route we take. We can cut through into France and take the bridge over to Dover. We can cut through Belgium, Holland and then into France and take the bridge to Dover. Or we can head north, get to the coast and pay for someone to sail us over. That way we avoid any international border and the checks that come with it. I'm sure we can find someone with a boat to get us there, if we look hard enough."

Melnik started to laugh, frustratingly amused by what seemed like a crazy plan. "I thought so, it's madness. Paying someone with a boat? You really think someone would be crazy enough to agree to it?"

"Everything can be bought for a price and we've got hundreds of thousands in gold bullion."

"Which is worthless to most!"

"Unless they know where to go where it can be used, and we can organise that."

Melnik still wasn't convinced. Even if they went with Frick's plan and travelled to the British Territories either by road or sea, the one question Melnik had was, "Why? Why the Territories? What's there for us that'll keep us safe."

Frick hesitated. In a way it pained him to say it as it conflicted so much with both their ideologies. "The Menorah."

Melnik's eyes widened in horror. "The Menorah? The… Menorah? You've lost your mind. What the hell makes you think they'll keep us safe?"

Frick was expecting a more explosive reaction from the fiery Ukrainian. He had no doubt that she could explode in an even more spectacular fashion so he had to be clear and concise in his logic. "I know how mad it seems but let's face it, we have two things in common with them. Firstly, we are now wanted people who the Reich would not hesitate to wipe out in a heartbeat. Secondly, we are wanted people because we all share the same views on Hitler. Ultimately, we want the same outcome. To remove Hitler. So in that respect, they would be the most logical people to offer us protection."

"Have you not forgotten one thing? Like, for instance, the fact we're both Nazis and they're Jewish? Have you not seen this as just ever so slightly problematic?"

Of course he had and she wasn't wrong. "I know and of course I see it as problematic. Look, The Syndicate was a combination of Nazis and communists. Historically two enemies. But look how we came together when we discovered we had a common cause. Maybe I'm thinking we could achieve the same with The Menorah. Also, we can offer them something in return?"

Melnik scoffed. "Really? Like what? What can two fugitive Nazis offer a group of Jewish terrorists whose people we are indirectly responsible for virtually eradicating from the face of the planet? What could we possibly offer them Richard?"

"Support in Europe."

"What?"

"What happened in Berlin may have failed but there's remnants of The Syndicate still out there. And we have contacts in the east where we can get more weapons from if needs be. The Menorah don't have much of a platform outside of the Territories. With our help, they could have. The Syndicate might be over but there's nothing to say it can't return in a different form. In return, they offer us protection."

The two went quiet while they both digested what Frick had just said. "So assuming we were to make it to the Territories, how do you propose we find The Menorah?"

Frick shrugged. "I don't know. I remember seeing some intelligence a few years ago relating to somewhere in London. An estate by the river which might be a good place to start."

"What makes you think they wouldn't just shoot us dead on the spot."

Frick shrugged again. "I can't guarantee that. But can you guarantee the same wouldn't happen if we tried to get to the Ukraine?"

They both fell silent again as they continued to ponder over their options in order to stay alive. It was a sleepless night for both of them and as they sat in the kitchen in Turgenev's house the following morning, it seemed as though Melnik had come to terms with the fact that getting home to the Ukraine was simply not a possibility.

"I don't like it Richard. Not one bit but I can't see that we've got much choice."

"We really don't. I wish it could be different. Does this mean you want to head to the Territories?"

"Not really. But I don't see what choice we've got. I think we'll be lucky to get as far as the coast but we've got to try."

"We'll make it. One way or another we'll make it. We have to."

16

IRON FORTRESS AND THE BLUEBIRD

JUNE 1979 — THE BERGHOF, BAVARIAN ALPS, GERMANY

The new Führer sat on the terrace of the Berghof enjoying the beautiful summer afternoon sun and the light breeze blowing in from across the Alps. It was the same place where, many years before, his father had brought to a very sudden end an innocent game of soldiers that he was playing, berating him in the process with yet more accusations of weakness and foolishness and how he would never lead his precious Reich. A lot of time had passed since that fateful day in 1962 and he was no longer the stuttering idiot his father had accused him of being. In many ways, he wished his father could see him now — sat on the terrace of the Berghof, looking out onto the snow-capped peaks of the Alps having defeated those seeking to overthrow him all within the space of a single evening some months beforehand.

He hadn't seen Rudolf Hess since his failed attempt at a coup with his international squad of militants, but he hoped the aging former Deputy-Führer was living uncomfortably in his final elderly years (which he indeed was) wherever he had been incarcerated. He didn't know where that was and cared little. The plotting of his current Deputy-Führer Götz Koch had been brought to an abrupt end on the very same night and he was now required to report to the young Führer whenever he was summoned to do so. Unlike his father, who afforded the highest-ranking members of the NSDAP a certain amount of autonomy, the young Führer wanted to know absolutely everything of all members of his cabinet. Koch was now being watched very closely and it was only by the sheer grace of God that he too had not been executed at the same time as the members of Hess' Syndicate on the steps of the Chancellery building. This had been a political move to once again not give Japan any indication whatsoever of any unrest from within the Reich, and after all, his father had thought very highly of Koch and he had served his father well during his time as Deputy-Führer. There was no denying that. He therefore remained in his position... for now.

It was Zappa who had impressed the Führer the most in recent months though. Although initially appointed by his father to weed out The Syndicate, Zappa had managed to stumble almost by accident onto the rumours surrounding the second less bloody coup attempt to be led by Götz Koch. On reporting this back to the new Führer, the decision was made to let Koch carry on with his behind the scenes plotting and to finally bring his master plan for domination over the Reich to an abrupt end on the same night as Hess' equally doomed attempt — two birds, one stone.

Zappa had blended in beautifully amongst the disgruntled dissenters. It hadn't taken him long to have Richard Frick fooled and when he finally got to meet Hess for the first time, it was before he had taken up residence in Hermsdorf and he was still living in exile in Austria. Hess had presented himself as nothing more than a bitter old man, still furious at his removal from the position of Deputy-Führer. Initially, Hess had a deep mistrust of Zappa (or Pietro Casati as he was at that time), the high-ranking Italian politician. Hess' guards kept Zappa captive in Hess' small mountain retreat, periodically interrogating him in an attempt to determine his intentions and that they were indeed genuine. Zappa endured a lot. Hess had seen weaker men crumble under much less pressure but this man was strong. He was determined, he shared Hess' vision and by the time his captivity had ended, Hess was convinced that Pietro Casati could be implicitly trusted. Indeed, his high position in the Italian government could be advantageous, and while Hess had yet to unveil any concrete plans, he did have Casati marked for a position of some description in the new Reich, such was his previous experience of politics at a ministerial level.

Zappa had Hess fooled, such was his expertise, leaving him horrified and livid on the eventual revelation that he had been responsible for thwarting the uprising of The Syndicate. To identify the marginally less militant plan of Koch and the other high-ranking officials within the NSDAP was somewhat of a bonus. The young Führer had deliberately maintained his trademark awkwardness for the duration of Zappa's assignment and no one had known any different. The surprise, shock and impact of the undercover IUI operation had, in the ensuing months, well and truly solidified the reputation of the young Führer and within a very short period of time, there was no doubt whatsoever as to who was now leading the Reich and all talk of coups, uprisings and discontent had been brought to an abrupt end. The Empire of Japan would never even know that anything amiss had ever occurred in the first instance and remained none the wiser of the internal wrangling — aside from the thwarted, botched coup attempt by The Syndicate. Financially, Giovanni Zappa was highly rewarded for his services to the Reich and afforded an extended period of leave for his efforts before being redeployed on another assignment with the IUI and it was on that June day in 1979 that he was summoned to attend the Berghof for an audience with the Führer to find out what that assignment would be.

The Führer's mother had been so proud of her son and that he had finally risen to the challenge of becoming the leader of the Reich. She had worked tirelessly in the months following the attempted coup, traversing the globe and doing her best as the ambassador and poster girl for the Reich, promoting her son and the legacy of her husband. Her efforts continued to keep Japan totally unaware that there had been any major internal unrest in the first instance. Eva Hitler continued to remain blissfully unaware that her own son had poisoned his father and equally unaware that she too would meet a less than desirable fate. The timing had to be right though. In the early stages of his rule, she was proving to be too useful and he needed her but his disdain and hatred for her remained simmering below his outward acceptance of his mother. Even though she didn't know it, she was on borrowed time but she was too valuable at the moment to be dealt with. She would be dealt with though, all in good time.

The young Führer's guests turned up later in the afternoon. The first to arrive was Governor-General Klaus von Hindenburg of the British Territories. He was not to know when he arrived at the Berghof on that summer day that he would leave with a document that would change the very course of world history — but that was some months away from that particular moment in the Bavarian Alps. Von Hindenburg greeted the Führer in the same way as he had done his predecessor, with a Nazi salute. Shortly after von Hindenburg's arrival, the Führer's other guests filtered in — Alois Brunner and Governor-General Adolf Eichmann arrived together shortly after von Hindenburg, with Giovanni Zappa being the last to arrive. Brunner's greeting was much different and informal and involved an almost fatherly hug for the Führer and the two seemed delighted to be in each other's company. Eichmann's greeting was as per the other governor-general and involved a Nazi salute, as was Zappa's. Once the greetings had been carried out, the men were provided with refreshments by the staff within the Berghof and the group moved into the Führer's study to discuss the business they had been assembled for in the first instance and there was much to discuss.

The Führer was the first to speak as the men settled themselves for the meeting. "Thank you, gentlemen, for coming today. We have much to discuss. Klaus, let's start with the issue in the British Territories. What progress is there in relation to our 'friends' in The Menorah? We've managed to stop Hess and his syndicate. I want The Menorah dealt with next."

"Mein Führer, the police intelligence services have made progress. They have managed to root out moles within the Ministry of Media, Propaganda and Information. Those who have tried to smuggle information out of the ministry itself. We have undercover officers positioned throughout the various ministries making sure there are no further breaches."

"How have these people even managed to get positions in the first place Klaus? It was my understanding that our vetting procedures for any ministerial position are watertight. Clearly not it seems."

"I apologise, Mein Führer. Our procedures are indeed very stringent. Some of the strictest in the world if I may say so—"

"So what's the problem? Why do these people continue to slip through the net? Under your very nose?"

Von Hindenburg was being put under pressure. He was, after all, accountable for what was happening within the British Territories and was answerable to the Führer. He hesitated before responding, "Mein Führer, these people are… clever. As we adapt, so they adapt with us. Believe me, it pains me to think that they still manage to infiltrate some of our institutions. Please be reassured, we have the best, and I mean the best, intelligence agents working to route them out."

The Führer at this stage decided to turn his attention towards the Italian IUI agent who had impressed him so much back in the February of that year. "I appreciate that these people are clever, Klaus. I saw how much of a frustration they were to my father. I'd like to take a different approach in an effort to solve these problems gentlemen and that's why I have invited Herr Zappa here today." The Führer turned to address Zappa personally. "I would like you, Herr Zappa, to accompany Governor-General von Hindenburg back to the British Territories and set to work at playing these Jewish bastards at their own game. I want you to penetrate the very core of The Menorah, in the same way you so expertly did with The Syndicate. Find out who this 'Hebron' is. Root this golem out. At any cost." He almost spat over the word 'golem' as he said it such was his disdain for Hebron and The Menorah.

"It would be a pleasure, Mein Führer, I would be honoured to help in whatever way I can," responded Zappa proudly.

"There is one more thing, more so for you, Klaus, and you, Herr Zappa."

"Yes, Mein Führer," von Hindenburg responded with interest.

"I have received separate intelligence to suggest that someone you may know has made their way to the Territories."

All the men present at the meeting were intrigued as to who this may be, including Zappa. "May I ask who this may be, Mein Führer?"

"Frick. And that Ukrainian bitch of his. It's my understanding they have been sighted in London. I'm not a gambling man, Herr Zappa, but if I were, I would wager that those pair of traitors have ended up in London for a reason."

"Mein Führer?"

"I think they may be looking for sanctuary within Governor-General Hindenburg's borders." The suggestion left all in the meeting lost for words. Why would two Nazi rebels possibly think they could find sanctuary in the British Territories?

"Forgive me, Mein Führer," von Hindenburg began, "but why would you think they would be seeking sanctuary in the Territories? Who is there that could offer them protection?"

The Führer had had the same thought process as Frick when he suggested to Melnik in the February of that year that The Menorah may be able to protect them as, after all, they were fighting a common cause even if their ideologies were somewhat different. The men all listened intently as the Führer explained the logic behind why he believed Frick and Melnik might have turned up in London.

When he had finished, he turned once again to Zappa. "Herr Zappa, do you think Frick knows who you really are?"

Zappa thought it over. In theory, there was no reason for Frick to know his true identity. Frick had made a run for it before it was revealed to those who were captured that Pietro Casati was not Pietro Casati at all. All those members of The Syndicate were dead and Hess was in prison so there was no way that Frick or Melnik would know that Casati was actually Zappa.

"I see no reason why he would know, Mein Führer. None at all. The only people who knew who I really was were the ones captured at the steps of the Chancellery. Neither Frick nor Melnik were amongst them."

The Führer took over. "We rounded up many in Berlin that night and they were dealt with, the rest we can assume fled back east into the former Soviet Union, with the exception of those two. How would you like to assume the role of Pietro Casati again, Herr Zappa?"

Zappa nodded approvingly. "More than happy, Mein Führer. It would be the best identity to use to not only infiltrate The Menorah but to also get to Frick, assuming he is in London with the Ukrainian."

"Excellent. Then you'll head to the Territories where Governor-General von Hindenburg will provide you with everything you need. No expense spared. One last thing Klaus, are we still making an effort to discredit The Menorah?" This was an interesting question. As Peter Fewtrill had identified in the British Territories, the police had been responsible for carrying out attacks against members of their own and then putting the blame onto The Menorah. Little did Peter Fewtrill know at that moment in time where the instruction to do so had come from.

"Yes, Mein Führer."

"Keep up the pressure, Klaus. I believe it's been quiet for a while. Maybe it's time for something big to happen. Lots of casualties. Innocent ones, if you see my point?"

"Yes, Mein Führer. I will see to it when we get back to the Territories."

The Führer then turned his attention to Brunner and Eichmann. "Gentlemen, we turn our attention to the Liberty Front and the border with Japan. What news?"

Eichmann was the first to respond. "Mein Führer, the IUI continue to be active across the country and we have had many successes in infiltrating the Liberty Front. Like Herr Zappa, the IUI in East America has proved to be an invaluable tool in our fight. We have a large team with operatives operating throughout the country. The tunnel network between Mexico and East America has been dismantled which, as you know, was the source of a lot of weapons to the Liberty Front." The Führer nodded as he had indeed heard all about the tunnel network and the problems it was causing. "However, like their counterparts in the British Territories, their tactics are clever, they adapt their methods continually. Their influence continues to run across East America."

"And the leadership, Herr Eichmann?" Eichmann wasn't sure how to respond. The Führer would be disappointed at his response and he was hesitant, much to the frustration of the Führer. "Herr Eichmann? The leadership?"

"I apologise, Mein Führer. We are still no closer at this stage to identifying the leadership of the Liberty Front. Such is the size of East America, whoever it is can hide with relative ease. Please, be assured that the IUI are working round the clock to find out who they are so we can deal with them appropriately."

The Führer was not happy and remained mildly frustrated at Eichmann's response. He didn't know how his father would have reacted to this news but he chose to move on to his namesake and good friend Alois Brunner. "Maybe you can give us an update on your progress, Herr Brunner. Hopefully your progress in these matters has been a little more... meaningful."

Brunner beamed ecstatically. He relished any opportunity to boast about the prowess of his precious weapons division. It was another chance for him to wallow in a sense of his own self-satisfaction and over-inflated ego, characteristics that had left him deeply unpopular and disliked within the NSDAP. Zappa found Brunner immediately abhorrent. He was liked by Eichmann, tolerated by von Hindenburg but well-liked by the Führer — the one person whose opinion mattered above all others.

"Our satellites have indicated a build-up of military in Idaho to the west. Evidence suggests an airbase and mobilisation of Japanese infantry towards the border with Wyoming. I dare say that had events in Berlin taken a different turn, our Japanese friends just may have made a more ambitious move. Because of your brilliant plan, along with Herr Zappa of course, this was averted."

The Führer sat silently contemplating and the study remained in silence. The other men cringed a little inside as Brunner so blatantly praised the accomplishments of the Führer, almost as if the events in Berlin in February were something he had achieved single-handedly.

"If the Japanese want to mobilise, maybe we should as well? I want the Wehrmacht mobilised towards the border but I want it done discreetly. I don't want the Japanese knowing what we're doing." A pained look came across Brunner's face indicating that there may be a problem with this plan. It did not go unnoticed by the Führer. "What is it? Is there a problem?"

"Potentially."

"What is it?"

"We can send the Wehrmacht towards the border with Idaho, in theory."

"In theory?"

Eichmann (who was fully aware of the issue Brunner was thinking of) spoke up. "Mein Führer, there is a sizeable Indian reservation, in Wyoming, which borders Idaho and the Japanese military build-up. If we move in, they need to move out. Quietly as well, if we are to not attract any attention from across the border."

"And why is this a problem?"

"Mein Führer, I fear they may be reluctant to relocate. The Japanese will be watching. If we are to move in discreetly, they need to move out. Discreetly. I'm not sure they will. It is, after all, their ancestral homeland. I'm not saying that it *will* be a problem, but it could be."

In his inexperience, the Führer could not quite comprehend what the problem here was. In his mind, all he could visualise were red Indians dancing around fires and tepees. Why would this be a problem? The reality, however, was very different indeed. The Elk Valley Indian Reservation in Wyoming was huge and stretched up to the border with the Japanese Empire in Idaho. The Indians had always remained elusive and had never involved themselves in the Second World War or, indeed, the partition of America between Germany and Japan. In return, the Reich allowed the Elk Valley Indians to live in relative peace. Times had changed though and they needed to vacate their reservation to make way for the Wehrmacht.

"Will they not just… move?"

Brunner and Eichmann hesitated. The answer was — no. This had to be conveyed to the Führer in a marginally more positive way. "It may be difficult, Mein Führer," Eichmann responded. "They're a proud race. As I say, it's their ancestral homeland. It won't be easy trying to convince them to move."

The Führer laughed. "It's ridiculous. What is there in Wyoming anyway that's of any interest?"

None of the men responded and the room fell silent as they all pondered over the latest problem. After a minute or so of silence, Brunner spoke once more. "We could offer them an alternative. Somewhere else to live. There's plenty of space in Wyoming that they could go. Maybe if we offer them a decent enough alternative and new places to live, they'll go."

"And if they don't accept, Alois?" the Führer asked.

"We shouldn't be hasty. Let me see if I can convince them to move peacefully. If I can't get them to move, maybe we can discuss other options at a later date. I can make a call to my personal assistant and get him to start work on it."

The Führer nodded. "Fine. I want you to keep me updated. I understand you have something else to share with us Alois. For the rest of you, this is something my father started work on many years ago but he never followed it through so I recently instructed Herr Brunner to reactivate the project."

Brunner beamed again. He did indeed have something else to share with the Führer and the two governors-general but this was not for Zappa. "Mein Führer, this is a sensitive eyes-only document. I don't mean to be rude but this will not concern Herr Zappa."

Zappa was excused from the meeting and he left by offering a Nazi salute before exiting the study to leave the other men to discuss the top-secret dossier that Brunner had brought along for them to see. The men all sat in silence as they scanned through the pages of the document. It had been lovingly prepared by Brunner and contained many years' worth of work and study carried out in top-secret by scientists within his weapons division. Much of it was very technical but they got the idea as they read through it. After some time scanning over the pages, the men finished reading the dossier.

"Well, it looks very impressive, Alois," the Führer began. "Wouldn't you agree, gentlemen?" Eichmann and von Hindenburg nodded in agreement. They didn't understand a lot of it but could clearly see that a lot of work had gone into the preparation of the dossier. "A lot of this is very technical. Maybe you could tell us in simpler terms a little bit more about this Iron Fortress and Project Bluebird."

17

THE CHAINS OF COMMAND

By early July 1979, Klaus von Hindenburg had returned to the British Territories with Giovanni Zappa in tow, the latter with a very specific mission to pursue. While von Hindenburg made his way back to the Palace of the Governor-General, Zappa was transported to a flat in Hendon — in north London. This was to be his home for the foreseeable future, a base from which to start his enquiries into all things relating to The Menorah, and as equally important, the potential whereabouts of Richard Frick and Bohdana Melnik. The property was nothing special. A small studio on the top floor of a converted Victorian property with marginally more character than the hundreds of Reich constructed concrete towers. Within the flat, Zappa found all the intelligence files deemed necessary and relevant by the police. It wasn't a great deal, but it was enough for him to at least make a start. Frick and Melnik had been spotted in an area called Themse Marschland. Zappa had not visited London before, he had never had a need to, so this area was not familiar to him but he figured that it was possibly a good place to begin after he had thoroughly dissected all the intelligence delivered to him. For the next few months, he was now back to living his alternative persona — Pietro Casati.

Supt Rolf Becker had received the telephone call to his house early in the morning. He had been summoned. The car came to collect him one hour later and he made sure he was ready in plenty of time for he had no desire whatsoever to keep the governor-general waiting. Becker had been meeting secretly with von Hindenburg for many years now, receiving orders from him and delivering them to the best of his ability with the resources he had.

It had been some time since he had heard from the governor-general and he assumed it would be something of great importance, which it indeed was.

On arrival at the palace, Becker was escorted in through a rear entrance and ushered directly into the governor-general's private study area, a large and lavish room where members of the cabinet met as and when required to do so. Von Hindenburg greeted Becker with a firm and friendly handshake.

"Herr Becker, thank you for your time. I trust your journey was smooth? And my apologies for the early hour at which we called you."

"Thank you, Governor-General, the journey was fine, thank you. Please, there is no need to apologise for the early hour. I'm at your disposal as and when you require me."

Von Hindenburg smiled broadly. "Excellent, thank you, Rolf. Please do sit down." The governor-general signalled for Becker to take a seat on the other side of the large desk in the study which Becker duly did. "May I get you some refreshments? Maybe some tea?"

"No, thank you, Governor-General."

"As you please. Now, you're no doubt wondering why I have called you here?" Becker nodded in response. "I have just returned from Germany and a meeting with the Führer at his private residence in the Alps."

"And may I ask how the Führer is? I trust he is well after the events of earlier this year."

"Yes, Herr Becker, the Führer is indeed well. His father, God rest his soul, would be a proud man if he could see him now. He has risen to the mantle of Führer perfectly. He asked what our progress with The Menorah issue was. We discussed it at some length and I wanted to appraise you of the conversation we had. If that's all right with you?"

"Of course, Governor-General."

"Excellent. Well, first things first. We have an agent of the IUI staying here in London. His track record is exemplary; he was one of the agents who helped to uncover the plot by the traitor Hess. Fast becoming something of a celebrity with the Führer. Anyhow, on instructions of the Führer himself, he has been ordered to try and infiltrate the ranks of The Menorah. For security and secrecy purposes, I hope you understand that I cannot reveal his identity. To anyone. At least not until his mission is complete."

"Governor-General, forgive me for interrupting, but are we to cease our own intelligence operations with the police?"

"For now, Rolf, yes. The Führer wants to take a different approach in order to try and get inside The Menorah. Also, the Frick issue makes things, how can we put it? Interesting."

"May I ask how so, Governor-General?"

"We don't believe Frick, and that other one, know that our man in the IUI had anything to do with dismantling Hess' little group. In fact, we're pretty certain Frick doesn't know. This might allow our man easier access into The Menorah. If that's where Frick and the Ukrainian have headed to and if they don't know that our man is IUI."

"So there's a lot of assumptions?"

"Well, yes but orders are orders Herr Becker. If the chains of command dictate it, who are we to question it?"

"Indeed, Governor-General."

The two men took the time to discuss the Frick and Melnik issue and the intelligence the police had gathered on them before moving on to the next issue that von Hindenburg wished to discuss with Becker.

"The next issue the Führer and I discussed were our continuing efforts to discredit The Menorah. It's been a while since anything was carried out. In fact, from what I recall, Cleveland Street was the last mission. The Führer wants efforts to discredit to recommence. As soon as possible."

Becker nodded in approval. It had been a while since such orders had been issued. Before the new Führer came to power, the orders came directly from his father (via von Hindenburg). The instruction to detonate a device outside Cleveland Street had come from the new Führer, deliberately timed to give the impression The Menorah was trying to create irreversible instability on the back of the death of the late great Adolf Hitler — and to subsequently discredit them in the process. Since this time, he had found himself somewhat preoccupied with Hess, Koch, his mother and everything else involved in ensuring a secure transfer of power. Now he had had a few months to settle into his role, the Führer had deemed it necessary to recommence the engineered attacks.

"May I ask where the Führer wishes to target, Governor-General? Are we to go for another one of our own?"

"I'm pleased you asked, Rolf. On this occasion, no. The Führer wants it to be something big."

"Big, Governor-General?"

"Yes, Rolf. Big. Maximum casualties. He wants those bastards in The Menorah finished. That, and our IUI man, we are hoping will not only expose who they are and find out who this Hebron is, but they will be universally hated and loathed by the wider population."

Becker understood very well what von Hindenburg was saying. The Führer wanted any foothold (no matter how small) The Menorah had made in the psyche of the British population to be well and truly destroyed in a single act of terror. An act so terrible that they would be viewed as nothing more than hardened terrorists, even by the most sympathetic minds. It would have to be something much larger than Cleveland Street and something where the casualties would have to be less discriminate — and there had to be lots of them. This combined with whoever the man in the IUI was, the Führer was clearly hoping would bring about the eventual death knell for The Menorah.

At the conclusion of the meeting, Becker was transported back to his place of work in Ladbroke Grove. As he arrived, he was greeted by his secretary Sally. Becker greeted her back before making a request of her. "Sally, I need you to make a call to someone for me, please."

"Of course, who do you need me to call?"

"I need you to make contact with DS Dean Fellows. Tell him that I need to see him as a matter of some urgency and that I have a very specific task for him. He'll know what I mean."

PART 3

EICHMANN'S AMERICA

18

THE PILOT

MAY 1980, SOMEWHERE ON THE WYOMING PRAIRIE, EAST AMERICA

He was lost. Well and truly lost. It had been the best part of two days and nights since he set off from the border with the Japanese empire, leaving behind his new-found friends of the Elk Valley Indian Reservation, and he had not seen a single soul since. The dust still hung heavy in the atmosphere obscuring the sunlight and making any form of navigation near impossible. Despite Mike Morgan's military training, he had not been trained for this particular eventuality. He was hungry, thirsty and exhausted — both physically and mentally. The determination to continue was strong. The determination to seek some kind of retribution for the events of the preceding weeks and months was also strong. His strength, however, was failing and rapidly. He had not eaten for days and had hardly had anything to drink with the exception of a few sips of dirty contaminated water from a spring he had stumbled upon during his journey across the prairie.

As he collapsed to his knees in exhaustion, he coughed heavily. His lungs ached but he couldn't tell if it was because of the sheer amount of dust in the air or something more sinister. The hints of blood in his sputum were indicative that he was beginning to suffer in the same way as his parents had done years before. Mike didn't know how much longer he could continue or even if he was heading in the right direction. As he knelt in the soft yellow grass gasping for air, he reflected on the last few years of his life and was almost amused at how he had ended up out there all alone and how drastically his life's journey had altered in such a relatively small space of time.

1st FEBRUARY, 1972, HIGHWAY 132, TEN KILOMETRES WEST OF JEFFREY CITY, WYOMING

Mike Morgan's fate was sealed over eight years earlier as he and his wife, Hannah, were returning home to Jeffrey City after meeting with friends a few miles away for dinner. They had met with Cliff Boon and his wife, a colleague of Mike's. It was getting late as they drove down Highway 132 back towards their home. As they drove, they passed by the Elk Valley Indian Reservation. He had never had anything to do with the Native Americans, they very much kept themselves to themselves in their own contained society on the reservation. Similarly, no one tended to bother them. The Reich Police of East America were happy for them to remain within the boundaries of their reservation but it wasn't entirely unknown for the Indians to receive a decent amount of undue harassment from the authorities if seen venturing too far from their land. Such was life in America in the years following the war, with discrimination and segregation remaining rife throughout the country against minority and native races. Mike didn't think anything of it as he drove with his wife past the reservation that night and little did he know that within a few years, he would become involved with the Native Americans in a way he never would have imagined at the time.

Mike Morgan was born on the 21st October 1940 in Oklahoma to a farming family. He had grown up in Eichmann's America, and as with the European population born after the war, he knew little else other than what he was taught at school. The United States had been a gross capitalist nation, heavy handed in its approach to foreign policy, ruthless in its ambitions to expand its influence across the globe, keen to finance and support the Jewish threat and led by a succession of brutal presidents posing a dire threat to world peace and proving to be a formidable enemy of Hitler's Reich. In school, Mike was taught that America sought to destroy Germany with the atomic bomb and had worked tirelessly to develop the necessary technology to do so but they failed and the great German Reich was able to strike first and this, combined with the almost simultaneous invasion to the west by Japan, finally brought about an end to the evil America and all it stood for.

As he was growing up on the farm near Watonga, Oklahoma, he remembered the struggles the family encountered. Radioactive fallout from Der Befreier I & II had spread across the country in the years following the war. If the crops on the farm didn't fail as a result, they were often stunted due to contamination and unfit to withstand human consumption. He remembered the dust created by the blight of the crops. He remembered how sick his mother and father had both become. He remembered his father coughing up blood on a regular basis. He remembered his mother cursing the German Reich and putting the blame on them for the dreadful situation the country was in. He remembered many others in the locality becoming sick and frail in the dust storms that regularly devastated the state. He remembered the day when his father put a shotgun in his mouth and killed himself. He remembered seeing the German liberators driving through the streets in their armoured vehicles adorned with flags of the swastika. Most of all, he remembered seeing the jet planes flying overhead.

As part of the German occupation, the Nazis had installed a new airbase on the outskirts of Oklahoma City. A staging post for German aerial operations across America to target former military forces of America intent on resisting the new Nazi rule by mounting a guerrilla campaign against the occupying forces. Sometimes at night, he would sit outside of the farmhouse and hear the planes flying overhead. In the distance, he would see the flashes followed by a series of loud cracks as the Nazi bombers dropped their load onto the enemy. At first, the tracer fire from the anti-aircraft guns on the ground was common — although it never seemed to hit the target high in the sky. Over time it became less common as the mighty Luftwaffe systematically brought its enemy down and destroyed its very capabilities. Eventually, the bombing stopped altogether and the nights would be quiet, with the exception of the occasional cricket chirping into the night or his father doubled over in agony once again as he coughed uncontrollably. Mike remained entranced by the Luftwaffe and one day aspired to become one of them.

By the time Mike was thirteen, Adolf Eichmann had been appointed as the governor-general of East America. He didn't know a lot about Eichmann at the time other than the fact he had been a top-ranking officer of the SS back in Germany and an architect of the solution to the so-called Jewish problem. It seemed as though the Jewish problem was the catalyst that began the war, certainly in Germany, due to the greed of the Jew and the fact they horded all the wealth in Germany, creating an enormous divide. At least that was what school taught him. Alongside tales of armed Jewish militia terrorising neighbourhoods across Germany; looting, raping and destroying at will. All for their own personal gain. Despite the tolerance of Hitler, any olive branch offered was cruelly turned down and after several attempts at peaceful negotiation, Hitler had no choice but to retaliate in order to protect Germany from nothing short of an armed Jewish insurrection.

Adolf Eichmann was considered a hero. The SS officer was appointed by the Führer himself to coordinate the round-up and deportation of Jewish usurpers from across Europe. He earned himself a fearsome reputation but was also highly effective in his methods and the Führer was happy with the results Eichmann was able to bring about in relation to solving the Jewish problem. He became a highly decorated war hero. In the years following the war, Eichmann became a close friend of Argentinian President Juan Peron and spent five years living in the South American nation in a luxury villa in Buenos Aires. By 1950, Eichmann had been persuaded by the Führer to return to Germany in order to consider a career in politics as a senior member of the NSDAP and by 1953, he had been appointed by Hitler to be the new governor-general of East America. Mike Morgan remembered the appointment well. It was greeted with celebration (at least that's what the news reported anyway) and Eichmann proudly pledged to rebuild America promising that it would never be a remote outpost of the Reich, but an industrial and military powerhouse instrumental in consolidating the reputation of the Reich throughout the world.

Throughout his time growing up, Mike Morgan continued to have a fascination with planes and the Luftwaffe and by the time he was sixteen, he had signed up to join them. The training was gruelling and the sixteen-year-old boy from small town Oklahoma grew up — and toughened up — quickly. As well as learning how to pilot some of the most advanced fighter jets on the planet, the Luftwaffe were trained to survive extreme situations on the ground, as well as be skilled with weapons and hand-to-hand combat.

The first year of training was alongside the Heer. The ground forces that had swept across Europe like a plague of locust during the war, decimating everything in their path; trained to survive any situation. Individual killing machines. By the time he was seventeen, he had leapt from an aeroplane and parachuted to the ground safely hundreds of times. He had trained in Germanic Russia during the harsh winter learning how to survive in the wild with little more than a knife and the clothes on his back. He had been part of many simulated beach invasion scenarios (similar to the New Year's Day invasion of Britain) and had vomited in the landing craft on every occasion as it navigated its way across the choppy waters of the English Channel. As he approached his eighteenth birthday, he was finally able to fly inside a fighter jet alongside a trained Luftwaffe pilot.

He remembered this first flight. It was a Messerschmitt ME-300. During the war, one of the technological advances pioneered by Germany was the jet engine. In the 1930s, the Messerschmitt ME-262 was the first jet powered combat aircraft constructed, able to achieve speeds of up to five hundred and forty miles per hour. As the 1930s progressed, aeronautical engineers improved and further developed jet technology and by the beginning of the war, Germany had amassed a fleet of over five hundred Messerschmitt ME-285A jets. Capable of speeds up to nearly eight hundred miles per hour and easy to manoeuvre in the air, the Luftwaffe were able to outrun and outgun the British RAF with ease: often bombing military targets in Britain with little to virtually no warning. They could fly higher, faster and for longer than other combat jets and the Luftwaffe became as feared as the Heer. The speed and G-force of the Messerschmitt ME-300 made Mike Morgan pass out the first time he flew in one. The German pilot had laughed loudly at seeing the teenager's eyes slowly roll up into the top of his head as he performed a near vertical take-off at pushing nine hundred miles per hour. In order to really let the young man know what he was in for, he levelled out at a height of thirty thousand feet and waited for him to regain consciousness, which he soon did. At which point, the German pilot took the jet into a near vertical nose dive whilst simultaneously performing a number of barrel rolls. Mike vomited into his oxygen mask. The German pilot howled again with laughter until he finally decided to land the fighter. Mike spent the next half hour vomiting violently at the side of the runway whilst the other pilots looked on at him with much amusement.

Despite returning to his barracks covered in his own stomach contents, Mike Morgan remained undeterred. His maiden flight in a fighter jet had proved to be perhaps the most liberating feeling of his entire life. Following a further two years of intense training (both in a simulator and in the real thing), Mike Morgan gained his wings — and excelled. By the time he was twenty-five he had completed countless missions. The majority of these were conducted over American soil involving strategic bombing raids against a new and emerging group of terrorists known as the Liberty Front. Throughout the 1960s, they had become more organised on the ground but were no match for the Luftwaffe. Despite the numerous raids on Liberty Front safe houses, it only served to drive them further into the more inaccessible areas of East America making the missions of the Luftwaffe more and more challenging as the years went on.

Some days, Mike Morgan just liked flying and sometimes he would seek any excuse to get into his jet and perform a solo flight across America. He remembered flying high above New York. Far enough away from any lingering radiation created by the bomb dropped years before but close enough to see what it had done. He had seen pictures of New York in books and he found it hard to imagine that it was the same city he was now seeing himself. The scene of devastation stretched as far as the eye could see and while it shocked and somewhat depressed him, he couldn't help but think that it was also oddly beautiful in the most morbid way. The famed Statue of Liberty remained in place in New York Harbour, albeit missing the arm that used to hold the torch aloft. Largely forgotten about in Eichmann's America, she had remained the inspiration for the Liberty Front who had taken the name from Lady Liberty herself. One day he flew west to the frontier with Japan and looked down on the huge border wall separating East and West America. A dead straight giant white monolith constructed by Japan to follow the state boundaries between the east and west of the country; thus demarcating the boundaries of the two respective empires. Inadvertently he ventured into Japanese airspace one afternoon and was met by an anti-aircraft missile fired from the other side of the border wall. His skills as a pilot were sufficient enough to see that the missile was avoided — he wasn't lucky enough to avoid a dressing down from his commanding officer on return to the airbase.

In 1967, Mike Morgan had been promoted to the rank of Major (the British equivalent of a Squadron Leader) and while he remained a well-respected and revered pilot of the Luftwaffe, he had decided to spend less hours in the air and more time training the fresh blood wishing to follow in his footsteps. His mother had by now also become very sick and unable to manage the farmhouse in Oklahoma. Her lungs were riddled with cancer from years of breathing in the contaminated soil. The farmhouse was in disrepair and despite holding on, the cancer would eventually claim her life, but Mike figured better that than taking your own head off with a shotgun. The land was worth little and was eventually purchased by the Reich for reasons that never really became known to Mike, particularly due to its low monetary value.

With a promotion — and the death of his mother — came a reason to move on and so Mike found himself moving north up to Wyoming to work for the Ministry of Aeronautics and Weaponry. The ministry was headed up by none other than Alois Brunner, Adolf Eichmann's right-hand man. He only ever met Brunner once and he never liked the man. He was arrogant and rude, disliked in many circles, but he was also known to be ruthlessly efficient when he needed to be. Mike's exceptional skills as a pilot and his track record in the Luftwaffe made him an ideal candidate to work for this ministry and he was engaged in a number of aeronautical weapon development projects, most notably the development of the Iron Fortress. A new spy plane so highly developed and weaponised, that not even a squadron of Luftwaffe would be able to take it down. It was while he was living in Wyoming he met his soon to be wife, Hannah Miller. Following a quick courtship, the two were married in 1969 and lived happily in Jeffrey City, Freemont County, Wyoming — within a sensible travelling distance to Mike's workplace at an outpost of the ministry (and Luftwaffe airbase) in nearby Saratoga. Many of his friends and colleagues frowned upon the relationship he had with Hannah (although Cliff Boon was not one of them).

As Mike was driving them home after a night with Cliff and his wife, his attention was diverted to the blue flashing light that had appeared in the rear-view mirror of his car. It was the police.

"Damn it," Mike said, clearly frustrated.

His wife had been dozing in the passenger seat and was alerted by Mike's frustration. "What is it?"

"Police. I think I was going too fast."

As Mike pulled the car over to the side of the road, so the police car stopped behind them and the driver got out of the car and approached Mike's side. Mike wound his window down and placed both his hands on the steering wheel in the ten and two position. The officer leant into the car and shone his torch into Mike's face. He was a middle-aged man (Mike guessed in his early fifties) and wore the typical jet-black Police uniform emblazoned with the swastika on each shoulder. His breath wasn't terribly fresh as he leaned forward to examine the occupants.

"Evening, sir. Do you know why I stopped you tonight?" he questioned, actually in a rather friendly tone.

"Was I going too fast?"

The officer smiled politely and nodded. "Sorry, sir, wouldn't be doing my job if I didn't pull you over. May I see some ID please?"

"Yeah sure."

Mike reached into his pocket to retrieve his military ID and handed it to the officer who surveyed it under the light of the torch. The smile on the officer's face broadened significantly when he realised he was speaking to another Reich guy. A high-ranking member of the Luftwaffe, nonetheless.

"Luftwaffe, are you?"

"Yep, that's me."

"All right! I see you guys coming over my house all the time. Hell, sometimes I think them engines o' yours gonna break my windows it's so damned loud. Jeez!" The two men laughed jovially as clearly the realisation of Mike being a member of the Luftwaffe was a nice little icebreaker. "Well, listen. I'll let this one go for tonight and you be on your way. Just watch that speed. Say, who you got in there with you?"

Up until this point, the officer had not paid any attention to Mike's passenger but he leant further in and shone the torch over and into Hannah's face who looked back in sheer terror. The officer examined her for a few seconds and the smile vanished from his face and he took on a much more serious tone. He holstered the torch and signalled to the other officer who was still in the car to come and join him.

Hannah reached over and grabbed Mike's hand. "Mike." She was panicked.

"It's OK, don't worry," Mike replied reassuringly.

The officer leant back into the car and addressed them both. "I need you to step out of the car please, sir."

"Officer, look, I'm sorry I was going a bit too—"

"Sir, I need you to step out of your car. Right now." There was a rising sense of urgency in his voice. "Your lady friend too."

"It's my wife," Mike corrected the officer.

"I don't care who she is. Get out the vehicle, little lady, and step over here."

Mike looked over to Hannah and nodded to her as if to indicate that they should do as they were told. So they both got out. The other officer had joined them by this point. He had swaggered over from the police vehicle and was a younger man who looked like he possessed an air of some arrogance about him. The sort who would likely shoot first and ask all the questions later. Indeed, his hand hovered by his holstered sidearm as if this may be the case. His arrogant demeanour seemed to vanish as he set eyes on Hannah as she rounded the front of the car to join her husband. His expression had turned to one of shock — not because she was eight months pregnant, but the fact that she was mixed-race.

"Holy shit!" he exclaimed. "What do we have here?"

The second officer ushered Hannah over to him at the rear of Mike's car while officer number one continued to engage with Mike.

"You got anything in the car you wanna tell me about, Luftwaffe?"

"Like what?"

"Oh, I don't know. You been hiding her in there, maybe you hiding something else we don't know about?"

It was absolutely evident why an initially innocuous and routine stop was unfolding into such a drama, and it wasn't because Mike had been driving too fast. It was because his wife was mixed-race and in Eichmann's America, mixed-race partnerships — while not outlawed — were very much frowned upon. He had been warned by some of the other pilots not to marry her. Some had mocked him. Others had abused him. Some had been knocked clean out by Mike for showing such disrespect. Eichmann's police were also notoriously heavy handed when dealing with any person of race. A mixed-race woman pregnant with a white man's child was nothing more than a red rag to a bull for the two officers. An opportunity to exert their authority, however justified it may or may not be.

"Don't be stupid, we're just going—"

Mike didn't have time finish his sentence as, without any warning, the officer punched Mike below the ribs immediately winding him and sending him to his knees beside the car. For a slightly older man, he delivered a surprisingly hard and fast blow to the fitter younger man. The next thing Mike knew, the officer had pulled his holstered sidearm and had it pointing towards his forehead. Hannah had begun to scream as the other officer had forcibly swivelled her round and pushed her up against the side of the car yelling at her to raise her hands, no doubt revelling in the opportunity to dish out some kind of justice.

"Don't you move a goddamn muscle, Luftwaffe," the first officer sneered at Mike as he eyed him intently in his winded and shocked state on the ground. "Search her, would you. Let's see if she's carrying anything she shouldn't be. Apart from a white man's child."

He was clearly getting some enjoyment from the situation and Mike guessed that this probably wasn't the first time the two officers had taken enjoyment from harassing someone of colour. Mike glanced over at his wife who was clearly distressed and was weeping uncontrollably and pleading with the other officer to leave her be, whilst also highlighting the fact she was pregnant. Her pleas were ignored.

"Shut your mouth, quit squealing like some kind of farm animal." He moved in close to Hannah and whispered in her ear, "I promise I'll be gentle."

With that, he kicked Hannah's legs apart, forcing her to let out a panicked yelp, and dropped to his knees. With both hands, starting from the ankles, he began to frisk her legs in some kind of mock search.

"Nothing to see down here. Maybe I should move up a little bit? What do you say?" Hannah was now beside herself with fear and couldn't even muster up the strength to respond as the officer moved his hands up towards her thigh and into her skirt. "Why you getting so upset for? I thought you liked white meat?"

All the while, Mike looked on, currently powerless to act, for fear of receiving a bullet to the skull. As much as he wanted to leap up and rush to the aid of his wife, his gaze remained fixed on the officer holding the gun with both hands steadily to his head. Similarly, his gaze remained fixed on Mike as he smiled to reveal a gross set of yellowed front teeth that were no doubt the reason behind his terrible breath. Their eyes locked. Mike was waiting for the right time. He needed to act quick but he also had to time his next step with split-second precision.

The officer with the gun was desperate to look to see what his colleague was up to but doing so proved to be a mistake. For him at least. As soon as he momentarily averted his gaze, Mike Morgan struck. With his left hand, he palm-struck the officer's right arm. This served to immediately move the gun away from his forehead. Instinctively, the officer pulled the trigger of the firearm which let a bullet off into the side of the car. At the same time, the force of Mike's palm strike fractured the man's radius of his right arm forcing him to drop the weapon. As this happened, Mike swept upwards with his right fist and using the force of the lift as he left the ground, punched the man underneath the ribcage to the right side of his body. The shot was so perfectly timed and aimed with such precision that it perforated his liver and sent him sprawling onto the ground in nothing short of absolute agony. Seeing where the firearm had landed, Mike dropped once more to the ground, retrieved the weapon, rose to his feet and pointed it towards his wife's aggressor.

"Step back!" Mike yelled at the man who immediately froze. "Now!"

"All right. Take it easy, I didn't mean no harm. I was just messin'."

"Get your hands in the air and step back."

The man (who hadn't quite made it as far as Hannah's buttocks, but wasn't far away) rose and cautiously put his hands in the air. Mike made eye contact with his wife and signalled with his head for her to move back towards him which she promptly did. As she did so, the officer moved his right hand towards his holster as if to reach for his sidearm and this was immediately met by a shot from Mike. The bullet was aimed with such precision that it skimmed the man's left ear and made him freeze in fear. His breathing quickened as did the pace at which his hands went back up into the air. He stood still as Mike approached him, not once lowering his weapon as he got closer. He daren't move for fear of getting a bullet right between the eyes. Embarrassingly, he also realised at that stage he had unwittingly wet himself. Then he saw stars and finally nothing but black as Mike hammered the butt of the sidearm into his face, knocking him into an unconscious heap onto the road in a puddle of his own urine.

Mike disarmed the now unconscious officer and proceeded back to the one he had incapacitated moments before, who was now writhing on the floor whining like some kind of wounded animal. On his way back, he unloaded the magazine from each sidearm, emptied the chamber and threw them both into the darkness of the surrounding Wyoming prairie. He went to check on his wife and hugged her reassuringly before asking her to wait in the car. He then went and stood over the injured man who, when he saw Mike, raised a hand and began to beg.

"Please. Please don't kill me. I got a family. Please don't."

Mike knelt down next to the man, and reached for his radio which was attached to his uniform on the shoulder. He took it off and placed it on the man's chest before saying, "Call it in." He then rose and went back to his car to sit with his wife and await the arrival of police backup.

The way he figured it, the situation could've been played out one of two ways. He could've made the choice to not intervene and allowed his wife to have been sexually assaulted by two blatantly racist police officers. Ultimately, they would've walked away alive from the situation and Mike would've kept his job at Brunner's Ministry of Aeronautics and Weaponry. His wife would've been traumatised probably for the rest of her life, and no matter how much they may have complained, the police would not have followed any complaint up based purely on the skin colour of his wife. Mike was too proud to allow this happen. There was no way in the world he would kneel there and allow any other man to do that to his pregnant wife.

So Mike Morgan played the situation his way and brought to a swift conclusion what would've been a life changing assault on his wife. As a result, he lost his job and spent the next four years of his life in prison. It would have been a lot longer had he not been attached to the ministry and its reputation in the Reich. He missed the first four years of his daughter's life. He could've run from the situation after it had happened but there was no way he would've escaped justice. The two officers had identified him as a member of the Luftwaffe and he had a mixed-race wife. Such was the rarity of a partnership like this anywhere in America, let alone in the Luftwaffe, he would've been tracked down in under a day and his punishment would've been twice as harsh.

Upon his release from prison, Mike returned to live with his wife and daughter, Rebecca, in a shabby rented apartment in Jeffrey City. Before his jail term, Mike had been fortunate enough to purchase the couple a nice property in the same town. Nothing massive. Just a little two-bedroom house in the suburbs with a nice garden and plenty of space but this had to be sold when Mike was convicted. Hannah, who did not work at the time, needed money in order to find a new home and pay for the upbringing of a new baby. By the time her husband was released from prison, the money had dried up. Hannah spent her time working a low paid waitressing job at a local diner while balancing the demands of childcare. She had cried into her husband's arms when he finally returned to the new home. Partly in relief at his return, partly in despair at the dreadful situation they were in and it was at this point that Mike Morgan pledged to get the family out of such dire straits — by whatever means possible.

19

MTS LTD

OCTOBER 1976, SARATOGA, CARBON COUNTY, WYOMING

Mike Morgan wasted no time whatsoever looking for work upon his release from prison. It hadn't been the nicest four years of his life by any means but he coped. Based on the set of skills he possessed, he began to look for work in the security sector but few interviews were forthcoming due to his criminal record. One particular position caught his eye, that of a Security Consultant for München Towers Security (MTS) Ltd. He had heard of the company and had certainly seen them advertised; however, he knew little about them other than the fact they provided security solutions to other companies and businesses in the form of personnel, alarms, security cameras and arranging secure transport of sensitive goods and materials where necessary. He deemed it highly unlikely he would end up getting a job with them, let alone an interview but he had to try. For the sake of his family, he had to at least try. To his surprise, he was invited to attend an interview only five days after posting his application form.

So, Mike Morgan found himself sat in the bare room opposite a panel of three men on a rainy October day in 1976. The headquarters of MTS Ltd were located on the outskirts of Saratoga, not far from where Mike used to work — when he was still employed at Brunner's Ministry of Aeronautics and Weaponry — and a short drive from where he was living in Jeffrey City. The building was pretty nondescript but was surrounded by a fence covered, in various places, with security software and a rather bored and overweight looking guard at the gatehouse who looked as though he would fall asleep at his post at any point. The room Mike was in had high ceilings and the walls were completely bare. In the intermittent periods of silence between the questioning he was receiving, the gentle hum of the air conditioning could be heard. Each man had in front of him a small dossier, Mike assumed it was all the details pertaining to himself. What made the panel interesting was the presence of a black gentleman. He had been the quietest of the three men but to see a man of colour on the management panel of a private security firm was highly unusual. As Mike knew from personal experience, the Reich were discriminatory towards most people of colour, resigning them to the more menial jobs in society with a continued policy of segregation. Nothing had changed during his time in prison. To see (and hear) him identify himself as a co-director of MTS Ltd came as a surprise. Mike had donned his finest suit and tie that complimented his muscular frame. He was clean shaven and he had gelled back his short black hair and he was a naturally handsome man with deep green eyes. The interview had seemed more like an interrogation at times but for such a position in such an esteemed company, Mike guessed they had to be thorough. He could tell that the interview was reaching its logical conclusion and deep down inside, he had everything crossed for some success. He felt as though he could certainly do with some.

"I think, Herr Morgan, we're almost done and I'm sure my colleagues would agree that you've got a very impressive work history."

"Thank you," replied Mike to the gentleman sat to his far left. He was the oldest of the panel and the director of MTS Ltd — Elias Frank.

The middle man on the panel, co-director Giselher Mollath, continued, "I wholeheartedly agree with Herr Frank. And you present yourself very well indeed. A man who would be loyal and committed and I, well… we I should say, we like that about you very much."

"Thank you, Herr Mollath," responded Mike. "I appreciate your time and the kind comments."

"There is one thing though." It was the black gentleman to his right this time. Co-director Leonard Savoy. "It says here in your documentation, that you were involved in an incident a few years ago."

"Incident, Herr Savoy?"

"Yes, something to do with a police officer of the Reich? Would you care to elaborate?"

Mike most certainly did not wish to elaborate but there was no way to gloss over this one. It was always going to come back and haunt him (particularly as he had served prison time) and it would've been terrible wishful thinking of him to think it wouldn't. One way or another, he would have to face up to this one and explain the 'incident' in question and hope that the panel could see past this and see him for who he really was and what he was capable of. Mike cleared his throat before continuing.

"It was, how can I put it? It was a mistake. A heat of the moment incident that shouldn't have happened. I had a confrontation with a—"

"Confrontation?" interrupted Giselher Mollath. "It says here you spent four years in a Reich penitentiary for assaulting not one, but two police officers of the Reich. What sort of confrontation was this exactly, Herr Morgan?"

Mike paused before considering his next words. "He, one of the officers involved, was heavy handed towards my wife. We were driving and the officer in question pulled us over. Speeding violation apparently. Anyhow, he manhandled my wife in an inappropriate manner. I asked him not to, he ignored me, I stepped in and things got… well, things became… heated."

"Heated?" questioned Leonard Savoy. "You broke one officer's arm and ruptured his liver. And you beat the other one unconscious. Sounds a little more than heated to me."

"I think beat is a little strong. I only hit him once—"

"With the butt of a gun."

"Well… yes. I was defending my wife. I admitted I over-reacted during my trial and put a guilty plea in. This was taken into—"

Savoy raised his hand in a bid to silence Mike.

"The problem is, Herr Morgan," Elias Frank continued, "is that we need people we can trust."

"You can trust me Herr Frank. I would work for you, there would be no problems, I guarantee it."

"Oh I have no doubt at all about how hard you would work for me and your credentials are second to none. We welcome former military personnel and in fact, we consider former Wehrmacht to be some of our best employees. But this…" Frank held up a page from Mike's dossier (what he assumed to be the page relating to his conviction), "this, Herr Morgan, is problematic."

"You see," continued Savoy, "we need people on our team we can trust. And this is why we think your application may be problematic. We can't have one of our operatives becoming heated. This would jeopardise an operation or assignment. Maybe even put the reputation of the company in danger. Do you see why this makes it difficult for us to hire someone like you? Irrespective of your credentials?"

"I understand your reservations. I really do. Nothing like that happened before or has happened since. I just want a chance."

"Can we trust you, Herr Morgan?" queried Mollath. "Can we really trust you?"

"Yes," responded Mike without any hesitation. "Yes you can!"

Less than an hour later, Mike was sat alone in a nearby bar gently caressing a large shot of whiskey on ice. He had taken a small sip but had since sat staring into the glass watching the ice cubes dance on the surface of his drink serving to both cool and simultaneously dilute the whiskey. Another failed interview, another disappointment, another tough conversation to have with his wife, Hannah. She had stuck firmly by her husband through thick and thin. She had stuck by him during his prison sentence. She stuck by him even though he was absent during the birth of their daughter as a result of his incarceration. She had stuck by him as their financial situation had subsequently become so dire they had to give up their home. She had stuck by him through everything. Good, reliable, trustworthy and ever patient Hannah. Although, Mike wondered how long her patience would last.

"Mind if I take a seat?" The voice snapped Mike from his whiskey daydream and he looked up. "Sorry, didn't mean to startle you. Do you mind?" Leonard Savoy gestured towards the empty seat next to Mike at the bar.

He wondered why this man, who had less than an hour ago rejected him during the interview, had suddenly appeared at the bar beside him. Of all the bars in all the towns! "Go ahead," responded Mike nonchalantly.

"Thanks," said Savoy, taking a seat next to Mike. He raised his hand as if to gesture over the barman who promptly came over and stood opposite Savoy. "I'll have what he's having. Get him another while you're at it."

The barman scoffed, "Can you read, son?"

"Yes, as a matter of fact, I can. Why do you ask? Oh, and I'm not your son."

"Because last time I checked there was a great big sign on the front door saying your type ain't welcome in here. Yet here you are."

Savoy laughed out loud. He then turned towards the door looking confused before continuing, "My type? And what's my type exactly?"

"Don't you get smart with me, boy! We got rules so I suggest you—"

The barman was cut short rather abruptly as Savoy slapped what looked like an identity card onto the bar in front of the barman. Mike didn't see the card in its entirety but managed to make out the words 'München Towers', the swastika logo and a photograph of Savoy. The barman took a few moments to inwardly digest what was in front of him before reluctantly submitting.

"All right then. Coming right up."

"Apology accepted," replied Savoy which was met with a reluctant nod of acknowledgement from the barman.

Mike was impressed. He had seen people of colour stand up to prejudice but every time (with the exception of this particular occasion) it had never ended well. More often than not, defiance had turned to aggression which had turned to violence. Clearly, Savoy was in a position to demand respect despite the colour of his skin. This was almost unheard of in Nazi East America. It did, however, beg the question of what exactly he wanted and why he was here. And so began their conversation.

"How can I help you, Herr Savoy?"

"Leo. Call me Leo, please. Herr Savoy is too formal for my liking. I just wanted to say I'm sorry you didn't get the job."

This confused and intrigued Mike greatly. Had he really come all this way to apologise for him not getting a job? This seemed unlikely.

"You're telling me; you came down here to apologise to me because I beat up some asshole of a Reich officer for molesting my wife?"

Leo laughed, "Careful! Criticism of the Reich carries a mandatory prison sentence. Six months minimum last time I checked."

"Been there, done that, do I look like I care?"

Leo laughed again, "No you don't."

The barman arrived back with their drinks and left them in front of Leo who responded by leaving a small pile of Reichsmarks for the barman.

"So, Herr Savoy... sorry, Leo. Why are you here?"

"I want to offer you a job."

Mike looked quizzically at Leo. "I thought I wasn't a suitable candidate."

"You're not. Well, not for that job. To be honest, you wouldn't have been cut out for that anyway. A man of your skills is destined for, how shall we say, greater things. Much greater things. If you're interested of course."

Mike was indeed interested. He was in a desperate situation and in dire need of some form of financial support. As well as being interested, he was also intrigued by this somewhat mysterious proposition from this equally mysterious individual.

"OK, I'm listening. What is it you think I'm destined for?"

Leo laughed and patted Mike on the shoulder before continuing, "That job at MTS, I only do that part time. I have interests invested elsewhere. You see, I front an organisation that deals with more covert security problems involving more sensitive individuals."

Mike looked at Leo quizzically. "Covert and sensitive? Are you trying to recruit me as a spy?"

He was actually being facetious and said this with amusement in his voice. Leo appreciated the humour and laughed before responding.

"Well, you're not too far away to be fair, Mr Morgan," Leo replied before taking a sip of his drink. "I know from your previous work that you're more than familiar with the Liberty Front. I dare say you've dropped a few bombs on them during your Luftwaffe years."

Mike nodded in agreement. Leo wasn't wrong. "A few."

"Well, they're still out there. The bombs did the job at the time but the times have changed. The Liberty Front has changed. America is a big place and they've found places to hide. They've also taken an element of inspiration from The Menorah by infiltrating areas close to the Reich and using this against us. You know The Menorah, right?" Mike nodded. He had heard about them and how over the years their methods had become ever more sophisticated and cunning. "Thing is, what started out as a few guys with guns has turned into something a lot more dangerous. I think in many ways, we underestimated the intelligence of the Liberty Front.

Whatever we've thrown at them they've managed to adapt. Every bomb dropped, every member killed, they regroup and come back at us stronger and we need a different strategy. One that penetrates into the very core of the Liberty Front."

"And what would that be?"

"The organisation I work for sends people like me and you — trained individuals — deep undercover. So we don't do your normal in and out bombing raids. Our operatives go under for months, if not longer, to root out members of the Front. We've been fighting these assholes for years now and still, we don't know who leads them, we don't know where their HQ is, we don't know who supports them. In reality, what do we know about them?"

Mike shrugged. "Not a lot, by the sounds of it."

"Exactly! Not a lot. We need to dive deeper. But we can't just send anyone in. We need people with skills, resilience. Someone able to blend in to any environment no matter what. Someone able to build the trust of someone and then put a bullet in between their eyes without a second thought."

"And you think that's me?"

"Potentially. We can't just send anybody into a deep cover situation. Whoever we send in needs to have a specific set of skills, as in military skills. Survival skills, someone who is able to blend in to their surroundings and adapt if needs be yet someone who is willing to bring a mission to what we would deem to be a logical conclusion. And then walk away."

Mike sat with his drink in front of him gently swilling the rapidly melting ice around in the glass. It certainly sounded like an interesting opportunity but he still had questions.

"So what's MTS then? Is that some kind of a front to find people like me?"

"Kind of. More often than not, it's 'people like you' that apply for a position within a security firm, and like I say, you demonstrate the skills we're looking for. But we look for suitable candidates anywhere and everywhere. We recruit across America and we have operatives working for us in Europe too. And further afield than this. All depends on where the need is. Wherever we identify a need, that's where we plant our operative."

Mike was still intrigued. Leo Savoy clearly wasn't operating an American-based agency (if that's what it was) but what seemed like more of an international based operation.

"Who are you, Mr Savoy?"

"What do you mean?"

"I mean, who are you really working for? Is this secret service? Or Gestapo?"

Leo laughed hard and continued to be somewhat amused by Mike. "Gestapo? No, they were well and truly disbanded back in the fifties. Not fit for purpose. Let's just say we're the…" He trailed off, as he thought how to finish the sentence, "we're the successors. But on a more widely distributed scale. People like the Front and The Menorah, as I said already, they've become clever over the years. While, traditionally, the Front may have stayed in America and The Menorah in the British Territories, this isn't necessarily so any more. They spread themselves out over a larger area. Which is why we need a particular type of expertise to penetrate the ranks."

Mike nodded as he continued to listen to what Leo had to say. "OK. So what's in it for me?"

"Are we talking money?"

Mike nodded in acknowledgment. That was exactly what he was talking about. After all, he had lost all of that as a result of his criminal conviction and time spent in prison.

"You would be compensated more than generously for your work. All of our operatives are. So that nice little house you lost all those years ago, doesn't matter. Because you'll be able to buy a bigger and better one. And that nice little wife of yours? She can give up the job at the diner. You'll be earning plenty to support her too. We can look at wiping that record of yours as well. That little incident with those two idiots? We can make it disappear. Permanently."

It was at this stage that it really hit Mike. This man meant business. Not once had he divulged any information about his former house to Leo. Similarly, he had never once mentioned that his wife worked as a waitress at a diner. This man clearly knew things about Mike and had done all his homework. Further to this, no one was able to make a criminal conviction disappear unless they were in a position of some privilege and influence in the Reich. Leo Savoy was clearly in such a position if he were to ever make good on such a claim. Indeed, to erase his criminal conviction would only serve to benefit Mike and his wife and this was beginning to look like an offer that may be too good to refuse.

"You have my attention, Leo. I still have a lot of questions to ask though. Before coming to any decision. You understand that, right?"

"Absolutely. I would have questions too. Tell you what," Leo paused as he reached into his pocket to retrieve what looked like a business card which he placed in front of Mike, "come to this address tomorrow morning at nine o'clock."

It was indeed a white business card which had nothing on it but a finely printed address. Mike didn't know where this was but he could find it out easily enough if needs be.

"If you're there," Leo continued, "we'll talk some more and I can introduce you to some of the team and look at getting a contract drawn up. If we don't see you tomorrow at nine o'clock then, no hard feelings and all the very best to you. How does that sound?"

"I'll take it into consideration."

"Good."

Leo downed the rest of his whiskey in one gulp before placing the empty glass back on the bar for the disapproving barman to come and collect. He then extended his hand towards Mike who shook it firmly.

"It's been a pleasure, Mike Morgan. I have a feeling we'll be seeing each other again very soon."

With that, Leo got up and began to walk away leaving Mike to silently look at the business card that had nothing but an address on it. There was one final thing that he wanted to query.

"So, if this is such a secret and sensitive operation coordinated by the Reich, why did they recruit... you?"

"What do you mean?"

"A black man."

Mike didn't hesitate in responding to Leo when asked what he meant. Leo clearly knew enough about Mike to know who he was married to and the discrimination he (and his wife) had faced as a result of nothing more than skin colour. In fact, it came as no surprise to Leo at all that Mike should feel the need to question such a thing as, in Eichmann's America, black people didn't take up positions within the Reich, surely?

"That's a very good question considering we aren't even allowed to drink in the same bar as a white person or even legally share a bathroom with you. So the Front would never suspect a black person as an infiltrator. Which, I guess, makes me the perfect candidate for any secret and sensitive operation coordinated by the Reich."

With that, Leo smiled at Mike and left the bar, leaving Mike to ponder further over the conversation he had just had with the mysterious Leo Savoy. He finished his whiskey and was about to leave before deciding to have one more to ponder a little further. He then returned home to his wife and child. Hannah looked tired and sad yet there was a glimmer of hope in her eyes when her husband walked through the door later that evening.

"Well? Any joy?" she queried, desperately hoping to hear that he had been offered a job.

"Maybe," Mike responded, "just maybe."

20

INFILTRATION UND INTELLIGENZ

It hadn't taken Mike Morgan long to decide to take Leo Savoy up on his invitation to visit the address passed to him on the business card. The day following his failed interview at MTS Ltd, he set off to find the address given to him. It was a remote nondescript house, approximately fifteen miles to the west of a town called Casper, Natrona County, Wyoming, just off the I26. Tucked away and discreet, no one would know it was there unless really looking for it. The house was of wooden construction and stood two-storeys tall. It looked like it could've been a farmhouse and in later times, Mike learnt that it was simply a property used by the Reich for various purposes including regional meetings of police or Wehrmacht officials, a meeting location for government officials or — in this case — for recruitment purposes.

The house had to be approached down a long dirt track that cut through the surrounding grasslands. It appeared to have a large amount of land that was being tended to by a number of workers; cutting the long grass in the gardens or looking after the flowers, generally making sure the property looked presentable to anyone coming in from the outside. Leo Savoy was sat in a wooden chair at the front of the house enjoying the fresh, yet slightly chilly, morning air. The dew lay on the surrounding grass, yet to be burned away by the morning sun and he wore long sleeves and sunglasses to protect his eyes from the glare of the morning sunshine. Leo cheerily greeted Mike as he drove cautiously towards the house.

Once inside, Mike was introduced to three other people — two men and a woman — who all turned out to also be part of the same organisation. Mike was made to feel welcome in the house but he still had a lot of questions that he wanted answering by the people who he was now faced with. In fact, he had barely slept the previous night, such was his curiosity.

The Gestapo (created by Hermann Göring in 1933) was officially disbanded in 1955. Following the appointment of a number of governors-general across Europe and America and the rapid suppression of any armed resistance, the Gestapo was no longer deemed necessary. The emergence of The Menorah and the Liberty Front in the 1960s forced Adolf Hitler into a rethink. Initially, military strikes against Menorah and Liberty Front targets appeared to have the desired effect but in reality, they only served to make both groups rethink their tactics and move them further underground in order to ensure their own survival. As well as continuing with an armed insurgency against the Reich, both groups became cleverer and started to perform infiltration operations of their own deep into the heart of Reich institutions in order to destabilise from within. The Reich had to play them at their own game.

By 1963, Hitler had created a successor to the Gestapo. A top-secret Reich ministry known only to those within the highest circles of the Reich. The Ministry of Infiltration and Intelligence (Ministerium für Infiltration und Intelligenz) or the IUI. Set up again by Hermann Göring (on the orders of Adolf Hitler), the top-secret ministry was designed to recruit the most highly skilled and specialist military minds from across the world with the aim of eventually infiltrating deep into the Liberty Front and The Menorah. Leadership of both groups had remained largely unknown. Although the mastermind behind The Menorah was known as Hebron, in reality nothing else was known about him or her. Even less was known about the leadership structure behind the Liberty Front; with intelligence services not even having a name let alone anything else. The rise of both groups had begun to worry Hitler somewhat and the establishment of a new top-secret agency was deemed an appropriate measure to counteract such a threat.

By the early 1960s, the IUI had recruited Leo Savoy to its ranks. He hadn't had an easy ride in order to get there. He was born into an America in 1935 that was highly segregated with seemingly little opportunity or hope for anyone of colour. His parents were unable to find regular employment in Chicago and the family lived in relative poverty with short periods of homelessness. When Leo was only six years old, he remembered (albeit vaguely) the evacuation of Chicago as a deadly poisonous cloud approached the city from the east. He didn't know it at the time but in later years, he realised that the cloud was the radioactive fallout from Der Befreier I & II slowly working its way inland. The very same toxic cloud that would go on to leave Mike Morgan's family farm in near ruin in subsequent years. The family managed to escape Chicago but under Nazi rule, life wasn't much better. They eventually settled in Minneapolis in 1945 when the German occupation was very much in full swing. His mother and father found work in Minneapolis; his father working in a canning factory and his mother cleaning some Nazi general's house. Although they had some money, discrimination and segregation remained an issue. Leo did not attend school but was taught to read and write by his mother, who did the best she could under the circumstances.

When he was eighteen years old (and the same year Adolf Eichmann became governor-general of East America), Leo Savoy decided to join the Heer. It seemed as though there were few other opportunities to pursue (certainly in Minneapolis) and anyone could join the Heer irrespective of the colour of their skin. After all, the Reich needed as many people in their ranks as they could possibly find. Like Mike Morgan and his experience of training in the Luftwaffe, Leo Savoy had to grow up and toughen up quickly. With segregation remaining rife in Eichmann's America, things didn't seem much better in the Heer. Young black recruits (of which there were only a few) had to sleep in their own barracks and were regularly subjected to the most heinous abuse from other soldiers. Although he never saw it happen himself, Leo was aware that some black soldiers had committed suicide such was the level of torment permitted, but he was determined to not become another statistic. As he watched other recruits around him fail, Leo excelled in all areas. He was a tough candidate. Physically and mentally strong with an athleticism not seen by many of the other young soldiers. He showed a particular skill for sharpshooting and hand-to-hand combat and was able to tackle a number of people at once (and more often than not come out on top). His superiors were impressed at the young black man as he progressed through his training but one particular incident stood him out above and beyond the rest of his fellow soldiers, an incident that ultimately determined the path his life would take, thus eventually leading him to the IUI.

It was December 1962, and despite having been in the Heer for many years, Leo Savoy had not progressed past the rank of Soldat (the British equivalent of a private). Leo's unit had been sent to carry out a routine patrol of a town called Colby in Kansas. There had been reports of Reich police being targeted by what may have been an armed militia, possibly Liberty Front insurgents (but this was not known for certain at the time). While it had been quelled by the police, the Heer was called in to provide reassurance and a visible presence of firepower to deter further attacks. The ambush was sudden and unexpected. There was nothing suspicious about the car parked to the side of the road as Leo's small unit passed it. It didn't look suspicious and it wasn't parked illegally or awkwardly. The lady sat inside was waiting for someone (or so it seemed) and smiled politely as Leo walked past. When the patrol was approximately two hundred metres further along the street, the car sprang into action. It accelerated towards the patrol and as it passed them, the bomb inside the trunk detonated, killing the driver and all but two of the patrol (Leo being one of the two survivors). Leo's panicked calls for back-up were answered within minutes and the two survivors were evacuated.

It was at this point that Leo decided to go AWOL. He had seen four of his fellow soldiers immediately blown to pieces in a devastating attack. The fifth he wasn't sure would survive his injuries despite receiving medical assistance from Leo on the spot. Filled with rage, he dressed in civilian clothes, took only his sidearm and a single magazine of ammunition and headed back into Colby on foot. With what little money he had, he took a room at a local guesthouse and posed as a traveller forced from his home by the Reich. It didn't take long for rumours of the black man in Colby to circulate (as well as his reasons for being there in the first instance) and within a very short space of time, Leo had become acquainted with a small group of dissenters. Outspoken critics of the Nazi occupation and vocal supporters of the Liberty Front. Within a week, Leo had ingratiated himself within the group and eventually identified those responsible for carrying out the bombing of his unit and the death of his colleagues. Worryingly, Leo also became aware of a further plot to carry out more attacks on the Heer — who remained in the area providing support and reassurance to the local populous.

The group had tuned out to not be Liberty Front, but Leo was under no illusion whatsoever that they would likely align themselves to the group given half the chance. It seemed more like they were a very disgruntled group of townsfolk with minimal access to weaponry and technology yet they had enough to make a crude set of explosives and to arm themselves sufficiently so as to cause the Reich a minor headache. Leo had arranged to meet the group that night at the local bar after it closed its doors. An amateur move at best, Leo thought to himself. A more organised operation would at least have the sense to meet at a more covert and remote location. Nevertheless, he would have them where he wanted them. From discussions, he reasoned that there would be ten of them in total. A mix of men and women, most of them young to middle age. He would have to assess the logistics of what he was planning to do when he got there. So that night, he hid his sidearm in his belt under his shirt and set off to the bar.

He made a point of being late so he could gauge everyone's position when he arrived. They weren't happy and he apologised profusely. Disappointingly, he had miscalculated. There were twelve people. A minor inconvenience. His attack was over in under a minute anyway and left all twelve people dead. Such was his precision as a sharpshooter that not a single bullet had been wasted. He gauged almost immediately who was armed and who looked like they would pose the biggest problem and took them out first. A couple tried to rush him but he found himself able to despatch them without too much difficulty with his bare hands. The older members of the group came last and they offered little in the way of resistance. One woman had managed to flee the bar and was midway across the street. As Leo took aim at her back, he wasn't too sorry to see that she had run into the path of an oncoming car and was swiftly cut down and killed almost instantly. When the carnage was over, Leo checked each body. They were all dead but the noise had attracted the attention of others in Colby — as had the drama of the woman being run over in the street. It was getting risky to stay where he was so before anyone got too close to the bar, Leo fled out the back and into the dark.

He had been gone from the barracks little over a week and was immediately placed under arrest and detained. He was questioned rigorously by his commanding officers who also went on to investigate the incident in Colby. Those in command weren't necessarily sorry about what he had done that night but still, he had broken protocol. He had gone AWOL on a daring and foolish mission and would have to be punished.

His actions, however, had piqued the interest of Hermann Göring. The story of the rogue black soldier single-handedly infiltrating a militia and subsequently killing all twelve of them had spread like wildfire. Whilst many believed it to be nothing more than an elaborate fabrication, Göring decided he wanted to investigate it further and so found himself personally paying a visit to Kansas and the barracks where Leo Savoy was being detained. The black soldier impressed him immediately. Yes, he had defied orders, and in any other circumstances, this would have been an offence worthy of imprisonment. However, this was not any other circumstance. So angered had he been, he had single-handedly despatched an entire militia. What impressed Göring the most was his ability to infiltrate the group with such ease and in such a very short space of time in order to yield such results. He would be the perfect person to join the new ministry that he had been ordered to take the lead with. The main obstacle was the Führer. He would need convincing.

On his return to Germany, Göring met with Hitler to explain the situation in depth and how the black soldier's colour could, under these circumstances, work in the favour of the Reich as no one would possibly suspect a black person to be an undercover agent. To Göring's astonishment, Hitler was surprisingly agreeable to his suggestion, even going so far as to request to meet Leo Savoy in person. So it was that orders from the very top were made to have Leo Savoy released with immediate effect and flown to Berlin for an audience with Adolf Hitler himself. Whilst remaining relatively unfazed by most situations, Leo was filled with a sense of dread whilst stood in front of the Führer. He was significantly taller and broader than Hitler but was still intimidated by the smaller man who eyed him up and down with what seemed like a reluctant suspicion. He had remained stood to attention with his gaze fixed forward, being instructed to not make direct eye contact with the Führer under any circumstances whatsoever. He was joined by a young Italian soldier also under the radar of Göring as a potential member of the new ministry. Giovanni Zappa had too been eyed with steely suspicion by the Führer and had seemed equally anxious of the whole experience. Nevertheless, both men eventually met with the approval of the Führer and Göring vigorously shook their hands in delight as his new team was finally beginning to take shape as 1963 dawned.

In subsequent months and years, Göring's team began to grow as members from (mainly) across Europe and some from America were recruited into the IUI, all of whom possessed a variety of military skills and an exceptional track record in their field of specialism. Acting on intelligence, the IUI would skilfully infiltrate cells belonging to The Menorah or Liberty Front and live amongst them as one of their own, gathering ever more vital intelligence and then striking to destroy them as and when appropriate to do so. No matter how deep the IUI went, the leadership of The Menorah and the Liberty Front always remained oddly elusive and always just beyond reach. Hermann Göring passed away in 1968 but was replaced by Fynn Schmid — a former general within the Heer.

After carrying out numerous covert operations for the IUI across Europe, Leo Savoy was eventually deployed back to Eichmann's America where, by the mid-1970s, he had taken a step back from years of operational activity and begun to seek out newer, younger and fresher recruits. By being deployed to work inside München Towers Security (MTS) Ltd, Leo was able to meet and question potential former military recruits, who may be suited for bigger and better things. Upon receiving Mike Morgan's dossier, Leo was immediately impressed. A recruit to the Luftwaffe from a very early age with an impressive track record, he seemed like perfect IUI material. Looking deeper at his record, Leo could see that the pilot had already carried out bombing raids against Liberty Front targets. Therefore, he was unlikely to feel too bad about taking more of them out given half the chance. He could see that he had finished his military career working for Brunner's Ministry of Aeronautics and Weaponry, a somewhat specialist field which, although he knew relatively little of, recruited only the very best scientific and military minds. A rather prestigious role if ever there were one.

However, there was the abrupt end to his decorated career with a prison term for assaulting two police officers of the Reich. Initially, this had troubled him. After all, the IUI didn't want hotheads. It didn't want those who lose their cool at a moment's notice. So what was it that had made a normally rational, level-headed pilot break one officer's arm, as well as rupture his liver, and knock another one unconscious with the butt of a gun leaving him requiring ongoing medical treatment? Being in the position he was in, it didn't take Leo long to find out what he needed to know in terms of Mike Morgan's personal life and he was immediately sympathetic. He had married a mixed-race woman and had been defending her that night.

Leo understood immediately, for he had experienced exactly the same racial profiling and discrimination throughout his life, from childhood into his days in the Heer. If anything, this said to Leo that Mike Morgan was loyal at least. Honest as well, as indicated by the fact that instead of fleeing the scene and denying all knowledge, he had calmly put all weapons well out of harm's way and requested that one of the injured officers' radio their colleagues for assistance. Although injured, in agony and confused, the officer had willingly done just this while Mike Morgan went back to his car and sat in it patiently waiting to be arrested and dealt with accordingly, which he was. Although Leo did think that a helicopter and a total of eleven armed officers was maybe a little on the excessive side. To Leo, Mike Morgan ticked all the boxes.

Militarily skilled, able to follow and complete orders, knowledgeable, loyal and honest. Everything the IUI was looking for. As for the prison sentence? He figured he had gone AWOL years before and killed twelve people in the process. How was a four-year prison sentence much worse than this? Under the circumstances, it seemed almost justifiable.

So it came to be that Mike Morgan's questions were answered that day by the IUI representatives gathered in the house outside of Caspar and he gladly accepted his new position within the IUI. Within a few days, he had bid his tearful wife and daughter an emotional goodbye as he headed off on what would be his first assignment. He didn't know when he would be back but he knew that when he did return, he would be financially a lot better off. In fact, he didn't return until March 1977.

Hannah was elated to finally have her husband back. Physically, he had changed. He had lost a lot of his previous muscle mass in the months since he had been gone and he had grown a long beard that tickled her face when she hugged him. He was quieter as well. She assumed he was tired but at night he was distant and he would often lie in bed for hours simply staring at the ceiling, seemingly deep in thought. She knew he was forbidden to discuss his work and she wouldn't ask but she couldn't help but think that her husband was troubled or that something he had seen or done in his line of work had troubled him. She didn't know for sure.

By the summer of 1977, the couple had moved to a larger property. A house with a nice garden in a nice neighbourhood. Hannah didn't ask Mike how much he had been paid, but it was enough to maintain a much nicer life. The beard went over time and the weight went back onto his body, but he remained distant and almost trance-like at times which continued to worry Hannah.

In reality, Mike was troubled. Troubled by the very nature of his missions which involved him working hard to gain the trust of, often times, seemingly nice and normal people. Sometimes, the people he was tasked with pursuing and infiltrating were not as nice by any means but it bothered him considerably that he had to bring about the end of someone's life for simply having an opinion. It left him questioning his new role and whether it was what he really wished to pursue in the longer term.

As the months wore on, so Mike would be periodically called into action, never really knowing what he would be required to do or how long he would be gone for. Only knowing that whatever he was called to do, it would ultimately have to end in the killing of someone, whether that be by his own hand or indirectly via the hands of someone else in the IUI. As 1979 approached, rumours were becoming rife about the failing health of the Führer although Berlin refused to either confirm or deny rumours relating to this. As in European circles, concerns were also forthcoming in relation to the suitability of Hitler's successor, his son, and it was in August of 1978 that Mike was once more called back to the house in Caspar where a small team of IUI members had been assembled; some of whom he recognised, some of whom were not familiar to him. The meeting was being led by Leo.

"Gentlemen, thank you for coming. I know some of us have met, some of us haven't, so, for the benefit of everyone let's just do some brief introductions before we get going. You all know me, I'm Leo and this is…" Leo began to go round each member individually as a way of introduction, "…Terry Ostler; former Heer — British Territories, we've got Mike Morgan; Luftwaffe, Andras Varga; Hungarian Heer and Walter Huber of the Kriegsmarine. Gotta have at least one homosexual on the team haven't we!"

The joke directed towards the German mariner Huber made everyone laugh.

"Right, down to business, gentlemen. Now, as you probably all know, there's rumours that the old man is unwell and doesn't have long left. That's all they are. Rumours. Nothing more, nothing less. The problem is, we think the Front are going to capitalise on this in the coming weeks and start causing us a few headaches. Now, recently I've been in touch with police intelligence and we've got information coming in about the emergence of some new cells. I can't say how reliable the intelligence is at this stage but considering the current climate in Europe, I think we need to act and determine how reliable it is ourselves. And deal with it if there's a significant threat."

"Where are these cells, Leo?" questioned Varga.

"OK, like I say we've got a few so I'll be sending you each out to an individual area to do what you do best. Some of you, I've got a lot of leads for. Some of you, not as much and — if I'm honest — it could lead to nothing. In which case you'll be back for Christmas." The group all laughed again. "Some of you, don't get your hopes up for getting back before the end of the year. Anyway, let's take a look at where the intelligence is pointing us to."

Leo had preprepared a map of East America and had it hanging at the front of the room. He had taken the time to annotate the map to identify the locations of where the suspected Liberty Front cells were believed to be operating. He allowed the group time to examine the map and ponder before continuing.

"OK. So, the first one is here in Midland, Texas. Just outside of Odessa. We've got intelligence that would indicate movement of something (we aren't sure just yet) from the border with Mexico to the Gamblin district."

"When you say something, what do you mean?" asked the British man, Ostler.

"Honest answer? We don't know. Surveillance cameras along the road between Odessa and Juarez have been pinged one too many times for the police's liking. Same few vehicles each time travelling the same route going to the same place."

"What are we talking here? We talking cars? Trucks?"

"Well, that's why its suspicious. It's a set of three commercial vehicles. Travelling on false plates. Suspect maybe transporting arms from Mexico, maybe something else. Maybe nothing."

"Why have the police not pulled them?"

"They were told not to. If it's something weapons related, it's ours. The police would be too heavy handed. Ask Mike here, he knows all about that. By the time they had gone in, suspects would've moved out. Along with any weapons — if that's what it is. So it's one for us. And you know what Frank, I'm pleased you've asked so much about this one because it's yours. Get your bags, go to Texas, see you next year!"

Again, the room laughed at the sense of camaraderie amongst them. One by one, each member of the team received their own individual briefing but were also provided with a dossier relating to each individual case containing all the gathered intelligence on each particular location and — if available — photographs of suspects, vehicles or buildings involved. Mike was last to be briefed by Leo.

"OK, saving the best until last. Mike Morgan this is yours. Nice one for you. You're going to Iron Mountain Lake, Missouri. Heard of it?" Mike shook his head. He had never heard of the place. "Me neither until now. It's in the middle of nowhere but police have recorded reports of suspicious activity at a house near the lake. I don't have a lot to go on with this Mike. Let's take a look…" Leo began to flick through the few notes he had on Mike's case. Leo started to laugh sarcastically, "Wow. You got your work cut out for you here Mike. Reports of suspicious comings and goings. Suspicious vehicle stopped in the area, occupant behaving strangely and gunshots heard late at night."

"Is that it?"

"Afraid so."

The room began to erupt in laughter again.

"Why the hell has this come to us, Leo? I mean, seriously, why?"

Leo shrugged before responding, "I don't know Mike. I really don't. It could be they've had incidents in the area before maybe. It could be the fact it's such a remote location and they aren't used to people acting so strangely. I don't know is my honest answer."

"Leo, it sounds like a waste of time."

"Mike, I agree. I really do. But they've identified it as an area of interest, so…" Leo shrugged as if to say his hands were bound and there was nothing he could do about it.

"Well, all right. I'm coming for you if I'm not home for Christmas."

The room all chuckled again before taking their dossiers and leaving to prepare for their missions. When he arrived home, Mike read the dossier in as much detail as he could but couldn't identify anything that jumped out of any particular interest. In his mind, he suspected it would be nothing more than a wild goose chase. Suspicious people, suspicious vehicles and shooting in the middle of the night. Sounded like any rural place in East America to him. If the Reich were going to pay him to sit out in the countryside for a few weeks though, who was he to complain?

The following day, he bid Hannah and Rebecca goodbye and set off on the long journey to Missouri. He made sure he had packed everything he needed and had retrieved a particular set ID documents from his safe. Produced by the Reich they were virtually fool proof, only detectable as fakes by those with significant expertise. As soon as he set off on his journey, he was no longer Mike Morgan. For the next few months, he would be Bernard Garcia.

21

IRON MOUNTAIN

As in Europe, the news of Adolf Hitler's death broke in East America on the morning of Monday 29th January 1979, and just like in Europe, much of the country was in mourning over the news. The occupants of the house on the northern shore of the Iron Mountain Lake, however, were not. While there were tears, they were tears of joy as an elderly, balding and bespectacled Adolf Eichmann delivered a solemn address to the nation across all television channels on the morning of the 29th January whilst also declaring a period of national mourning. The occupants of the house hugged one another in joy and shouted in celebration at the news of the death. Bernie Garcia was amongst them and had been staying in the house for some weeks now. He had been awoken by the celebratory noises in the house that morning and immediately joined in with the jumping and shouting and even managed a few celebratory tears of his own. Mike Morgan had mastered his act during his time with the IUI and had managed to successfully convince his hosts he was Bernie Garcia from a very early stage.

Mike had arrived in Missouri towards the end of the previous August 1978 and immediately headed to a motel on Highway N, approximately one mile from the Iron Mountain Lake. He checked in as Bernard Garcia and handed over all the necessary documentation that was checked and cleared without any difficulty. On his first full day in Missouri, he decided to trek over to the Iron Mountain Lake to begin to survey the situation concerning the house on the northern shore. The lake was easy to find as was the house — the very same house identified in his intelligence dossier. Following the shore of the lake to the south in order to avoid detection, Mike took up position on the eastern shore approximately half a mile from the house and (under cover of the surrounding foliage) surveyed the property and the surrounding area through his binoculars. It seemed as though a family lived in the house: a woman, a man and their two young children. They seemed happy and looked innocent enough from a distance but he knew he would need to wait this one out if he were to identify anything of any suspicion and worthy of a follow up. Mike noticed that the northern shore ascended up into a wooded hillside. This would make a better observation point and it also faced onto the rear of the house, which might provide a better insight into any activities of a questionable nature.

Returning to his motel the same day, and gathering together everything he needed for a few nights in the woods, Mike set off again back towards the lake the same evening — but under the cover of darkness. He wouldn't need much and he was well trained to survive in the wild for a prolonged period of time. What he did take with him was disguised as fishing equipment so he would not arouse any suspicion from the proprietor of the motel as he headed out again. The evening was warm and after a few hours of careful trekking, Mike had found a perfect position on the hill, above the lake house, where he could carry out more in-depth observations.

Over the next three days, Mike captured everything he needed to. For the most part, they seemed like an ordinary family. The lady, who he assumed was the mother, would leave early each morning taking the children to what Mike assumed was school. The children would return — with the mother — later in the afternoon. In between the children leaving the house and returning again, the two adults didn't seem to venture very far too often. At first, Mike struggled to really ascertain exactly why this had been flagged up by police intelligence and considered the whole concept of police intelligence somewhat of an oxymoron. On his third day of surveillance, a vehicle drove up to the lake house along the narrow road on the western shore of the lake. It was a utility truck and two rather large burly looking men were within it. They appeared to be good friends with both occupants as when they arrived at the house, there was much hand shaking and friendly hugging. On checking the plates, this was the vehicle mentioned in his intelligence dossier, the one reported as acting suspiciously in the area. On the outset, there was nothing visibly suspicious but Mike's interest was somewhat piqued by the removal of a large trunk from the rear of the truck. It was lugged by the two men into the house and no one was seen again for a few hours. Mike waited and watched intently.

Later in the day, the woman disappeared as usual to go and collect the children. She was usually gone for at least an hour. As soon as she left, the two burly men and the male occupant of the house brought the trunk out to the rear of the property. Out of sight of prying eyes — or so they thought. Mike was positioned perfectly to now watch their every move and after three days, he was finally watching something potentially noteworthy. As the trunk was opened, the male occupant of the house looked inside and started nodding approvingly. He then reached in and removed what turned out to be one of the many automatic weapons inside. Jackpot! Mike began snapping away with his camera, zooming in as closely as he possibly could to get some good shots of the weapons. He could see why they had arrived with a trunk now as not only had they arrived at the address with automatic firearms (including what looked to Mike to be military grade assault rifles), but a wealth of ammunition, and most worryingly, what looked like shoulder-mounted surface-to-air rocket launchers. Enough to take on a small army. The sparse intelligence initially presented to Mike was now all falling into place. As the woman returned to the house with the children along the same track on the western shore of the lake, the men packed away the newly delivered arsenal and it was placed in a large wooden outhouse to the very rear of the garden of the property. The door was locked and shortly after, the two burly men left the lake house in the utility truck.

Mike pondered over his next move. This was certainly a situation worthy of infiltration, there was no doubt about this. Before he moved to this stage though, Mike wanted to know more about the two burly looking men and their utility truck. More so in terms of how much of a threat they would pose to any future action he took. Mike figured that anyone able to acquire such a hoard of advanced weaponry would likely be very unsavoury, probably quite dangerous too. Figuring them out would determine any next steps taken.

For now, he had had enough so he left his hilltop position and headed back to the motel. On his way back to his room, he had a quick chat with the proprietor who keenly enquired about how his fishing expedition had gone and how the lake had never been the same since the two atomic bombs years before. What *had* been the same since that happened? In the dimly lit motel room that night, Mike carefully developed the photos taken earlier that day and hung them up to dry once removed from the trays of developing fluid (that he had brought with him as part of his work). The latent images became visible and Mike was pleased with the results. The faces of all three men were clearly identifiable as was the utility truck and its plate. Pleased with his work, Mike took a warm shower and settled down for the night.

The following day, Mike enquired with the motel proprietor where the nearest police precinct was located and was informed that there was a sizeable headquarters in the town of Bismarck, some six miles to the north of the Iron Mountain Lake so he proceeded there. When he arrived, he presented his IUI identification card to the counter clerk and requested to converse with someone in the intelligence department. His identification was scanned to confirm who he was and the clerk immediately telephoned through to Lieutenant (Lt) Daniel Paris, the chief officer in Intelligence. Lt Paris welcomed Mike into the department placing himself at his disposal. Mike presented the photographs of the three men he had photographed the previous day and asked Lt Paris if he knew who they were and if he had any previous intelligence pertaining to them. As well as possessing fingerprint technology, the Reich was also a world leader in facial recognition software, and after scanning all the pictures, it didn't take long at all to ascertain who the men were and to recover all previous information held against them.

The three men it turned out were related. The two burly men were brothers. The other man in the house was their cousin. The files printed out made for interesting reading.

MISSOURI STATE – REICH POLICE OF EAST AMERICA – NOMINAL DATABASE

Nominal ID	122776Y
Name	HOWARTH, Clayton Robert
Alias	Clay, Robbie
DOB	21st October 1929
Current Address	No fixed abode
Previous Addresses	3456 Rhodes Dr, Glendale, MO, 64222-6574 (Aug 63 – Sep 76) 32 Hanson Way, St Louis, MO, 63122-342 (Mar 51 – Jan 63) 161 Garrison Pkway, Branson, MO, 65322-999 (Oct 41 – Jul 50)
Convictions	3rd July 1945 – assault with a weapon. Fine and warning 14th August 1945 – assault with a weapon. 6 months youth detention and rehabilitation. 23rd February 1955 – theft from store and assault of Reich officer of East America. 4 years detention and rehabilitation. 17th September 1966 – assault on police officer whilst drunk. 6 years detention and rehabilitation.
Intelligence (starting with the most recent logs)	**457654** – February 2nd 1978 – driver of 510HJC with passenger nominal 239877J (HOWARTH, John Ryan). Unable to explain where they were heading or where they had been. Aggressive to police when stopped. Believed false plates. **443654** – January 15th 1978 – seen associating with nominal 8765123F (GEORGE, Reginald Arlo), believed involved in illegal activity within and around border of Mexico. No stop. Intelligence purposes only. **399765** – November 1st 1977 – passenger in 510HJC. Vehicle spotted near Mexican border, El Paso, TX. Travelling alone. No stop. Intelligence purposes only. Believed false plates.
Associates	HOWARTH, John Ryan (brother) GEORGE, Reginald Arlo (friend/associate) NEAL, Edward James (cousin) PHILBY, Patrick Finlay (friend/associate) HOWARTH, June (wife – believed deceased) HOWARTH, Andrew Morgan (father – believed deceased)
Vehicles	510 HJC Mercedes M150 pick-up truck (1974) – driver and passenger

MISSOURI STATE – REICH POLICE OF EAST AMERICA – NOMINAL DATABASE

Nominal ID	239877J
Name	HOWARTH, John Ryan
Alias	JR, Johnny, Johnny-Ryan, Big H.
DOB	22st March 1932
Current Address	Not known
Previous Addresses	11 Harris Av, Glendale, MO, 64222-6523 (Jul 60 – Oct 73) 765 Jefferson Park Blvd, St Louis, MO, 63122-312 (Feb 55 – Jun 60) 161 Garrison Pkway, Branson, MO, 65322-999 (Oct 41 – Jul 50)
Convictions	1st January 1952 – assault and battery. 6 months detention and rehabilitation. 18th April 1954 – assault and battery. 9 months detention and rehabilitation. 21st February 1961 – assault of Reich police officer. 2 years detention and rehabilitation. 8th July 1969 – theft from store. 6 months detention and rehabilitation. 3rd November 1971 – criticism of the Reich. 6 months detention and rehabilitation. 9th December 1974 – criticism of the Reich. 6 months detention and rehabilitation.
Intelligence (starting with the most recent logs)	**457654** – February 2nd 1978 – passenger of 510HJC with driver nominal 122776Y (HOWARTH, Clayton Robert). Unable to explain where they were heading or where they had been. Aggressive to police when stopped. Believed false plates. **433229** – June 16th 1976 – associating with nominal 358912H (NEAL, Edward James). Questioned by police outside Red Harris Bar and Grill, MO. No explanation given for being in area. Advised to return home. HOWARTH was aggressive towards police. Approach with caution. **246235** – July 27th 1972 – spotted entering Burns Motel, El Paso, TX with nominal 122776Y (HOWARTH, Clayton Robert) and believed PHILBY, Patrick Finlay. Entered 13:11 departed 13:44. Non are local to El Paso.
Associates	HOWARTH, Clayton Robert (brother) NEAL, Edward James (cousin) PHILBY, Patrick Finlay (friend/associate) HOWARTH, Andrew Morgan (father – believed deceased)
Vehicles	510 HJC Mercedes M150 pick-up truck (1974) – driver and passenger

MISSOURI STATE – REICH POLICE OF EAST AMERICA – NOMINAL DATABASE

Nominal ID	358912H
Name	NEAL, Edward James
Alias	
DOB	16th June 1945
Current Address	The Lake House, Iron Mountain, MO, 64322-1276
Previous Addresses	Not recorded
Convictions	Not recorded
Intelligence (starting with the most recent logs)	**433229** – June 16th 1976 – associating with nominal 239877J (HOWARTH, John Ryan). Questioned by police outside Red Harris Bar and Grill, MO. No explanation given for being in area. Advised to return home. HOWARTH was aggressive towards police. Approach with caution.
Associates	HOWARTH, Clayton Robert – cousin HOWARTH, John Ryan – cousin
Vehicles	Not recorded

Mike had obtained what he needed and what he was reading would be plenty enough to determine his next move. The Howarths seemed like the ones to watch. Between them, they had racked up a range of convictions — mostly for violent offences, some against officers of the law. At least Mike had one thing in common with the brothers. Uncorroborated intelligence of them making trips to and from the Mexican border could possibly explain the trunk of weaponry. Mike thought back to the meeting he had sat in on in Caspar. Frank Ostler's assignment was related to potential gun running across the Mexican border, it wasn't entirely inconceivable that what was happening at the Iron Mountain lake house was linked to this. Only time would tell. Edward Neal had a lot less against his record and certainly nothing of a criminal nature. Just one intelligence log linked to his cousin.

Mike thanked Lt Paris and kindly reminded him that he was bound by the Secrets Act and under no circumstances was he to divulge any information relating to the conversation they had just had or the information passed over to him. This was duly acknowledged. The two men shook hands and parted company. Before leaving, Mike enquired with the clerk at the front desk where the nearest fishing tackle shop was and he was directed accordingly.

The fishing tackle shop wasn't too far from the police precinct and Mike purchased everything he needed. He could now fill his bags with actual fishing related paraphernalia, not with all his surveillance equipment. Back at the motel, Mike placed his Reich ID documents into the safe located in the room and replaced them with all identification relating to Bernard Garcia. He arranged his fishing equipment for the following day, plotted a route back to the lake, went for a five-mile run, showered and went to bed.

He rose early the following morning and ate a small breakfast of slightly stale blueberry muffin (from the small convenience store adjacent to the motel) and a marginally tepid coffee. He then drove back to Iron Mountain Lake but this time, he located the narrow track on the west shore that, if followed for long enough, would lead directly to the lake house. The entrance to the track was off Parkway Drive and was signposted as a private road. He already figured this but he ignored it and carried on anyway. Once onto the track and driving parallel to the lake he slowed to a crawl before identifying an area where he could not only park his car safely (so as to not obstruct the track) but also in an area where he could access the banks of the lake with ease. It was here that he got out and began to set himself up for a day's worth of fishing. He had fished once or twice when he was younger but had never had much luck. Oklahoma's radioactive dust storms had done little for the wildlife in the area. It was a quiet day and he was far enough from any major highway to not be disturbed by the rumbling of vehicles. The air was still, the occasional bird flew overhead, the even less occasional fish leapt from the water before splashing back down. For somewhere so lush, it surprised him at how quiet and devoid of significant life it seemed to be. He made sure he had parked his car in such a way that it would be perfectly visible to anyone driving down the track — a deliberate and intentional move.

He sat fishing all morning but it remained quiet by the lake. The woman (whose name he still didn't know) left the lake house at her usual afternoon time. It seemed as though she hadn't spotted Mike on her way out but on her way back an hour or so later, she shot him a brief and curious glance. He remained in position wondering if anyone would come to investigate; no one did. As the evening began to set in and the light started to fade to give way to darkness, Mike packed up and headed back to the motel.

He did exactly the same the next day although, this time, he found a spot a little further along the track — ever so slightly closer to the house. He also set up earlier, in the hope the woman would maybe spot him on her way out in the morning. She never appeared though and Mike figured she had perhaps set off earlier than usual and he had missed her. Nevertheless, he set up his fishing equipment and settled down for another day. It was early in the afternoon that he heard a vehicle rumbling down the track, from the direction of Parkway Drive. As it approached, Mike could hear that it was a heavier type of vehicle, something larger than a car. His assumption was correct and in fact, it turned out to be the Howarth brothers in their utility truck. Unlike the woman who had not spotted Mike the first time the previous day, the brothers spotted Mike immediately and slowed the truck to a crawl. Mike couldn't tell which brother was driving. There wasn't much of an age difference and looks wise, they looked similar with long straggly beards and large portly frames. The Howarth brother in the passenger seat eyeballed Mike intensely as the truck passed him by. Mike raised a hand in acknowledgment and smiled politely before the utility truck sped off up towards the lake house.

The truck returned about thirty minutes later and this time, the driver eyeballed Mike who, again, smiled and waved politely as they passed him by. He had been noticed three times now. This was good, this was what he wanted. If this didn't elicit the reaction he was after, he would come back again tomorrow but this time set up position even closer to the house. He needn't have worried himself because within an hour of last seeing the Howarth brothers, Edward Neal had come along to investigate the mysterious fisherman who had set up at the side of the lake.

He was a small man (in comparison to his brutish looking cousins). He was thirty-three-years-old and wore a casual cotton shirt, blue jeans and had fair hair, combed neatly and parted to the right. Unlike his cousins, Edward Neal's approach to the stranger was a little friendlier — if not still a little suspicious

"Hey. How you doing?" he asked politely as he approached Mike.

"I'm good. How are you?"

"Yeah not so bad thanks. You do realise this is private property?" Edward Neal had now stopped next to Mike who remained seated.

"Is it?" Mike said in mock surprise.

"Afraid so. There's a sign at the start of the track back there. Maybe you missed it."

"Ah gee. I'm so sorry. I didn't realise. The guy at the motel said there was a lake nearby I could fish, I just assumed it was here. I'm so sorry. Listen, give me a minute and I'll be on my way. I'm so sorry."

"Hey, look, no worries. You take your time."

"Thanks."

Keeping his act up, Mike began to clumsily pack away his gear giving Edward the impression he was feeling embarrassed at having being caught out fishing on private property. Mike had to work quickly yet carefully so proceeded to keep the conversation going.

"I've travelled all the way down from Columbus for a bit of a break."

"Is that right? You're a long way from home."

"Yeah. Nowhere to fish up there these days."

"Yeah?"

"Well, not since the bomb. Place is becoming more and more of a wasteland thanks to those Nazi bastards." There was silence. Mike carried on packing up. "Sorry, forget I said that. I shouldn't have... sorry."

"You don't have to apologise," Edward replied. "You're not the only one who thinks the same, trust me. Before the war, this lake was full of fish. Now? You're lucky if you catch a car tyre, let alone a fish. You notice how quiet it is round here?"

Mike actually had noticed this (with the exception of the occasional bird and singular splash in the water of the lake).

"Yeah I did notice."

Edward came in closer, seemingly quite keen to tell Mike more. "Before the war, you wouldn't have been able to hear yourself talk over the sound of the birds. Look at it now…" He cast his gaze out across the silent lake and the surrounding area.

Mike paused in thought and the two men remained silent momentarily. "You grew up here then?" Mike asked.

"Sure did. Iron Mountain born and bred. I mean, not the house up there but the area yeah. My wife inherited the house. From her father. He passed some time ago now."

"Nice and out the way I guess."

"You bet."

"Out of the way of those Nazi bastards right? Am I right?"

Edward looked at Mike and started to laugh. "Yeah plenty out the way." There was another pause before Edward continued. "So what brings you all the way down to Missouri?"

It was serious cover story time for Mike. "Well, truth be told, I got into a little difficulty with… them. You know, Nazi police. I won't go into it. It's a long story but—"

"I've got all day," Edward interrupted.

Mike hesitated, again in mock reluctance at having to tell the story to Edward. "Well, they pulled me over one night for speeding and got a little, how shall we say, heavy handed. Trouble is, for them, I got a little heavy-handed back and they came off worse!"

"For real?" Edward sounded genuinely surprised.

"Yeah. So, anyway, I'm getting out the way for a while. Wait for the heat to die down and then I'll head back. Problem is, Columbus is crawling these days with Reich. There's no escaping it. At least not in the big cities."

Edward nodded silently in agreement before rejoining the conversation. "So you here alone?"

"Yeah, just me."

"What about family or job back in Columbus?"

"No family. Well, I mean, just a brother back in Columbus but we aren't too close. I'm just living off my Heer pension these days."

Edward looked shocked and almost taken aback by what he had just heard from the fisherman and Mike saw this and raised his hands as if to placate Edward who he had clearly just shocked by mentioning he used to serve in the Heer.

"It's OK," Mike said reassuringly. "I was discharged years ago. Injury. Anyway, for what it's worth, they were some of the worst years of my life."

This seemed to calm Edward down who became visibly more relaxed. "You had me worried for a minute there."

"Sorry, didn't mean to worry you. It's a chapter of my life I'm not particularly proud of to be honest. I saw things that no man should see."

"Things? What sort of things?" Edward asked quizzically.

Mike took a deep breath and exhaled loudly, appearing to Edward to be uncomfortable at the prospect of having to discuss a past life. His act was good and upon seeing how uncomfortable Mike looked, Edward immediately apologised.

"I'm sorry, that was intrusive of me. I'm sorry."

"No, no, it's fine. Let's just say I saw the Reich do things that nobody should ever see. And you know, I'm grateful for the pension and all that. But I'm not sad to no longer be a part of it all. Anyhow, I've troubled you for long enough. I'll be on my way."

Mike started to make his way back to his car, all the while waiting in anticipation. He loaded the trunk and was about to get in and drive off when Edward spoke to him again.

"What's your name?"

Mike turned to face Edward. "Oh, I'm Bernard. Bernard Garcia. Everyone calls me Bernie." He extended his right hand and likewise Edward extended his and the two shook hands.

"I'm Edward Neal. Look, I'm sorry if I was a little abrupt with you."

"Hey, no bother."

"How long you in the area for, Bernie?"

"However long it takes for the Reich to get bored of trying to find me I guess. Or until they do find me. Either way. And as long as the pension keeps coming."

"Why don't you drop by the house later? I live just at the end of this track. Come and meet the wife and kids. Seems to me you've had a bit of a rough time of it recently, plus, I feel bad for kicking you out when all you were doing was trying to fish."

Mike was hesitant but again, it remained part of his act. "I don't know. I don't want to intrude. What will your wife think? Bringing some strange guy into your home?"

"You're not a strange guy. I know your name and you know mine. Besides, she'll understand."

"What about them other two guys in the truck?" Mike was of course referring to the Howarth brothers.

"Oh them? They were just visiting. So? What do you think? Come by later, say seven o'clock? I'd feel bad if you didn't."

Mike thought on it for a few more seconds before responding, "All right, seven o'clock it is."

That evening, Mike smartened himself up ready to go to the lake house. His mission was only just beginning and he had to tread carefully. If Edward Neal and his cousins were indeed Liberty Front, getting in would not be an easy feat. He had to sweet talk them and continue to try and convince them that he was a disgruntled former Reich soldier, traumatised by what he had seen forces of the Reich do, and on the run from the police for assaulting two heavy handed officers.

At the lake house, Edward Neal spoke to his wife when she returned from the school run. Carmen Neal was intrigued by her husband's encounter by the lake, yet also cautious.

"Are you sure about this, Eddie? We don't even know this guy."

"I know, I get that and I understand why you might be a bit worried. All I'm saying is, let's get him over and you can see for yourself what you think. If you think there's something not right, we leave it there. End of."

"I just don't get what you think is so special about him, that's all."

"He's ex-Heer. He'll have skills. Military skills and we need people like that. All that stuff out back that JR and Clay brought over? A lot of that is wasted on us. Give that stuff to a soldier though?"

"Ex-soldier."

"OK, ex-soldier but we need people with that sort of experience if we're going to stand any hope or any chance of even moderate success. And I think it's worth a shot."

"And have you spoken to JR and Clay about this?"

"No."

"Do you think you should?"

"I will, if or when the time comes. For now, they don't need to know."

Carmen was still not entirely convinced but she trusted her husband implicitly. She greeted Bernie Garcia into her home at seven o'clock that evening. He was dead on time and well presented. He had even bought the family a bottle of wine, not a cheap one at that. Bernie Garcia was polite and charming and a perfect gentleman. She found him to be a physically attractive man and could see that he was physically fit (as a military man would likely be). He remained reluctant to go into great depth about his days in the Heer but they were able to ascertain that he was medically discharged after seven years after suffering an injury whilst on duty. Since then, he had lived in Columbus, Ohio (happy to live off his Wehrmacht pension which proved more than generous). As the drinks flowed, so everyone's tongue began to loosen and it became clear that Bernie, Edward and Carmen all shared a common dislike and distrust of the Reich. Even though Mike was feeling the effects of the alcohol, his guard never dropped and he remained in character throughout. By the time the evening was over and he had left, Carmen was feeling more positive about her husband's new friend. Mike had told the Neals where he was staying and that he would be there for a little while longer and they agreed that another meeting should be forthcoming.

After drinking a little too much, Bernie bid his new friends goodnight, left his car parked outside of the lake house and staggered home. The motel wasn't far and it was a nice evening for a walk. Besides, he wanted to leave his car with the Neals. He knew full well they would probably, even as he walked back to the motel, be checking it out and doing a search on the plate. He had deliberately left the car doors unlocked in anticipation of them searching the vehicle for anything that would identify him. They would find exactly what they were looking for. A driving licence in the name of Bernard Garcia from Columbus, Ohio. He also knew that this information would no doubt be escalated to a higher power within the Liberty Front and that they too would perform further checks on Bernard Garcia. Like The Menorah in the British Territories, the Liberty Front had their methods and ways of finding out what they needed to. But it would all check out. Bernard Garcia would be exactly who he had said he was and an outstanding warrant for his arrest was in circulation for the former solider currently living on a Reich military pension now hiding out in rural Missouri.

Mike arrived back at the motel and slept heavily that night, satisfied that he had done a convincing job in the role of Bernard Garcia. The following day, he walked back to the lake house to retrieve his car. No one was home but an envelope had been left pinned to the front door with a handwritten note in it apologising for not being there and indicating that the key was in the envelope, which it was. He sat in his car and opened up the glove compartment. Without a second glance, he could see that his belongings had been tampered with as they weren't positioned in exactly the same place he remembered deliberately positioning them. They had done exactly what he suspected and hoped they would do. As he drove back to the motel, he knew the ball was now very much in their court. He would not initiate any further contact. He would wait for them to contact him — should they wish.

As he drove off, Edward and the Howarth brothers watched him leave from behind a curtain in one of the top rooms in the house.

"You sure about this guy, Eddie?" Clayton Howarth asked his cousin.

"Yeah. I think he'll come in handy, Clay. Real handy. Also, leadership says he checks out."

22

BISMARCK

The celebrations at the Iron Mountain lake house went on into the evening of the 29th January 1979. The Howarth brothers joined the Neal family (and Bernie Garcia) in the late afternoon and much alcohol was consumed. Such was the remote nature of the lake house, there was no danger of their party being discovered by the police. If it were, no doubt the punishment would be very harsh indeed, after all, mere criticism of Hitler would meet with a mandatory prison term so who knew what having a party to celebrate his death would result in?

The Neals had two children: nine-year-old Daisy and six-year-old Clarence. They both took to Bernie from an early stage. He had engaged with them both beautifully and proved himself to be a natural around children. Carmen remained surprised that he had never managed to find a life partner of his own and settle with children but he brought it down to his traumatic time in the Heer and fear of his own mental suitability to commit to a long-lasting and loving relationship. Carmen did not probe any further but willingly allowed Bernie to engage with her own children who had grown fond of Bernie, over time, and he of them.

Exactly as he hoped, Edward Neal made contact with Bernie again within a few days of his first visit to the lake house. He called the motel Bernie was staying in and once again invited him over to visit; an invite that Bernie duly and graciously accepted.

Over the following weeks, he was able to find out a little more about the Neal family. The lake house had belonged to Carmen's father, who had been a school teacher. Carmen's mother had died shortly after she had been born, leaving Carmen as an only child to be raised single-handedly by her father. She always knew the lake area as a quiet place and struggled to picture how it was the way her father had described it — bustling with life. By all accounts, Carmen's father had witnessed the decay of the area as a result of Der Befreier I & II and it also seemed as though he too eventually succumbed to years of exposure to the toxic air drifting across the country. When he did pass, the house went to his only daughter, Carmen, and now acted as an idyllic family home at the shore of the lake. Carmen did not work, a decision both her and her husband had made when they decided to have children.

Edward, however, worked from the lake house as an accountant, managing a variety of books and accounts for several small business owners in the area — one of whom was the proprietor of the motel Bernie had stayed in upon his arrival in the Iron Mountain region. It was only in the weeks following the end of the Iron Mountain mission that Mike found out Edward Neal had been skimming money from his various clients over a period of many years in order to finance his other less desirable activities — charging for services not required or carried out seemed to be a recurring theme on analysis of his financial records.

It was some weeks into his relationship with the Neal family that Bernie was finally introduced to the Howarth brothers for the first time. They weren't likeable or particularly welcoming but all the same, Bernie smiled politely (as he had done when they passed him fishing on the lake) and shook their hands. Neither said a lot to him at first but would just glare at him with nothing more than utter contempt. Edward was apologetic, bringing his cousin's behaviour down to a severe mistrust of anyone with any links to the Reich. After all, they had both had enough experience of the Reich and therefore had collectively enough reasons to loath anyone remotely associated with it. As time wore on, they became marginally more friendly towards Bernie but he still felt as though there was a distinct lack of trust.

By the end of 1978, Bernie had become well and truly incorporated into the Neal family. He had been invited to reside at the lakeside house, which was large enough to have a self-contained annex. Initially used for Carmen's elderly father in his final years, it was no longer being used and was offered to Bernie at a cheaper rate than the motel he had been staying in. The biggest breakthrough came in December of 1978 when Edward and

Carmen sat Bernie down one night and cautiously explained their involvement in the Liberty Front. Bernie sat and listened carefully before finally saying how pleased he was to have found this out and that in many ways he had suspected, based purely on their dislike of the Reich and everything associated with it. What pleased Bernie even more was the invitation to join the Liberty Front and become one of their operatives. Bernie had wept tears of joy and hugged both of them exclaiming how honoured he would be to be part of the organisation.

Under the guise of Bernie Garcia, Mike Morgan's mission was going exactly as he planned. His hosts had eventually confirmed their involvement in the Liberty Front and had also shown him the trunk full of weaponry. Bernie had stood over it in mock awe and the haul had actually been considerably more sizable than he had initially thought when he was perched atop the hill in the early stages of his mission.

In December of 1978, Edward, Bernie and the Howarth brothers had taken a long drive into the Missouri wilderness, miles from any known civilisation and away from prying eyes. With considerable expertise, Bernie had demonstrated how to use some of the weapons and showed off his military skills, which only further served to solidify his reputation within the small cell. The Howarth brothers were physically large and strong, there was no denying that. However, their skills with a range of weapons remained limited. Bernie took great pleasure not only tutoring them on how to handle and use a range of assault weapons, but also putting them through a rigorous set of military-style drills until they could barely move, such was their exhaustion. He remained cautious in relation to trying to ascertain where the weapons had originated in the first instance but after several discreet enquiries, he did eventually come to the conclusion that they had indeed come from somewhere and someone in Mexico, smuggled underneath the giant border wall through an elaborate set of tunnels constructed deep into the Mexican side of the border, and equally deep into the American side.

As 1979 dawned, Bernie saw the new year in with his friends at the lake house but Edward had become distracted. Bernie had noticed him taking increasingly frequent private phone calls that he would answer in his study area. A hushed discussion with his wife would usually follow and Bernie also locked onto the fact there was a safe in Edward's study room that he would see him regularly going in and out of. Bernie was skilled in many things but cracking a safe was something he was not trained to do. The Howarth brothers still paid regular visits in their utility truck to the lake house. They remained stand-offish with Bernie but had begun to converse with him a little more over time.

A week before the death of Adolf Hitler was announced, Bernie told the Neals he was going to take a trip into Bismarck to purchase some new fishing equipment. It wasn't questioned by anyone so he set off. Instead of heading to Bismarck, he actually headed towards Belgrade where there was a diner (just outside of the town) on old Route C. He was pretty sure he hadn't been followed but took all the necessary precautions ordinarily undertaken to shake a tail. He didn't think Edward or Carmen would attempt to follow him, but the Howarths? The air of mistrust between them made Bernie wary that they may attempt such a tactic. Bernie found the diner easily enough and pulled into the carpark. As he entered, he immediately spotted Leo who was sat behind a table at the other end of the diner nursing what looked like a coffee.

The two men hugged each other; it had been some time since they had seen or communicated with one another. It drew some disapproving glances from the few patrons in attendance but they didn't care. Bernie was, for the first time in several months, now back to being Mike Morgan of the IUI. The two men talked at length. Leo listened intently as Mike explained everything he had discovered. He had retained the photographs of the Howarths (hidden out of sight during his time with the Neals) and now presented them to Leo, accompanied by their respective intelligence and criminal records. Mike explained to Leo about the cache of military grade weapons and his suspicions that they had been run from the border with Mexico. He also explained about the tunnel network mentioned to him but was unable to identify a specific location as this had not been divulged to him at any stage.

"Don't worry about the tunnels, Mike. As you know, we've had Ostler looking into the Mexican connection so that's one for him. These names on the intelligence — Philby and George — well, Ostler has his eye on them and we're sure they're involved in something tunnel related. I will tell him to leave your Howarth boys alone though, should they venture down that way again. They're for you to sort out and I think we need to keep them in circulation and figure out what they're up to in this part of the country."

"There's something else going down too."

"Go on."

"Ed's been talking to someone on the phone. I don't know who but something about it isn't sitting quite right. He's also putting something into a safe. Could be nothing but…"

"What does your gut tell you, Mike?"

In all his years of experience, Edward's activity indicated only one thing to Mike — that it was suspicious and he rightly said so before adding, "Trouble is, there's no way I can get into that safe in the study to see what he's trying to hide."

Leo pondered for a little while thinking over the direction the operation could take from here. It seemed to both men that something less than desirable was brewing, and they had to find out what it was.

"Can you get a bug into the study, Mike?"

"Yeah, I don't see why not."

"All right. I think that's the next step. We need to figure out who he's talking to and about what. Have they given you any idea about who's giving the instructions?"

"No. Nothing. From what I can gather, access to the leadership circle is only granted to a certain few. I may be a part of the Front, I may have trained those asshole brothers how to use a gun, but I haven't carried out an operation for the cause. Who knows how long I could be in there for before I'm given access to the leadership."

"So, you've not heard any names?

"Sorry, Leo. These guys are tight-lipped. They're discreet and they're good at what they do and at covering their tracks."

Leo pondered for a few more seconds. "All right. I'll get the technical guys to check out the telephony. See if we can trace who's calling and from where. In the meantime, get a bug in that room and monitor the chat. Could be they're under orders to carry out an operation. Certainly seems as though there's some kind of mobilisation going on."

"Leo, one more thing."

"What is it?"

"They have children. Two of them. They aren't involved in this in any way. Whatever happens, I don't want them hurt. I can get them out of there if needs be."

Leo nodded in agreement and appreciation for what Mike was saying. "It's fine. You don't need to worry about that."

With that, the two men parted company once more but not before Leo returned to his car in order to retrieve a bugging device and associated equipment for Mike to plant in Edward Neal's study room. When he returned to the lake house, he was once again Bernie Garcia. The two children were home from school and ran to greet him with great big smiles on their faces. He had grown very fond of the children, and deep down, was desperately worried about what their ultimate fate would be. He had, however, raised his concerns with Leo and at this point, there were more pressing and urgent matters to attend to.

That night, Bernie crept out from the confines of his annex at the lake house and made his way to Edward Neal's study room on the ground floor of the house. It was into the early hours of the following morning, and all had been quiet within the house for some time now. Edward never locked the door to his study, he had absolutely no need to, for he trusted everybody in the house implicitly, Bernie included. The bugging device was a small receiver, that was easily attachable to the underside corner of Edward's desk. It would remain there undetected for the duration of Bernie's stay and the battery was such that it would no doubt last even longer than this. The advances of Reich spying technology were as advanced as its weapons programme and world-renowned. It was an easy enough task completed within a matter of minutes. No one would ever know that Bernie had even moved from his room that night. To accompany the receiver was a small ear piece that Bernie ensured remained on his person at all times. At the first indication of Edward taking a phone call, all he would need to do was place the earpiece in and he would be able to hear everything that was being said.

He had to wait a little longer than he had originally hoped for the first call (after the bugging) to come through. It was shortly after the announcement of the death of Adolf Hitler that the telephone rang and Edward excused himself and made off into his study to take the call. Making his own excuses, Bernie made his way outside indicating he was going to take a walk around the lake. As he left the house, he inserted the ear piece and began to listen intently to the conversation Edward was having with whoever had called him.

"...I understand, I do think we should wait a little longer though. His death will have put them on higher alert than usual... no, I see... in principle I agree, but Clay and JR have both checked it out. I mean, they've been in there themselves enough times in the past. So they know the layout but apparently the outside has reinforcements and... yes, I know there's no guarantee of that but unless you can send us reinforcements... Bernie? I'm not sure he's ready. We usually give the new operatives at least a year before their first mission, to be sure they're ready... Yes... Absolutely, his skills are second to none. He had Clay and JR working up a sweat anyway... It's the missiles... they're the ones... yeah... he's the only one of us with any experience and it's those we need to use if we're to do a frontal assault on the building otherwise we're just shooting into a brick wall which would be... and... he..."

Bernie had walked a little out of range and was losing reception so he turned and walked back towards the house, stopping and looking over the shore innocently while he listened on to the phone call — the reception remained a little sketchy.

"...I'll get it looked into and we're heading for end... mo... and we'll see if... I'll discuss with... and... we'll... Tomorrow..."

The transmission then cut off altogether. The conversation hadn't given a great deal away but it had given away enough for Bernie to conclude that an attack on somewhere was indeed in the pipeline but he still had many unanswered questions: where was the target? Who was the target? When was this scheduled to take place? It was the following day when Bernie decided to once more take a trip to Bismarck for more 'fishing equipment'. Whilst in the town, he located a public telephone box and — after once again making sure he had not been tailed — made a call to Leo on a secure line to relay the intelligence he had gathered from the bug. Regrettably, there had been no success on tracing the origins of the phone call to the lake house. The Front had scrambled the line, although the technical staff at the IUI were unsure exactly how they had achieved this, making it untraceable. Bernie had made the deduction that it was the Front leadership Edward had conversed with and clearly, they were taking all necessary precautions from their end to avoid detection.

The instruction from Leo was clear. Wait it out a little longer and try to ascertain what, if any, the potential target might be. It had become clear from the intelligence gathered from the call that in ordinary circumstances, newcomers to the Liberty Front were not afforded the luxury of operational duty for at least a year after officially joining. Would Bernie's military skills and positive impression in terms of his military style and abilities negate such a long probationary period? Bernie thought long and hard over the subsequent days about what he had heard and what he could deduce from the conversation. With only hearing one side of the chat, and with the intermittent reception, it wasn't an easy task. It was something or somewhere the Howarth brothers were familiar with. They apparently knew the layout and it was somewhere they had visited often enough in the past. It was also likely to be reinforced and a frontal assault of some description required (possibly with the shoulder-mounted missiles from Mexico). It wasn't easy but Bernie deduced that it was possibly a police precinct that was being referred to. He knew the previous records of the Howarth brothers and knew that they were no strangers to the law and had indeed notched up several dealings with the police between them over the years. After referring back to each intelligence record acquired from the Bismarck station, there was a trend. The arrests would have resulted in a period of short detention at the same station. In Bismarck. Was this the target? Had the brothers deliberately committed a string of minor (yet arrestable) offences in order to gather their own intelligence on a specific Reich target? He felt as though it was all becoming a little clearer, but he needed that confirmation — enough to be sure. He needed more intelligence of his own. Also, would Edward make an approach of assistance to Bernie in order to help operate some of the more advanced weaponry required? When was the deadline to complete any potential operation? Frustratingly, the transmission from the bug had cut out when it seemed as though this may have been revealed. If the plan of this cell was to be thwarted, Bernie needed to know this.

After pondering over the recent events, Bernie made the decision to turn his attention to the Howarth brothers. Bugging them was not an option. From each of their records, it was difficult to ascertain an exact location or fixed abode for each brother or indeed which one would be best to bug, or even if both of them could be bugged. Further to this, he had not built up anywhere near the same level of trust with them that he had with the Neal family, so getting close enough to bug them would be incredibly difficult. He could tail them though. From the phone call he had monitored, JR and Clay had 'checked it out' so maybe they would check it out again? Whatever 'it' was. Bugging was not an option, tailing them was certainly on the table. However, another problem was presented as he didn't know for sure where they lived so where would he pick them up from? Tailing them from the lake house would be too obvious. He knew they always travelled together in the same vehicle. Options were to wait for them on a local highway or, if Bismarck was indeed the target, could he wait it out for them there? Waiting by the side of the highway could be risky. They knew his vehicle and it would be incredibly likely they would spot it. Maybe waiting it out at Bismarck would be the better option?

Bernie didn't make a decision immediately but instead, sat tight and waited for whoever had called the lake house to call again. But no call came. The Howarth brothers still periodically visited but any discussions still did not include Bernie, and Edward still did not make any approach to him asking for any assistance militarily or otherwise. As time pressed on, it seemed to Bernie as though his probationary period may indeed be extending to the full year but he didn't have that much time.

With not much else to currently work with, Bernie made the assumption that the deadline for whatever was being planned would be the end of February so without further ado, he decided to set up some surveillance of the Bismarck Police Precinct. Edward and Carmen didn't seem suspicious when Bernie explained that he had to leave for a few days and return (with some caution) back to Columbus. His brother had become ill. It looked like a radiation related illness and certainly bore all the hallmarks of it. He seemed genuinely upset but promised to keep in touch and that he would return as soon as possible. Edward and Carmen urged him to be careful with a reminder that he was still a wanted man but Bernie seemed defiant and certain that, with the recent death of the Führer, the authorities would be distracted with other matters. So off he set, back to Columbus, Ohio to visit his gravely ill brother.

Arriving in Bismarck, Bernie went straight to the Parkway Hotel in the downtown area. He chose this particular location due to the private underground parking lot attached to the hotel. He wasn't far from the lake house and had to keep his car well out of sight. Everything he did from here on would be done via foot travel only. Bernie checked into his room, although he didn't anticipate using it a great deal. As the sun was beginning to set, Bernie set off to the Bismarck Police Precinct. It sat on a busy road and indeed, as per the phone call, it was more heavily fortified than it had been the last time he had visited. Metal railings were erected at the front of the building meaning no one (with the exception of the extra armed personnel) was able to get within about ten feet of the main entrance — or indeed access any part of the front of the building. The few steps leading up to the main doors of the police precinct were being guarded with a walk-through metal detector placed at the very foot of the stairs. In addition, anyone wishing to enter the building was being directed via a one-way system that would navigate them around the metal barricades in place, through the metal detector where a couple of armed officers would await with a fingerprint scanner to cross-reference any details returned with any identification papers. It seemed security in the centre of the town was certainly more prominent but this was to be expected given the recent news. It had been a long held belief that dissident groups would likely take advantage of any instability caused by Hitler's death — which wasn't too far from the actual reality of the situation.

Opposite the police precinct (and on crossing the busy main stretch) was a row of store fronts: a mini-market, a small diner, an electronics store and a dentist. Bernie stepped into what looked like the most central to the police precinct, which happened to be the diner. An old portly gentleman stood behind the counter at the diner and politely greeted Bernie as he walked in. After enquiring, Bernie was informed that he was indeed the proprietor (a Mr Phillips) and he promptly closed the diner when shown the Reich ID. Upon request, Mike was shown the upstairs of the property which was a vacant apartment now full of boxes and other items clearly in storage. At the window looking out into the street, Mike spent some time looking up and down. Coverage was perfect. It was a dead straight road and he would be able to see anyone or anything approaching from a distance. The view directly outside the diner onto the sidewalk was also more than adequate. This location would be perfect. Mike sat Mr Phillips down, who then listened intently as Mike explained that he would be using the apartment above the diner for an indefinite period of time. Mike reassured

Mr Phillips that he would not be seen and that his business would not be affected in any way whatsoever. In return, Mr Phillips was not to discuss Mike's presence in any shape or form to anybody, for fear of reprisals from the Reich. Mr Phillips had lived long enough and seen enough to know exactly what Mike meant and so he calmly (and honestly) agreed to comply with Mike's instructions. Later that evening, Mike returned with his surveillance equipment (disguised in his fishing bag) and began to set up in his new home above the diner; and so began another long haul surveillance operation to determine if the Bismarck Police Precinct was to be a target of the Liberty Front.

Being a military man, as well as a member of the IUI for a number of years, he figured that if the Howarth brothers were carrying out their own surveillance, it would likely be in the evening and night time hours when the streets were quieter and there were fewer prying eyes. So he restricted his rest periods to short naps during the daylight hours. He had received enough training in the past to cope with minimal rest. Any other time, he remained with his gaze fixed out into the street and the police precinct opposite. The Howarth brothers did not disappoint. As he correctly predicted, they made their first appearance into the twilight hours of Mike's second day of observation. Their utility truck rumbled past the police precinct at around six thirty p.m. and Mike sprang into action, furiously snapping away with his camera and zooming in and out to capture as many images as he could. The truck indicated to turn right into one of the streets off the main drag where it performed a U-turn and pulled up on the same side of the street as the police precinct about two hundred metres from Mike's position.

Zooming in and out using his camera, Mike could get a decent enough view of the brothers and what they were doing. It seemed as though they were heavily in discussion with one another and pointing and gesticulating towards the precinct. At times, they both looked on thoughtfully; other times they seemed locked in discussion or debate. About what though could not be determined. On that first evening, they stayed in position for about twenty minutes before making a slow drive past the precinct and heading off. It appeared to attract little attention. The brothers returned (discreetly) another three consecutive evenings at roughly the same time. On each occasion, they would pull up at the side of the street, far enough away so as to not attract any attention from the precinct and each time they would remain in position discussing something. Only twice did the brothers exit the vehicle. The first time, JR crossed the street and walked slowly along the sidewalk before stopping opposite the building (almost underneath where Mike was positioned). He leant himself up against a nearby lamppost, giving the impression he was nothing more than an innocent civilian casually waiting for someone. Mike snapped away furiously at JR. He didn't stay long; only for about five minutes. Any longer and he risked attracting the wrong sort of attention.

When JR returned to the truck, he could see the brothers were once again discussing something and Mike was frustrated that lip-reading was not amongst one of his skills. The second time one of the brothers exited the vehicle was the following evening. This time it was Clayton and Mike was stunned to see him enter the one-way system of metal barriers as if to attempt an entry to the building itself. Mike was so taken aback by Clayton's actions that at first, he genuinely thought the brazen brother was about to launch a solo attack. He leapt from his observation position by the apartment window and rummaged in his kit bag for his sidearm, his intention to put a stop to Clayton. When he glanced back out the window to see the progress Clayton had made, he could see that he had been stopped at the metal detector. Mike waited. The armed guards were remonstrating with Clayton, and although he couldn't hear exactly what was being said, he could hear that their voices were raised. They were clearly arguing about something. After a few seconds, two of the armed guards grabbed an arm each and forcefully ejected Clayton away from the steps of the building. Clayton turned around, flipped them a finger and uttered a profanity of some description before walking back in the direction of his brother in the utility truck.

Mike breathed a sigh of relief, stood down and resumed his position. He watched as the utility truck once more took a slow drive past the police precinct and disappeared into the night. This would turn out to be the last time the brothers visited the location. Mike assumed that Clayton's attempts to get into the building were more of an attempt to gauge the level and effectiveness of the heightened security situation, which he had managed to achieve successfully. After two further nights of inactivity, Mike decided to return to the Iron Mountain lake house to see if there had been any further developments of note. He sensed that whatever was being planned by the cell was getting ever closer, and as the month of February wore on, he could feel an ever rising sense of urgency in his latest mission.

He hadn't utilised his room a great deal at the Parkway Hotel in downtown Bismarck. Only the secure parking lot to make sure his car remained well out of sight. On the morning that Mike left the apartment above the diner, he thanked the proprietor and once again reminded him of his obligation to not discuss his presence with anyone. He then put all of his equipment back into the trunk of his car, checked out of the room he had hardly used and headed back to the lake house. Edward was not in when he returned but Carmen was. She didn't question Bernie too much and could see that he was clearly a little upset that his brother had passed away the day before and that he was sad that he couldn't hang around in Columbus for the funeral, such was the situation regarding his outstanding arrest warrant. She allowed Bernie to quietly retreat to his annex. She would leave it for her husband to discuss the finer points of the operation when he returned with his cousins later that day.

23

THE MORALITY OF WHAT WE DO

"I'm sorry Eddie, I'm not having that. I don't agree!" JR Howarth shouted angrily at his cousin who by now was despairing.

"We set ourselves a target of the end of the month and they won't be happy if it isn't done by then."

"I don't care. The leadership can damn well wait. I don't want him involved."

"Jesus! Why not JR?"

"Because I don't trust the son of a bitch. Plus, ain't it meant to be a year before anyone new is considered for operational duty?"

"Ordinarily yes but—"

"But nothing, Eddie. That's final."

There was a pause in the heated argument that was taking place. Edward and his two cousins had met up in a bar not far from Bismarck, away from prying eyes, to discuss the upcoming operation; however, discussions were not progressing as well as Edward would've liked at that stage.

"What about you, Clay?" Edward questioned the other cousin. "What do you think about him?"

Clayton sat and stared up at the ceiling in thought, clearly pondering over how to respond, "I gotta admit, I'm not wild about the guy. But I see why you wanna use him. He's got experience, I'll give him that much, and hell, we could do with that." Clayton turned to directly address his brother.

"JR, you telling me you're gonna use them missiles without blowing yourself to shit?"

"How difficult is it? Put it on your shoulder, aim and fire."

"Oh right," his brother came back, "that goddamn easy is it? We got two missiles, JR. That's it. Two. We ain't got time to be going back down to the border to get the beaners to give us more. Plus, we ain't got the funds. What if you screw it up? Shooting those things? What then JR? You shoot them things into the sky and not into the front of that building, then we are dead. All of us."

JR didn't verbally respond but continued to shake his head in disagreement.

"Look," Clayton continued, "we saw it ourselves last week. They've upped the security. There is no way in hell we're getting anywhere near that building just us with guns in our hands. They gonna cut us down before we even get close. Now, blow the goddamn front off the place with them missiles? Who gonna be the sitting ducks then?"

"He's got a point," added Eddie.

"I just don't understand why they want it done now. Why now Eddie? Why can't it wait until the heat has died down?"

"I don't know, JR. And that's not my decision to make either. You know that. Either way, I think the only way to get in and do what we got to do is to blow the front off the building. And for that I think we need Bernie."

JR remained silent and was clearly furious with the prospect of allowing Bernie to have any involvement in the operation.

"Look, JR, I take responsibility. I invited him in, it's all on me and I'll explain this to leadership."

JR thought it over for a moment longer before knocking back his drink in one gulp, slamming the glass back down onto the table and getting up to leave.

"I don't like it, Eddie. I don't like it one little bit. It's on your head, all of it. Just you remember that."

JR then left the other men sat at the table and he exited the bar. The other two took JR's reaction to be a reluctant approval of Bernie being involved in the operation. Little did they know that JR's instincts about Bernie were indeed correct.

That same evening, the moment Bernie had been waiting for finally came. Edward sat him down and explained that they were going to carry out an operation. The target? The police precinct at Bismarck. All the evidence Bernie had tirelessly gathered was beginning to finally piece itself together. His months of hard work were reaching fruition. Bernie sat and listened calmly and quietly as Edward explained in detail what the plan was. He had allowed Bernie into his private study (the same room Bernie had bugged) and retrieved a set of documents from the safe (the same one Bernie had always been unable to access). It turned out Edward had been storing blueprints of the precinct. Detailed floor plans of the entire structure. In theory it was a simple plan.

The concrete building was only accessible to the front. The rear was made up of a separate and secure police parking lot, fenced off and an extra barrier to have to penetrate. Entering via the front entrance was the only viable option. Once in, take out the bottom floor through a lightning fast armed assault. Take them fully by surprise to maximise the number of casualties. Easy in theory but the increase in security at the front had caused a problem. Leadership (whoever this was) were unwilling to reschedule. They wanted it done. Edward continued to explain that in order to penetrate the front of the building, they wouldn't be able to shoot their way in. They would have to blow their way in and they needed Bernie's help to do this. Edward explained that even if the building was not so heavily fortified, they would probably still need his help. His experience with the smuggled weapons was invaluable. They simply could not afford, under any circumstances, to waste the precious missiles that they had acquired and they would prove instrumental in the success of the mission. Bernie agreed to help without hesitation.

The following evening, the Howarth brothers came over to the lake house and all four men convened in the study area to begin discussing and finalising the logistics of the operation. The date was finalised as the night of the 26th February 1979. The group would drive to Bismarck and position the utility truck approximately two hundred metres from the station. Bernie would exit the vehicle with the surface-to-air missiles. These would be disguised in a large backpack to avoid arousing suspicion. Once positioned opposite the station, Bernie would launch one missile at the front of the building, no doubt sending the security into mass confusion (if not killing them first). The second missile would serve to blast a large enough hole in the front of the building to allow access to Edward and the brothers. The launch of the second missile would be the cue for the other three men to speed towards the scene in the utility truck.

Under covering fire, from Bernie, the assault on the building would begin in earnest. The plan from there was to enter the building. Theoretically, there would be minimal resistance at this stage as it would have been blown to pieces already. The police building was two storeys and Edward and Bernie were to clear out the ground floor with the Howarth brothers making their way up the stairs to deal with whoever was on the first floor. Maximum casualties, maximum impact. Another blow to the Reich's continued presence in America.

Upon exiting the building, they would make off in the utility truck which would be destroyed at a location to be determined. It was already on false plates, which would make it difficult to trace its precise origins. The Howarths knew full well that intelligence would likely link them to the truck (when located after the operation in its destroyed state, which it inevitably would be) but their alibis would be watertight. There would be enough evidence and witnesses to link them to a location far away from Bismarck. To their knowledge, the truck had been stolen.

On the 23rd February, Bernie found himself at the diner outside of Belgrade again having contacted Leo on a secure line. Here, he presented all his evidence and findings to Leo who looked through it all approvingly.

"Mike, this is great. You've done a great job. As always!"

"Thanks."

"This will save a lot of good lives. Plus, we've got more leads on the Mexican connection so we'll hopefully be shutting that down within the next few days. No more guns in tunnels. Philby and George will be apprehended in due course. So, you'll be setting off at about ten p.m. on the 26th?"

"That's right. With a trunk full of smuggled weapons."

"I need to get final authorisation from Schmid but I can't imagine there'll be an issue so we'll come along and meet you at the house on the 26th. How does that sound?"

"Look forward to it."

And so the 26th February came round and Edward, Bernie and the Howarth brothers readied themselves to set off on their mission. The day itself was quiet and nondescript. Carmen left the house in the morning to take the children to school and returned shortly afterwards. Edward and Bernie took a leisurely walk around the perimeter of the lake. He had spent many months with the Neal family and had missed his own terribly. Like any other mission, he had been unable to make any contact with Hannah or his daughter. While he was on a mission, he had to emotionally detach himself from his family at the risk of compromising the very fabric of the operation. On any given mission, he had to constantly remind himself that he was not Mike Morgan; he was always someone else, whether that be Bernard Garcia or some other Reich fabricated identity. As much as the occasional loneliness bothered him, he had little choice. Other employment options had remained non-existent and his longing to provide a good life for his family and secure a financially viable future for his daughter outweighed the sacrifices he had to make in order to achieve this. Physically and mentally his missions were draining. He would always be physically and mentally exhausted at having to maintain his act for such a long period of time and while at first, the ultimately bloody end to any mission never bothered him too much, he was beginning to tire of the violent endings to his missions. Often at his own hand, sometimes at the hands of others.

His time with the Neal family only served to bring forth a feeling that had, up until that point, remained relatively dormant. One of guilt. Some of his assignments had been alongside people who remained thoroughly unlikeable on every level. Much like the Howarth brothers. But this assignment was different. The Neal family were likeable. Edward was a gentle and otherwise placid man and his wife even more so. They were, to the untrained eye, a normal and loving family. Both law abiding and upstanding citizens of the Iron Mountain community and well known and equally liked within the community. On the outset, it never would've been obvious or conceivable that either would be capable of committing the atrocity they were about to commit. Then there were the children. Mike had never been on an assignment that involved children. The Neal's loved their children and it was obvious that they wanted nothing but the best for them and their future. They were kept well away from the dodgy dealings going on at various hours of the day and seemed to be almost blissfully unaware of what their parents were doing. Mike had grown fond of the children and had started to look upon them almost as if they were his own. It was almost as if he had let his emotional guard drop. The one barrier that helped to keep each assignment in perspective. This troubled Mike greatly and he often thought to himself, what would become of the children when this was all over? From what he could ascertain, there were no other family members close by who would take them in the aftermath. So what then? Were they destined to spend the rest of their childhood in some grim Reich orphanage alongside all the other orphaned children of Liberty Front members? Would they even stay together? Or would they be torn from one another in yet another cruel twist of fate? It remained an unknown.

Over time, Mike had also formed a close bond with Carmen. He didn't want to and under other circumstances this may not have happened but he shared a lot in common with her. They were mutually attracted to one another and Mike would often wonder what things would be like for them in a different life. Their respective pasts were also remarkably similar and equally tragic. Carmen had grown up in the Iron Mountain lake house with her father, who succumbed to debilitating cancer as a result of the radioactive fallout that swept across America in the years following the war. She had watched the health of her father gradually falter until he was no longer able to care for himself adequately. The lake and the surrounding area used to be full of so much life: birds singing, the lake almost bursting with fish, deer roaming wild. Now, the area was a shadow of its former self. Even Mike had picked up on this in the early days of the Iron Mountain operation. The animals were the first to go and Carmen remembered seeing dead fish floating atop the lake and washing up on the shores, only to be picked apart by scavenging animals who themselves would end up sprawled out dead on the track leading to the lake house. The trees suffered next, shedding their leaves at irregular times and becoming discoloured as the radiation drifted in from the east. Over the years, the trees recovered but the wildlife was still a shadow of its former self. A cruel legacy created by an equally cruel regime. In his guise as Bernard Garcia, Mike never revealed the true nature of his past but he sympathised greatly with Carmen, for his own past was similar in so many ways. The lasting legacy of the atomic bombs was something that would live with him forever. He had seen his father take his own life, his mother slowly succumb to radiation sickness and what should have been a prosperous farm rendered virtually worthless, only to be acquired by the Reich for a pittance of what it should've been worth. Deep down, Mike knew this was morally reprehensible but the great Reich and how it fought to free the world from oppression was all he knew. Why would he want to ever be so critical of it? His position with the IUI had afforded him a different perspective on the state of Eichmann's

America, and as he penetrated deep into the heart of the Liberty Front, he was beginning to see a different side to the story. People driven to commit horrific acts through desperation. People driven to commit such acts through hatred of the Nazi regime and the atomic legacy left behind after the war.

Mike had often reflected on the flight he did when he was a member of the Luftwaffe that took him over New York. As eerily beautiful as the devastation had been, he wondered to himself how many people in the city were just ordinary people like his parents or Carmen's parents? How many of the people wiped out within the blink of an eye had been simply going about their business, having no political allegiance or involvement whatsoever in the war raging in other parts of the world? How many of those people truly deserved to die? As his emotional guard had slipped during his time at the lake house, so he thought more and more about these things. All the missiles he had fired, all the bombs dropped. All the lives he had taken. Who were they really? Were they people like Carmen and Edward? His missions left him increasingly quizzical and seriously questioning his own future role within the IUI.

Daisy and Clarence were put to bed at their usual time on the 26th February. Shortly after they retired, the Howarth brothers arrived and the men began to ready themselves for the mission. They were all dressed in military fatigues and had balaclavas ready to ensure they kept their faces hidden from view. The trunk with the weapons was hauled into Edward's private study area (away from the children and far enough away so it would not wake them up) and they began to sort the weapons and accompanying ammunition. Bernie was tasked with looking after the shoulder-mounted surface-to-air missiles and was also armed with a machine gun and a sidearm. Enough to blow open the front of the police precinct and contribute to the subsequent assault. Leo and the rest of the IUI had been tipped off and had liaised on Parkway Drive approximately thirty minutes before Edward, the Howarths and Mike were due to set off. They had shut Parkway Drive in both directions and operatives had been positioned discreetly around the perimeter of the house to seal off every escape route. An aerial presence was considered but in such a rural space, this was deemed too much of a risk, potentially inadvertently revealing the presence of the IUI. As Leo and his team got into position, the weather decided to take a turn for the worse, the clear night sky clouded over and a thunderstorm began to sweep through the Iron Mountain area.

As the thunder erupted in the night sky, Mike began to feel apprehensive. He was pleased the children had been put to bed. While he doubted they would remain asleep through the ruckus of IUI agents storming the lake house, he could at least try to make sure they stayed out of the way (in his capacity as an insider). His heart sank as both children came downstairs, frightened by the thunderstorm that had started. By this time, all weaponry required had been loaded into the utility truck but the children were confused as to why the men were all wearing military-style clothing. They didn't question Edward's explanation that they were heading out to the lake for a spot of night fishing. Mike glanced at his watch. The IUI would be arriving within minutes and the children were not supposed to be there. Carmen had gone to the kitchen to go and warm them both some sugary milk in an effort to settle them back down again, and while Edward and the Howarth brothers talked, Mike followed them into the kitchen. As he followed, he glanced out of the front window that looked across the lake and track leading to the house. Headlights had appeared in the distance. It was them. The other men hadn't noticed yet, but they would before too long. He had to move fast in order to make sure the children were out of harm's way. Carmen had gone to the refrigerator which was in a smaller utility area beyond the kitchen. The children were sat patiently at the kitchen table waiting for their mother to return. Mike went into the utility area and took Carmen by surprise.

"Bernie! You made me jump," she chuckled at the surprise of him suddenly appearing.

"Carmen, you need to get the children back upstairs. Now."

Carmen looked at Bernie and could see the urgency in his expression but was simultaneously confused. "Why?"

"Please, Carmen, just get them upstairs. Right now."

"Bernie... I... don't understand. What's going on?"

In the distance, the engine noises were getting closer and the other men had also picked up on their presence and were beginning to question what was going on. As they got closer, the sense of rising panic in the house was palpable, and as the realisation of what was happening began to unfold,

Bernie and Carmen could hear the men running into the study area in order to retrieve some of the remaining weapons from the trunk.

Without any further warning, Mike said to Carmen, "I'm sorry."

He then quickly swivelled her round and placed her in a choke hold, sending her to floor unconscious (yet unharmed). Without further ado, he rushed back into the kitchen to retrieve the children who were becoming frightened at the events unfolding metres away from them. He took each one by the arm and pulled them along through the living room. By this point, the living room was being pelted with bullets as the IUI had taken up position outside and started peppering the front of the house with lead. Although, unbeknownst to Mike at the time, this had been largely in response to JR Howarth who, in his heavy-handed way, had charged outside and opened fire on the IUI convoy before they had even come to a halt. Mike and the children all ducked as the bullets whizzed past and embedded into the interior walls of the house. Shards of glass and woodwork splintered around them as they tried desperately to avoid being hit. Edward and Clayton had taken up position by the now completely smashed front window and were firing out towards the convoy who had set up spotlights that had rendered both men virtually blind.

Mike was halfway up the stairs with the children when the stun grenade came through the window. The flash of light and the bang knocked them all down as they climbed the stairs and momentarily blinded and deafened them. The effects of the grenade sent Edward and Clayton sprawling across the carpet clutching their heads in agony, leaving them lying amongst the detritus blown onto the floor from all areas of the house. The children were in shock, not knowing what was going on and all were left disorientated. Mike and the children lay on the stairs for a few seconds and as Mike's senses gradually returned, he could hear the sound of shouting and footsteps coming from outside. The IUI were coming in. Time to get moving again. He grabbed both children and half dragged and half led them into one of the bedrooms and placed them into the bed. They were both clearly visibly distressed so Mike tucked them both in under the duvet and gently reassured them that they would be all right and there was no need to worry.

The shooting downstairs had come to a halt and all that could be heard was the rain rattling on the roof as it continued to fall heavily outside. Mike closed the door of the bedroom and made his way down the stairs to survey the aftermath of the raid. As he proceeded down, one of the masked agents spotted him and swivelled round pointing his gun at Mike.

"Don't you fucking move! Show me your hands. Now!"

Leo marched in behind him and lowered the man's arms. "Lower your weapon, he's one of us." The man did as he was instructed to do by his superior and continued to secure the area. "You OK, Mike?" Leo questioned.

Mike breathed a sigh of relief. His mission was at an end, "I'm good. The children…" Mike trailed off and indicated to Leo with his head that the two children were upstairs somewhere to which Leo acknowledged.

"OK, we'll send someone up."

Clayton and Edward had by this point been bound on the floor amongst the glass. He could see Clayton was particularly bloodied and he assumed had taken a bullet (maybe two) but couldn't see whereabouts he had been struck. Edward looked relatively unharmed and the agents had located a still unconscious Carmen in the utility room. She too had been bound and was being dragged out by two of the agents. Both Edward and Clayton had seen Mike descend the stairs and the realisation that he was in fact an infiltrator was beginning to sink in.

"You bastard," Edward sneered. "You bastard! We trusted you. Brought you into our home and this is what you do?"

Mike didn't respond as Clayton decided he also wished to chip in. "We shoulda listened to JR. He knew this fucker was no goddamn good." Clayton then turned his face up towards Mike. "I'll kill you, you hear? I'll kill—" He was abruptly cut off as a hood was placed over his head and tightened at the neck.

Edward and Carmen were afforded the same treatment and all were dragged outside and forced to kneel at the foot of the steps in front of the house as the rain continued to fall all around them.

JR was dead and sprawled out awkwardly in a heap at the front of the building. The back of his head was missing and it was clear that he had been despatched quickly. Mike wasn't too sorry. JR had remained suspicious and hostile towards Mike throughout and Mike remained under no illusions that JR would potentially show little hesitation to kill even perfectly innocent people if he had to. Mike had always suspected an element of psychopathy about JR. Not so much his brother but JR was a nasty piece of work who would've probably ended up dead eventually, irrespective of whether the mission to storm the precinct had gone ahead or not. The IUI agents had swarmed all over the utility truck and had begun to retrieve the cache of weapons (as well as those weapons left over inside the trunk). Leo and Mike walked out of the house together.

"Good work, buddy," Leo praised Mike as they walked out. "How are you feeling? Pleased it's over?"

"You bet."

"Well you did a great job. We'll get everything we need retrieved from the house and then we can organise a debrief. There's nothing more you need to do now."

Mike said nothing as he was contemplating. He had saved the lives of countless individuals. He had brought down a terrorist cell from the inside. So why was he not feeling good?

"Why don't you go wait in the car, Mike? Take a moment. Looks like you need it."

Mike proceeded to the lead vehicle in the convoy and took a seat in the passenger seat where, through the rain, he looked on at the house and the family he had called his own for so many months. The rain obscured his view as it ran down the windscreen of the car but he could see that the remaining three adults were all kneeling on the ground next to one another, hooded with hands firmly bound behind their backs. There they remained under the careful guard of two IUI agents. After a few minutes, another IUI agent exited the house with the children. He was holding each one by the hand and gently guiding them out of the front door. Mike was relieved. He had managed to get them out of the way and they had not seen much of the carnage unfold. Unfortunately, they had to walk past a very dead JR. Maybe they wouldn't realise it was their parents who were kneeling bound and hooded? Either way, they would be taken from the scene to the safety of another location.

What came next horrified Mike beyond words. The children were positioned next to their parents and with a shove made to also kneel down. The flash of light and the crack of gunfire took even Mike by surprise as the two guards standing over their prisoners opened fire, and without any further warning, cruelly killed not only Edward, Carmen and Clayton but also Clarence and Daisy bringing his mission in Iron Mountain to an abrupt, unexpected and traumatic end.

24

PUT TO THE TEST

The men who had met in the remote house in Caspar in August 1978 had all completed their missions by early 1979. As March came around, it was decided to come back together in the same location to discuss their next assignments. All men had returned from their missions triumphant in their respective success. The gun running operation from Mexico (and the associates of the Howarth brothers — Philby and George) had been shut down and the tunnel network destroyed. This would be a massive blow to the military capabilities of the Liberty Front. An attack on a Reich police precinct had also been foiled. Something that would've been facilitated through the use of the smuggled weapons from across the border. Everyone was very much wallowing in their own crapulence; all except Mike Morgan.

Mike had returned home to Hannah and Rebecca after his mission in Iron Mountain and had hugged them both so hard and wept uncontrollably. Part of it was the sheer relief at seeing his family again but a larger part was his sadness and despair at seeing two innocent children shot in front of his very eyes. Their only crime? Guilt by association. Something that they didn't ask for and a fate that they certainly did not deserve. Still loyal to the code of the IUI, Mike did not discuss his mission and Hannah did not ask but she could see that her husband was troubled. Very troubled. More troubled than he had been on his return from previous missions. He would not sleep but simply gaze into space. He was quiet and clearly struggling to engage with his daughter. He would disappear for hours on end as he walked and walked in quiet contemplation of what he had experienced and witnessed in recent months; continuing to question the morality of what he was doing.

Mike had remained distant from his colleagues in the IUI. He didn't know who had shot the children or who had ordered it. He suspected it was an order that had come from higher up than Leo but he wasn't certain. As well as being grief stricken beyond words, he was angry, and in a way, almost wished he knew who had been responsible for giving an order to execute two innocent children. Why had Leo not stopped it? He had expressed his concern over the safety of the children and it seemed that Leo agreed with his concerns, at least at the time. Or was this just an act? A way to keep Mike comfortable in the operation that he had made so much progress with over the months. He assumed he would never know. When the call came to reattend the house in Caspar in March 1979, Mike set off. Albeit with reluctance.

It was the same troupe as before at the house and Mike was the last to arrive. The men were all chatting and exchanging various tales and stories of missions gone by and they all seemed happy and comfortable enough in one another's company. It seemed very much like a celebratory event and several beers were being exchanged amongst the group of men.

Leo greeted Mike as he walked in, "Here he is! We've been waiting for you. Grab yourself a beer. Just having a quick catch up before we get started."

Mike retrieved a beer and was approached by Walter Huber, the former member of the Kriegsmarine who Leo had joked about the last time the men were together at the house.

"How you doing, Morgan?"

"I'm good, Walt. How are you?"

The two men exchanged pleasantries and began chatting casually. Mike didn't know Huber all that well. He had had a few dealings with the Kriegsmarine during his training and his sessions involving the choppy waters of the English Channel but beyond this, he hadn't dealt with them much at all. Huber, it turned out, had commanded a fleet of warships and was held responsible for coordinating a long term mission to stamp out the illegal running of weapons across the Gulf of Mexico from Central America to Liberty Front sympathisers in mainland America. While much of Central and South America remained under the rule of strongmen fascist dictators, weapons smuggling remained big business and while there were still people prepared to pay for the weapons, so the business continued to thrive. Assigned to help put a stop to it, Huber led a small fleet into the Gulf to hunt down the smugglers. Possessing a brilliant strategic mind, this was achieved, as was the shelling of Liberty Front positions along the Texan coast (dropping points for the smugglers). Huber's actions were believed to have severely compromised the capabilities of the Liberty Front, certainly in the southern states, and had also brought him to the attention of Hermann Göring's successor in the IUI, Fynn Schmid. Recruited to the IUI in 1974, the forty-year-old Huber proved to be a valuable and loyal addition to the team although, he continued to miss his home country of Germany and one day longed to finally retire to the land of his birth.

Leo joined them after a while. The last time Leo and Mike met was shortly after the Iron Mountain mission was brought to a conclusion. Mike had been debriefed and the mission finally signed off. All evidence from the lake house was collected, the weapons and the safe (as well as its contents) retrieved, and from what he understood, the house was subsequently destroyed and the land acquired by the Reich in a final message and blow to the leadership of the Liberty Front who undoubtedly would find out before too long what had happened.

Mike seemed distant with Leo who picked up on this and expressed concern for his friend and colleague.

"What's up, Mike? Everything OK?"

Mike hesitated. Everything was most certainly not OK and it hadn't been OK since the conclusion of the Iron Mountain mission.

"We need to talk, Leo."

"Sure. Walt, excuse us for one moment, would you?"

The two men stepped outside of the house. It was a beautiful spring day and the sun felt warm as they stood outside in the fresh air.

"When I met you that day in the diner outside of Belgrade?" Mike questioned. "Do you remember that conversation?"

"Erm, yeah I remember. Why?"

"What did I say about the children?"

"The children?" Leo sounded surprised to be getting questioned about this.

"Yeah, the children. What did I say to you?"

Leo hesitated. "I don't know. It was a long time ago Mike. What did I say? Remind me."

Mike was getting increasingly frustrated at the conversation and pointed accusingly at Leo.

"You said the children wouldn't be hurt. I told you there were children there and that they had nothing to do with it. You said they wouldn't be hurt. Then I sit there and watch them get their heads blown off in the middle of the night."

Leo looked back at Mike, clearly shocked by his sudden outburst, initially not really sure how to respond. Mike remained with his angry gaze fixed on Leo, waiting in anticipation for a response.

"Mike… I… I don't know what you want me to say."

"Did you order it?"

"What?"

"Did you order them to be killed? Did it come from you?"

Leo was now also getting frustrated. In terms of hierarchy, he was higher up the chain than Mike and was under no obligation to explain anything like that to Mike.

"You need to be careful, Mike," Leo warned.

Mike lurched forward, grabbing Leo firmly by the collar pulling him forward.

"Did you order it?"

With a swipe upwards of both his arms, Leo knocked Mike's arms away from his collar and shoved him away to the chest with both hands.

"Back off, Mike! I don't have to explain to you who ordered that and it's not your place to ask. I give out the orders. You follow them."

"Bullshit, Leo!"

"No, Mike, it's not bullshit. It is what it is."

"What? It is what it is? What the hell is that supposed to mean?"

It was Leo's turn to lurch forward and roughly grab Mike by the collar and get into his face.

"These people would kill you and your wife and kid in a heartbeat. Don't you ever forget that. We do what we do to keep everyone else safe."

"Even if it involves killing kids?"

"Yes! Even if it involves killing kids."

The two men angrily eyeballed one another for a few seconds before Leo released his grip on Mike and the two men separated and each took a step back. Mike was still agitated but was feeling marginally calmer following the release of anger and tension that had built up since the end of the mission. Both men were breathing heavily not really knowing what direction the conversation would take from this point. Leo was the first to recommence the conversation.

"Do you remember the Miami incident? 1975?"

Mike wasn't sure initially what Leo was talking about but when he thought about it, he did remember it as it made the national news. He had been in prison at the time it had happened but it was all over the television that was located in the communal area (behind a cage). It was a coordinated Liberty Front attack on a military base. Two perpetrators had driven a truckload of explosives through the entrance gates and then detonated it at the heart of the base, killing eighty-eight service personnel. It was one of the deadliest attacks against the Reich ever carried out by the Liberty Front.

"Do you remember the names of the people involved?"

While he remembered the incident, he couldn't for the life of him remember the names of those responsible for carrying it out. "No."

"Well I do. They were brothers. Dennis and David Petersen."

Mike shrugged in confusion. "So? What's this got to do with anything?"

"Because I knew them! That's why. Do you want to know how I knew them?"

"Surprise me," Mike responded sarcastically, not knowing where the conversation was going. Leo slowed down and took some deep breaths before continuing.

"In 1965, I was assigned an operation in Tampa. There was intelligence to suggest a household on the outskirts was involved in something it shouldn't have been. Much like what you've seen in Iron Mountain. They were a family. Nothing special to look at but the father it turns out was also a skilled chemist. So much so that he was making bombs and other explosive devices for the Front in a laboratory he had set up in his garden outhouse. The stuff this guy knew and could do was unbelievable. He was a clever guy. But he was also one dangerous son of a bitch that we had to take down. We think he was involved in the deaths of hundreds of soldiers and police over the years, what with his little homemade bombs. So we took him out and his wife. But we spared the kids. His two sons. Dennis Petersen and David Petersen. They were only young at the time. Eight and ten I think. They didn't know any better. So they were put into care and that's the last we ever heard from them. Until they drove a truck full of homemade explosives into a military base ten years later and killed God knows many people, including themselves."

"What's you point, Leo?"

"My point is, Mike, things like this, they're engrained into the heads of these people — from a very early age. I met those two boys and they were the sweetest kids you could ever hope to meet. At least on the outside they were. But all they did was follow in the footsteps of their father a few years later and kill all those people. Using the same knowledge as their father."

"That doesn't mean to say the Neal kids would've been the same."

"You don't know that! These people, they're inherently evil. On every level. They would take the eyes out of your own child's head given half the chance. We deal with the problem at its foundations. Now I'm real sorry that you seem to have given even the slightest shit about those kids. But you've got to start thinking a little more realistically. For every one of them we let go, it's doing nothing but planting a seed that won't grow into anything too pretty. It's in them and there's nothing you or me can do about that."

"Other than kill them you mean?"

"Whatever it takes, Mike. Whatever it takes."

The two men stood opposite each other absorbing the conversation they had just had. When the dust had settled, Leo extended Mike an olive branch.

"Look, Mike. This isn't an easy job but it's all for the greater good. You just need to keep telling yourself that." Mike nodded in what looked like reluctant agreement. "Come back in. Come and have a beer. Catch up with the guys. Let's start this again. What do you say?" Mike hesitated. "Come on, Mike. Beer's getting warm in there."

Mike nodded before quietly adding, "OK." The two men walked back inside the house where Mike took a cold beer and sat listening to everyone's next assignment, his own included although it was about to be unexpectedly changed later that day.

As the meeting ended, everyone went their own way with the exception of Leo and Walter Huber, the latter of whom had noticed the minor altercation outside the house earlier in the day.

"Do we have a problem, Leo?"

"I don't know, Walt. I've never seen him like that before. I might change his assignment."

"To what? You got something else in mind?"

"Maybe. A little test to see where we stand with each other — to make sure we're still fighting for the same side."

Before Mike had a chance to prepare for his new assignment, he was visited by Leo. Mike invited him in and he joined the Morgan family for the evening. His visit was twofold. Firstly, to clear the air and make sure that there were no lingering issues likely to cause any further tension — which there were not. Secondly, Leo wished to inform Mike of a slight change in assignment. Due to the length of the Iron Mountain assignment and the mental and physical pressures of it, Leo put forward an alternative assignment. One that would be shorter, less tiresome and that would also afford Mike experience in an area he had not had a lot to do with. It was an interrogation mission of some captured Liberty Front suspects. They had been pulled over in a car outside of Laramie, Wyoming by two police officers due to a minor speeding violation. In the process of the stop, one of the officers was shot dead by the occupants. The other officer managed to unload his sidearm into the rear tyres of the vehicle causing it to veer off the road and crash into a lamppost; thus rendering the occupants incapacitated. Upon detaining the suspects in police custody, it had become clear that they would be of interest to a higher power so they were turned over into the custody of the IUI and were currently being held in another IUI satellite safe house in the San Juan Forest just outside of Durango, Colorado. Leo sold it as an opportunity for Mike to upskill himself in the interrogation techniques used by the IUI and that it would only be a short, yet lucrative, assignment. Especially if they were able to ascertain what they could from the captives. He was also informed that the assignment was being headed by Walter Huber, the former member of the Kriegsmarine. Thinking about the duration and mental and physical toll of recent events, Mike agreed and set off the following morning for the forest outside

Durango. It was a journey just shy of six hundred miles and it was well into the same night that he finally arrived.

The satellite house was more of a glorified and large log cabin. It was well into the forest itself, sitting in a clearing approximately three miles off the main highway — hidden well out of the way of what little other habitation there was in the area. While not tremendously obvious to the untrained eye, the approach was covered by a network of security cameras that were being monitored from the house. The cabin was in a neatly prepared circular clearing that had a diameter of about one hundred metres and the perimeter was demarcated by a wooden fence. Unlike many of the IUI or Reich associated compounds or properties, it was not surrounded by the usual razor wire or electrified fences. This particular property was far enough away from anyone or anything else and was covered more than adequately with cameras that there was no need for much else. Huber was waiting to greet Mike as he arrived. He was pleasant enough and showed Mike to a smaller cabin sitting to the left of the main house. There would be no interrogation tonight. It had been a long day and Mike was told to get some rest and the work would begin in the morning when he was a little more refreshed. The cabin was comfortable enough with all the modern facilities expected. He didn't know at the time but there were four of them in total: himself, Huber and two other IUI agents who he had not met before — they introduced themselves as Dunn and Kilby. Each man had their own room within the cabin and they were taking it in turns to watch over the captives to ensure they attempted nothing untoward.

The following day, Mike took a light breakfast before being guided into the main satellite house by Huber. Although a large cabin of log construction, the interior presented itself as a lot more modern. As Mike had suspected, there was a surveillance room where the various security cameras could be monitored and what looked like a series of cells — most of which were unoccupied with the exception of the two currently being taken up by the captives. It was a man and a woman, Mike guessed both in their early to late thirties. Both were bruised and bloodied but their wounds had been tended to and treated. Again, Mike figured the injuries were as a result of the car crash they had been involved in following the murder of a police officer. They wore dark blue jumpsuits and other than the visible injuries, seemed to be in otherwise good health. They were both awake and sat on the edge of their respective beds looking back at the captors in front of them.

"This is Henry McNamara. And this is his lovely wife Kate McNamara. Shot a police officer but don't seem too keen on saying much more than that at this stage."

"We told you everything we know," the woman said in a bitter sounding voice. "So why are you keeping us caged up like this?"

"Well, you see, the problem is, Mrs McNamara, we don't believe you. When you start telling us the truth, then we might think about upgrading you to the presidential suite." Huber laughed at his own joke.

Mike remained curious as to why they were here. "So they shot an officer, right?"

"That's right."

"So what makes you think they might be Front? Could it not have been a random attack?"

Huber shook his head. "No. We've got other intelligence of their vehicle acting suspiciously and meeting up with people in undesirable circles. I can show you all that—"

"Yeah! And it's bullshit!" the man shouted upon overhearing the conversation.

"Yeah, yeah, course it is. So anyway, I can show you what we got on these two. There's definitely something they're hiding from us. I know there is. Give it an hour, let's get set up and we'll get started."

Mike had a proper opportunity to meet the other members of the team, Dunn and Kilby, who had been questioning the couple for the past few days. Huber was keen to discuss Mike's role in the upcoming activities and was keen to emphasise that interrogation was not about torturing but more of a psychological process with both captives being placed in situations designed to break the spirit rather than the body. The first of these methods was to mask both of the captives and take them into a darkened room towards the rear of the house. Here, they both had a wooden board tied between their arms and were then made to squat. Mike and Huber then stood over them forcing them back into position at the first sign of either of them faltering. All the while the two men questioned their captives over and over again: what's your association with the Liberty Front? Where were you going on the day you killed a police officer? What's your opinion of the

Reich? Mr and Mrs McNamara were proving to be surprisingly resilient and still did not provide the answers the men had hoped for — but they had more methods and techniques to try out on them.

Then came the sleep deprivation. Masked in the same room, forced to stand in an upright position with hands held above their head. Further to this, the most unpleasant sounds were unceremoniously blasted into the room at a very high volume. Any sign of movement from the position resulted in one of the men charging into the room and placing them back into position. After several hours, they were removed one by one for another intense interrogation in a separate room within the cabin. Henry lasted thirty-eight hours before finally collapsing on the floor. Kate lasted a further fifteen minutes before also collapsing in sheer exhaustion. They were dragged from the room and placed back into their cells.

Less than one hour later, Henry was awoken and once more dragged from his cell. This time, he was placed on a table and bound so he was unable to move. Mike had this time being tasked with leading the questioning.

"What's your association with the Liberty Front, Henry?"

"Fuck you!"

"Henry, it can go one of two ways. This can be over very quickly if you just tell us what we need to know. If you do tell us what we need to know, I can make arrangements. We can cut a deal. We can protect you. Just give us what we need to know."

"Are you deaf? I said fuck you!"

Mike nodded. "As you wish."

Without further notice, a towel was placed over Henry's face by Huber and held firmly in place. Mike then began to pour water over the towel covering Henry's face. Henry immediately began to flail around (as much as he could in his bound state) on the table, choking and gagging on the water as it flowed over the towel. Within about thirty seconds he felt himself begin to lose consciousness but then, almost as soon as the waterboarding started, it stopped and the towel was removed from his face. He spluttered furiously and gasped for precious air. No sooner had he regained his composure and the men repeated the process again. And again. And again. Yet Henry still did not give. The same procedure was carried out for his wife and again, she would not give up or divulge anything of any particular value.

At the end of Mike's fourth day at the forest satellite house, he was preparing himself for a good night's sleep when there was a knock at his door. It was Huber.

"Hey, Mike. Sorry, I know it's late but we need your help."

"What's up?"

"Come along to the house. Back interrogation room. Shouldn't take long."

"OK, I'll be there shortly."

Mike got himself prepared before making his way back to the house. In the interrogation room were the McNamaras who were once again bound to a chair and being watched over by Dunn. He was instructed to leave by Huber and he shut the door behind himself as he left. Huber nodded to him on the way out, which struck Mike as being a little peculiar.

"What is this, Walt?" Mike enquired.

"We haven't had much luck with these pair. But we've got one more thing to try. Call it a wildcard if you will."

Huber lightly knocked on the door which was opened by Dunn (who had, moments before, left the room). This time he wasn't alone. He had in his grasp a young child, a girl. Mike's initial impression was that she was about nine years old. Her hands were tied behind her back and she was gagged and looked incredibly distressed. She was pushed into the room and grabbed by Huber who once again instructed Dunn to leave the room and shut the door. The McNamaras were beginning to look visibly distressed at seeing the entry of the child.

"Mike, let me introduce you to our new friend. This is Rachel McNamara. Daughter of our very own Mr and Mrs McNamara."

"What is this, Walt?" Mike asked again.

"Like I said, Mike, it's our wildcard." With that Huber thrust the girl towards Mike who caught her before she fell to the floor. He had taken on a distinctly nasty tone. "Kill her."

The McNamaras both wailed and began begging for their daughter to not be hurt.

"What?"

"I said," Huber stepped closer to Mike and paused before continuing, "kill her!"

Mike looked at the parents and then at the child. She was terrified. Utterly petrified and although she was unable to speak — due to the gag — the look in her eyes spoke for itself. It was a look almost begging Mike not to go through with the instruction to kill her.

"Kill... her!" Huber sneered again, "or I kill you." With that, Huber raised his sidearm and pointed it at Mike's head.

Mike was left with little choice. He pushed the girl away and she fell at her parent's feet. The tears were flowing from all of them now. Mike unholstered his sidearm and aimed it towards Rachel but Huber standing there pointing his weapon at his head was putting him off. He concentrated as hard as he could.

"Pull the trigger!"

The McNamara parents were deafened by the single gunshot discharged by Mike and equally blinded by the flash of the firearm. As they came around in the moments following the gunshot, they were horrified at the sight in front of them. Dunn and Kilby, who had moved outside of the house and were stood in the clearing, looked at one another and smiled approvingly. It seemed as though Mike Morgan had passed the test set for him by Leo.

25

TIME TO LEAVE

Huber lay slumped against the blood-spattered door. He was dead. He was an accomplished operative, no doubt about this but he was Kriegsmarine. He would clearly out-skill Mike on the sea but in terms of land-based combat? Mike was superior to his colleague and he knew this. With lightning speed, Mike had swivelled on the spot and discharged his firearm with precision right between Huber's eyes. At the same time, with his left hand he grabbed Huber's firearm before he even had a chance to pull the trigger. He was dead instantly. Mike immediately turned to the bound people in front of him with his finger over his lips indicating at them to be silent and remain so. He pushed himself up against the door listening. There was no sound, no indication that the single shot had aroused any suspicion. It was likely the other two men thought it was the shot intended for Rachel (which indeed they did) as they continued to lurk outside waiting for Huber and Mike to return. When Mike was sure it was safe, he began to search the corpse of Huber and found what he was looking for — a small knife. He then went firstly to Rachel and cut her free and removed the gag. Henry was next, followed by Kate. The family embraced each other in joy.

Mike continued to hush them before Henry turned to Mike asking in both astonishment and confusion, "Why?"

"It doesn't matter. It's time to leave, that's all you need to know. Do you know how to use this?" He directed Huber's firearm towards him.

"What?"

"Can you use it? Yes or no?"

Henry hesitated, taken aback that his captor was now offering him a weapon. "Yes."

"Take it," Mike replied, handing it to Henry holding it by the barrel as he extended his arm towards him.

Henry took it and then looked at Mike. "What's stopping me from killing you?"

"Go ahead. I probably deserve it but you won't get out of here alive if you do."

"And we'll get out alive if I don't?"

Mike shrugged. "Honestly? I don't know. But shall we at least try? Or would you rather sit here and wait for them to come back?"

Henry didn't ponder over the options for long. "OK. So what now?"

"I need to go and get the keys for my car. You need to wait here until I get back and don't make a sound. Understand?"

The family nodded in agreement with Mike, who pulled the bloodied corpse of Huber away from the door and cautiously opened it. The corridor was empty and the building seemed quiet. He exited the interrogation room and shut the door behind him and made his way into the corridor. Before he exited the building, he stopped at the entrance to the surveillance room. This would be problematic. Everything he was about to do would be captured by the security cameras that covered virtually every angle of the compound. He peered outside into the clearing. The other two men were stood not far from the sleeping quarters, chatting between themselves with seemingly no suspicions as to what was happening in the main building. Mike proceeded into the surveillance room and looked around. He wasn't familiar with the equipment but he had to disable it prior to continuing. After a few seconds of frantically searching, he noticed a fuse box mounted on the wall behind the wealth of screens that decorated the wall. It was not locked and Mike opened it up. He had to be careful not to flip the switch for the entire compound as this would arouse suspicion. Luckily, each circuit was carefully labelled and the label 'Camera' would be indicative that he was about to flick the correct switch. He held his breath and flicked it up almost half expecting all the lights in the compound to go out and the shooting to begin. Thankfully, all the screens in the room went black and the whirring sound of the wealth of computerised equipment ceased immediately. Perfect!

Mike now had to negotiate his way from the main building to the living quarters to get his car keys. Beyond this, he wasn't sure how this would play out (but suspected it would involve an element of shooting in order to achieve the final goal). With confidence in his stride, he holstered his sidearm and exited the building and walked across the clearing towards the living quarters. Both men spotted him.

"Hey, Mike. How did it go?" Kilby queried.

Mike stopped by both men and began to engage them in friendly conversation, giving them the impression that nothing at all was amiss.

"Everything went to plan. It's dealt with. They're giving all the information to Walt that we need. He'll be out shortly."

"All right. Does he need any help?"

"No, he's got it all under control."

With that, Mike continued towards the living quarters and retrieved his car keys. He wished that Dunn and Kilby would just move out the way. There was no possible way he could convince them to do so without eliciting the wrong kind of attention.

Nevertheless, Mike proceeded back to the main building with a light jog cheerily saying, "Forgot something," as he passed the two men who acknowledged him with a smile — still not suspecting a thing (or so Mike hoped).

Back at the interrogation suite, Mike slowly opened the door. Henry was stood behind it pointing the gun at Mike but lowered it when he saw who it was. Mike gently shut the door and began to address the family in a lowered tone.

"OK, listen up. There's two of them out there in the clearing. I won't be able to get them to move anytime soon so we'll have to catch them off guard and get them to surrender their weapons. They don't suspect me so I'll do it. Come with me but wait for my cue at the front door. Take these." Mike handed Henry his car keys, "and get to my car. It's the blue Mercedes-280 parked just behind the front gate. Get them in there and wait until I've secured the two out there. Understand?"

"Got it."

The four of them left the room and made their way to the front door. They stopped there and Mike peered out. Dunn and Kilby had gone.

"Shit!"

"What is it?" Henry asked.

"They've gone."

"Where?"

Mike looked around and could not see for the life of him where they had gone.

"Where?" Henry asked again impatiently.

"I don't know!"

Mike thought hard. Without knowing their position, he didn't know how to proceed. If he knew for sure they were in the living quarters, he could probably get them to the car and make a getaway without them even noticing. If they were lurking elsewhere in the compound grounds, that could prove a little more problematic.

"OK, let's go. Stick close to me and I want you to bring up the rear. Got it?" He was referring to Henry when he requested eyes to the rear which Henry agreed to.

So they set off cautiously across the clearing. They had approximately fifty metres to travel before reaching Mike's car. They proceeded with caution and were all light underfoot. It was a still night and all that could be heard was the gentle night breeze as it meandered through the surrounding trees of the forest. As they got closer to the living quarters, Mike became more anxious. Is this where they were? Would they come out and see what was going on? The quarters remained ominously quiet though. As if by some kind of miracle, they made it undetected to Mike's car and they all thought they were home and dry.

In their excitement they didn't see that Dunn had emerged from the rear of the main building having gone behind it to urinate into the night. Seeing what was unfolding, he unshouldered his machine gun and began to let off bullets towards the party. A bullet ripped through Mike's left shoulder, knocking him forward onto his car. Immediately he swivelled round, dropped to his knees and began to shoot back.

"Get in!" he yelled at Henry and his family. "Get in! Go! Now!"

The covering fire Mike was providing afforded Henry time to get his family into the car, start the ignition, slam it into reverse and then lurch forward out of the gate and away from the compound down the track. Dunn had diverted his fire towards the car and the bullets shattered the rear windscreen and penetrated the trunk.

Sat on the rear seats, Kate pulled her daughter's head into her lap in order to protect her from the bullets as they hit the car. Eventually they were far enough away not to receive any more fire and by this point, Dunn had turned his attention back to Mike who was attempting to take cover behind the perimeter fence and surrounding undergrowth.

Alerted by the sound of gunfire, Kilby had emerged from the living quarters but immediately caught a bullet in the leg in Mike's returning fire that cut through his femoral artery. He only realised when he began to feel faint and his limbs began to weaken as the blood rapidly drained through his wound. He managed to discharge one brief burst before collapsing onto the floor and rapidly expiring.

Henry and his family had made it about half a mile up the forest track and it was pitch black either side of the car.

"We've got to go back!" Kate screamed at Henry.

"What?" Henry responded in shock as he kept his eyes forward and his foot firmly on the gas.

"We've got to go back and get him, Henry."

"Are you crazy? I'm not going back there!"

"Henry, he helped us get away. Go back for him. Please!"

Henry kept driving before slamming on the brakes, hitting the steering wheel aggressively and yelling, "Shit!"

"Henry, please. Go back. Please."

Reluctantly, Henry performed a three point turn on the track and headed back towards the compound.

Dunn had pinned Mike down in the undergrowth. Mike had a single magazine for his sidearm and was using his bullets sparingly but he was under heavy fire from an automatic weapon and his sidearm was no match for it. Further to this, the shock of being shot was beginning to set in. The pain was evident as was the loss of blood which was now significant. He knew he had to get away and figured that, in the melee, his best bet would be to wait for Dunn to reload and then scarper into the darkness, although he doubted he would get far. So he hunkered down in the undergrowth and waited for the whizzing of the bullets to cease. When they did, he glanced up. Dunn was indeed reaching for another magazine in his utility belt. Mike prepared himself to move.

As he was about to run into the forest, the car came tearing through the gate and headed straight for Dunn who, like a rabbit caught in the headlights, stood there waiting for the inevitable to happen. He was thrown into the air and went tumbling over the roof of the car landing about ten feet behind it. The car skidded to a halt and for a moment all was still. But there was still life in Dunn who had begun to twitch and then lift himself off the ground. Seeing this, Henry rammed the car into reverse, hit the gas and reversed over Dunn leaving him in an awkward-looking crumpled heap on the ground. Henry stopped the car by the fence where Mike had been hiding and wound the window down.

He spotted the wounded Mike immediately. "Get in!"

Despite the pain, Mike pulled himself up with support from the fence and ran towards the car. He opened the front passenger side door and slumped into the seat awkwardly. Henry performed another three-point turn and sped back up the track towards what he hoped would be freedom. All Mike remembered as the car sped into the night was the panicked shouts of Henry and Kate as well as the crying of their daughter as he slowly slipped into unconsciousness.

Back at the compound, it was deathly quiet. Huber lay dead in the interrogation suite. Kilby lay dead outside the living quarters and Dunn was still sprawled out in a heap, with his body broken in many places. After a few hours, his hands started to twitch as an element of life crawled back from the very depths of his soul. He wasn't finished just yet…

26

ELK VALLEY

SEPTEMBER 1979, ELK VALLEY INDIAN RESERVATION, WYOMING

In the early hours of the morning, the car pulled off the main highway and began to follow the dirt track that led into the Elk Valley Indian Reservation of Wyoming. It proceeded with caution and at a low speed so as to keep the volume to a minimum and thus minimise the risk of detection although, the area was vast and the populous spread out far across the prairie so this would be unlikely, particularly at this hour of the day. Nevertheless, the car and its occupants proceeded with the caution they knew they should. After travelling for approximately two miles into the reservation, the car pulled from the dirt track and came to a halt. The four IUI agents exited the vehicle without talking to one another. They were dressed in black military fatigues and proceeded immediately to the trunk of the car. Inside was a large quantity of weapons and ammunition. Two of the men shouldered a flamethrower each and the other two men took a machine gun with enough magazines to easily complete their mission. It was a quiet night and other than the sound of the men preparing their equipment, nothing else could be heard on the prairie other than the gentle night breeze rustling through the long grass. Once they were geared up, the men checked one another's equipment and began their silent trek across the prairie towards their final target. Balaclava clad and carrying their weaponry, they walked silently in formation through the grasslands in the dead of night. In the distance they could see their final destination. The faint orange glow of Chief Brave Hawk's small settlement.

THREE MONTHS EARLIER

"Shit!" Daniel Bauer cursed as he drove, once again, into the Elk Valley Indian Reservation. "Shit, damn it, shit, damn!"

He had turned off the main Highway and was taking the dirt track leading deep into the prairie onto the reservation. He hated the journey and the bumpy track which was no doubt doing the suspension of his car absolutely no favours whatsoever. Every bump in the track was accompanied by an expletive or curse. It seemed as though he had visited the reservation hundreds of times in the past few weeks. He had started to even dream about the place — about getting swallowed up by the never-ending prairie, the grassland that stretched as far as the eye could see, with nothing in it other than… grass. Although never coming to any harm in his dreams, the sheer frustration of seemingly walking in a never-ending circle through the grass with no purpose or destination was in itself the stuff that nightmares were built on. His purpose today was clear, the prospect of success less so.

After what seemed like an eternity, the first signs of settlement in the boundaries of the reservation came into view. A single house in a clearing on the prairie, accompanied by a stable. It was a simple property, single storey and wooden in construction, lacking any of the amenities present in a more modern building. This was the home of Chief Brave Hawk of the Elk Valley Indians, one of the many chiefs to live on the reservation who, like many of the others, shunned the luxuries and modernity associated with a life in the twentieth century. Brave Hawk was a spiritual leader within the tribe. Elected to his position due to his wise nature and years of life experience, Brave Hawk had lived on the reservation since his birth sixty-four years earlier and continued to reside there, in the house he built with his wife. The same house that Daniel Bauer was now approaching.

Bauer pulled up outside the chief's house who promptly came out to greet him. They were familiar with one another and had met a number of times over the past few weeks to negotiate the relocation of the tribe to a different part of East America. The discussions had commenced almost immediately after Daniel Bauer's boss — Alois Brunner — had returned from his meeting with the Führer at the Berghof in the June of that year. Daniel Bauer was Brunner's personal assistant and had been for nearly ten years now. He neither liked nor disliked Brunner. He was aware of Brunner's reputation amongst his peers but he found it easier to keep his opinions to himself and to simply carry out his orders without question. He worked for Brunner at the Ministry of Aeronautics and Weaponry, and like Brunner, was based at the same airbase Mike Morgan was stationed at, prior to his arrest, in Saratoga. From the beginning, Bauer's instructions had been quite clear. Make contact with the leadership in the Elk Valley tribe and convince them to move their people out of the reservation. The reason being, the Reich wished to move in and exploit the wealth of natural resources in the area (primarily oil in the ground) — which of course was not true but the Reich did not want the Indians knowing the real reason for wanting them to move. In return, the Reich would offer the entire population new homes in a similar area. At no cost whatsoever to the tribe with more than generous financial compensation for their sacrifices. Surely a deal too good to be true?

So it came to be that Daniel Bauer made contact with the spiritual leader, Brave Hawk, who from the very beginning was resolutely stubborn: refusing every offer put on the table by the Reich. Bauer had been forbidden from making contact with any of the other Indian chiefs but Brave Hawk had met with them and all had shared the same opinion as their spiritual leader. The land was not for sale, they would not be bought or sold and they would not allow their homeland to be exploited simply for the financial gain of the Reich. While it may have been just land to the Reich, it meant a lot more to the tribe. In reality, Bauer knew this which only exacerbated his frustration at having to drive onto the reservation yet again with what would ultimately be the last deal the Indians would be offered. Brunner had been patient but his patience was now beginning to wear thin. The amount of financial recompense being offered to the tribe had almost doubled since Bauer's first visit but the chief would not budge — Bauer knew that before he had even pulled up outside the chief's house. The futility of it all was almost amusing. Nevertheless, he was under orders and he had to visit the reservation one final time.

Brave Hawk was a welcoming man and the two sat in the chief's house discussing the latest offer.

"I hear what you're saying, Mr Bauer, but the land isn't for sale and we don't want to move. No matter how much money you offer us. We aren't moving. I'm sorry, I know this is not the response you want to hear but we aren't moving, we won't move."

Daniel Bauer once again sighed (inwardly and outwardly) over this response despite it not been entirely unexpected. The offers had dried up.

"Well, I have nothing more to offer you. Herr Brunner has been more than generous in what he's prepared to offer and this is the best you'll get. The homes we are prepared to provide for you are all preconstructed with all modern amenities, almost like a purpose-built society. Further to this, the financial compensation package as you can see is more money than you could ever wish for."

Brave Hawk found this final comment patronising but remained calm for he could tell that Bauer was simply following orders on behalf of someone called Brunner (who he didn't know of, and cared little for).

"Mr Bauer, we aren't so ignorant that we don't know what money is and I, along with the other chiefs, are grateful for the generosity of your Reich." This was a lie. "But no sum of money could possibly compensate us. So, if you please, take the offer back to your Mr Brunner and tell him that we politely decline."

With that the chief pushed the latest dossier presented to him back across the table towards Bauer. He rose from his chair and moved gracefully towards the window that overlooked the small, modest settlement and surrounding prairie. Without turning back to look at Bauer, he continued.

"This is our land. My father was born and raised here, as was his father, as was his. And so it continues. This is not just my land; this is our ancestral homeland. One that we have fought and died for. One that my ancestors fought and died for. Thousands of my people died for the right to be here. And let's not forget Mr Bauer that in recent years, many more of my people have suffered at the hands of your Reich."

"How so?" Bauer questioned, feeling rather confused by the accusation.

The chief turned back round to face Bauer. He always looked so lacking in emotion and serious, deep down it saddened him greatly thinking of all those who had died on the reservation as a result of the Reich.

"Your bombs in the east, Mr Bauer. They poisoned the very air that we breathe and I have seen more people die as a result of that than I care to remember. The legacy of what you did in the east is something that will haunt me, even into the afterlife. And the giant white wall to the west has only served to separate us even further from our people."

The chief was referring to the giant border wall with Japan that followed the state boundary between Wyoming and Idaho.

"We didn't build that," Bauer interjected, seemingly in defence of the Reich.

"I'm not saying that you did. But it seems as though my people are pawns in your war games. We're stuck in the middle of your Reich here in the east and Japan, on the other side of the wall that cuts through my country like a snake. Dividing my people."

"I'm sorry you feel that way. As I say, that was Japan's idea, not ours. And it isn't about us treating you like pawns in any kind of game with Japan."

"Isn't it?"

"No. I've explained this to you again and again. What sits underground on this reservation will provide enough fuel for East America for hundreds of years to come."

"You believe that do you? You truly believe that we have hundreds of years' worth of oil under our very feet?"

"Yes."

"Well, my people have been here for a lot longer than your Reich and we didn't know it was there," responded the chief sceptically.

Even he had serious doubts about the reasoning behind the Reich wanting to make a claim on the territory. How did they even know there was all that oil under the ground anyway? He was not aware anyone had ventured onto the reservation to carry out a survey of any description. He wasn't stupid and was almost convinced in his own mind that the 'natural resources' card was nothing more than a ruse, a cover story.

"We belong here, Mr Bauer. Your Reich won't convince me or any of my people otherwise, and with the greatest respect, we won't leave. No matter what the price."

"I won't be back with another offer. I'm under strict instructions that this is final. No more offers, no nothing. You do understand that, right?"

"And what then, Mr Bauer? Will your Reich force us to leave?"

Bauer paused to consider his answer. He didn't know for certain how the Reich would respond, but he had a suspicion of what may happen.

"The Reich will make that decision, not me. I don't know how they will choose to respond."

Brave Hawk scoffed at the woolly response. "A very diplomatic response, Mr Bauer. No matter. Your Reich can do what it wishes from here but mark my words — we won't be giving up. At least not without a fight. We have defended our land for centuries and will continue to do so."

"You're messing with a power that you don't understand, Chief. You think the Reich will be as diplomatic as me? I don't think so! Do yourself a favour, accept this offer. For the sake of your people, if nothing else. Please."

The rising sense of urgency in Bauer's voice amused the chief who laughed gently.

"I sense your Mr Brunner will not be very pleased with your continued lack of progress? You fear him. I can tell in your voice." He wasn't incorrect — although Bauer did not admit it. "We were here long before you, we will be here long after you've gone. Now I suggest you take this... proposal, or whatever it may be, and return back to your Reich."

Bauer began to gather his belongings together. The meeting was over and he had done his level best to convince the stubborn chief to persuade his people to move but he had not succeeded. When he had gathered together his belongings, Bauer made his way back to the car before shaking the chief's hand that had been politely extended to him. The chief had always been very courteous. Stubborn, yet courteous.

"For one so wise, you're making one hell of an unwise choice," Bauer said before getting into his car.

The chief shrugged nonchalantly. "Hell. That's the word isn't it? The word to describe what you would turn this place into should my people roll over and take your money. Safe journey, Mr Bauer. Oh... and please don't take this the wrong way but I hope, in the nicest possible way, that we don't have cause to meet again."

The two men parted company and Brave Hawk watched carefully as Bauer made his way off the reservation, leaving a trail of dust in his tracks as he drove away into the warm afternoon sun on the prairie. As Bauer drove off to report his findings, Brave Hawk couldn't help but feel fearful, despite the stoic and calm stance he had taken against the agent of the Reich, Bauer. There would be ramifications as a result of his actions. This he knew. What he didn't know was what those ramifications would be or when they would happen. This remained an uncertainty but he knew he would be foolish to think otherwise. There was a metaphorical storm on the horizon and Brave Hawk knew he had to prepare his people for what was about to happen. While the reservation had remained largely untouched by the Nazi occupation of East America, it had been on his mind since 1941 that they would one day begin to encroach onto Native American land. This had never been a possibility in his mind but an almost certainty — after all, the Japanese had done so with their border wall. He knew the Reich was ruthless, he knew they had systematically virtually eradicated an entire race in Europe, he knew Adolf Hitler was ruthless and he suspected his son was equally (if not more) ruthless and ambitious even though he knew very little about him.

While the Reich rattled their sabres to the west, so the Empire of Japan rattled theirs back to the east, with the reservation stuck somewhere in the middle. Was there really a vast wealth of natural resources to be exploited and pumped from the ground? Maybe — but he strongly suspected not, as no one outside of the reservation had ever expressed an interest in the land before. Was this actually an attempt by the Reich to gain influence on the borders of the Japanese Empire? This seemed more likely to the chief, and what seemed equally likely was the fact that the Reich wanted to pay off his people, make as little fuss as possible and get the war machine of the Reich moved to the Japanese border, again with the least amount of fuss possible. Thus putting Japan on the back foot. Japan would more likely notice if the Native Americans started making a fuss. This would give them time to mobilise their forces and devise a suitable strategy to counter a Nazi threat. Power play between two empires, with the Native Americans caught in the middle as nothing more than pawns in a global game. His assumptions were correct.

What worried Brave Hawk now was exactly how the Reich intended to go about getting the indigenous population out of their homeland without the Japanese noticing what was going on. The promise of money had failed. The promise of new ready-made settlements in other parts of East America had failed. Every other incentive offered by the Reich had thus far failed, leaving few options remaining other than ones involving force. Brave Hawk knew that his people were outgunned and outnumbered. Massively. But he would be damned if he, or any of his people, would simply stand aside and let the war machine rumble onto the prairie. Something would be unleashed, and soon. He would travel to Elk City later that day to report the findings of his latest meeting to the other tribal chiefs. For now, he retreated to his house to carefully consider what the tribe's next move could be.

As Bauer trundled his way back up the dirt track towards the highway, he once again cursed and swore at every bump in the road. This time his cursing was significantly more aggressive due to the fact his latest, and final, round of negotiations had failed. Brunner would not be happy and he would likely be on the receiving end of his discontent. He didn't have to wait too long to find out how he would react, for Brunner himself had ventured onto the reservation and had parked his car on the dirt track approximately one mile away from Brave Hawk's house. Bauer was surprised to see that Brunner had ventured out onto the reservation and he couldn't just drive on by pretending he had not seen his boss. Reluctantly, he pulled off the track to join Brunner.

Brunner said nothing, he just stared across the landscape. Prairie stretching for as far as his sunglassed eyes could see. As he surveyed the beauty of the landscape, he listened carefully to what he was being told by Bauer who had arrived a few minutes previously following his meeting with the chief. The outcome wasn't what he wanted to hear. They wouldn't move — it was not entirely unexpected. Bauer had been overtly apologetic, even when he had finished explaining the situation, clearly feeling a modicum of responsibility for the chief's refusal to move. Brunner waved his hand at Bauer to silence him. He continued staring across the landscape, deep in thought.

"I don't get it."

"Excuse me, Herr Brunner?"

Brunner gestured with his arms, indicating the surrounding land. "All this, Bauer. All this! It's just... grass."

"I know, Herr Brunner. It goes far beyond what it is in materialistic terms. It's their ancestral home land."

Again, Brunner waved Bauer silent. He wasn't interested in tales of ancestral home lands. He had come out to the reservation to see it for himself. Grass as far as the eye could see wasn't impressive and he thought to himself that it would look a lot better with thousands of tons of military hardware rolling down the dirt track deep into the heart of the reservation. Brunner sighed and turned to return to his car. He had travelled there alone, which was highly unusual as he always travelled with an armed escort.

"I think we will have to get a little more persuasive, Herr Bauer."

"Persuasive, Herr Brunner?"

"Yes. More persuasive. Maybe then they might get the message."

27

PERSUASION

The four IUI operatives had trekked in silence for nearly an hour across the prairie. The two men armed with machine guns walked in the middle flanked by the men shouldering flamethrowers. There was an air of some apprehension as they approached their final target, the home of Chief Brave Hawk. The stubborn tribal chief, too proud and stupid to accept a more than generous offer from the Reich. All negotiations had failed and Alois Brunner had come to the decision that more forceful persuasion would be required in order for the tribe to vacate the land and allow the Reich to move in to rape the land of its so called 'natural resources' (or move the Wehrmacht in, which was their real intention). Before setting the four men off on their mission, Brunner's instructions had been implicit. Remove the head of the snake. Strike at the heart of the tribe. Show them that the Reich meant business and that they were not afraid to go straight for the leadership. The remainder of the tribe would surely fall like dominos once the respected spiritual leader, Brave Hawk, was removed. So it was, that the four men set out on their mission to assassinate the Indian chief.

    The four men halted when they reached the perimeter of Brave Hawk's property. In front of them stood the house the Indian chief shared with his wife. It was a simple building, constructed over several months by the chief himself. A one-storey wooden building, nothing fancy but enough to provide shelter for his family and to protect them from the elements during the harsh Wyoming winters. It was a cool night and smoke billowed from the chimney of the wooden house and the interior was dimly lit, more than likely by the light of a paraffin lamp or similar. The chief had largely shunned all modernity, preferring rather to stick to a more traditional way of life. He therefore lived in the isolated house on the prairie, away from the more populous Elk City where a more sizeable portion of the tribe lived. To the right of the main house was the chief's stable building where he kept and tended to his horses.

On arriving at their destination, the four men carefully surveyed their surroundings. All was deathly quiet and there was no indication of anybody wandering around outside of the house. The four stood silent, surveying their surroundings to ensure that they had not been seen before commencing their mission. The man with the flamethrower to the right-hand side of the group looked to his left at his three colleagues and gave them a nod as a signal for the operation to begin.

The jets of fire from the two flamethrowers were the first things to be seen — one from the right of the group and the other from the left. Like two dragons spitting fire, the flames roared through the Wyoming night immediately beginning to incinerate the wooden structure of Brave Hawk's house. In an instant, the two middle men opened fire with their respective machine guns, riddling the building with bullets. The searing heat from the flamethrowers was making the four men squint, their eyebrows and lashes becoming singed. Still, their attack on the home of the Indian chief was relentless and the flames continued to flow; the bullets continued to fly. Bits of wood splintered up into the night air, the rattle of the bullets against the wooden panelling of the house was deafening alongside the roar of the fire from the flamethrowers.

Only when the gunmen had exhausted three magazines each did the attack come to a halt and the flames from the throwers stopped. The smell of burning wood and gasoline lingered in the air and thick black smoke rose into the night sky, obscuring the light from the moon above. The four men lowered their weapons and surveyed the fruits of their labour. A house (and a home) reduced to nothing more than a bonfire of searing heat within the space of minutes. The attack happened with such ferocity, there could have been no survivors, even if the chief and his wife had attempted to escape to the rear. They wouldn't have made it. Even if they had have made it, the heat of the fire was so sudden and intense, it would've incapacitated them within seconds. If it didn't kill them immediately, it would have injured them seriously enough for them to perish of their injuries before daybreak and long before they could make it to the sanctuary of Elk City.

The men remained in position ensuring that no one would appear from the flames. There was a crash as the roof of the wooden building collapsed inwards on itself as the beams underneath deteriorated in the heat. The job was done. They were about to leave when two peculiar sounds pierced through the crackling of the burning building. The first sound was a momentary whoosh of air followed by an almost immediate metallic like clink. The men all heard it and turned to face one another, clearly confused by what had made such a strange sound. Nothing was immediately obvious to the men as they looked at one another and then surveyed their surroundings. It took the man on the right (the leader of the group with the flamethrower) a few seconds before he heard a trickling sound, like the noise a small water feature in a pond would make. He swivelled round in surprise but could see nothing. As he did so, the texture of the ground underneath his military boots had noticeably changed. It had become soggier and softer and the smell of gasoline had become noticeably stronger.

The second arrow that flew out of the darkness from the direction of the stable was different. Different in that the tip carried fire. In that split second, the realisation dawned on the man on the right as to what had happened. Someone had pierced the gasoline tank on his back with an arrow, shot so discreetly and with such precision that none of the men were immediately aware that it had happened. This allowed the tank to drain its contents around the feet of the man. The second arrow (fired with equal precision) was aimed at the man's feet with the sole purpose of igniting the highly flammable gasoline and incinerating him where he stood.

Seeing his very existence flash before his eyes, the man was barely able to mutter, "Fuc—" before the fiery arrow made contact with the gasoline setting off an explosion.

The flamethrower man was blown up almost immediately, scattering his body parts around the perimeter of Brave Hawk's property. The force and close locality of the explosion sent the other three men sprawling through the air and toppling in an unceremonious heap a few metres away from the scene of the explosion. All three were burnt from the explosion, although the man to the immediate left of the explosion had fared the worst. His bare hands were burnt and blistered as the heat of the burning gasoline had heated the metal of his machine gun to an unfathomable temperature.

His scalp was also burnt as was the right side of his face. All three were bloodied as a result of their exploding colleague, whose fate had been sealed rather swiftly.

As the three men lay on the ground attempting to regain their composure, the most severely burnt man screamed in agony, "Light it up! Light it up goddamn it!"

With that, they all struggled to their feet and the other man with the flamethrower immediately opened fire in the direction of the stable, spewing flame and fire on the roof of the building. The other two men (the severely burnt man in considerable pain) followed suit by opening fire with a fresh magazine towards the stable. While the attack was not as ferocious as that on the house, it was enough to ignite the stable and the men brought their attack to an end when a single magazine had been expended.

They stopped and surveyed the result of their actions. This time, they did not stand easy. In fact, they stood poised to resume their defensive attack with guns raised and targeted towards the stable that continued to burn in front of them. Through the flames licking away at the remains of their colleague, they could see nothing other than more flames rising from the stable. The man with the burnt face was breathing heavily. His military senses had him on high alert. He was about to issue an order to move forward and secure the area when there was another whoosh through the air. This time, it was followed by a sickening crack and a thud. He turned around to see the other man with a flamethrower on his knees, hands round his throat desperately attempting to remove another arrow fired, again with superior precision, from the darkness to the other side of Brave Hawk's burning house. The arrow had been so precise that it had nicked the man's jugular on its journey through his neck and blood was flowing from the wound as he gurgled and gasped for precious oxygen.

Instinctively, the two remaining men began firing in the direction of where the arrow had been fired from. The bullets from their machine guns traced their way into the darkness seemingly not managing to contact anything of significance but instead, fading rapidly into the night and dropping to the ground some distance away. After emptying another magazine into the night, the men remained stood ready. The other man with the flamethrower was motionless on the ground. In the ensuing flurry of gun fire, he had bled out rapidly and had slumped face forward into a pool of his own blood, his body dead and starved of oxygen. The breathing of both men had intensified. This was not the mission they had expected. This was meant to be a simple in and out, routine operation. Torch the house of the Indian chief and get out of there. Instead, they were now the ones under attack from an invisible enemy. The two remaining men stayed poised with their weapons raised; waiting for someone or something to appear from the darkness. The crackling of the burning buildings continued and the pungent smell of burning flesh and gasoline lingered. Their training had prepared them for many eventualities but none like this. An invisible enemy armed with a bow and arrow wasn't part of any military handbook they had read.

The next attack was equally surprising and ruthless as the previous two although was different in that it was not an arrow (alight or otherwise) that emerged from the darkness of the night. This time it was a tomahawk, again from the direction of the stable. The precision was once again second to none and it killed one of the machine gun wielding men almost immediately as it penetrated the back of his skull, blade first. This left the burnt-faced man with blood and fragments of brain spattered over his face as his last remaining colleague also fell to the floor dead in a pool of his own blood. Instinctively, the remaining man adjusted his footing, swung round and began firing blindly once again into the darkness before exhausting his remaining magazine.

No sooner had he finished blind firing when yet another arrow fired from the darkness penetrated his right bicep femoris but this one felt different. Why had this one been aimed at the leg? If they wanted to kill him they could've done with ease and this had been proved by the number of bodies and amount of flesh in the vicinity. This was a shot that felt like it was meant to injure or immobilise. Or both! Either way, the burnt face man had no desire to find out what the real intention was so he threw his spent machine gun down onto the prairie and began to make off back towards the car, far in the distance. The arrow that had penetrated the rear of his leg had gone deep making it too painful and awkward to pick up much pace. The tip of the arrow had struck the bone making proper mobility impossible. Still, he hobbled as best as he could. If he could make it far enough into the darkness, he would be safe and out of harm's way.

The arrow to the other bicep femoris stopped him in his tracks though and he fell to the floor in agony. He reached down to try and remove the arrows but such was the deliberate nature of each shot, they were simply too deep and forcibly removing them would rip his legs to shreds and cause him to bleed profusely, likely to death. He was well and truly immobilised. He struggled to his knees and turned to face the burning building before drawing his sidearm and firing towards it. The final arrow knocked the Luger from his right hand as it penetrated his wrist. The force of the impact catapulted the Luger far enough away that he was unable to move fast enough to retrieve it and take up his defensive stance.

In that moment, burnt and bleeding, he realised his fight was over. He remained slumped on his knees still facing the burning building where he got first sight of his attackers. Two of them appeared from the direction of the stable and a third had appeared in front of the burning house from the other side. They walked forward slowly before coming together in the middle of his vision. From the silhouette they were making in front of the burning building, two of the figures were wielding a bow and an arrow and the middle figure seemingly wielding nothing. They walked forward in unison. When they were about a metre away, the middle man bent down and picked up the burnt man's Luger that had been dropped as a result of the arrow shot. They took a couple more steps forward before stopping in front of the burnt man.

Slowly, and in considerable discomfort from the burns and other injuries, the burnt man raised his head to finally face his assailants. In the middle of the group was Brave Hawk. His face was expressionless and steely as he stood over the injured man staring back down at him. Little did he know, but the two men flanking Brave Hawk were his sons. Although not the same age, they were almost identical in looks with a tall muscular stature, long shoulder length dark hair and the same steely expression of their father. Brave Hawk looked at the Luger he had retrieved from the ground. As he suspected, agents of the Reich. The swastika embossed onto the grip was a dead giveaway. But Brave Hawk wanted to know exactly who was responsible for this atrocity.

"Who sent you?" questioned the chief, but the burnt man wasn't prepared to divulge any information. While his training hadn't accounted for bows, arrows and Indians, it had prepared him to resist during any form of interrogation. He said nothing but looked directly into the eyes of the chief.

"Who sent you?" the chief repeated. The burnt man again stayed silent.

Clearly stuck at an impasse, Brave Hawk did not hesitate and raised the Luger and with a flash of light shot the man in between the eyes and watched him fall sideways onto the ground. He knew deep down who was responsible for issuing the instruction to kill him and his family, and in time, they would be dealt with. There was absolutely no doubt about that. He threw the Luger back on the ground and the three men turned around and walked away into the darkness.

28

A DIFFERENT APPROACH

The four IUI agents did not report in to Brunner which immediately raised concerns. The day following the attempts to forcibly persuade the Indians to move out, Daniel Bauer was once more despatched to the Elk Valley Indian Reservation to find out what had happened and where the four operatives were. So he set off once again down the bumpy dirt road towards the chief's house — swearing and cursing as his car once again bounced up and down on the uneven track. He noticed their car first, seemingly abandoned on the track leading into the reservation approximately one mile away from Brave Hawk's house. He stopped and pulled up alongside it and got out to see if anyone was inside, which they weren't. Bauer immediately became concerned. This wasn't right. He wasn't a military man with a military mind but what he did know was that IUI operatives didn't just vanish without explanation. Something had happened here — he sensed something sinister. He was in two minds as to whether to continue on to Brave Hawk's house at all but he was under instructions from Brunner which if disobeyed, would have very serious ramifications indeed. He had no choice but to continue on with his journey.

He was about to get back into his car and continue down the track further into the reservation when he noticed the smoke rising in the distance. Something was burning and this only compounded his deepest fears over the true fate of the operatives. He remained hesitant but again, he had to continue. Brunner would not accept it if he returned back with his tail between his legs. So he got into his car and once more proceeded up the bumpy track into the reservation, although he continued with much caution and trepidation.

The Indians had removed the bodies by the time Bauer arrived at the scene but he was met with the smouldering remains of Brave Hawk's house and stable. He pulled up and got out of his car surveying the wreckage and was still none the wiser over the fate of the four operatives; although, it would appear that they had completed at least one part of their mission. So where were they? As he walked cautiously round the perimeter to see if he could find any evidence of their whereabouts, he trod in something that made his foot slip. He looked down and saw that he had trodden in what looked like some kind of animal dung. As he cursed and rubbed his shoe on the grass to remove it, he realised it wasn't dung at all. It looked like some kind of animal entrails. He stopped and looked at it in disgust. It was then that he heard the flies buzzing around and as he looked closer, he could see a multitude of the insects buzzing around what looked like other animal remains within the vicinity. Little did he know he had trodden in the remains of the flamethrower-wielding IUI operative who had exploded the night before. The smell then hit him. It had only been a few hours but the heat of the day coupled with the presence of the flies had made the remains rather pungent and he backed away with his hand over his nose and mouth, trying not to gag.

As he made his way back to the car, it was then that he saw Brave Hawk and his two sons. After disposing of the bodies, the chief and his two sons had waited in anticipation of the arrival of someone else to come and check to see why the men from the night before had not returned. As predicted, someone had arrived — in the form of Daniel Bauer. Bauer froze where he was. The chief was still very much alive, even if his property was now nothing more than a smouldering pile of wood, and he did not look like a happy man.

"What happened here?" Bauer asked.

The chief stepped forward towards Bauer while his two sons remained in position, fixing Bauer with their expressionless gaze. "You failed, is what happened here, Mr Bauer."

"Where are they? The men that were sent. Where are they?"

The chief shrugged nonchalantly. "You don't need to worry about them anymore."

"My God, what have you done? Why couldn't you just take up the offer and move out?" Bauer was becoming increasingly agitated. "You don't know what you've started. He'll send more, you do know that don't you?"

The chief remained calm. "Tell him he can send as many people as he wants. They'll all meet the same fate as the ones he sent last night."

The chief seemed fearless yet also ignorant as to who and what he was dealing with. "You won't win, Chief. I'm telling you that now, you won't win. You can't possibly win. And I can't help you now. Not anymore. This is out of my hands."

Brave Hawk stepped forward and came face to face with Bauer who, while terrified of the approaching chief, remained motionless.

"You can tell the coward that you work for that we treat this as a declaration of war. He can send all the men and tanks in that he wishes, but as I've said to you more times than I care to remember — We. Will. Not. Leave. Now go. And for your own sake, Mr Bauer, don't bother coming back. Our negotiations are over."

The chief turned and walked away back towards his sons leaving Bauer relieved that he was being allowed to leave unharmed yet still frustrated that, despite all his efforts, the chief remained too stubborn to move out of the reservation.

"It won't be more men and tanks, Chief," Bauer shouted after him. "It'll be something else, something bigger. You've made a terrible mistake." The chief was unwavering and kept walking without turning around to engage with Bauer. "You're a fool!" These were the last words Bauer would speak to the chief.

Bauer was convinced that Brunner would be furious when he returned to the office at The Ministry of Aeronautics and Weaponry to report his findings. He hadn't seen the bodies (and he hadn't realised that he had walked into the remains of one of the men) but he was convinced the IUI operatives were all dead. He sat opposite Brunner in the latter's private office and explained everything that had happened and Brunner listened patiently without interrupting. When Bauer had finished, Brunner sat quietly thinking whilst simultaneously spinning a pen in between the fingers of his left hand. The Indians had refused to move out of the reservation, despite his best efforts to convince them to leave peacefully. He needed them to move. One way or the other, he needed them to move so the Wehrmacht could be moved in to secure the border with Idaho. Any hopes that this would be achieved without attracting the attention of the Japanese seemed to be failing.

"Bauer, step outside please. I need to make a call. Wait for me outside and I shall call you back when I'm finished."

"Certainly, Herr Brunner."

Bauer stepped out of Brunner's office and took a seat where his personal secretary was busy working. Brunner picked up the phone and made the call. The Führer had told Brunner to call him at any time of day, no matter how early or late, in order to discuss the Wyoming issues and the mobilisation of the Wehrmacht. It was late at night back in Berlin but the call was transferred immediately to the private bedroom of the Führer who sleepily answered the call.

"Alois, it's Brunner. I am sorry to have woken you."

"It's not a problem, you know that. What is it?"

"It seems as though our efforts to persuade the Indians to vacate the reservation have failed."

"How so?"

"They killed four of our IUI operatives last night. The chief is still alive, and by all accounts, I think he wants to go to war with us. I don't think we can continue negotiation with these savages anymore."

The Führer sighed heavily. This was disappointing but not entirely unexpected. He had known from the beginning the Indians were stubborn.

"What are the options from here?" the Führer asked of his namesake.

"Whatever we do, it will attract the attention of the Japanese. I don't think there's any way we can avoid that now. The military are on standby and ready to move in on your orders."

There was silence as the Führer stopped to think about this. Brunner was right. There were no more diplomatic options available and any action taken from hereon in would no doubt attract Japanese attention but that was unavoidable.

"Where are we with the Iron Fortress?"

"The Iron Fortress is ready for a manned test flight; we have no date set though."

Again, there was silence as the Führer thought carefully. "And Bluebird?"

"Bluebird?"

"Yes, how far away is it from becoming operational?"

Brunner thought carefully. He had met with Professor Erich Bagge (one of the leading scientists working on the Bluebird Project and architect of the Nazi nuclear program) earlier that very week to discuss the progress of the project. It wasn't ready and wouldn't be ready for some time.

"The last time I spoke to Professor Bagge, it was only at a fifth of its capacity."

"But could we deploy it? If we needed to say... test it?"

Brunner thought this question over. The Iron Fortress was ready to fly (at least on a test level) but discussions about even testing Bluebird had not come into focus as yet.

"Well... in theory, yes, but I would need to check."

"Even at a fifth of its capacity, would it be enough to get the attention of the Japanese, do you think?"

This was an unknown entity but if the data gathered by Bagge was correct, it would almost certainly get the attention of the Japanese.

"Potentially, but it's still very much of an unknown. The capacity and yield are still being researched in depth."

"When can it be ready?"

"The Iron Fortress or Bluebird."

"Both. When can they be ready?"

"The Iron Fortress can be prepared to fly in a matter of weeks. We need more time for Bluebird."

"How much time?"

"I don't know Alois, I honestly can't say."

The Führer's final order was clear. "We stay away from the reservation. Under no circumstances are you to send in any more men. We'll move them out the other way and at the same time we'll give Japan a demonstration of what we're capable of. Maybe then they'll learn to keep their ambitions in check and stay away from our border. I want Bluebird operational as soon as possible, even if it is only at one fifth of its capacity. Once it's ready, we'll conduct the first test. Within the reservation. You put as many resources into getting it ready as soon as possible. Do you understand?"

"Yes, Alois, I understand."

With that, the call was ended. Brunner smiled to himself. The project he had worked so tirelessly on would be coming into fruition and while only a test, he was looking forward to witnessing for himself the results of years of effort and work. A lot of manpower would need to be diverted into the project in order to ready it but he would ensure it was ready to mobilise at the earliest opportunity. Brunner called Bauer back into his office.

"We won't be sending anyone else to the reservation. Not anymore. We have different orders."

"May I ask what they are, Herr Brunner?"

"The Führer wants to test Bluebird. On the reservation."

"Bluebird? Herr Brunner, what is Bluebird?"

Brunner laughed. "Oh, you'll see, Bauer. All in good time, you'll see."

Back at the Elk Valley Indian Reservation, Brave Hawk knew full well there would be repercussions for the events of the previous night. They would come back although he didn't know exactly what form that would take. He knew they were more heavily armed but he had proved, during the attack on his house, that modern doesn't always win over traditional. The four now very dead IUI agents had been proof enough of this. The problem was, Brave Hawk was not sure the tribe could now take on the Reich without firing a single shot in the process. In the aftermath of the attack on his home, the chief and his wife had retreated into the sanctuary of Elk City, where the bulk of the population of the Elk Valley Indian Reservation lived in more modern conditions than those of the chief.

In total, it was estimated that in the region of twenty-five thousand people lived across the reservation and word had spread quickly about the attack on the tribal leader's home, ultimately bringing in other tribal and clan leaders spread across the reservation in a singular show of solidarity against an act of aggression. The group of leaders had met at the home of Brave Hawk's eldest son — Tauri — where Brave Hawk was residing, temporarily, he hoped. The mood was one of much anger and discontent and it didn't take long for the conversation to turn to one thing — revenge.

"It's bad enough that they invade our country and then drop their bombs. The same bombs that have killed hundreds of our people over the years." Chief Black Smoke, the medicine man, was of course referring to the after-effects of Der Befreier I & II years before. "Now they want to come onto our very doorstep so they can plunder the land, our land, of all its value? Not in my lifetime."

There were chants of agreement in the room where the leaders had assembled before the medicine man continued, "And then they dare to attempt to kill one of our own! It means only one thing as far as I'm concerned." Again, there were nods and more chants of agreement to what the man had said.

"I agree," continued Chief Snow, another revered and respected leader within the reservation. "This cannot be ignored and we must act. Otherwise, what next? How much more of our blood are they willing to spill before they stop?"

Brave Hawk raised his hand to settle the crowd so he could speak.

"I understand and I agree but we have to act with much caution. We are easily outgunned and outnumbered."

"We have guns," shouted out one of the other leaders which was met with more roars of agreement. No doubt each clan had its own cache of weapons available.

Again, Brave Hawk raised his hand in order to settle the angry crowd. "No doubt. We all have our own weapons within each of our respective clans but it isn't enough. If they come into the reservation again, I fear we will not be able to hold them off."

"So what do you suggest?" queried Black Smoke.

Brave Hawk paused before continuing. "We strike first. We assemble the warrior brotherhood and I propose we go straight for who was behind this in the first place."

"And who is behind this?" asked Chief Snow.

"His name is Brunner. And he will pay for what he has done. One way or another, he will pay. And in doing so, it will be a message to them all to stay away from what belongs to all of us here in this room."

The leaders in the room again all chanted in agreement at the proposal to go straight for Brunner and discussion commenced almost immediately to come up with a plan as to how they would achieve their goal to successfully target Brunner. In the meantime, all leaders present agreed to arm anyone willing to answer the call to arms in the event of another unwanted incursion onto the reservation (as well as mobilise the numerous warrior brotherhoods scattered across the reservation). There were no more incursions and little did the people of the Elk Valley Indian Reservation realise that Brunner had something much larger and more destructive planned for them that they would never be able defend against — but the Indians weren't done yet and things would get a lot bloodier before the Iron Fortress was ready to fly.

29

THIS IS WHERE WE END (FOR NOW)

1979 had proved to be a memorable year for everyone. The death of possibly the greatest world leader to ever have lived had undoubtedly taken centre stage in the minds of most people across the globe.

In von Hindenburg's Britain, the doubts Peter Fewtrill had about the morality of the great German Reich had been well and truly confirmed and his involvement with The Menorah continued — as did his involvement with the young lawyer, Susan Scott, whose husband he had discovered was also the perpetrator of an act of mass murder. Frustratingly, he remained sworn to secrecy, somewhat of a necessary evil for the time being. He also remained close friends with the undercover police officer Danny Want, and his role within the Propaganda Department at the Ministry of Media, Propaganda & Information continued, where he was able to access further sensitive information relating to the activities of the Reich in the years after the war and feed this back to Hebron and others within The Menorah. Little did he know that he was soon to stumble upon two rather particular and very interesting pieces of information — firstly, evidence relating to another, and more terrible, act of Reich engineered mass murder, and secondly, a top-secret dossier relating to a secret and highly advanced Reich weapons programme to be tested somewhere in East America — something called Iron Fortress and Project Bluebird.

In Hitler's Germany, the new Führer had surprised all within his inner circle with his ruthless efficiency in quashing not one, but two coup attempts. Rudolf Hess remained in prison, living out the rest of his days with the memory and misery of seeing his son killed in front of his very eyes. With no leader, many members now dead and the coup thwarted, The

Syndicate was officially disbanded with any survivors attempting to flee to the east, and the relative safety of the former Soviet Union. With the exception of former NSDAP member Richard Frick who, along with another member of The Syndicate, had successfully bribed their way to the British Territories seeking out sanctuary amongst The Menorah, closely followed by Italian super-spy, Giovanni Zappa. The Führer's mother continued to tour throughout Europe in the remainder of 1979, tirelessly promoting her son whilst also remaining blissfully unaware that he had planned for her the same fate that had ultimately brought about his own father's demise. The Führer was feeling optimistic about the future and the time was nearing to finally witness the long awaited test of a project initiated by his father many years earlier. A project that would eventually change the very course of history and secure the future of the Reich across the world once and for all — Iron Fortress and Project Bluebird.

In Eichmann's America, former pilot (and member of the team behind the development of the Iron Fortress) Mike Morgan's new career had not gone to plan with the requirements of his missions clashing with his stronger sense of moral duty. His unexpected captivity would eventually come to an end with a rather surprising outcome; taking his life in a direction he never thought it would — placing those closest to him in imminent danger at the same time. Little did Mike Morgan also know that his path would eventually cross with Chief Brave Hawk of the Elk Valley Indian Reservation in Wyoming and that he would enter a desperate race against time to convince the people of the reservation to come to a decision before falling victim to something he knows all about and the devastating implications of it — Iron Fortress and Project Bluebird.

Little did anyone know that their lives would eventually be brought together by a secret weapons project conceived by the former Führer. Little did they know that the latter end of 1979 into 1980 would prove to be quite so eventful.